THE RWANDAN HOSTAGE

CHRISTOPHER LOWERY

The second book in the African Diamonds Trilogy

URBANE Publications
urbanepublications.com

First published in Great Britain in 2016
by Urbane Publications Ltd
Suite 3, Brown Europe House,
3/34 Gleamingwood Drive,
Chatham, Kent ME5 8RZ

A CIP catalogue record for this book is available
from the British Library.

Paperback ISBN 978-1-910692-96-7
Kindle ISBN 978-1-910692-98-1
epub ISBN 978-1-910692-97-4

Cover design and typeset at Chandler Book Design,
King's Lynn, Norfolk

Front cover images sourced through
royalty free photo libraries:

© Subbotina Anna | shutterstock.com (*burnt paper*)
© Peshkova | shutterstock.com (*concrete room*)
© Jag_cz | shutterstock.com (*flames*)
© Nadya Lukic | istockphoto.com (*hands*)

Printed and bound by
CPI Group (UK) Ltd,
Croydon, CR0 4YY

urbanepublications.com

The publisher supports the Forest Stewardship Council® (FSC®), the leading international forest-certification organisation. This book is made from acid-free paper from an FSC®-certified provider. FSC is the only forest-certification scheme supported by the leading environmental organisations, including Greenpeace.

Dedicated to my parents, Christopher Dawson (Kit) Lowery and Lilian May (Lily) Lowery

Thank you. For everything.

My thanks for their advice and assistance go to:

SWITZERLAND:

My beloved wife Marjorie, 'red liner in chief', cutting down my wordy phrases into bite-sized chunks.

My dear daughter, Kerry-Jane, whose experience in Rwanda was the genesis of this book and whose editing was essential to its authenticity.

Martin Panchaud and Sig Ramseyer.

SPAIN:

Mo & Barry Nay

UK:

Mike Jeffries and my nephew Nick Street.

And especially to my publisher, Mathew Smith, at Urbane Publications, who had faith in my first book and encouraged me to finish this one (and start the next one).

Oh, what a tangled web we weave,
when first we practice to deceive.'

Sir Walter Scott, 1808

There's many a slip 'twixt cup and lip.

Old English proverb

PROLOGUE

April 6th, 1994
Kamenjye Neighbourhood, Kigali, Rwanda

It was six forty-five on a warm, airless evening. Darkness had fallen. Cigarette smoke drifted out of the open windows of the three lorries and music could be heard, the same song being played over and over, a kind of folk music mixed with a rap beat that sounded right across the valley. The tarpaulin-covered army trucks were driving at only sixty kilometres an hour, heading eastwards away from the city on the Kanombe Military Hospital Road, along the north side of the airport runway. At the end of the airport property, they turned to the south, driving along several smaller roads through the Kamenjye neighbourhood. The drivers dimmed their lights as they left this populous area, passing Basanza Cemetery and heading up a dirt track on Colline Karama. The occupants weren't so much concerned with noise as with unnecessary light. The sound of the engines increased as they began the slow climb up the incline on the way to the upper slopes. The children playing by the roadside ran after them for a little while and the inhabitants of the shacks pointed and chattered until they were out of sight, then resumed their evening conversations amongst themselves.

Each vehicle contained an officer and four soldiers of the *Forces Armées Rwandaises,* the Rwandan Armed Forces, as well as two wooden crates, about two metres long. The officers were members of the Hutu *akazu* movement and the soldiers, dressed in ill-fitting army uniforms and carrying AK-47 assault rifles, were all specialists in *Interahamwe* training – professional murderers. In the first truck, two men, dressed in European civilian outfits, smoking Gitanes and wearing sunglasses, sat alongside the officer on the driver's bench seat. They leaned over to the open window so that the incoming fresh air, although not cool enough to be refreshing, at least blew away the stink of the soldiers' sweat.

The music was coming from the *akazu* controlled radio station, *Radio-Télévision Libres des Mille Collines* – Thousand Hills Free Radio-TV. The song, '*Nanga Abahutu,* I hate Hutus', was sung by Simon Bikindi, a Hutu extremist. Bikindi's lyrics berated those Hutus who failed to continue to supress the Tutsis and maintain the power they had gained during the 1959 revolution. This ideology was indoctrinated in Hutus of all walks of life, especially those in the army, who were taught to recite verbatim a 1992 army memorandum, which defined the Hutu's enemy as 'the Tutsi, inside or outside the country'. Mutual racial hatred was the common currency of Rwanda and there was nothing the intervention of the outside world could do about it.

During the years since the revolution, hundreds of thousands of Tutsis had fled, settling in refugee camps in the huge and populous countries surrounding their homeland. There were now over half a million of them in Zaire and Tanzania and in their smaller neighbours, Uganda and Burundi. Rwandan exiles were amongst the largest communities of refugees in Africa. Many had been born in the refugee camps and what little they knew of their country, known as the 'Land of a thousand hills,' was learned only from hearsay and traditional songs and stories repeated by the older generation who still had vague memories of the tiny, magical land, lying like a beautiful island in the Great Lakes region of eastern-central Africa.

Inside the country, there was little opportunity for the Tutsis to change their fortunes, but in 1987, a growing movement of refugee exiles in southern Uganda had created the Rwanda Patriotic Front, and they had other ideas. In October 1990, four thousand Tutsis of the RPF invaded Rwanda with the intention of replacing the Hutu regime. The invasion was a catastrophic failure, which would have far-reaching and horrendous consequences that no one could possibly have imagined.

Dar es Salaam International Airport, Tanzania

In the luxuriously equipped cabin of the Dassault Falcon 50, the eight VIP passengers settled back in their seats as the plane taxied towards the runway for their short flight to Kigali. The private jet, a gift from Francois Mitterrand, the French president, to Juvénal Habiyarimana, the Rwandan Hutu president, was carrying them back from a one-day summit meeting of regional African leaders in Dar es Salaam. In addition to Habiyarimana, there were three senior members of his cabinet and his personal doctor, as well as Cyprien Ntaryamira, the newly elected president of Burundi, with two members of his government.

There was only one flight attendant on board, Marie-Ange Lemurier, a shapely black woman from the French island of Réunion, with thick brown burnished hair. A young aide de camp, Benoît Umotomi, seconded as a security officer, was sitting beside her in the spare flight attendant's seat. His name was a throw-back to the fifty years of occupation by Belgium which Rwanda had suffered prior to independence in 1962.

The purpose of the summit meeting had been formally announced as a debate on the problems faced by Burundi since the assassination of the previous Hutu president, Melchior Ndadaye, after only two months in office. However, Habiyarimana had been mercilessly harassed once again by his African counterparts for his prevarication over the signing of the Arusha Peace Accords. This agreement, which was effectively a power sharing coalition between the Rwandan Hutu government and the Tutsi Patriotic Front, had been published in August 1993, but never signed by Habiyarimana and it seemed it never would be. The presence in Rwanda of the French and Belgian UNamir peace-keeping force was a sign, albeit a feeble sign, of the interest of the international community, but more especially the UN, to avoid yet another African disaster, but it wasn't yet working.

Habiyarimana was trapped between the extreme members of the *akazu* Hutus, who would never agree to share power with the Tutsis, and the African and western powers, who insisted that he had to. Whichever way he moved he would lose, and after eleven years in power, he didn't want to lose, but he was running out of time. He refused the glass of champagne offered by Marie-Ange and closed his eyes and tried to sleep as the triple Garrett turbofan engines roared to life and thrust the aircraft up into the night sky.

At the end of the track the three trucks pulled into a circle on a desolate grassy plateau that had been cordoned off with red and white tape that morning. The plateau faced north-east, towards the presidential palace, about three kilometres away. It was now pitch black and the lights of the runway at the airport could be seen, at about half that distance. The approach to the airport was from the East, going across in front of their position and directly over the palace on its final descent. At a command from one of the men in civilian clothes, the twelve soldiers formed themselves into a cordon around the vehicles, holding their rifles at the ready. The officers unloaded the crates from the lorries, opened them up and placed the contents on a large plastic sheet, laid out between the trucks. The two civilians supervised their work until they were satisfied with the placement of the equipment. They tested each piece to ensure it hadn't been damaged in transit then they prepared them for use.

"*Bon. Tout est prêt. Attendez notre signal.* Everything's ready. Wait for our signal." One of the men took out a pack of Gitanes and offered them round. The men and the officers sat smoking quietly, surrounded by the trucks and the cordon of guards. The time was seven thirty.

* * *

At five minutes past eight, the French pilot announced that they would be landing in ten minutes. Marie-Ange collected the empty champagne glasses from the passengers and ensured they were buckled into their seats. After depositing the glasses in the small galley at the back of the aircraft, she went into the toilet just opposite.

At ten minutes past eight, the air traffic controller at Gregoire Kayibanda International Airport repeated his instructions to the pilot of a United Nations C-130 Hercules transport plane which was approaching the airport. "Please make a turn to your starboard, descend to twenty-five thousand feet, take a holding pattern to the north and await further instructions. Another aircraft has been given priority over your slot time." The weekly Belgian Hercules flight was carrying UN troops, part of the UNamir contingent stationed in Rwanda, who were returning from leave. The pilot responded affirmatively and the plane banked away into the clear, starlit sky to leave the airspace clear for the presidential plane.

"You are cleared for approach, Falcon Fifty."

"Roger that, tower." The Falcon pilot started to line up for his approach. Habiyarimana was exhausted. The Burundi president and even some of his own officials had continued to harangue him during the flight and he had spent the last hour trying to find good reasons to defend his procrastination. He leaned back in his seat, wondering how he would be able to hold them off for much longer. He would consult his wife, Agathe Kanzinga, the power behind his throne, when he arrived home.

"Quick, quickly now!" Marie-Ange pushed Benoît, the aide de camp, down onto the toilet seat. His trousers were around his ankles. She hoisted her short skirt, pulled down her panties and straddled him. "We'll arrive in a couple of minutes and I have to be present for landing."

On the hillside, the group were listening to the voice of the announcer of *Radio Milles Collines* berating his audience for not taking decisive action against the Tutsi enemy. He suddenly stopped speaking for a moment then announced that the presidential jet was coming in to land. A selection of classical music began and the commentary ceased.

"*Ça y'est. Allons-y!* Let's go!" The plain-clothed men barked out orders and picked up two of the Russian-made 9K38 *Igla-type* surface-to-air missile launchers, loaded up with their 9M39 missiles. Each man held a weapon in place, facing the presidential palace, which was exactly on the approach path to the airport. At between three and four kilometres, the target would be well within the range of the *Igla* missiles. The army officers had the remaining weapons loaded and ready, but they knew if the first shots missed, they would be unlikely to get another chance.

Everyone in the group was motionless, listening intently and scouring the skies with narrowed eyes. The UN transport plane had appeared a few minutes ago, but had turned away without landing and was no longer in sight. "*Voilà. Là bas!*" One of the civilians pointed towards the airport. They could discern the faint lights of the Falcon circling from the north side of the airport all the way back to the south of them, then turning into a final approach path from the east that would take it across their line of vision. The muted sound of the aircraft's engines became louder in the silence of the night. They watched the lights approach them until the aircraft was almost level with their position, about three and a half kilometres away.

The two men adjusted the range finders on their weapons, squinting through the sights at the dual infra-red images that would enable the rockets to seek out the aircraft's heat track. "*Tirez!*" The first missile streaked away, its fiery tail lighting up the hillside. The second followed a couple of seconds later, arrowing after the first, straight towards the Falcon.

"*Oui, Oui!* Yes, Yes! Keep going! Faster, faster!" Marie-Ange cried out as she and Benoît began to climax at the same time. He was already holding her tight with his hands around her middle, but she grabbed him around the neck with both hands to hold herself in position.

President Habiyarimana was dreaming. He was piloting a helicopter and could hear the rotors spinning faster and faster. It was almost out of control, but Agathe, his wife, was giving him instructions through the headphones. He felt reassured. His wife was always right.

The first missile struck the Falcon just behind the portside wing, ripping off a two metre section, exposing the toilet area. Marie-Ange and Benoît, still sitting in the coital position, were sucked out of the gaping hole in the fuselage and hurled through the air, clinging to each other in abject terror.

The impact pushed the wing upwards and the tail section down, directly into the path of the second rocket. The tail was completely blown off by the explosion of the missile and landed in splinters on the western end of the runway. The forward section of the aircraft was immediately engulfed in flames as the fuel tanks erupted and the remains of the Falcon spiralled like a flaming comet in a deathly descent towards the earth, ironically smashing into the ground just short of Habiyarimana's presidential palace, the bodies of the ten remaining occupants strewn outside the landscaped gardens.

The soldiers loaded up the three lorries with the remaining material and they trundled quietly off back down the mountain on their way to the Kanombe military barracks. After a few minutes, the classical music on the radio stopped and the announcer said, in a respectful tone, "We have just learned that the presidential aircraft has crashed, resulting in the death of our beloved President Habiyarimana and several of his government members."

Then the slaughter started.

FEBRUARY, 2010

ONE

Geneva, Switzerland

***La Bise* is a French word meaning 'The kiss'. It is also the name** of the cold, sharp wind from the east which regularly sweeps across central Europe, especially Switzerland. Local people will tell you that it always appears for one, three or five days, but everyone knows it can blow for a week or more. It was blowing strongly as the young woman climbed out of the taxi in front of the private bank in Plainpalais at nine twenty-five on a freezing cold February morning. She pulled her coat tighter around her against the chilly air, grateful for its warm cashmere fabric and hurried across the pavement and through the massive double doors.

"*Bonjour,* Madame Bishop, I hope you are well." The man waiting in reception shook her hand. "Welcome back to Klein Fellay. Everyone is here, expecting you. Please follow me."

They entered the lift and he pressed six. "Did you have a pleasant trip, Mme Bishop?"

"As usual, Mr. Schneider, but a more pleasant prospect this time."

"Indeed." He nodded his head. "It has not been an easy time for you. I understand. It's been rather a difficult period for us here at the bank also." When the woman said nothing, he took out a handkerchief, blew his nose loudly then continued, "May I say that I admire your determination and courage in fighting this matter and I'm personally delighted that it has been resolved in your favour."

She smiled grimly. "Thank you, Mr Schneider. Then we're both delighted." Jenny Bishop didn't like Eric Schneider and she didn't like Klein Fellay. The litigation was the only reason she still had her accounts there, *but that's going to end today,* she told herself.

They exited the lift and she handed her coat to a woman assistant. Schneider led her to what she assumed was the bank's main conference room, extravagantly large, with a high painted ceiling featuring a baroque scene, nudes, angels, cherubs and all. The room was beautifully furnished, with a number of recognisable old masters on the walls. Jenny had attended several meetings at the bank and each time it seemed they found a larger and more opulent ambience to display their wealth. *Designed to impress and intimidate,* she thought, *but it won't work this time.*

Four men and a woman were already seated at a magnificent Boulle baroque style table, made for Louis XIV, inlaid with tortoiseshell and red leather veneer. Twenty Hepplewhite armchairs were placed around it, which to Jenny looked rather incongruous. The table was set with eight leather writing pads, two on one side and six on the other, each with a matching ballpoint pen and pencil. Jenny shook hands with them all then sat with her lawyer on the client side of the table. Schneider sat on the other side with his boss, Emile Bluchner, the bank's Chief Executive, and the four lawyers.

Six to two, she registered suspiciously. *Why so many when the matter's already resolved?* Her own lawyer, Sylvestre Prideaux, smiled confidently at her and poured her a glass of water. Prideaux was reckoned to be the best of Geneva's new breed of techno-lawyers, specialising in the recent phenomenon of cybercrime; embezzlement, fraud and robbery over the Internet. He had been recommended by a Swiss colleague of José Luis Garcia Ramirez, her Spanish lawyer, and she had hired him a year after the dreadful experience with d'Almeida, the psychopathic murderer. That was when she had finally come to terms with the death of her husband, Ron, his father and his partners and the catastrophic events she and her friends had lived through at the Angolan's hands. After months of wrangling, she was still fighting to recover the money he had stolen from her and this was her last attempt to settle the matter before the court case, scheduled to begin in March.

Bluchner himself served coffee to everyone and there were a few minutes of general conversation as they settled in their places. Jenny had met all of them before, except for the female lawyer and knew their style, what to expect from them. The men had always deferred to Bluchner, adding only legal footnotes to his long monologues about new technology, client protection and bank liability. She listened carefully to the woman's few remarks, trying to gauge her attitude to the meeting and anticipate her position on the litigation. To Jenny, she sounded self-opinionated and bossy.

Finally Bluchner opened the meeting. "Mme Bishop, thank you for coming to meet with us today and I hope that it will prove to be worthwhile for everyone concerned." Jenny said nothing and he turned to the woman lawyer. "Mme Wyss, can you please summarise the bank's proposal for Mme Bishop."

"Certainly Herr Bluchner." The woman cleared her throat and started reading from a set of notes in a fast staccato rhythm with a Swiss German accent so strong that Jenny couldn't understand half of what she said. What she could understand was that she, Mme Wyss, had been brought in to deliberate on the extent of the bank's liability and she proposed to do this by reference to the few available precedents in the field of financial fraud by Internet.

After a minute or two of this incomprehensible rhetoric, Jenny sat forward and said, "Please don't continue Mme Wyss. I can't understand you and I don't want to listen to any more long legal speeches. I've had almost a year of them already."

Prideaux, her lawyer, put his hand on hers as if to say, *hold on, don't interrupt,* but she pulled it away and went on, "Mr Bluchner, I came here today because you advised my lawyer that you acknowledge that an error was committed by your bank in making a transfer without proper authority. If that is the case then there is no need to examine precedents or to make any kind of a proposal. You must simply reverse the transfer and we can both pay our lawyers and forget the matter. If not, then we're going to proceed with the court case scheduled for next month. It's as simple as that."

"But Mme Bishop, the fact that we agree that an error was committed doesn't settle anything. We must decide on reciprocal culpability and discuss the amount of appropriate damages. Please let Mme Wyss continue with her analysis and our proposal."

"We deny that there is any reciprocal culpability." Prideaux was now on his feet. "My client and her two companions were held at gunpoint and forced to disclose their PIN numbers. The perpetrator had already received the security codes from one of your own employees and he sent all of the information himself via your Internet Banking System. Your bank therefore executed a transfer of twelve million dollars based upon improper instructions. Subsequently, Mr Peterson, one of your clients whose account was pillaged, was shot dead by the villain who then also died in the fracas." He stopped for a moment, letting this last awful statement hang in the air.

"The law is clear on this matter. Your duty to your clients is to only operate their account with instructions received from the account holders themselves, not from a third party, unless they are in possession of a power of attorney, which we know is not the case. Please inform me where my clients' culpability arises in this case."

Mme Wyss sat forward and started speaking to Prideaux in French, with an even stronger Swiss German accent, a hard grating sound to Jenny's ear. She caught the words "*Internet*" and "*PIN securité*".

"Please speak English Mme Wyss, my French and Swiss German are a little rusty," she said.

The woman looked at her contemptuously and continued haranguing the lawyer until Bluchner called for order. Everyone sat back down and lowered their tone, but within a moment the conversation became heated again and continued for several minutes, each side trying to make their point against the other, until Jenny stood up and banged on the table.

"Stop this arguing immediately. You sound like a bunch of market traders trying to settle the price of a second hand fridge. Please listen to me carefully, because my return flight to London leaves in two hours so I don't intend to stay here much longer.

Prideaux, who knew Jenny and her temper quite well by now, put his hands over his eyes and sat back in his seat. The others, shocked, said nothing and waited for her to speak.

"Firstly, you have agreed with my lawyer that you made an error in making the transfer of twelve million dollars. You didn't specify the error, but Mr Prideaux is right, it is because none of the account owners, neither I nor Adam Peterson nor Leticia da Costa actually sent any instructions to you and this has been confirmed by the police investigation.

"Secondly, I know that the bank has a professional liability indemnity policy in place for two billion Swiss Francs, for just such errors as this. That should be enough to cover my claim.

"Thirdly, thanks to the stupidity of the actions of the UBS, after its sixty billion dollar bailout, the Swiss banking system is under immense scrutiny right now, not just by the United States, but by Europe and even here within Switzerland. I don't think your parent bank, the International Bank of Paris, would be very happy to see their Swiss subsidiary's name all over the international press and on TV in connection with a Geneva law-suit involving cyber-fraud, a serial murderer and two very unhappy clients who have lost twelve million dollars because of an error that you admit was your fault."

She squared up to Bluchner, looking him straight in the eyes. "Mr Bluchner, if you want to fight, then you're going to have to fight my way, because I don't have two billion francs of insurance. I came here to collect my money and get on with my life. If I can't do that, then I'll have to find my satisfaction in some other way."

Jenny sat down, shivering with fury and fright, in equal measure. Prideaux put his hand over hers again, this time to signal, *well done*.

"So, Mme Bishop." Bluchner took a deep breath. "You're saying it's twelve million dollars or a battle?"

"Exactly, Mr Bluchner. But a battle on my terms."

TWO

Geneva, Switzerland

An hour after Jenny's impassioned speech, Mme Wyss placed a three page document in English before her on the table then turned and walked away without a word. Sylvestre Prideaux read it over carefully and nodded his agreement. Jenny read it for her own satisfaction, registering mainly the sentence; *KF agrees to rectify the error by crediting, with immediate value, the amount of Twelve Million US Dollars to the aforementioned bank account in full and final settlement of TAC's claim against it.*

She fleetingly thought of making a further argument for accrued interest but decided that she had had a pretty good run for her money. *Don't push your luck, Jenny,* she thought. *Besides, interest rates are so low it makes very little difference. We've won, that's all that counts.* Jenny took out her own pen and signed the agreement, in triplicate, on behalf of The Angolan Clan, the business created by Charlie Bishop, her father-in-law, over thirty years before, bringing success and wealth to the members for many years before being targeted by a pathological genius, ending in catastrophe and death. *There, Charlie,* she said to herself. *I got our money back for you. I hope you're proud of me, getting the better of this crooked bank.* She pushed the papers over to Bluchner, who signed them without comment.

"Thank you everyone. That concludes our business and you'll be receiving further instructions from Leticia and I, properly signed, in due course." She got up and went over towards the door. Only Bluchner came to shake her hand.

"I'll just tidy up here, Jenny." Prideaux was still fussing over the papers on the desk. He shook hands with her and turned back to his administrative work. "My secretary will send copies of everything together with my invoice in a day or two."

I'm sure she will, thought Jenny. *There's the first chunk of the money gone and I did most of the work myself.* Her agreement with the lawyer was an hourly consulting fee plus one per cent of the settlement. This was going to cost her and Leticia almost two hundred thousand dollars. She shrugged resignedly and replied, "Thank you, Sylvestre. *Au revoir.*"

"Let me accompany you, Mme Bishop." Schneider opened the door for her and they went to reclaim her coat from the cloakroom. Stepping into the lift, he once again pulled out his handkerchief, this time only to wipe a bead of sweat from his forehead.

"May I say something, Mme Bishop?" He held the handkerchief against his mouth and she could smell the fragrant after shave he had sprinkled on it.

When she nodded, he said, "I have never witnessed such a magnificent performance in my life. Mr Bishop would have been proud of you. I must say I miss his visits, and now I suppose I'm going to miss yours too."

"Thank you, Mr Schneider. I'm pleased it's over, but thank you for your kind words."

They walked to the door and he asked if she needed a taxi.

"I don't think so. A walk in the fresh air will do me good. Goodbye Mr Schneider."

Jenny shook his hand and walked away, pulling the collar of her coat around her. It was still bitterly cold. There was a taxi stand on the corner of *Rue Jaques-Balmat* and she climbed thankfully into the one waiting cab, giving the driver an address in *Pâquis,* the red light district on the other side of the lake. She hadn't wanted Schneider to know where she was heading. Switching on her mobile she texted two words, '*12 million*', then sent it to Leticia, in Spain. She couldn't know that it was the same as the message sent by d'Almeida, the murderer, to Esther, his girlfriend, just before he died.

Good job I got her to agree to joint signatures, she thought to herself. Unlike Jenny, Leticia was a new born big spender, revelling in the fortune she'd inherited from Charlie, her former lover and father of her son, Emilio. Hopefully Patrice, her French fiancée, who was a banker, could advise her well enough to cover her expensive tastes. *Anyway, this money's going to be safe,* she thought, then put the matter from her mind for the moment.

Jenny hadn't told the truth about her airline booking. She had a reservation on a Swiss International flight to Malaga at two thirty, which gave her enough time to make two more visits before leaving this freezing place. As they passed over the lake on the *Pont du Mont Blanc* the *Bise* brought the air temperature down to well below zero and she admired the fantastic shapes created by the frozen waves as they were blown along the sides of the *Lac Leman.* The taxi pulled up in front of a six storey building and when Jenny rang the bell, one of the heavy double doors swung back, revealing a young man in a dark blue suit.

"Madame Bishop. How nice to see you again. Please come inside from the cold." He ushered her into the reception area and shook her hand.

"Gilles Simenon. What a surprise. I didn't think you'd still be here after almost two years. Young people change jobs quite a lot these days."

"It's not so easy to get a good job here anymore, Mme Bishop. The economic problems are starting to affect Switzerland now, like every other country. So I'm glad to be in a secure position with a very good company. I suppose you wish to visit your safety deposit box?"

"Yes please." Jenny signed the large book that Gilles opened for her. "Is Mr Jolidon still in charge?" She asked, as they walked to the lift which he opened with a code on the key pad.

"He is, although he spends a lot of time in the offices on the other side of the building. We're a bit short handed because they've cut some staff. That's where he is now. Do you want to see him?"

"No, it's not necessary." Jenny was relieved. She neither liked nor trusted the manager.

They descended two floors then went through two sets of steel doors into the massive circular vault. Gilles removed a key from the cylindrical rack in the secure key cupboard and inserted it into the top lock of box 72 and turned it. Jenny took two keys from her purse, each with an elastic band on it, one green, which she turned in the middle lock, the other yellow, which opened the lower lock. Gilles turned away as she entered fifteen-eleven- forty-five on the keypad and the door clicked open.

"Excellent! I'll wait for you upstairs Mme Bishop." The young man closed the security doors behind him and left her alone in the vault.

She took out the steel box and placed it on the large central table, self-consciously looking around to ensure there were no prying eyes, even though she knew the room was virtually hermetically sealed. She removed Charlie's battered old briefcase from the box, opened it and laid the ten chamois leather pouches on the table. Untying each one, she spilled the contents into ten piles on the table top.

Jenny hadn't been back to Ramseyer, Haldemann since April, 2008, almost two years ago, when she was accompanied by Leticia and Adam Peterson, just before his tragic death at the hands of d'Almeida. Her breath was once again taken away by the burst of brilliant light reflected from the ten miniature pyramids of Angolan diamonds in front of her. *Beautiful, but deadly,* she mused, not for the first time. Henrique's diamonds had been the source of great wealth and happiness and great poverty and revengeful jealousy in equal measure.

Because of the long drawn-out dispute with Klein Fellay, Jenny had never found the time or the energy to move them to another safety deposit facility, as she'd originally intended. Now, she realised, she might just as well leave them where they were.

No one else knew she had both keys and she intended to keep it that way. She had taken the second key from Adam because she didn't fully trust him. There were parts of his story which didn't ring true and he had lied about the terms of the contract with Charlie. Who knew what might have happened if he had survived the confrontation with d'Almeida?

The immense fortune they were inheriting was also causing her more and more concern. She knew that great fortunes and happiness don't always go hand in hand and subsequent events had proved her sixth sense right. Leticia, who had given her the other key, was too young and inexperienced and she had taken it from her to avoid inviting any further tragedy in their lives.

Jenny didn't consider that the diamonds belonged to her. She thought of them as belonging to no one. They would stay untouched and unannounced in the vault until, God forbid, there ever there came a day when one of her or Leticia's family needed them, then they'd still be there.

She trickled the diamonds through her fingers back into their pouches and replaced them in the briefcase. Before closing up the box, she picked up a felt bag and took out a framed newspaper article with a photograph. *Olivier and Charlie,* she smiled ruefully, *if only you'd known how it would end.* She sighed and replaced the box in its cubby hole and locked the door then pressed the bell to recall Simenon.

"Will you be returning soon, Mme Bishop?" He asked as they went up in the elevator.

"I don't think so. Why do you ask?"

"It's just that the annual rental fee will become payable again at the end of this year. I was just looking at the file. It seems that the previous owners usually paid five years at a time to avoid any complications, since we didn't have an address for them. I've printed out an invoice with the payment instructions and the amounts for one to five years."

"Thank you, Gilles." Jenny took the invoice from him. She had completely overlooked the fact that fees were payable and, unlike a bank, there was no account to debit to pay them from.

Gilles saw her eyes open wide at the amounts listed. "Yours is quite a small box, Mme Bishop. The larger ones are much more costly."

"Small mercies, Gilles," she said, thinking about what was in the box. She had looked up some data about diamond prices before coming over to Geneva and knew that prices had fallen by about twenty per cent since 2008. But twelve hundred carats of finest quality Angolan diamonds should still be worth between ten and fifteen million dollars at today's full wholesale price. She told herself that the fee wasn't unreasonable. It was a bit like an insurance policy and fifteen million dollars' worth of diamonds would cost a fortune to insure. "I'll make arrangements to transfer five years of fees when I return home."

She folded the invoice and put it into her handbag as he opened the door for her.

"Thank you Mme Bishop. I hope you have a safe flight home and an enjoyable weekend."

"The same to you, Gilles. It's been a pleasure to know you and I wish you lots of success in the future."

She turned and walked off in the direction of Cornavin railway station, impervious to the resentful looks of the underdressed women freezing in the doorways of the bars and night clubs. She had one more appointment and she was looking forward to it.

Jenny hurried along the Rue de la Gare, pausing for a moment outside no. 362 with a feeling of nostalgia. The IDD offices had been closed down shortly after the d'Almeida tragedy and all the documents and paperwork packed into boxes and moved to a storage facility. The name was no longer among those on the mail boxes.

She pulled her collar around her neck and continued for another hundred metres to the corner of the Rue du Mont Blanc, where she went into the Banque de Commerce de Genève. Mme Aeschiman, the manager, came out to reception, greeted her warmly and escorted to her office.

"It's a while since you've been to visit us, Mme Bishop. I hope everything is well with you and Mme da Costa?"

"Things are finally getting back to normal, thank you. That's why I came over to see you."

The two women talked inconsequentially for a few moments, then Mme Aeschiman opened up a file on her desk. "Well, I've prepared everything as you asked. You'll need to fill out quite a lot of forms then I'll call in our Head of Portfolio Management, M Philippe Jaquelot. "

Thirty minutes later, Jenny had arranged to transfer her own and Leticia's funds from Klein Felly into new accounts with the Banque de Commerce and opened an account for the twelve million dollars from the Angolan Clan settlement, *'In trust for Emilio Salvador da Costa'*, with both her and Leticia's signatures. With M Jaquelot, the investment advisor, she agreed on a conservative, low risk portfolio strategy and her business at the bank was finished.

She thanked Philippe and Valerie, as she now knew them and took copies of the documents for her UK tax accountant and the remaining forms for Leticia's signature when she got back to Marbella. They shook hands and Jenny walked out to find a taxi at the station rank to take her to the airport.

At Ramseyer, Haldemann, Claude Jolidon, the director of the safekeeping department was examining the signature book. He turned to Gilles. "I see that Mme Bishop was here this morning."

"I asked her if she wanted to speak to you, M Jolidon, but she said it wasn't necessary. She sent her best regards, to you," he added, untruthfully.

"You should have called me," Jolidon said, rather petulantly. "Was she alone?"

"Yes she was and she seemed to be in a hurry."

"Really? And Mme da Costa wasn't with her. Was she able to open her safety deposit box?"

"Yes. She had both keys with her, but I'm sure she didn't remove anything. Anyway, she was only here for a few minutes and I knew you were busy. She's going to pay five years of fees when she gets home," he said brightly."

"That's alright Gilles, but next time, please call me. It's been two years since I've seen Mme Bishop. I would have liked to say hello."

Jolidon walked away, a thoughtful look on his face. He took his coat from the wardrobe. "I've got a lunch appointment. I'll be back by three o'clock." His car was parked near the Richemont Hotel. He drove off in the direction of the French frontier and pulled up in front of the Hotel du Lac, in Divonne.

"*Bonjour,* M Jolidon," said the well-built man at the door of the Casino de Divonne.

"*Bonjour,* Hervé. The new man had been guarding the casino entrance for only a few months, but his visits were so frequent that he was already well known to him. He walked through the gaming rooms to the offices at the back and knocked on a door.

"*Entrez!*" A voice called out. Jolidon went into the office and closed the door behind him.

Jenny took out her mobile and called Linda, at the kennels in Ipswich. Because of the break in her journey to visit Geneva, she'd had to leave Cooper, her West Highland Terrier in the UK. It seemed that he was well and enjoying his stay, as he always seemed to. As she put the phone back in her pocket, a text message came up. It was from Leticia. It said '*Well done, Jenny. Gracias y hasta luego*'.

She sat back and made herself comfortable in the taxi for the twenty minute ride to Cointrin airport. Her day's work was accomplished and she felt rather pleased with herself. Now she could get away from this freezing cold weather and down to the warmth of Marbella.

THREE

London, England

The woman shivered as she walked quickly along Jermyn Street, behind Piccadilly, and entered the Cavendish Hotel. She made her way to the Petrichor Restaurant and left her outdoor coat with the hostess, glad to be inside. The fabric wasn't as warm as the weather deserved. "No thanks," she replied when the Maître d'Hôtel asked if she wanted a table, "I'm meeting someone here." She looked around the busy room, ignoring the admiring glances of several male customers, until she spotted her lunch appointment sitting at a corner table by the window. He stood up when he saw her and pulled aside a chair.

"Thank you, Arthur," she said and he leaned forward and kissed her on the cheek. She had put on a close-fitting blouse and skirt for the 'date', from a fairly limited choice. Sitting down, facing him across the table, her impressive bust line was subtly revealed by two undone top buttons. "And thank you for inviting me for lunch. I've heard it's a wonderful restaurant."

"One of my favourites, nowadays. The chef is an old friend of mine from the River Room at the Savoy. That was before they destroyed its lovely ambience with a facelift, of course."

The man must have been in his late fifties, with a comfortable paunch under his baggy, worn tweed coat and a dark blue and green striped tie tucked into the top of his trousers. He wore tortoiseshell framed spectacles and had a generous, rather French looking moustache.

"A smidgeon of Laurent Perrier?" She nodded and he waved the waiter over to pour a generous flute for her and a fill up for his own glass.

Looking around, the woman saw one or two faces she recognised from the newspapers. "Keeping up with the right company, I see. *Santé*. Here's to us." They clinked their glasses and sipped the champagne. "That tastes good."

Neither broached the subject of their meeting until after he had ordered her lunch. "Just leave it to me. I know exactly what you'll enjoy." She was happy to do so. Her fine wining and dining days had been few and far between of late.

"Now, my dear," he said, when the waiter had taken their order. "Judging from your call yesterday and your immediate trip to these shores I am bound to assume that you have some important revelation for me. I beg you not to leave me in this dreadful state of suspense for one single moment longer."

The woman looked carefully around the dining room, leaned forward across the table and said, "She has the keys and nothing has been taken."

"You're sure? Absolutely sure?"

"*Absolument!* She has never been back until this week and she opened the safe but removed nothing. Everything is as it has been for the last two years."

The man's eyes gleamed from behind his spectacles. "And you have received this news from a reliable source?"

"The best possible source. It comes directly from the Director of the Safe Keeping Department himself. It will cost us a small commission of course, but my connections through Divonne Casino have finally borne fruit."

"They have indeed. Then I think we deserve another glass of

Laurent Perrier before we partake of our delicious repast and discuss our plan in somewhat more detail." He counted on his fingers. "We have four months to get ourselves organised." Raising his glass again, he said, "To a very profitable partnership, my dear."

Just before three o'clock the woman reclaimed her coat and bid Arthur farewell with a modest peck on the cheek. She walked up Piccadilly and into Fortnum & Mason's tea department. As she waited to pay for the expensive tin of leaves, she selected a speed number on her mobile. "*Cheri*," she said, "wonderful news. Arthur is up for it. He'll manage the whole business. With my help, of course. He bought me a delicious lunch and couldn't take his eyes off my *poitrine*. He's even invited me to the ballet next Thursday, at the Royal Albert Hall. It's Minkus's *Don Quixote* with Simon Ball. I think he's falling for me."

"So, he's hooked. Good. Be careful to keep him at a distance and on the boil. Did you get an idea of the cost?"

"He's going to call me when he's prepared an initial plan, but he wants to move very quickly."

"Now I have to make sure I can get the money."

"Phone me when you're sure. And you need to contact the doctor also. There's a lot to be done in a fairly short time."

"I'll call you as soon as I can at your hotel and I'll see you next week."

"I can't wait. I love you. Goodbye." She paid eight pounds twenty for the tea and walked out towards Piccadilly underground station to take the tube back to her three star hotel in Bayswater.

Monte Carlo, Monaco

Prince Muhammad Samir Ismail Abdullah El Moutawakel Bensouda took too large a swig of his Glenmorangie single malt and swallowed uncomfortably, trying to supress a cough. The smooth ten year old whisky wasn't helping his frame of mind. It was well after midnight and he was sitting in the member's bar of the Monte

Carlo Casino in Monaco, a quiet haven, subtly removed from the bustling throng of wealthy and not so wealthy gamblers and tourists who still crowded the gaming rooms and public areas. Bensouda pondered his situation. The tables hadn't been kind to him tonight. In fact they hadn't been kind to him for the last year, any of them. Macau, Las Vegas, Divonne, London, he'd contributed heavily to their record profits and gone a long way towards squandering the impressive fortune he'd inherited.

He took an envelope from his inside pocket, unfolded the letter and reread it for the umpteenth time that day. Although he was becoming used to receiving threatening letters from his many creditors, he was obliged to take this last one extremely seriously. If he lost the family home in Spain his very life would be at risk, even his siblings would not tolerate that level of profligacy. He ordered another whisky from the tail-coated waiter and sat quietly reflecting on the rapid erosion of what had seemed like an inexhaustible mountain of wealth. *Perhaps it's time to stop gambling and find a more reliable source of income,* he told himself.

Bensouda finished his drink, left a hundred Euro note as a tip and walked unsteadily out to the entrance hall. At least they weren't hassling him to pay for his drinks. He'd already paid through the nose on the tables, the drinks were on the house, even the great number he consumed while throwing his money away.

His chauffeur drove up to the entrance and helped his employer into the back of the Rolls Royce Phantom. The drive back to his hotel at that time of night was less than a half hour, unlike during the day, when it could take several hours along the beautifully picturesque but hopelessly congested coast road. He tried to focus on his problems, making mental commitments, not for the first time, to stop drinking and gambling, lose weight and get back into competition shape. After a few minutes he dozed off and was woken by the door being opened by the concierge of the Hotel Negresco on the Promenade des Anglais in Nice.

"*Bonsoir, M. le Prince.*" The Rolls drove off towards his driver's lodgings and the concierge led him through the lobby towards the elevators. "*Vous avez votre clef?* You have your key?"

The man took the key and inserted it into the panel and pressed the top floor button.

Bensouda took a one hundred Euro note from his pocket and folded it into the concierge's hand.

"*Merci et bonne nuit, M. le Prince. A demain.* Sleep well. I'll see you tomorrow." He returned the key and the lift doors closed.

Bensouda managed to open the door of the suite, walked across the wide entrance hall into the principal bedroom, kicked off his shoes and fell onto the king size bed. The curtains were open just enough to show the lights on the promenade around the Bay of Angels, but he didn't see them. He was already dead to the world.

DAY ONE

SUNDAY, JULY 11, 2010

FOUR

Johannesburg, South Africa

The score in the World Cup Final was Netherlands 3 - Spain 2. No goals yet, just yellow cards. The noise in the FNB stadium, Soccer City, was unbearable, almost worse after the half-time whistle had been blown than during the match itself.

"Those bloody vuvuzelas! They should be banned. I'll be surprised if I don't get a burst eardrum by the end of this match." Emma Stewart held her hands over her ears to try to block out the incessant blast that seemed to emanate from the throat of every one of the 90,000 fans who packed the stadium.

"Never mind, Mum. Just think of the headlines in the Newcastle Herald; '*Local writer struck deaf during World Cup Final*'. That's pretty cool." Her son Leo stood up and stretched painfully, trying to get the circulation restored after sitting with his knees under his chin for the last hour. Emma's books sold reasonably well, but not well enough to afford seats with enough leg room to comfortably accommodate his six foot three frame. But he wasn't complaining. Just being at the final was a terrific reward for his eight grade 'A' GCSE passes the previous year. At age fifteen, Leo was not only tall beyond his years, but clever enough to be already submitting applications to the best universities in the UK. With any luck, he'd have three or four 'A' levels under his belt and be an undergrad in a top college before he was eighteen.

"I have to go to the loo," he announced. "Can I get you anything? A drink, hot dog, whatever?"

"I'll come with you. I need to stretch my legs too and I don't think I can sit for another hour without a toilet break."

They fought their way along the aisle to the main thoroughfare then followed the signs through the masses of football-crazy supporters to the toilets.

"Wait for me here," instructed his mother. "It's bound to be bedlam in the Ladies. Don't budge until I get out."

Five minutes later, Emma struggled out of the door, still wiping her hands dry on her handkerchief, and swept the crowded area with her keen gaze. She couldn't spot the easily identifiable tall slim figure of her son. After a few minutes wait she realised the crowds were returning to their seats for the second half. *That silly boy,* she said to herself, *he just doesn't listen to me at all.*

She made her way back to their aisle but Leo's seat was vacant and he wasn't to be seen. Supressing her exasperation she went back to the toilet area and asked an attendant to look inside for a tall teenager.

"No one", he reported.

She visited the drinks stand, the hot dog stand and every other place she imagined he might be – but he wasn't. When she came back into the stadium, play had resumed and she could see around their seating area more easily. She anxiously scoured the crowded rows one after the other but she couldn't pick out his tall figure. Leo was nowhere to be seen.

Another attendant directed her to the security office, which was near to the main stadium entrance. A young black woman listened to her story and showed her into a small ante room. A burly, hard looking white man in a creased linen suit came in. He looked like a sand bag with arms and legs.

"I'm Marius Coetzee, head of the security company. What's wrong?" His skin was pock marked and his breath smelled of stale cigarettes. He spoke in an arrogant manner with a strong Afrikaans accent and didn't seem to be particularly interested in Emma's problem as he lit up a small black cheroot.

"It's my son. I can't find him," she said, trying to supress the feeling of panic that was invading her. She explained the circumstances and described Leo. "He's fifteen, slim and very tall, it should be easy to spot him, but I can't."

"Mrs. Stewart. Do you know how many people there are in that crowd? There's more than ninety thousand. Your son could be anywhere in the stadium, it's the size of a small town. Maybe he met someone he knew and he's sat with them, or he's still in the lavatory, or he went to get a coke."

"You don't understand, I told him...."

He interrupted her response, "Lady, it doesn't matter what you tell teenagers these days, believe me, I know all about it. I've got one of my own in there and I haven't a clue where she is." His manner seemed to imply that he didn't care either and neither should she. He went on, "Have you tried his mobile phone? Even though it should be switched off."

Emma fished two mobiles from her bag. "I switched them both off and put them in here. He hasn't got his with him."

"Well, you're just going to have to wait in your seat until the game ends and hope he turns up. Or you could go down to your gate and watch for him to come out."

"And that's all you have to say? I thought you were head of security?"

For the first time the man looked slightly abashed. "Have you got his passport?"

"They're both in the safe in our hotel room."

"A photograph?"

She shook her head. "No,wait." Switching on her mobile, Emma found her photo album and scrolled through the latest pictures. "Here. Taken yesterday." She showed him a snap of Leo standing by the hotel pool.

"Right. Send it to my phone, here's the number, and I'll have it circulated to the guards throughout the grounds. There's over a thousand of them. Someone might have seen him." She noticed he avoided asking the obvious question. "Now go and wait in your seat until the end of the game. If he doesn't turn up, come back here just before full-time and one minute after the final whistle I'll make an announcement. I doubt if anyone'll hear it in the chaos, but it's all I can do at the moment."

Reluctantly Emma followed his advice. She sat on tenterhooks for the rest of the game, repeatedly peering around the stadium, watching and listening to the raucous behaviour of the crowd, trying not to think of how vulnerable she and her son were in this tough and unforgiving country.

A half hour after extra time was over, Emma and Coetzee were still standing by the stairwell watching the last of the crowd making their way out. She had hardly registered the second half of the match and was already running down to the security office when Andrés Iniesta's goal for Spain in the 116th minute caused the crowd to errupt with delight. The security man had waited until there was a slight lull in the pandemonium after the final whistle, so his announcement over the Tannoy system was more or less audible, but Leo hadn't turned up.

"What now?" She turned to the security chief, the mounting panic in her mind now showing in her sharpened tone. "What do we do now?"

"Well he must have left the stadium at some time, because he's certainly not here."

"Then we'll have to look at the videos from the CCTV cameras at the gates. We must be able to spot him if he left."

"Mrs. Stewart." Coetzee looked even more jaundiced. "There are twenty gates here, twenty, and it's almost two hours since you lost him. It would take a night and a day to look at all the footage. It can't be done."

"Very well then. So what do we do, in your expert opinion? What's next in the operations manual?"

He gave her a sharp look. "What do you do for a living?"

"I write books, but.."

"What kind of books?"

"Thrillers, crime stories, that kind of thing, but I don't see.."

"I'm just trying to get to know you. It's background. It could be important. You should know that if you're a writer. Anyway, which hotel are you staying in?"

"It's a small hotel, the Packard, near Mayfair."

"I know it. We'll call there now, see if they've seen him."

He led the way to his office which stunk of cigarette smoke. "What about your daughter?" Emma tried to break the ice a little. "Don't you have to take her home?"

He shrugged and moved some papers around on the desk. "She texted me. Her mother picked her up. She lives with her."

"Oh, I see. Sorry, I just assumed.." *So that's his problem,* she realised.

"It's OK. Anyway, how long have you been in SA?"

"We were in Cape Town for a week and the last three days here in Jo'burg."

"Right. Where did you stay in Cape Town?"

"The Best Western Suites Hotel. I booked it online. Same for the Packard. I can't afford expensive hotels."

"When did you make your bookings?"

"Almost a year ago. It's the only way to get flights and rooms at a reasonable price."

He gave a rare smile. "Too right. You got the Packard number handy?"

Emma gave him her key card and he dialled the number and asked for Leo Stewart's room.

The number rang out for a while, then the telephonist came back on the line. "There's no reply. Do you want me to try his mother's room?"

She came back on the line again, "They're not in the hotel. They were booked to go to the match and the coach hasn't returned, so I doubt they're back yet."

"Pass me the duty manager, please." Coetzee avoided Emma's gaze as he waited. "Barry, Hi, it's Marius Coetzee." He quickly explained the problem. "Mrs. Stewart's here with me now. Have you seen the kid, Leo?" He listened again. "Well, if he turns up, call me right away, OK?"

He lit up another cheroot and stared across his desk at Emma. "Now, Mrs Stewart, I want you to dig in your memory and be absolutely honest with me about what your son's been doing for the last two weeks in South Africa, where he's been, who he's been seeing and anything that's happened which would explain his behaviour."

"What do you mean 'behaviour'? Are you completely mad? My son is missing. That's not a behavioural characteristic. Something has happened and he's somehow got lost amongst ninety thousand people. He's fifteen years old and still at school, for God's sake! He doesn't know anyone in South Africa, never mind Johannesburg. We came here a week ago for the football and he doesn't even know the way back to the hotel, because we came on a special coach." She put her hand to her mouth, "And he hasn't got enough cash with him to get a taxi. If that's your idea of behaviour then it's a waste of time continuing with this conversation." She stood up, her rage overcoming her anxiety. "Where's the nearest police station? I'm going there right now to see if I can find someone who talks sense."

Just then, Coetzee's phone rang. He listened for a moment or two, looking at her intently, then gave a sharp order in Afrikaans. "Sit down, Mrs. Stewart. I'm sorry about my last question. But kids these days are into everything; drugs, guns, robbery, it's just unbelievable. I'm only trying to find out what kind of a kid he is that might explain him going missing. Anyway, it seeme he might have been seen. One of the guards is on his way up. His name is Jacob Masuku. Be nice to him, we might strike lucky."

Neither spoke until a small, wiry black man of about fifty with frizzy hair and a security badge on his shabby shirt came into the room. He started jabbering away in a kind of pidgin English, showing the photo on his mobile and gesticulating. Emma couldn't understand a word he said.

She jumped up from her chair. "What's he saying? Has he seen Leo?"

"He says he saw a young person like the one in the photo leaving the stand at half time."

"What? That's not possible. He was waiting for me. I was only three or four minutes in the toilet."

"Wait. He's not finished. Just wait until he's finished please."

The guard continued his story, waving his arms and rolling his eyes, glancing sideways at Emma.

Coetzee stopped him and asked a question, the same question, twice. The man nodded vehemently. "Yes Boss. Sure Boss." He said in plain English, looking again at Emma, who was shifting around nervously on the hard seat.

"Right. Mrs Stewart, please just sit still and calm down." He cleared his throat. "This man says he saw your son at half time. He says he's sure, because he got a very good look at him. Leo was leaving the stadium by gate number fourteen."

"That's the door near where we used the toilets." She paused and looked at the guard. "Why did he wait all this time? Why didn't he come up when you sent the photo?"

"He didn't switch his phone on until just now, to call his wife. They're all the same, they don't like to leave them on in case the battery goes down. I don't know why we issued the bloody things in the first place."

"But why was Leo leaving? It doesn't make any sense."

Coetzee dumped the remains of his cheroot in the ashtray. "He says Leo was unconscious, or asleep. He was pushed out in a wheelchair!"

FIVE

Johannesburg, South Africa

"He says there was a white man in a dark shirt with a badge on it and a woman who looked like a nurse and they pushed Leo out the stadium gate in a wheelchair. He's certain of it."

Emma jumped to her feet. She was in a state of complete shock. "What's he talking about. Why would he be in a wheelchair? It's total madness. There's nothing wrong with him at all, he's the healthiest person you could find." She turned to the guard and grabbed his arms. "You're lying! Why are you lying? Where's my son?" What have you done to my son?"

The guard fell back, trying to release himself from her desperate grasp. "Boss! Boss!" He cried out, afraid of hurting this crazy Englishwoman and getting into trouble.

"Mrs Stewart. Stop that now! The man's just telling you what he saw." He pulled her away from the terrified guard. "Just calm down and stay in your seat. If he's the only person who saw your son we need his help and you're not going to get it like that."

Emma sank back down in the chair, her mind a turmoil of emotions. As if in a dream, she listened to Coetzee cross examining the security guard until he seemed convinced of his story. He took the man out and sat him in the ante room then returned and closed the door. Took a bottle of brandy and a glass from a drawer in his desk and poured a couple of fingers.

"Here, drink this, it'll make you feel calmer."

She pushed the glass away. "I don't want to feel calm. I want to find my son."

"Well, the guard says he seemed to be completely unconcious and they wheeled him out about half way through the break. He didn't speak to the man and woman, just assumed they were medical staff, which isn't smart since there hadn't been an emergency call. But these security guards are frightened of anyone who looks important, so he just kept stumm, until he saw the photo on his phone."

He lit another cheroot and blew the smoke away from her. "Now. Tell me about Leo's evening. This was a big occasion for him, wasn't it? Had he met some friends, taken a drink or two? Experimented with something maybe?"

"I already told you he doesn't drink or take anything. He's still at school and he doesn't know anybody here. You must know better than me that there was trouble near the hotel just after we arrived, Two men were shot in the street. Do you really think I would let my son go out and make friends in a country where people get shot in front of your hotel? Don't be so idiotic. Why do you keep asking stupid questions?"

"OK. I'll ask a less stupid question. Why didn't you tell me Leo's father was black?"

Emma had been waiting for the question, but it still came as a shock. "Because it's not relevant. Not relevant at all. Anyway, it's clear from the photo I sent you. His father was black, but that's got nothing to do with him being abducted from your football stadium." She looked the man straight in the eyes. "Unless you've worked out a really clever theory without any facts to support it."

"Was his father South African?"

"No he wasn't and that's the end of this interrogation. I'm not the problem here, it's the lack of security in your stadium that's the problem." She got to her feet again. "Now, either take me to the police station or get a taxi to take me." She walked to the door, stopped, then turned back to him, her eyes alight. "Wait! Now it makes sense to look at the CCTV video for gate fourteen. We know the approximate time, so we should see something."

They found Leo on the video monitor at exactly 21:24, just when Emma calculated she would have been emerging from the toilets. As the security man had described, he was sitting in a wheelchair, his head thrown back, obviously completely out of it. A man, wearing a white cap and gauze mask, dark shirt and trousers was pushing the chair and a black female in a nurse's outfit, also wearing a medical mask, was leading the way through the crowded area. The camera was situated above the doors at the stadium exit, looking back along the corridor and the shot was about twenty seconds long until they went out of camera range.

Coetzee looked away from the screen at Emma. Her face was aghast, her hand to her mouth, breathing in short panic gasps.

"Who are they? Can you see their faces? Why are they pushing my son outside? What's wrong with him? Why didn't they come and find me? I was right there just a moment later." She paused, thinking about the scene. "There must be a vehicle outside if they are taking him in a wheelchair. An ambulance or a van or something. Is there a camera outside so we can see what they do? "

"The cameras outside are pointed at the turnstiles, in case of trouble at the gates. There's some in the car park, but I doubt they went there. They'd get him into the vehicle as quickly as possible, right outside the gate, but we don't have that covered." He re-ran the shot, slowing it down and peering intently at the screen. "I can't make their faces out. I've got no idea who they are and I don't recognise the badge the man's wearing. They're looking down and sideways, away from the angle of the camera. I'd say they knew it was there and they're avoiding it to hide their faces."

"So you're saying they don't want to be seen. They're taking my son against his will and they've given him something to knock him out. And no one saw anything on the CCTV monitor and the guard wasn't trained to say anything and we don't know where they've taken him. How could you let this happen in your stadium? What kind of a security manager or whetever you call yourself are you? Oh, my God. I don't believe this is happening." Emma collapsed into a chair, her eyes wide with fear.

"Mrs Stewart, you've got to calm down. There must be a reasonable explanation for all this. You told me there is no one in South Africa who has any interest in you or your son, so either he was taken ill, or it's some kind of mistaken identity. I can't be held responsible for everything that goes on in a stadium with ninety thousand football-mad fans inside." Coetzee sounded almost as frantic as Emma felt. "We need to get to the police and find out where they went and why. Just wait a moment."

He selected a two minute sequence from the video before and after Leo's appearance and burned it onto a CD. "I'll call the police right now and we'll take this CD down to the station. Come on, my car's downstairs." He pulled out his mobile phone and ushered Emma to the door.

Diepkloof, Gauteng, South Africa

It took them only 15 minutes to get to the Police Station at Diepkloof, since most of the traffic was going the other way, towards Joburg. The precinct appeared to be in a state of complete chaos, mostly full of drunken and bloodied soccer fans, but Coetzee's call seemed to have had some effect. They waited only a few minutes before Sergeant Nwosu appeared, looking smart and fresh in his beige trousers and cream shirt and carrying a brown cap. He was a good looking, tall, skinny man, smelling of a powerful after shave or perfume, his head shaved and gleaming with oil. It was now after midnight and Emma was embarrassed by her dishevelled, sweaty appearance, but the man smiled kindly and shook her hand.

"How do you do, Mrs Stewart, I'm sorry to hear about this problem. Please come inside and we'll talk about it. Our job is to help our visitors if we can, whatever the circumstances."

He led them into a small conference room with an old Sony laptop and a projector on the table top, pointing at a white wall. Coetzee gave him the CD and he loaded it and prepared the laptop. "I understand this concerns your son's disappearance from the game tonight?"

"It wasn't a disappearance, Sergeant. Just look at what happened." Emma braced herself to view the kidnapping again.

He adjusted the projector beam and the scene was visible on the wall, much larger and not quite so distinct as on the monitor in the security back room.

"There! There he is." Emma put her hand to her mouth again.

"You're sure that's your son, Leo?"

"Of course I'm sure. I'm absolutely certain of it. But I have no idea what's happened to him and who those people are. I left him five minutes before and he was absolutely fine."

"Hmm. I agree it's uncommon to get suddenly sick at fifteen years of age." The policeman reran the clip again, peering closely, as Coetzee had done.

Emma's mind was suddenly clouded by an intruding doubt. She couldn't put her finger on it, but something was nagging at her subconcious. Something she'd heard. *What was it?*

Nwosu stopped the clip with the frame of Leo lying back in the wheelchair. "I see he has African blood in his veins."

Emma switched back to the policeman's words and she shifted nervously on the seat.

"Now, tell me about his father? Where he came from, where he is? Just a few details so I can get a picture of Leo's background. It might help us to unravel this mystery."

All at once it dawned on Emma what the nagging doubt was. *'Leo, only fifteen years of age', he'd said. But I didn't tell him that and neither did Coetzee.* She quickly reran in her mind the security man's call from his mobile as they drove to the station. He'd mentioned Mrs Stewart and her 'young son, a schoolboy', who was missing and had possibly been abducted from the stadium, the guard's testimony and the CCTV shot of the 'boy' in a wheelchair. He'd never mentioned her son's name, nor his age. How did this policeman know these details? She shivered, her feeling of panic increasing, disbelieving and frightened at this latest revelation. *What in God's name is going on here?*

"Sergeant Nwosu, how did you know so many details about my son? Like his name is Leo and he's fifteen years old?" She looked intently at the policeman, to see his reaction.

"His details?" Nwosu coughed and glanced across at Coetzee, who gave an imperceptible shrug without looking away from the image on the wall. "I'm not sure why that would be important, but of course Mr Coetzee informed me when he called. We're both very concerned with your son's wellbeing and all information is vital to finding him."

Emma's brain was working overtime. Somehow this police sergeant had known about Leo without being told. He had known before they got there. Maybe even before the abduction. And Coetzee was involved. He hadn't asked about Leo being black, not until later and now his lack of reaction to her question wasn't normal, he'd never even turned his head. *In case he gave something away.*

"Mrs Stewart? Emma?"

"What did you say?"

"I was asking about Leo's father. I'd like to get some background on him. Where he came from, where he is now? Are you still together? Those kind of details can be vital to an investigation like this."

"Let me think for a moment. My son is missing and I'm trying to remain calm and rational and all you do is keep asking me questions about his father. Just leave me alone for a moment, please."

The two men sat back, Coetzee lighting up another cheroot, fiddling with his lighter, trying unsuccessfully to look nonchalant. Emma concentrated her mind, revisiting the last few minutes of conversation, trying to absorb and analyse what she'd heard, what she'd seen. Finally reaching a terrifying conclusion. *CONSPIRACY.* The word jumped into her mind. *These men are conspiring together. The head of a security firm and a police sergeant. Conspiring to abduct my son. But why? What's so important about a fifteen year old schoolboy? Why would anyone want to kidnap Leo?*

Old, almost forgotten memories came to her mind. Thoughts and worries she hadn't entertained for many years came flooding back. She tried to push them aside. To concentrate on the present. On finding Leo.

Her mind started racing again. *This is just too far- fetched. Don't let your crime novels start taking over your imagination. Conspiracies only happen in books and deranged minds. Kids just don't get abducted in crowded football stadiums. There must be some reasonable explanation to all this. And the last thing you want to do is to alienate these men. They may be your only chance of finding Leo, or at least keeping in touch with events. But don't answer any dangerous questions.*

Aloud she said, "Before we lose any more time we have to check with all the hospitals around. Leo must have been taken to a hospital or a clinic. If there was something wrong with him, he can't be very far. And you can put out an 'all points alert', or whatever you call it here, for the other police forces to look out for him."

"I've already set the wheels in motion. My assistant is calling the medical centres as we speak. He's also preparing a circular to email around. We do know what we're doing, Mrs Stewart. We're really quite capable." Nwosu looked affronted at being lectured to by this young woman.

Coetzee handed him his mobile phone. "Take this picture for the circular. Mrs Stewart took it just yesterday."

Emma was thinking furiously. "I want to call the British Embassy," she announced. "We have to inform them in the event of an emergency. We were given strict instructions when we got the travel documents. Can you get the number for me please?"

"Well, until we have some real information I don't think we can classify this as an emergency yet. It's only a few hours since Leo's disappearance and it's usual to wait twenty-four hours before taking that decision. Let's wait until we get feedback from the hospitals."

"But that might take all night. And if you don't think that a teenage boy being doped and kidnapped from your stadium is an emergency then I don't know what would qualify." She paused, trying to think clearly for a moment, then stood up and walked to the door. "Please call a taxi for me. I'm going back to my hotel. There's nothing I can do here and I need to make some phone calls. You can contact me if there's any news."

Nwosu looked worriedly at Coetzee. "But we still need a lot of information before we can carry out a proper investigation. Please sit down again Mrs Stewart so I can ask you further questions."

Emma struggled to remain calm and assertive. "Sergeant Nwosu. It's now almost one in the morning and I'm exhausted. I don't think anything I tell you tonight will change the situation. As you just said, let's wait for the feedback from the hospitals and we'll see what transpires before morning. If necessary I can come back and answer your questions then, but now I want to get back to my hotel."

DAY TWO

MONDAY JULY 12, 2010

SIX

Johannesburg, South Africa

Emma put down the phone in her hotel room. It was after three in the morning. Her last call had been to the British High Commission in Pretoria. Coetzee had dropped her off in front of the Packard Hotel after she had refused to answer any more of Nwosu's questions and told her a car would come to pick her up at ten in the morning to take her back to the station. He drove off looking quite disgruntled. Barry Lambert, the manager, was waiting in reception for her and asked if there was anything he could do. It seemed the hotel staff had taken a liking to Leo and they were concerned for his welfare. He tried unsuccessfully to console her then she took the keys to both of their rooms and went up to the seventh floor.

She entered Leo's room. It was as untidy as his bedroom at home in Newcastle, books and papers scattered over the dresser and night table, shirts and shorts lying on the floor and on the bed, towels hung over the bath and his toilet things all over the place. She looked around at her son's belongings and sat on the edge of the bed, tears pouring down her face. Taking one of his shirts she held it close, breathing in the familiar smell of his body, remembering the feeling of his energy and youth. *Oh, Leo. Where are you? What's happening to you?*

After a while Emma pulled herself together and went next door to her to her own room, stripped off and ran a warm bath. Lying back in the foamy water she forced her mind to revisit the events of the evening. *I've got to find out what's going on. Leo didn't just get sick and pass out, he's never been ill in his life. And the whole thing's just too slick. A wheelchair and two people appear from nowhere and push him out of the building. But to where, and why?*

A strange thought came to her mind. *It's almost like one of my thrillers, but the plot is backwards. I have to reconstruct it from scratch if I want to find my son. This isn't going to be easy. I've got to find Leo without telling the police things they don't need to know.* Even if there was something going on between Coetzee and Nwosu, they had the resources and it wouldn't do to get on the wrong side of them.

She towelled off and sat in her nightdress by the bed with her notebook. The A4 notebook she used to outline the plots and characters for her novels. Only this time it wasn't a novel, it was the real life disappearance of her only son. Emma had an almost photographic memory and formidable powers of observation. She cleared her mind then tried to dredge her memory of everything she had observed and remembered that evening, noting the events by time, by scene, by characters and by impressions or possible conclusions or motives for the abduction. For that was what she was now convinced had happened, her fifteen year old son had been abducted and she was perhaps the only person who could be trusted to find him. She started writing.

After filling three pages of the notebook, she opened her laptop and entered the user name and password for the hotel WiFi network. They had been going to charge her a daily rate for usage but the manager gave her a free pass when he discovered she was a writer. She went online and typed in, *Hospitals in South Johannesburg.* The screen showed three establishments close to Soccer City; *South Rand, Chris Hani Baragwanath* and *RLR Squalene.* She noted down the phone numbers and picked up the hotel phone, it would be cheaper to make local calls than to use her UK mobile.

The telephonist at South Rand asked her to hold on while she called the night duty supervisor to ask if he'd heard anything from the police about Leo. The answer was no. There had been no call or email from the Diepkloof police department or any other police department that night and there was no record of an admittance of a teenage English boy. The answer was the same from the other two hospitals. Emma had drawn a blank, but Nwosu had apparently done nothing.

She looked up the other police stations around the neighbourhood of Soccer City. There were ten of them. Randomly, she chose *Dobsonville, Kliptown* and *Meadowlands.* Summoning up her best South African accent, she called the first precinct. "Sorry to ring you so late, but I've been circulating a message about a missing British teenager and I'm not sure if I sent it to you. Would you mind checking for me?"

The operator came back after a few minutes. "We've had no emails or faxes about a missing boy. Why don't you send it again and I'll make sure it goes to the night sergeant right away." She called the other stations, but they had received nothing either.

Emma put the phone down after the last call and sat back, her heart in her mouth, stunned and scared to death by the implications of this news. Now she knew for certain there was a conspiracy to kidnap her son and the police were involved.

She thought back over the evening's events, putting the pieces together in her mind. Coetzee had taken her to see Nwosu, so they were definitely working together. Two people had taken Leo out and it was probably one of them who had put him to sleep. *That's at least four people and one of them was a policeman. How high up does this plan go? Nwosu's a sergeant, would he act without the authority of his superiors? Who else is involved?*

And all this planning and people just to kidnap my fifteen year old son! What reason can there possibly be? We seem to be trapped in the middle of some elaborate scheme, but what on earth for?

Emma assessed her situation. *I'm all alone here in this foreign country, without friends or connections of any kind and for some reason that I can't begin to comprehend, my son has been taken by a gang involving a police officer.* She forced herself to think clearly about her options. How could she find out more about the abduction without going through Coetzee or Nwosu? There must be a way to get around them and find the truth. She needed outside help and she needed it now.

She found the number for the British High Commission in Pretoria. This time she used her mobile, the hotel rates for long distance calls would be ruinous. A recorded woman's voice, very English, advised her that the embassy was closed, but in the event of an emergency she could be diverted to speak to a Duty Consular Officer at the Foreign Office Global Response Centre in London. She pressed 'one, hash', and a man's voice came on the line.

If Emma hadn't been so concerned and fearful about the fate of her son, she would have found the ensuing conversation almost amusing. After trying to convince Mr. Lawrence that a missing British teenager in Johannesburg who had been seen unconcious in a wheelchair being pushed out of Soccer City constituted an emergency, she finally gave up. And her refusal to answer questions she preferred not to answer didn't help her case at all. She thanked the man and rang off after ten minutes when she saw she was getting nowhere.

Emma lay back on her bed, her mind going over and over the problem, trying to find solutions until her head was splitting. If she couldn't trust the police and if the British Foreign Office was incapable of acting without an in depth interrogation, who could she turn to? Finally, she just couldn't think any more. Physically exhausted and emotionally drained, she switched off the light and lay in the dark, crying softly and thinking of her son. After a while, she fell into a troubled sleep.

It was six hours since Leo had been taken.

SEVEN

Johannesburg, South Africa

It was seven fifteen in the morning. Emma was hanging on for grim life as *Coetzee drove his Land Cruiser at over one hundred forty kilometres an hour down the De Villiers Graaff Motorway towards Diepkloof. Coming off the highway to the left they flew past Ridgeway and Glenanda, then turned up towards the South Rand Hospital. Coetzee stopped in front of the A&E Department and they jumped out of the car.*

"Leo Stewart?" He called to the attendant, who pointed down the corridor to the right, "Room seven."

They sprinted down the corridor and pushed the door open. The room was full of equipment; pulleys, automated medicine dosage machines, monitors, breathing apparatus, some of them making strangely musical sounds, like slot machines in an amusement arcade. A doctor was standing by the side of the bed, making notes on a tablet. The sheet on the bed was pulled up over the head of the occupant, who was lying motionless. There was no sign nor sound of breathing.

The doctor looked over at them. "I'm sorry," he said. "You're just too late." He pulled back the sheet to reveal the young boy lying there, still and lifeless.

"NO!" Emma sat up, sweat pouring down her face. "NO!" She cried again, then fell back on the bed, her body convulsed with helpless sobbing, her tears seaping into the bedsheets, already soaked from the sweat of her nightmare. She lay crying for several minutes, a vision of Leo in the wheelchair, unconscious and helpless, burning in her memory. Finally, she wiped away her tears on the bed sheet. *I must stay in control,* she told herself. It wouldn't help Leo for her to lie there wallowing in self pity. She got up to shower and clean her teeth. It was just before seven, she'd been asleep for less than four hours, but she had too many things to do to waste time on sleep.

Emma made herself a cup of tea with the hotel kettle and tea bags. There was no sugar, but a plastic capsule of cream and a biscuit. She realised she was starving. It was over twelve hours since she and Leo had shared a pizza in one of the cafés at the stadium. There was fruit in the room and she peeled herself a banana and went next door to her son's room. There was nobody about, but she locked the doors just in case. The empty room seemed dark and oppressive and she opened the curtains to let the early morning light in. She went through Leo's things meticulously, looking for anything that seemed out of place or unusual. Folding up his clothes carefully and gently, she placed them on the bed, unwilling to pack them into his suitcase. She found nothing untoward in the room that might explain his disappearance. Looking at the small pile of her son's belongings, tears started to prick at her eyes again but she overcame her emotion and went back to her room.

Emma finished the fruit while she went back through her notebook. Rereading her notes from the previous night, she was even more convinced that Coetzee and Nwosu were involved in Leo's abduction. What was more, they hadn't made a very good job of covering it up. Presumably they didn't expect to be challenged by a feeble English woman who wrote crime novels for a living. Their positions as security chief and police officer were guaranteed to give them credibility over a distraught mother crying conspiracy.

As she progressed with her line of thought and notemaking, her mind went off on another tack. Kidnappers didn't take people without a reason and the most common reason was money. In Leo's case there couldn't be any other explanation. He wasn't a celebrity or socially important, mixed up with a terrorist group or had any political connections. *He's just a bright schoolboy who likes football. But why would they assume I've got money? They must think crime writers make a fortune selling TV rights and movie scripts to Hollywood all day long. I wish! But I suppose as long as these people, whoever they are, think they can get money, Leo will be safe and looked after. You don't damage your only asset if you're putting it up for ransom. Ransom, that must be what we're looking at here. How am I going to face up to negotiations over the value of my son's life?*

Another thought suddenly came to her mind. A worrying detail she'd buried beneath the events of last night. She opened the safe in the wardrobe and took out their travel documents. Their BA return flights via London were booked for Wednesday evening, the day after tomorrow, and she was certain they were not flexible and non-refundable, even though they'd cost a fortune. She looked at her watch, it was now after eight. Quickly going online she got the BA office number at Johannesburg airport and called. The employee informed her that the bookings could only be changed in the event of a death or with a doctor's certificate of illness causing inability to travel. If she and Leo didn't turn up for the departure, they lost their tickets. One way tickets at short notice would cost almost a thousand pounds each, but all the flights were full for the next few days, it was World Cup week. Emma thanked her and rang off without trying to explain the circumstances, it was just a waste of time.

She took up her notebook again, assessing her financial situation. The cost of changing the tickets was more than she had with her and would eat up most of her bank account balance in Lloyds. In her purse she had almost four thousand rand - about three hundred pounds, plus another hundred and fifty in sterling. Four hundred and fifty pounds total, plus about seventeen hundred available in her UK account and a thousand on her credit card. This trip had cost her almost two thousand pounds, so she was getting very low on available funds. Her pension plan had been hammered by the crisis in 2008 and was starting to build up slowly again, but definitely not a cash option. Her apartment in Newcastle had a fairly low mortgage but raising money on it would take time she didn't have. She was due some royalties on September 30th and the first draft for her new novel was almost finished. That would bring in a deposit of forty or fifty thousand, which would assure their solvency until the end of the year, but in terms of ready cash, she had just over three thousand pounds.

Emma felt ill at the thought. She had to find someone who could advise or help her. Turning to a new sheet in her notebook she drew a line down the page to split it into two columns. She headed one, *MONEY*, and the other, *ADVICE*.

She went through a mental list of her friends and acquaintances, people who she could trust and people who had money. It was a very short list. The first name that came to mind was her publisher, Alan Bridges, owner of an independent publishing house in Edinburgh and her on-off boyfriend for the last five or so years. She put his name into both columns, although she knew he'd be full of sympathy and good advice, but not very forthcoming with money. He wasn't that well off himself. Maybe an advance on her royalties, but nothing earth shattering. A couple more names came to her, which she added, without much conviction. Friends who would probably declare their dying love and devotion but would be totally useless to help unless she could convince them to spring a small loan. And a small loan, she was beginning to realise, was not what she needed.

In terms of family, her options were even more limited. Both of Emma's parents had passed away, she was unmarried and apart from Leo, she had only one surviving relative, her sister, Jenny, who was three year's younger than her, born in 1972. That was before their parents' acrimonious and devastating divorce. She wrote *Jenny Bishop* in both columns, then sat back, thinking about her sister.

Jenny had lost her husband in a hit and run accident a couple of years ago. It had been a horrible time for her, since her father-in-law had then died in an accident in his swimming pool in Spain. She had gone down there for a couple of weeks and apparently everything had been sorted out without further incident. Emma knew Jenny's father-in-law was a wealthy man and she had told her, on a recent shopping trip in London, that she had 'come into a little money'. She had demonstrated this by being unusually generous with Emma. Obviously she knew not all writers are millionaires, most of them, like her, were just struggling to pay the mortgage.

In addition, Emma had come to recognise that her sister was a lot smarter than she. Originally a junior school teacher with a handful of 'A' levels and a BA in teaching, she had taken two years off to graduate from the London School of Economics with a degree in Sociology, then gone back to Sunderland to teach kids with learning difficulties. This had greatly impressed Emma. Her own forays into the NGO world of humanitarian endeavour had been instigated much more by a desire to escape from her unhappy childhood than to use her limited abilities to save the planet.

Jenny had then married well and after being widowed in tragic circumstances seemed to have reorganised her life. Emma had always thought there was more to her than met the eye. Jenny didn't say much, she just got on with things.

She was often at the house in Spain and had asked Emma to come down for a visit with Leo, but she had somehow not got around to it yet. She was too busy writing her books just to survive and provide her son with a stable home life and a good education. He was the clever one in her family, but now it was her turn. She had to be clever enough to find Leo and get him back from whoever had taken him.

Emma sat on the side of her bed in her shabby three star hotel room in Johannesburg as she tried to get to grips with the enormity of what was required of her. She looked in the wardrobe mirror and saw her pale reflection in the early morning light and she felt frightened and totally helpless.

It was ten and a half hours since Leo had been taken.

EIGHT

Ipswich, England

Jenny Bishop was waiting with her suitcase at the open door of her semi-detached in Ipswich when the house phone rang. She looked at her watch, it was just coming up to seven. *Who would call me at this hour?* When it continued to ring she stepped back into the hall and picked up the receiver. She immediately recognised the lilting north-east accent of her sister.

"Jenny, Jenny, it's Emma. Thank God you're there, I thought you might be away. I need to talk to you. Something terrible's happened and I don't know what to do. Can you call me back on my mobile? I'm still in South Africa and calls are so expensive and I've got no money." Her voice cracked and Jenny heard a sob.

"Calm down, Emma. I'm just leaving for the airport, but I'll call you straight back." She pressed the number on the screen and her sister came back on the line. "What on earth is wrong?"

Emma took a deep breath. "It's Leo. He's disappeared and I'm sure he's been abducted. It's all so complicated it'll take me ages to tell you. When can you call me back? Things are happening very fast here."

"What are you talking about? How can ...." Jenny looked outside. "Just wait a minute. I'm on my way to Stansted airport to fly down to Spain and my cab's arrived. Let me get in and I'll call you straight back again. Is that OK?"

"I won't budge until you call. Thanks, Jenny."

A black minicab drew up and the driver put her case into the boot while Jenny locked the front door then got into the back seat. Since she had 'come into a little money' she'd given up the coach ride to Stansted and negotiated a good price with a local taxi company, not much more than the coach fare but a lot more comfortable. She was still a low-maintenance person, but she'd decided she could afford a little more comfort. However she continued to fly with EasyJet, there were some things she wasn't yet ready to change. It was a grey morning and the countryside rolled past in a dreary blur, like a black and white movie slightly out of focus.

She checked her mobile, it was over ninety per cent charged up and the drive to Stansted was at least an hour, enough for a long conversation. She pressed the recall button. *What's happened with Leo?* She wondered, as the call went through. *Emma's not the type to panic, but she's definitely in a panic right now.*

"Jenny. It's so good to hear your voice. I'm at my wit's end."

"No problem, Emma. Now just calm down and tell me what's wrong. I'm in this cab for an hour and I've got nothing else to do but talk to you."

Jenny's first comment, after listening to her sister's story for thirty minutes, was, "This is too incredible to be true, it sounds like something from one of your books. You're absolutely sure of it?"

"That's exactly what I thought. Then I double checked my notes and went back through my memory and I'm absolutely convinced I'm right. You have to believe me. Leo's been taken by these people. I don't know why and I don't know where, but I know that's what's happened. What am I going to do? I've got no husband, no real friends, no idea of what I should do. You're clever. You know how to fight adversity, get things done."

Like her sister, Jenny had the habit of making notes about everything, though she'd recently started using an iPad and the

Notes App. She looked down the couple of pages she'd written in the cab and asked a few relevant questions. Listening to her quiet and authoritative tone, Emma started to feel better. She answered in a calmer voice, remembering and describing every detail that supported her story.

"There's no question that I'm right, Jenny. Otherwise, where is my son? He can't suddenly have decided to go walkabout. He's got no money and doesn't know anyone. Twelve hours ago he disappeared and he hasn't returned. If he hasn't been abducted, where is he?"

"Right, you're right. We have to assume you're not losing your mind. I'm sorry, I didn't mean that. It's just that it's all so unbelievable, such a shock. Who in God's name would want to kidnap Leo? I wish I was there with you, I know how helpless and alone you must be feeling. But I'm just on the end of a telephone, so between us I'm sure we can get this sorted out."

She paused, thinking hard. "If Leo has been taken, we're dealing with well organised and ruthless people, so you're going to have to be brave and decisive and we need to start taking some decisions right now. When are you supposed to leave?"

"The night after tomorrow. And if we miss the flight, it'll cost me two thousand quid which I don't have. This was a major decision for me, to bring Leo here for the football. It took all my savings and now I'm down to the bare bones."

Jenny made another note – *No money, no flights.* "What's the position with, er," she scrolled up a page on the iPad, "Coetzee and Nwosu?"

"I'm supposed to see them this morning, but I really don't want to listen to any more lies from them."

"Wrong, Emma. That's exactly what you do need to do. You need more details about what happened and they're the only two people who can provide them. You've got to fool them now just as they've been fooling you. What time is it now?"

"We're one hour ahead of you, so it's just before nine here and I'm supposed to be picked up at ten. What do you suggest?"

"Let's go through our notes again and pick out the points you can check. We need to be absolutely sure your theory is right and we need to try to work out how they did this and how we can prove it. We've got two days to find out what happened and contact someone at a higher level to intervene, otherwise we'll get nowhere.

"Now," she continued, "what about the guard who saw Leo in the wheelchair?"

NINE

Diepkloof, Gauteng, South Africa

Coetzee and Nwosu were in the policeman's office, also on the phone. The speaker volume on Nwosu's mobile was low, so they had to sit close to the phone and to each other. Coetzee wasn't keen on being so close to the black man, but their conversation wasn't for public consumption.

Coetzee was getting a tongue lashing from the person on the other end of the line. His short temper boiled over and he leaned across to the phone. "I already told you. I had to send that photo around. The woman might have asked one of the guards herself. And there was supposed to be a diversion on the other side of the corridor. The guard shouldn't have seen a thing. I 'm not responsible for other people's incompetence!"

The voice from the speaker was slightly deformed by some kind of acoustic software. But it was definitely a man's voice, chillingly quiet and calm. "Mr Coetzee, I do not appreciate my employees shouting at me on the telephone. Don't do it again. The fact is that the incident in the stadium was entirely under your management and it went wrong. There is now a witness to the event and I consider that to be an unwelcome deviation from our plans. In addition, Mrs Stewart should not have been aware of the circumstances of her son's disappearance until much later. It makes things very awkward."

"Once the guard had told us he'd seen the boy, I had to let her look at the recording. She'd already asked to see it. She's an intelligent woman."

"You'll have to arrange for the guard to be, let's say, unavailable for further information. He could be a fly in the ointment in our subsequent arrangements, or if he adds two and two together he might even try to profit from the opportunity. Please see to it immediately."

The two men looked at each other, Nwosu making a slashing action across his throat. He leaned over the phone, "Just leave it to me."

"Excellent." Despite the sound deformation, they could discern that the man spoke with a recognisable English accent. The intonation was so perfect that the two listeners suspected he might not be English at all, but hiding a foreign accent which might betray him. Neither of them had met him, Nwosu's original contact in April had been via a visit to his apartment by an intermediary, who arrived in a car with a Zimbabwean number plate. He came twice more then disappeared. He had been told to get Coetzee on side for a 'large transaction' and the promise of a lot of money had achieved just that. Further contacts were always made by emails, couched in innocuous, seemingly anodyne terms, or by telephone. The emails were sent from an ISP in Azerbaijan and the telephone calls came, usually at nine thirty in the morning, from an untraceable number. Nwosu had used his network of police contacts in several vain attempts to locate the source. In the absence of any other means of identification they called the man 'The Voice'.

Coetzee tried to avoid the police departments at all cost and had never encountered the policeman previously. He had quickly discovered that Nwosu was a corrupt and venal example of officialdom. In addition he was totally uninterested in sport. The security chief had been chosen as Nwosu's partner only because he had a security company and, vitally, the contract for the stadium security arrangements, including the World Cup Final. He had agreed because he was broke and losing money every month. His army pension pot had been almost eaten up over the last two years because he was an incompetent business man. Neither of them knew who the Voice was, what he looked like, where he came from, or where he was based. Funds, transferred from a bank in Panama City, appeared in their bank accounts without any sender's information or reference of any kind.

Lambert had arrived at the hotel in May and they had been ordered to contact him at the hotel. Details of the 'large transaction' had then been divulged to them and preparations had been put in place for various abduction scenarios. Coetzee didn't know who the target was until the day before the match and was shocked to discover it was a teenage boy. Now it was too late to regret his decision.

Relations between Coetzee and the policeman were not good. The security chief didn't trust Nwosu and the sergeant obviously despised him. Both men knew they were navigating dangerous waters, but the rewards were impressive. As always, greed, or in Coetzee's case, necessity, got the upper hand.

"Now," the Voice continued. "The boy, Leo. How is he?"

"He's in a safe place and he's OK. I saw him this morning. He's still sedated, but we've got very competent people monitoring his condition and there's nothing to worry about there."

"Please bear in mind that this young person is an exceptionally valuable commodity. To neglect to properly protect such an asset would bring deserved opprobrium upon your heads, followed by immediate and unpleasant consequences."

"We understand." Coetzee looked at Sergeant Nwosu and shrugged. *Who uses words like 'deserved opprobrium'* he asked himself. *This guy is from a very strange place.*

"And the Stewart woman. What's the situation?"

"She was so upset last night we didn't get anything much out of her. She went back to her hotel to cry herself to sleep. We have a man there and she hasn't budged. She's coming here at ten and we'll get to work on her then."

Coetzee interrupted the policeman. "What exactly do you want her to tell us? We need to know more about it, so we can ask the right questions, push her in the right direction."

The Voice sounded annoyed again. "I've already covered this point in detail with you. You should interrogate her remorselessly about her son and about his father. Who was he, what did or does he do? Where and how did they meet? Where was the son born? Where is the father now? Was she married to him, or was it a brief romance? Is he still alive or what happened to him? I want a full and comprehensive report from you by this evening without fail. You'll then receive further instructions as to the subsequent steps to be taken in connection with the boy."

There was the faint sound of someone speaking quietly in the background, then the man continued, "Don't hurt the woman. Her wellbeing is essential to the success of our programme. That will be all for now." The phone went dead.

"Did you hear the other voice? Maybe this guy isn't the big chief after all. We need to get to the bottom of this. This could be some kind of paternity thing. The boy's been taken off by the mother and the father's trying to get him back. He's got African blood, so maybe there's some kind of racial problem. There must be a lot of money involved and that's what we need to find out about. I don't like being in the dark and I don't like being treated like an imbecile by some arrogant shit who talks like Shakespeare." Coetzee lit up one of his cheroots and went to sit at the other side of the desk.

"Forget that for now." Nwosu said. "Call the guard and tell him I want to see him here in…" he looked at his watch, it was nine fifteen, "three hours. I'm sending him on a little holiday as a bonus for his good work."

Coetzee made the call, telling the guard that his sharp eyes had helped to locate the boy and he was to be rewarded with a bonus. The man was excited and relieved. After the woman's attack on him he'd been afraid he'd be sacked and now he would get a reward.

This was a good day.

"I've got to get back to check on the boy again." Coetzee went to the door. "I'll be here at ten thirty to talk to the Stewart woman. Keep her warm until I get here."

Nwosu watched him walk along the corridor, a cynical smile on his lips. *Idiot!* He said to himself.

TEN

Diepkloof, Gauteng, South Africa

Sergeant Nwosu came to meet Emma in the little reception area. "Good morning Mrs Stewart. I hope you're feeling much better today, after your awful night. I'm really sorry about what happened, but believe me, we're on top of the situation and I'm confident we can get your son back very quickly."

Emma followed him into the same room they'd been in the previous night. *He sounds like a second hand car dealer,* she thought. Aloud, she said, "Thank you, Sergeant. I'm sorry I got upset last night. It was all such a shock I lost control of my emotions." She saw that the laptop and projector were still on the table. *Good.* She sat next to the computer. The laptop was open with the screen saver running. It was a photograph of Cape Town, with Table Mountain in the background. The icons were listed down the left side of the screen.

The policeman looked fresh and polished, as if he'd had ten hours sleep and been to a barber before coming to the station. "Never mind, Emma. May I call you Emma?" He gave her what he imagined was an irresistibly trustworthy smile.

Emma tried to supress a shiver. After her talk with her sister, she realised how dangerous these people could be. She needed to get him out of the room for a few minutes. "Do you think I could have a cup of coffee, please? I was so exhausted that I overslept and I haven't had anything at all this morning. I suppose Mr. Coetzee is coming, so we have a few minutes to spare."

"I'll get it myself." He went out into the corridor, leaving the door ajar.

Emma leaned over the laptop, moved the cursor to 'Computer' and left clicked. The screensaver disappeared and the Hard Disk Drive 'C' icon came up together with the icon for Removable Disk 'G'. She breathed deeply with relief, no password was required and the CD must still be in the machine. As she moved the cursor over the 'G' icon she heard a step at the door. She turned in her chair with her back to the laptop and nodded to Coetzee, who came in ahead of Nwosu, carrying three plastic coffee cups. "Good morning and good timing Mr Coetzee. Just in time for coffee," she said, cursing her bad luck.

The two men sat opposite her, out of sight of the screen. "How are you today, Emma?" Coetzee was more polite than last night. "It's more than twelve hours now and we haven't heard anything from the hospitals or the other precincts, so we'll have to classify Leo's disappearance as an emergency and that requires a lot of paper work. I hope you're up to it."

"Anything that'll help to get my son back," she replied, "that's all that matters to me."

Nwosu commenced the questioning, starting with her and Leo's personal details. He filled the forms out by hand, with a black fountain pen, it looked to Emma like a *Mont Blanc. Strange,* she thought, *there's a laptop on the table and they must have a centralised computer system. Why is he writing everything down?* Then it dawned on her. Leo's abduction was not even in the system! They were keeping the case under wraps, so they could control it without any chance of interference from other officers. A disappearance would cause some questions in the station and they didn't want to answer them. The hair prickled on the back of her neck.

This is all just a pantomime, a show, but I can't afford to make a fuss. My son is in their hands. Jenny's right, I just have to play along.

She gave them the basic information they asked for, full names, nationality, address, dates of birth, mobile numbers for her and Leo and her email address. She'd also brought photocopies of their passports, but not the original documents. She thought they looked a little annoyed about this, but no comment was made.

Nwosu examined the passport copies. "So Leo is short for Leopold. That's an unusual name. Any special reason for that choice?"

Emma thought quickly. "He was one of my favourite uncles. I love the name."

"I see. And his place of birth was in London?"

Emma moved uncomfortably on her chair, "That's right. He was born at the University College Hospital. We've always lived in England."

"When did you plan to go back to the UK? I assume you've got return tickets." Nwosu took a diary from his shirt pocket. "Today's Monday the twelfth." He looked quizzically at her.

"Our tickets are for Wednesday evening, the fourteenth. We must find Leo before that, or I don't know what I'm going to do." She took out her handkerchief and wiped the genuine tears from her eyes. "I checked and there aren't any seats available anyway, everything's booked up. This whole thing's a nightmare."

"I'm sure we'll find Leo by Wednesday. We've got all of the police stations on alert, the hospitals and clinics advised, and we're planning a TV appeal for information if there's no news by tomorrow." At this, Nwosu's eyebrows raised, but he said nothing. Coetzee continued, "We're already working on several possible leads, but we need more information from you to point us in the right direction, confirm our suspicions. It's vital you tell us everything you can about Leo and his father."

"That's right," Nwosu added, "we need the details of Leo's birth, his father's name, nationality, date of birth, etc."

Emma had been worrying about how to get around these questions. She had to steer around the subject without revealing anything she didn't want to. "Let me tell you about my background," she said. "It will make everything much clearer to you."

Nwosu and Coetzee exchanged a look. Now they were getting somewhere.

"I joined the International Committee of the Red Cross in 1992, when I was twenty three. Well, it was actually the British Red Cross, because I was in London. Before that I worked for two years with a charity organisation in India to get some experience for the job. I started in 1990 in an orphanage in Mumbai, looking after children from one to twelve years of age and then in 1991 ...... "

Ten minutes later, she was still talking about her work in India and she knew she could continue for several more hours.

Finally, Coetzee interrupted her. "We're getting off the subject here, Emma. When and where did you meet Leo's father?"

Emma was working out how to get around this question when the phone rang. "Yes?" Nwosu listened for a moment then swore softly under his breath. He looked at Coetzee then said, "We'll be there directly."

He stood up and beckoned to Coetzee. "We've got a problem we need to check on, Emma. It'll take only a few minutes, OK?"

She nodded, "I'll get myself another coffee, if you don't mind."

"I'll bring you one," he went to fetch the coffee and placed it on the table beside her. He glanced at the laptop but it was on screen saver. "We'll be back in no time." He left the room and closed the door.

Emma stood over the laptop and hit Enter. The 'C' and 'G' icons came up again. She opened up the 'G' drive. There was only one item on it, labelled *Leo Stewart*. She was wearing a safari jacket with several pockets. Pulling out a USB memory stick she inserted it into the slot on the machine. The icon for 'Remote Device D' came up and she opened it up. It was the stick she always carried with a copy of the latest draft of her book, for editing when she was travelling. It had six gigabytes of capacity, with less than a gigabyte used. She was sure it would be enough.

She put the cursor over the *Leo Stewart* file and dragged it into the memory stick. It took just over a minute to copy, but it seemed like an hour, glancing over her shoulder to ensure that the men didn't return. Putting the stick back in her pocket, she closed the two windows and waited nervously until Table Mountain reappeared on the screen. She drained the coffee in one gulp feelingly quite elated. *Now, I'm doing something useful,* she thought. *Thanks, Jenny.*

As they walked along the corridor to the reception area, Nwosu whispered angrily to Coetzee, "That fucking guard, Masuku, is here to claim his bonus. I told the half-wit to come in two hours. We'll have to get rid of him. You'll have to do it. I'll stay with the woman. Shit! Why can't people just do what they're told?"

"What do you mean, 'get rid of him'? That's not my line of business. I'm a facilitator, not a fucking executioner."

"This is a police station, Coetzee. I can't let you interview Stewart alone. What if someone comes in? Nobody even knows she's in the building except us. One of us has to look after Masuku and it can't be me, so it has to be you."

Coetzee said nothing further until they found the little guard, sitting in reception. He jumped up, looking happily at them both, like a dog whose masters have just come back.

"Jacob Masuku, this is Sergeant Nwosu," announced Coetzee. The guard put out his hand, which was ignored by Nwosu. "He has some news for you. Some very good news. I have to get back to the stadium, so I'll leave you with him and see you later. Thanks for your help, I'll see you."

Nwosu looked at him with fury. "You can't ......", as Coetzee walked out of the station and got into his car without looking back.

Masuku hadn't noticed the altercation, he was too busy imagining what his bonus might be. Nwosu grabbed him by the arm and walked him outside. The guard was babbling. "Boss, what you got for Jacob? You got somethin' nice for me, eh? That kid was drugged, eh? I seen lots of kids like that before. Eyes up in their head. But I don't say nothin' to nobody, 'cos I know you got somethin' nice for me."

The policeman was swiftly weighing up the alternatives. He needed more information from Emma, but she wasn't going anywhere, at least not until Wednesday, if then. This guard was now becoming a dangerous nuisance and needed to be silenced. "Wait out here for me, Jacob," he said. "Sit on that bench over there and I'll be back in just a minute and we'll go collect your bonus."

Emma was sitting sobbing into her handkerchief, her head on the table, when he came back into the room. He sat beside her and took her shoulder. "Don't worry, Mrs Stewart. Everything is going to turn out alright. Things are never as bad as they seem. Just trust us and we'll get Leo back for you."

Nwosu could project a very tender image which women found comforting. He switched on his most charming expression. She turned to look at him. His breath was surprisingly sweet and his gaze was so intensely steady she almost believed what he said. Almost, but not quite. "Thank you, Sergeant Nwosu. I have every confidence," she replied.

"I can see you're very upset again. Maybe it would be better if we wait until this afternoon to talk. Why don't you go back to the Packard and come here at four o'clock. You can catch up on your sleep and I'm sure you'll feel better for it."

She mumbled her thanks and walked with Nwosu back to the reception. A taxi was just pulling up in front of the door. "I'll get him to take you to your hotel then bring you back at four o'clock," he said. "I'll charge it to the station account."

As the taxi pulled away, Emma switched off her phone's recorder then turned to look out the back window. She saw Nwosu walk across the driveway with a small, wiry black man. She knew the man. It was the guard, Jacob Masuku. She quickly took a snap of the two men with the phone as they were getting into a white Opel Astra with red and blue markings. Her taxi turned the corner and she settled into her seat.

It was fourteen hours since Leo had been taken.

ELEVEN

Gauteng, South Africa

Jacob Masuku didn't own a car. He had a clapped-out Triumph motor bike that he spent more time trying to fix than riding. He had seldom travelled in a modern car and never in a smart police vehicle. He was fascinated by the gadgets inside the car and giggled like a child when the radio crackled with a message. After multiple requests, Nwosu switched on the siren and the little guard leaned back, his eyes closed, imagining he was following a dangerous criminal in his souped-up getaway vehicle. This suited Sergeant Nwosu very well as he drove west from Diepkloof along the Moroka Bypass. Makusu was preoccupied with the car and his imaginings and he paid no attention to the journey.

After they'd driven for about fifteen minutes, he emerged from his reverie and looked around the outside surroundings. "Where we goin' boss?" He asked. "Where you takin' Jacob? Someplace nice, where I get my bonus? Where we goin'?"

"That's right, Jacob. I'm taking you to a secret place just along the road. It's where I keep my bonus cash. I don't take risks with it. It's for special services like the job you did for us. Then I'll drive you back to your house, or wherever you want to go. You're going to have the best day of your life, I promise you. You'll never have a better one." He smiled grimly at his own sense of humour.

Masuku settled back in his seat, luxuriating in the soft upholstery. "I knew you'd look after old Jacob," he said. "I told the wife, 'that policeman, he gonna' look after me, 'cos he know I seen the kid was drugged. He know Jacob's no idjit 'cos I don't say nothing 'bout it'. I told her it ain't my business where you take that kid. Jacob just wants his bonus."

"Where do you live, Jacob? Is it around here?"

"It ain't too far 'way. Robertville, off of Main Reef Road. You been there?"

Nwosu said nothing. He listened to the guard babble on as they passed the Libanon Gold Mine, about thirty kilometres from Diepkloof. He continued on Route 501 until he reached a farm track going north. They passed an old disused sand quarry on their left, with a dilapidated warehouse and a large pond in front of it and Nwosu pulled off the track beside the warehouse.

Masuku was starting to become nervous, "What we doin' here, boss? What's this place? Jacob don't likes the look of this place."

"This is where I keep my special bonus money, Jacob. I promised you your reward and you're going to get it. Trust me."

Reluctantly, the little guard got out of the car and followed Nwosu to the door of the warehouse. The policeman took out a key and unlocked the padlock on the door. He walked in, Masuku following nervously behind. The building was high and large, with a concrete floor and bags of cement and sand still stacked against one of the walls. An office, built from breeze blocks, the windows no longer in place, stood in the corner and Nwosu led the other man across to it. The place was cold, the flimsy construction and missing windows providing no insulation from the weather.

Masuku looked into the sparsely equipped office. There was a pile of plastic sheets, a large knife, some tools, lengths of steel wire and a coil of rope on the floor. On the desk were rolls of plastic tape and rubber gloves, a bottle of clear liquid. "I don't like this place, boss. Jacob gotta be headin' home now. We just forget 'bout the bonus. I didn't see nothin', I was just pertendin'. I don't want no bonus. Just take Jacob home now, boss. Please."

Nwosu smiled his charming smile, "I just want to know one thing before you get your bonus, Jacob. Have you told anyone else about what you saw in the stadium?"

Masuku was sweating profusely, wiping his forehead with the back of his hand. "I never said nothin' boss, like I told you. I ain't talk with nobody 'cept the wife. Anyways, like I said, I ain't seen nothin', so there's nothin' to tell. Boss, I'm sorry I made up that story." his voice began to shake, tears came to his eyes and he looked frantically at the door. "I just want to get a little bonus so I could take her 'way for a couple days. But it don't matter. We just forget it and you let Jacob go now. I can walk back, don't need a lift in your nice motor car. Just you let me go, boss, and we forget this whole thing."

"That's not possible, Jacob. It's just too risky." Nwosu took his Vektor SP1 pistol from the holster on his belt.

"Boss. Please boss! I promise I don't gonna say nothin'." Masuku lost control of his bladder and a dark patch appeared on the crotch of his jeans.

The policeman pulled the trigger twice and blasted the little guard backwards onto the concrete floor outside the office. He lay completely still, a pool of blood appearing from beneath him and gradually surrounding his upper body. Nwosu leaned over to check the pulse in his neck. There was none.

Sergeant Nwosu put on the rubber gloves from the office, went across to where the bags were stored and brought back a sack of cement in a wheelbarrow. He wheeled the cement over to a concrete step at the edge of the lake and dumped the sack onto the step. He then took a plastic sheet from the pile in the office and laid it alongside Masuku's body. Scrupulously avoiding any contact with the blood, he rolled the corpse onto the plastic and wrapped it tightly around, fastening it with duct tape. Upper torso first, he loaded it onto the wheelbarrow, the feet sticking out over the end. He wheeled the body over to the step and dumped it beside the cement sack.

Pushing the wheelbarrow over to the end of the warehouse, he returned with a large wooden box, which he placed on its side next to the dead man. He rolled the body into the box then manhandled it over, the open side up. Then he slit open the neck of the cement bag and poured the material into the box until it covered the corpse. With a hammer and nails from the office, he fastened down the lid of the box, tight. The lid had small holes punched into it, just enough to let a trickle of water enter, slowly but surely.

Nwosu looked carefully around the warehouse and checked the interior of his car, then returned to the step. He pushed the box over the edge of the step, until gravity took it and it slid into the murky depths of the lake, committing Jacob Masuku's soul to a concrete grave which would never be uncovered until the fifteen foot deep lake dried up or was emptied. He carefully put all of his tools and materials away then hosed down the floor of the warehouse. The concrete would soon dry out and there would be no evidence of how the last day of Jacob Masuku's life had ended. As Sergeant Nwosu had promised, 'You'll never have a better one'.

Emma got back into her room after braving the remarks of sympathy and encouragement from the hotel staff in reception. She would have liked to think their support might be useful, but she doubted it. She didn't know how wide Coetzee and Nwosu had spread their web and these people might be under their control. She was remembering Jenny's admonishment, "Behave as if everyone you meet there is your enemy."

She took her mobile phone and the memory stick from her jacket pockets and laid them on the desk, then opened her laptop to check her emails. There was nothing urgent or special to reply to. Some fan mail asking about her next book and no message from Jenny, but it was only eleven forty-five, so she wouldn't have arrived in Marbella yet. She inserted the memory stick to check that the clip had properly copied. The police station laptop was a Sony and hers was an Apple so she crossed her fingers that it was compatible. *Thank heavens,* it was just as clear and precise as the original. She didn't watch the film again, it would make her too distressed, just saved it to the hard disk, filing it, after some conflicting emotions, under *Pictures, Family, Leo's SA Trip.*

Taking up her mobile, she found the photo she'd taken. The two men were easily identifiable and she wondered what problem had caused Coetzee to leave and Nwosu to meet the guard. *Strange, it was important enough to interrupt my interview and get rid of me.* She emailed the image to her laptop and saved it in the same folder as Leo's clip, under *Nwosu & Masuku July 12.*

Then she played back the morning's conversations she'd recorded on the phone. The volume had been on maximum and the discussion could be clearly heard. She shivered again at the sound of the men's' voices lying to her and trying to find out about Leo's father. Using the 'Share' feature, she emailed the recording to her laptop and filed it under *SA Interview Nwosu & Coetzee July 12.* She'd been in the station for less than half an hour, but a lot of that time had been spent waiting, so she edited the recording to about fifteen minutes of conversation.

Next, she looked up the number of Diepkloof Police Station. It hadn't occurred to her to call there last night. Using the same pretence, she asked about a missing boy. She used her mobile to record the conversation. She'd downloaded a special app to do this, but it wasn't difficult. For the first time, she informed the operator of Leo's name. But the answer was the same. Nobody in the station had ever heard of him.

Emma rang off then replayed the recording. She sat back at the desk. *It's a conspiracy,* she thought, *I was right, it's a conspiracy and Leo is the victim. This is the final proof. Nwosu's own police department knows nothing about the kidnapping because he and Coetzee organised it. That guard Masuku must be involved as well. God knows how many more people are involved. But why?* She asked herself for the hundredth time. *Why on earth would anyone want to abduct my son? Well, now I've got ample proof of what's going on. I just need to find a way of using it.* She emailed it to her laptop and saved it under *Diepkloof Tel. July 12.*

Finally, Emma opened up Dropbox. She created a new folder, called *Leo Stewart* then went to 'Share a Folder' and entered Jenny's email address. She dragged the file she'd prepared with the four items, the CCTV clip, the photo, and the recordings of the conversations in the police station and the telephone call, into the *Leo Stewart* folder in the Dropbox. Then she went downstairs to get something to eat. She was famished.

It was sixteen hours since Leo had been taken.

TWELVE

Marbella, Spain

I've shared some of my files or folders with you. To open them, just click *the link(s) below.* Jenny found this message when she looked at her laptop in the office in York House, in southern Spain. The house, with its several hectares of surrounding land, was located on the Las Manzanás Golf Course, near Marbella. It had been her father-in-law, Charlie Bishop's house, which she'd inherited jointly with Leticia da Costa, a young Angolan woman who was the mother of Charlie's son, Emilio.

She opened up Dropbox and found the *Leo Stewart* folder. After studying the film clip and photo and listening to the recordings, she took her notebook and played everything through again as she typed her notes. Finally, she ran the film clip again, trying to see if there was something that stood out, something she may have missed on the first viewings. *Hmm, that's interesting.* She ran it through three more times, stopping it in the same places each time and making more notes. Jenny closed down Dropbox and sat thinking for a while then she picked up the telephone and made several calls.

It was three o'clock when she called her sister back on her mobile and Emma answered immediately. After a snack and a sleep, she was feeling more like her normal self, although her voice shook when she asked, "So, what's the verdict, Jenny? Am I crazy, or has my son been abducted?"

"You're definitely not crazy and I'm sorry I doubted you. It seems too incredible to be true, but I'm convinced Leo's been kidnapped and that Coetzee and Nwosu are involved. But what's more important is I'm also convinced you're in very grave danger and we've got to take immediate steps. We have very little time, so listen carefully and please don't argue."

"Why don't you Skype me? These calls are going to cost a fortune."

"It's not a good idea and you mustn't worry about the cost. Just listen and do what I tell you." Jenny adopted her school teacher voice. "First, go and check outside your door and make sure there's no one around. Do it now."

"There's no one in sight," her sister confirmed a few moments later.

"Good, lock it and bolt it with the dead bolt and keep it that way."

"Now," she continued, "go and sit as far from the door as possible, and speak quietly, so there's no chance of anyone hearing. Have your laptop ready so you can look at something."

"Right." Emma sat by the window, her laptop open on the bedside cabinet. "What's this all about? You're scaring me."

"Just taking precautions. You'll see why in a moment. Now, first question. Who does Leo know in Johannesburg?"

"No one at all. We've been here five days and apart from the staff in the hotel, we've never spoken to anybody except waiters and shop assistants. There was a shooting outside the hotel on our second day, so we've never even walked about outside, it's far too dangerous. We've taken the bus and a couple of taxi rides to see one or two attractions and then the coach to the football match. But I don't see what all that's got to do with his disappearance"

"Think about it Emma. I'm sure whatever was done to Leo must have been done by someone he recognised. He's too smart to let a stranger come up and stick a needle into him or do whatever it was to knock him out. So it must have been someone that he met at the hotel or somewhere else you've been. Someone he had confidence in. Now listen, I may have spotted something on the video clip. Play it again and tell me what you see."

"I'll pull it up. What do I have to look for?"

"There's a man who's in the picture at the beginning and then comes back into range at the end. See if you recognise him."

"Jenny, I've looked a thousand times and I haven't seen anyone I recognise."

"Look at it again. First you see the corridor between the toilet and the exit. It's exactly as you described, a huge crowd of people moving all over the place so you could hardly get through. And when you watched the clip you were looking only at Leo being pushed out, which is normal. It's what you wanted to see, so you didn't pay attention to the rest of the picture. If you look again carefully, you'll see a man move into camera range behind the wheelchair. He follows it until it's gone from sight and I think the guy pushing the chair actually turns to say something to him. Then he comes walking back from the exit again after Leo's gone. You can't make out his face because he's wearing a baseball cap but you can see he's got lots of curly black hair and a beard. He's in a black bomber jackets with silver stripes across the upper arms.

"It's not obvious, because he's underneath the camera and there are lots of people around him, but it's definitely the same man. He goes out of sight when the wheelchair gets near the exit, but gets caught again when he comes back in. Just what he would do if he wanted to make sure that Leo was taken out successfully, except he doesn't realise he's come back into camera range."

"Ok. I'm watching it now. When do I see him?"

"It's just as the wheelchair is coming through. If you look at the bottom of the picture, on the left, you'll see a great big black man in a red and blue shirt."

"I've got him."

"Next to him comes in the man in the baseball cap and it looks like the guy who's pushing Leo out is talking to him."

"In the baseball cap and black jacket. I see him now. Oh my God, I don't believe it!"

"Do you recognise him?"

"It looks like Barry Lambert, the hotel manager!" Emma glanced fearfully at the locked door. "So that's why he's been so friendly with us, especially with Leo. He offered to take him to Lion Park, but I put a damper on it. After the shootings in the street I didn't want Leo out of my sight in a city like Joburg, so I made up an excuse. Leo was furious, but I got tickets for us to go there with a tour bus on Friday. It was a wonderful day out. He absolutely loved it," she added sadly. "And I've just remembered, Lambert suggested taking us to the Gold Reef City amusement park tomorrow, for our last day here."

"Are you sure it's him, this Barry Lambert?"

"Let me run it through once more." She reran the clip, her heart in her mouth. "I think it's him. I can't see his face properly under the cap but there can't be two people like him with all that curly black hair and the beard."

"Then it must be him, it makes sense. He's the only person that Leo might have trusted because he's the manager of the hotel. And he has to be involved, otherwise he would have gone to help when he saw Leo in the wheelchair, but he did nothing. He and the other guy must have drugged Leo and stage managed this whole abduction."

"No, it's not possible. I've just remembered, when Coetzee called the hotel last night, he spoke to Lambert. If he was at the hotel, he couldn't have been at the stadium."

Jenny thought for a moment. "But it must have been at least an hour and a half after Leo was kidnapped that Coetzee spoke to him. He had ample time to get back and take the call. In fact, I bet that was a set up as well. Lambert has got himself an alibi if anything goes wrong, because Coetzee called him at the hotel in front of you."

Emma reran the clip once more. "I want to see him come back into the picture. Wait, the wheelchair has gone out... there he is again." He's walking back now. I recognise him and the jacket from behind. You're right, it can only be Lambert. He must have orchestrated the whole thing with the other man otherwise he'd have looked for me. He knew we were both there and he did nothing to help us." She put her hand to her mouth, not believing what she'd seen

After a few moments of silence, Jenny asked, "Are you OK?"

"I was just trying to work out how they drugged Leo so quickly. I know there are some very fast acting knockout drugs, but they have to be injected to take immediate effect. They only had five minutes or so before I came out of the loo."

"They must have been waiting by the toilets, it's logical, everybody goes at half time. Lambert sees you go into the ladies and knows you'll be stuck there for a while. They follow Leo in, get chatting to him, jab a needle or something into his arm then hold him up so he doesn't fall to the floor. The nurse comes in behind with the wheelchair and they cart Leo out. Job over in two minutes flat. Simple but effective."

"But Leo would have felt the jab. He'd have bashed him or called out or something. He wouldn't have just let them inject him without a struggle."

"That's why there were two of them. One of them must have held him from behind, hand over his mouth, so he couldn't yell for help. There's so many people milling about it wouldn't even have been noticed. This was well planned and well executed. If it hadn't been for that guard, Masuku, we might never have found out the truth about Lambert. He and Mr. X were the field agents and Coetzee and Nwosu are obviously involved at a higher level."

"And they probably originally intended to take Leo when Lambert invited him to Lion Park. Or," Emma reasoned, "they would have another chance if we'd gone to Gold Reef City with him. That's three alternative plans to make sure they got Leo." She sat back in shock and fright, absorbing the implications of such a well-organised plan. This must have been set up before we even arrived in South Africa. And now I'm staying in a hotel with the man who organised the kidnapping of my son and the only two other people I know in South Africa are his accomplices. My God!"

"Emma, pull yourself together and put those thoughts aside for now. We have to take immediate action and you have to listen to what I tell you. Are you alright?"

"I'm sorry, Jenny. I'm just dazed by all this. I brought Leo to South Africa for the biggest trip of his life, it cost me a fortune and now it's cost me my son. I just can't bear it. This is all my fault, we should never have come here."

"Don't be silly, Emma," Jenny said. "You haven't lost Leo. Look at the film. He's only unconscious. If you look really carefully at him in the chair, you'll see his eyes flicker. He's drugged, but alive. And that's the most vital thing. We're not dealing with a murder here, we're dealing with an abduction, just as you thought. That means when these people make their demands known, whatever they are, we can take action. We can get Leo back. But now we have to prepare ourselves for the next step and you can't do it from there."

"What do you mean?"

"I mean you're in terrible danger and the more you find out about Leo's abduction, the more danger you'll be in. Sooner or later the kidnappers are going to catch on that you won't tell them anything because you don't trust them and then God knows what they might do. We have to get you out of there now. Today."

"But how can I leave without Leo? I can't just abandon him here in Africa!"

"Just think, Emma. What can you do there? Nothing! You don't want to talk to the Embassy and you can't trust anyone else because they all seem to be in this together. You'll be much better able to do something in a safe environment where you can work in the open and not hide in your hotel bedroom. And I'll help you. I have some contacts and I'll help you to get Leo back and give these people the ransom they deserve – a lifetime behind bars. That's what we have to achieve. We can do this, Emma. Have faith in me and together we'll get Leo back." Jenny's voice had taken on a hard, calculating tone.

She was reliving an episode from her past, an episode in which only her strength and determination had saved her and her family. She was convinced she could do this.

"But I don't even have a plane ticket and the flights are completely full."

"I've already arranged everything. Don't worry about that. As long as you've got enough cash for a taxi ride, we'll have you safely out of there today. Just listen carefully, take notes and trust me.

"Now," she continued, before her sister could raise more objections, "What time are you supposed to see Nwosu?"

Jenny spent the next fifteen minutes explaining the arrangements she'd made on the telephone that afternoon, repeating every detail of her plan, patiently hushing her sister up every time she raised an objection, until she was certain Emma had understood everything.

"I don't know how to thank you, Jenny." Emma was weeping softly again. "I suppose you're right, it's the only way, but I just hate the idea of leaving Leo here in this bloody country."

"I'd be extremely surprised if Leo is still in South Africa, as a matter of fact."

"What do you mean?"

"I've been reading up on abductions. Apparently it's most common to take hostages out of the country where they were kidnapped and hold them in a different place. Not only does it make it more difficult to find them, but the international laws between countries complicate prosecuting the offenders if they get caught. Sometimes they move across borders several times."

"But I've got his passport. How can they take him across a border without his passport?"

"I don't think borders are too much of a problem to people like this. If Nwosu is involved you can be sure it's for good reasons and one of them would be just that, getting around bureaucracy and borders. So leaving South Africa doesn't mean you're abandoning Leo. You're going somewhere where you have more chance of finding help to get him back again. Just get your things together and follow the plan and I'll see you tomorrow."

She must have been a terrific school teacher, Emma thought to herself. She wiped her eyes and cleared her throat, decided now. "All right. I'll follow your instructions to the letter."

"There's one more thing, Emma, and I'm sorry if it's a very touchy subject, but we need to discuss it. From your conversation with Coetzee and Nwosu and what you told me about the British High Commission, there's something about Leo's birth, or his father, that you don't want to disclose. I'm convinced that's the reason for his abduction. I don't know why or how, but there's no other possible interpretation of their questions. They know something about Leo's father and that's what this is all about.

"I don't want to pry into your life any more than I want you to pry into mine, but I have to know what's going on here, otherwise I can't help. When we see each other you have to be completely open with me. It could make the difference between finding Leo or not. OK?"

Emma sighed. "It'll actually be a relief to tell you everything, Jenny. You'll be the first and only person to know the truth. Not even Leo knows, and you're right, it might possibly be of importance, I just don't know."

On that note the two women said their goodbyes, Jenny to make some more calls, and Emma to set out on the most dangerous journey of her life.

It was eighteen and a half hours since Leo had been taken.

THIRTEEN

Johannesburg, South Africa

At five minutes past four, Emma got into the taxi that had brought her back to the hotel that morning. She chatted pleasantly with the driver, but inside she was shaking with fear. The manager, Barry Lambert, had accompanied her to the door, asking again about her son. She managed to refrain from smacking him across the face, just replied, "I'm going back to the station now. They say they're following several leads, so I'm praying there's some news. I'll see you later, Mr Lambert."

Emma was wearing her safari jacket and carrying only her laptop bag with a change of underwear and a few cosmetic articles squeezed in beside her computer and Leo's notebook. She was reluctant to leave everything in their rooms, but there was no other choice to avoid suspicion. As the driver pulled away from the hotel, she said, "Please take me first to the shopping centre around the corner. I need something from the chemist."

The driver stopped on the corner by the entrance to the mall and she jumped out, carrying her bag. "I'll just be two minutes," she said, and ran into the building. It was bustling with shoppers, mostly Indian, who were the predominant residents of the area. She'd been there previously with Leo, stocking up on some filling snacks and drinks for a fast growing schoolboy. Walking quickly along the alleyway she turned the corner and went out the exit on the other side of the street. Continuing along the street she found the nearest taxi rank and climbed into an old blue Peugeot. The driver was a young Indian man with slicked down hair and a beaming smile.

"Where can I take you, lady?" He asked, in a sing song lilt.

"OR Tambo Airport, please."

Once they got out of the city centre, the traffic moved quickly and it took them only twenty minutes along Broadway Extension to get to the airport. Following Jenny's instructions, they went to the arrivals level. The young driver didn't stop talking from the moment they set off. He was interested in Emma; what she did, where she came from, was she married, did she have children, what was she doing in Joburg? *He should be working for Nwosu,* she reflected. He knows how to interrogate someone.

She said as little as possible and paid him off with a small tip, not enough to make him suspicious. As soon as he'd driven off, again following her sister's instructions, Emma went upstairs to the departures level and flagged down what looked like a vintage Mercedes with an older, sad looking black driver.

He looked wearily at her and just nodded when she said, "Wonderboom Airport, please."

The driver took the R21 north for about forty kilometres then turned onto the N1 to skirt Pretoria. As they were driving past Queenswood to the east of the city, Emma heard the sound of a siren coming up behind them. The driver looked in his rear view mirror and slowed down to the left side of the road. In the wing mirror she could see a police car approaching, siren blaring and lights flashing. She suddenly felt sick to her stomach. *Nwosu's found me. Somehow he's followed my trail. Dear God, what's going to happen to Leo and me now?*

The police car flashed past them and the driver pulled back onto the road and resumed his cruising speed. Emma's eyes were closed as she tried to pull herself together. *It's not far now, I can make it,* she said to herself, steeling her nerves.

It was just after five thirty when they pulled up alongside the main terminal building at Wonderboom. A sign on the wall outside the door said, ***MyJet Aviation, First Floor.*** Emma paid the driver from her fast depleting bunch of rand notes and walked nervously up the stairs.

"Good afternoon, I'm Mrs Stewart," she announced to the young blonde woman behind the desk.

"How do you do, Mrs Stewart. We've been expecting you. My name's Alison. Please sit down and I'll bring the forms over to you. Would you like a coffee?"

Diepkloof, South Africa

Coetzee was in Nwosu's office. They were arguing about Jacob Masuku, when they got the call from the first taxi driver. Nwosu went berserk, screaming at the man until he switched off his phone. It wasn't his fault if some woman decided she didn't want to go to the police station. He went home to watch the TV.

"That bitch, Stewart. She's been playing us along. We've had her in here twice and she's told us nothing and now she's on the run."

"Well don't stand there screaming and shouting. Get your bloody police force out looking for her." Coetzee was becoming tired of Nwosu. He was the antithesis of the security chief. Taller, better looking, smartly turned out and a great charmer. But all he really knew how to do was clean up after he'd messed up. What they used to call a 'wet work' guy in the SA Special Forces, where Coetzee had spent almost fifteen years before going private. "Get them onto the airports, the bus and train stations, hotels, B&Bs, every place she could possibly have gone or be hiding in. She's only had fifteen minutes and she doesn't know anyone, so she can't be far. Get the passport photo out there. Someone's bound to see her."

"I don't understand this," said Nwosu as he prepared an email with Emma's photo and a brief, fictitious account of *Emma Stewart, drug dealer on the run, to be captured and brought to Diepkloof without harm.* "Why would she run away when she doesn't know where the kid is? She's genuinely worried about him, but for some reason she decides to piss off without him. It doesn't add up. Unless she's on to us, but I don't see how."

"Women do strange things." Coetzee took a drag on his cheroot. "That's why I don't get involved any more. You look after them for years, take them on holidays, buy them a nice house, give them kids. Then they start acting strange, blaming you for everything, like you've stolen their lives. And then it's over. You don't know why, twenty years of your life and it's over. They've gone, they're not coming back and you're screwed."

Nwosu looked up from his PC but said nothing. He stored this information in his memory, just like he stored everything he saw and heard. It might be worth something one day, to know what had happened to Coetzee, how his wife had apparently walked out on him. *It might be valuable, provide leverage, who knows?*

"Right," he said. "These messages will be out on the street in five minutes. Where do you think she's gone, and why?"

"My bet? She said her tickets are non-flexible and she's got no money. I'd say she's somewhere in hiding, waiting for her flight on Wednesday. She doesn't know anyone, so she'll be looking for a cheap hotel. So I'd put money on her being somewhere near the airport. She probably went through the mall to the north exit and found the nearest taxi rank. You should get somebody to check with the drivers there. Maybe someone took her to the airport. That'll limit the search area."

"Good thinking," Nwosu begrudgingly complimented the other man. "I'll circulate the dispatchers and get the Mayfair cops to check the taxi ranks around the shopping centre." He made a couple of phone calls, then turned back to Coetzee. "What are we going to tell the Voice?"

"Nothing, for now. It's late in the afternoon and he's not going to call again today. If we find her by the morning, there won't be anything to tell him anyway." He stood up. "I'm going, there's nothing I can do here. Don't kill anyone while I'm gone."

Nwosu watched him walk along the corridor. *Arrogant swine,* he thought. *Masuku won't be the only casualty in this business. All in good time.*

FOURTEEN

Diepkloof, Gauteng, South Africa

The young Indian taxi driver called as soon as he returned to the rank and saw the notice posted by the phone booth. After he'd convinced the operator that he had important information concerning Mrs Stewart, he was put through to Sergeant Nwosu.

"How can you be sure it was her?" The policeman didn't want another embarrassing fiasco. There had been too many of them already.

"It was an English lady, about forty, right? She had a kind of accent, but definitely UK. Dark hair, pretty, in a safari jacket. First visit to Joburg. She didn't say much but I recognised the photo immediately. I picked her up from my rank beside the city library."

I should hire him for the force, Nwosu mused, echoing Emma's thought. "That's her. Where did you drop her off?

"OR Tambo Airport. Arrivals level."

"Arrivals? Are you sure?" The policeman was put off balance. *Why would she go to the arrivals when she was trying to escape?* "Did she have a bag?"

"I dropped her at the arrivals and she just had one of those shoulder bags. Looked like a computer bag."

"What time?"

"Four thirty."

Nwosu rang off and called the police station at the airport. *We'll get her,* he smiled to himself. He didn't call Coetzee. He'd been right and Nwosu didn't like it.

The security chief was sitting smoking in his office at the stadium. He was reflecting on the mess he'd gotten himself into. He'd gone along with the kidnapping only for the money. The divorce had been an expensive business and he still had his daughter's education to pay for. And the security business wasn't as lucrative as he'd anticipated. Mainly because he was a lousy business man. He wasn't tough enough in negotiations. He didn't like to nickel and dime or hire a lawyer to write his contracts. This World Cup deal was actually going to cost him money. He'd completely screwed up on the cost calculations, so his pension savings were going to take another hit.

The whole business with Leo and Emma was starting to weigh on his mind. Nwosu was obviously a villain through and through and the kid was just a pawn in a scheme orchestrated by people they didn't even know, using them to make money, a lot of money, he imagined. He knew Emma must be going through Hell and he could almost feel her pain. But he also knew that professional kidnappers didn't usually kill their victims. They delivered them against cash, or whatever else they were doing it for. *If I'm going through with this,* he decided, *I want more than the measly amount they've offered so far. This deal has to make a difference in my life, a big difference. I'll protect the asset and I'll deliver him safe and sound but I'll make sure I get properly paid for it.* The kid was young and healthy and he would make sure he survived the incident with nothing worse than bad memories, whatever happened to anyone else.

Even during his time with the Special Forces, Coetzee had never been keen on killing. He'd always tried to make sure someone else was doing the wet work. On the few occasions he'd been obliged to take a life, he'd hated it. Hadn't felt a thrill or a sense of satisfaction like many of his mates. He didn't like it and when he'd left the forces to set up his security consulting firm, he'd vowed never to be involved in it again.

But now he was back in the killing fields. The Voice had made it clear that anyone who got in the way of his plan would become 'unavailable'. That pathological maniac Nwosu had already done away with Masuku and bragged about it to him that afternoon. He'd been graphic in his description of the murder, right down to the poor guy pissing in his pants. Then he'd boasted about Masuku's widow's premature departure from this life caused by an accident with scalding water in her shack. "Dangerous places, these shanty dwellings," he'd laughed. "And if anyone does suspect foul play, they'll assume Jacob killed her then went into hiding. What I would describe as the perfect murders."

Jesus Christ, Coetzee thought to himself, *what a fucking sadist! And I'm stuck with him.*

Nwosu got the call from the airport police at six twenty. Emma Stewart had taken a taxi from the departures level at about four forty-five. The driver didn't get the message until he was back because the police had only checked the arrivals rank and he'd switched his radio off since it was his last drive for the day. Nwosu hadn't imagined that she might hail a taxi at departures. Coetzee would probably have worked that out, he thought, envying the man his thinking ability, but he said nothing. He was feeling foolish enough as it was.

The driver said he'd driven her to the Pretoria airport at Wonderboom. He'd left her at the main terminal building and she'd gone inside to the MyJet Aviation office. Nwosu thought for a moment. If he called them, she might get wind of it and flee. Better to get the police in right away. He picked up the phone and called his opposite number in Wonderboom Poort station, using the drug dealer description. They could have a car there in ten minutes, the sergeant responded. Nwosu sat back, praying he wouldn't have to tell the Voice they'd lost her.

At six twenty-five, Emma walked out of the airport terminal in the company of Shane, a smart, good looking pilot and Tasha, his co-pilot. They were both Australian, apparently there were lots of Ozzie airline staff all over the world. Alison was their daughter and they were the owners of the little private jet hire company. Today, Alison would act as flight attendant and they were going to spend a few days on a family holiday in Mauritius. Not having travelled with an airline where you got to meet the pilot or the owner, Emma was suitably impressed.

They were about to climb up into the plane when she heard Alison calling her. "Mrs Stewart. Can you come back for a moment? I think we have a problem."

A feeling of dread invaded Emma's mind. *I knew it was too easy,* she told herself. *They've managed to track me down.* She turned to go back to the building.

"We'll prepare for take-off, Emma. Take your time," Shane called, as he and his wife climbed the staircase.

Alison was apologetic. "Mrs Stewart, I've just realised you don't have a visa. I'm not sure you can fly without one. I'm sorry, but I've only been helping my parents for a few weeks over the holidays and I'm not really up on these things."

Emma had never felt so relieved. She thought quickly, "Let's look it up on the web. It's sure to tell us if UK citizens need a visa."

It took Alison a few minutes to locate the proper section of the site, only to find that she'd been wrong, English visitors didn't need a visa. Emma breathed a sigh of relief and walked quickly back to the plane.

At six thirty-five, a car from Wonderboom Poort screeched to a halt in front of the terminal building and two policemen ran up the stairs to the MyJet Aviation office. The door was locked and there was nobody there. A sign on the door said the place was closed for the rest of the week. They called Sergeant Nwosu, in Diepkloof, to report the news.

Emma was already fast asleep in the most comfortable armchair-bed she'd ever encountered, leaving South African air space on a

Dassault Falcon 2000 twin engine jet, next stop, Mauritius. She was safely on her way to rescue her son.

It was twenty-one hours since Leo had been taken.

DAY THREE

TUESDAY, JULY 13, 2010

FIFTEEN

Diepkloof, Gauteng, South Africa

Nwosu and Coetzee were arguing again in the policeman's office. It was Tuesday morning and the news was not good. Nwosu was looking for somebody to blame before they received the call from the Voice. After learning that Emma had probably taken a private jet from Wonderboom, he'd requested the flight details from airport flight control. There were very few departures from the airport and the only MyJet Aviation flight at six-thirty had filed Mauritius as its destination. Subsequent enquiries showed a booking for Emma Stewart on an Air France flight to Paris at midnight. Calculating four and a half hours for the Mauritius sector, he assumed she had made the flight, so he asked further questions which revealed a booking for Malaga, also with Air France, on their Tuesday morning flight. Knowing Emma didn't have money, he also discovered that the flights had been paid for with a Swiss credit card in the name of Jenny Bishop. Further investigation showed that this was Emma's sister, who had a home in Marbella.

"The bitch is in a plane on her way to her sister's house in Spain now and we're screwed. Why didn't you work out that she wasn't staying at the airport? It was too obvious, going there, and she wasn't due to fly until tomorrow."

"Sergeant Nwosu, you didn't even tell me she'd gone to the airport. If I'd known she got out at arrivals I might have been suspicious. But you didn't tell me." He looked sarcastically at the policeman. "I hope you're not looking for a scapegoat. 'cos I don't do scapegoat." He lit up a cheroot and went on, "You're probably right. When she wouldn't tell us anything, she must have already been plotting with her sister to get out, and now the bird has flown."

"These people you hired are all incompetent pricks. Lambert or the doctor or someone must have let the cat out of the bag and she's caught on that the whole thing's a set up. She's a crime writer and she's got plenty of imagination. The Voice isn't going to be happy with you."

"We're in this together Nwosu. If you remember, she cottoned on to you right away because you knew too much about her son. Not smart, was it?" He paused, enjoying the moment. "And neither Lambert nor the doctor was my choice, so don't play pass the parcel with me, it could blow up in your face.

"We're not telling the Voice anything. We're in enough trouble as it is. We've got to figure out what he wants to know, so we can work out why this kidnapping was ordered. It's time we started asking the questions. We've taken all the risks for a few thousand dollars and he's sitting there calling the shots.

"Just ask yourself, why would he kidnap a schoolboy whose mother doesn't have enough money to buy an airplane ticket? It doesn't make any sense. There's some bigger play here and we need to get to the bottom of it. I agreed to go into this for only one reason, money, and I'm not about to get short changed."

"Be careful what you say or do, Coetzee. Those guys are ruthless and I don't want to become their next problem."

The security chief laughed. "Sergeant Nwosu has spoken, eh? Well just think about this. Who wants the kid? They do. Who's got the kid? We do. That boy is staying glued to my side until he gets handed over to his mother and we see the ransom money paid.

We're holding all the cards and if they want us to play the game that means a bigger payoff."

Nwosu nodded begrudgingly. "OK. I wouldn't object to more money. You handle the conversation and we'll see what happens."

Coetzee walked out to get a coffee, past the conference room where they'd interviewed Emma. He checked the laptop, the CD was still in the machine. He ejected it and slipped it into his pocket, just in case.

Marbella, Spain

Emma's taxi turned right into the Las Manzanás Golf Course and drove past a security office towards Calle Venetia. The driver seemed to know the way. He drove around a high wall made of white stone and stopped at a pair of iron gates with CCTV cameras on each side. He was about to press an intercom button by a plaque that said, ***York House,*** when the gates slid back and he continued on into the property.

Jenny was standing on a terrace at the top of the drive. It seemed like half a kilometre away. *Wow! What a house!* Emma thought, mentally comparing it to her two bedroomed apartment in Newcastle, on Quayside, by the river, with a partial view of the Tyne Bridge. Perfect for her and Leo, small, but cosy, but this was a property out of *Hello Magazine.*

They drew up in front of the house and she climbed out into the arms of her sister, tears of relief in her eyes. "Welcome to York House, Emma. Oh, it's so good to see you. You must be shattered. Just leave your bag with Juan and come in with me." A balding man in a black tee shirt paid off the taxi driver then took her laptop bag from her. "*Buenos Dias*", he said and she shook his hand.

Jenny led her up to the terrace and into the house. "Would you like to freshen up first or have a coffee on the terrace and tell me all about your round the world trip."

Emma smiled wearily. "Coffee would be wonderful and I can't wait to give you a blow by blow account."

They walked through a large hallway out onto a wide, sunny terrace littered with settees and loungers. Emma gasped at the panoramic view. Swimming pool, gardens, golf course and the Mediterranean were laid out in front of her under the warm sunshine.

A large, happy looking Spanish lady was fussing with the cushions on the settees. "This is Encarni," Jenny introduced them. "She's the boss around here, so you'll have to be nice to her. *Dos cafes con leche, por favor, Encarni,*" she said, and the woman laughed and went into the kitchen. "Encarni loves my Spanish. She's the mother of Leticia, with whom I share the house," she explained. "It's a bit complicated, but I'll explain it to you when we've caught up on your travels and what's happened in Johannesburg. Now, sit down and tell me all."

Emma sighed and wiped her eyes. "It was a wonderful trip, thank you, Jenny. If only I hadn't been leaving Leo behind, it would have been the trip of a lifetime. But it must have cost you an absolute fortune. First the private plane, then the business class seat to Paris and to Malaga. I've never been so spoiled in my life. I suppose you fly like that all the time, but it was a very special treat for me."

"Good. If you're feeling rested and ready for the next stage, then it was money well invested." Jenny didn't mention that she almost always travelled with easyJet and always in economy. "How did you leave things in Joburg?"

"I did a runner, just as you suggested. Took two taxis and then the jet. I was terrified to look behind me, but as far as I know they didn't find out until too late. Once I got to Mauritius I was more relaxed. I knew they wouldn't have time to get a warrant or suchlike to stop me there. After that I just let myself be pampered and tried to think positive thoughts, but they've still got Leo and it's breaking my heart.

"I'm sure they must have wanted me too. That's what all the questions were about. You're right, there's something they want that I know or that I've got and I have an idea what it is but I can't think it's of any importance after all these years. Now that I've got away from them I suppose they're trying to work out what to do next."

Jenny waited until Encarni had brought their coffees then said, "Now, Emma. I think it's time you told me about Leo and his father. Maybe we can work out what it is they're after. She took her iPad to make notes. Take your time, we're in no hurry."

"Right." She took a couple of deep breaths and assembled her thoughts. "This is going back fifteen years, Jenny, so it's going to take a while and I'm going to have some memory gaps, but I'll do my best.

"After the genocide in Rwanda, I wanted to go down and help. It was such a dreadful situation down there. A million people massacred in just three months, most of them with machetes. The Red Cross wasn't ready to send people, but the *SOS Médicale,* it's a small French medical relief organisation, they went into action with a few teams and I was able to go down with them. It was March, 1995. I remember arriving there; it was a Sunday, a lovely, sunny day. Flying in over the mountains I thought I'd never seen such a beautiful place. Then I discovered what was waiting for me on the ground. I worked in a dilapidated, makeshift clinic, looking after young women and girls who were pregnant from being raped. It was too horrible to describe, but I really felt I was making a difference."

Jenny settled herself back into the settee and took a swallow of coffee. Her sister was in full flow now, finally able to tell the story she'd concealed for fifteen years, since the day her son was born. She would listen, take notes and learn, hoping to find the reason for Leo's abduction.

It was thirty-eight hours since Leo had been taken.

RWANDA

1995

SIXTEEN

April, 1995
Bumbogo, outside Kigali, Rwanda

"*Poussez, Mutesi, Poussez.* I can see the baby's head. One more big push. A deep breath, that's it. Now *poussez!*"

After ten years of non-use, Emma Stewart's school French wasn't exactly fluent, but in the circumstances, there was no room for misunderstanding. She concentrated on her midwifery duty and ignored the rancid, suffocating stink of sweat and filth in the makeshift clinic. Once a bicycle storage and repair warehouse, the building, near Kigali, the capital of Rwanda, had been 'converted' a few months previously to a 'Family Assistance Clinic'. It could accommodate fifty females. There were presently ninety of them in the building, most of them rape victims who had managed to survive the Hutu genocide. The sanitation system was still non-existent and a dozen battered tin baths of tepid water could hardly stretch to all the women and girls who hadn't bathed for days as they made their way to the clinic in the hope of giving birth to their child in some vestige of civilisation.

As usual, the decision to send any kind of help to Rwanda after the genocide was discussed by many governments at all levels and for many months. Meanwhile the country was in chaos as the new Tutsi leaders commenced their retaliation to the Hutu massacres. There was no government in place to run hospitals, schools, shelters, food programs, or factories. Public utilities; telephones, electricity and water had ceased to function. Most of the previous Hutu officials had either been killed or had fled to neighbouring countries. Perversely, the initial international help was provided to the Rwandans who had fled to refugee camps in Zaire, Burundi, Tanzania and Uganda and not to those who were still in Rwanda itself. In other words, the help was being provided mostly to the perpetrators and not the victims.

Non-government bodies, like the UN, the International Red Cross and *Médecins sans Frontières,* were stymied in their desire to intervene in the country. A few smaller, less orthodox organisations made the first moves. At that time Emma was employed by the British Red Cross, in London, but when she heard that a small, effective French charity group, called *SOS Médicale,* was to send in a few medical teams, she immediately applied for a position with them. With a little help, she managed to convince them her school French was good enough to pass muster and her previous work in a hospital maternity ward made her a suitable candidate. She was amongst the first volunteers to arrive in Rwanda in the aftermath of one of the greatest human catastrophes since the Second World War.

Her preparation period had provided her with many dreadful statistics; almost a million Rwandan people, both Tutsi and Hutu, had been massacred in the space of just one hundred days. Adult males now represented only twenty per cent of the Tutsi population and many families were now headed by women or even young children, because all the men had been slaughtered. Over one hundred thousand children had been orphaned. The majority of the population suffered psychological damage, either from being victims, seeing atrocities or being forced to commit them. Many of the victims remained disfigured and physically handicapped, making their reintegration into society an almost impossible task. Very few survivors were able to bury their relatives, perform mourning ceremonies or even see the remains of loved ones. Afterwards, *Ihahamuke,* a new word, appeared in the Rwandan vocabulary to describe the post-traumatic stress and grief caused by genocide.

The most astounding fact of all was that the Tutsis had then overthrown the Hutu government, to take control of a country where their own people had been almost wiped out.

Emma had digested all these facts and figures, but nothing could have prepared her for the devastating sight of the young female survivors, great with child, walking, stumbling or being helped towards the clinic, overcoming their fear and terror to try to bring their unborn child into the world in their home country. A country that had showed no mercy to them, but which was the only option they had to try to regain some kind of dignity and peace of mind, beginning with the most historical and natural role of women everywhere - motherhood.

She had already assisted several teenage girls to give birth, some more successful than others, but none of them had been as young as her present charge. Mutesi was just fourteen. Thirteen when she'd been raped the previous July, when her luck ran out, and she, her father, mother and eight brothers and sisters were caught by a group of Hutu *Interahamwe,* the so-called 'self-defence' organisation that led and coordinated the atrocities after the death of President Habiyarimana in April. Ironically and sadly for Mutesi and her family, it was only a few days before the killing frenzy came to an end, at least the Hutu part.

Along with about forty other Tutsi men, women and children, the family had fled from their home in Rukara, one of the most eastern villages of Rwanda, about seventy kilometres north east of Kigali and close to the lakes on the Tanzanian border. A final murderous wave of Hutu violence was washing closer and closer to their isolated village, leaving no survivors. They crossed the hilly terrain along the western edge of the Akagera National Park and were hiding in the Gabiro High School, supposedly under the protection of the school staff. They were hoping to make their way across the park into Tanzania, unaware that already forty thousand of their tribespeople had been slaughtered or had committed suicide on the banks of the nearby Akagera River, their bodies being swept through the park in the fast flowing river and deposited in Lake Victoria.

Just after nightfall on the Saturday evening they were to make their escape, a dozen machete-wielding Hutus were let into the building by the teachers. After raping the screaming women and adolescent girls for hours on end, with the men and children forced to watch, the *Interahamwe* finally hacked every member of the families to death in a frenzied bloodbath. Everyone, except Mutesi.

Over the last two days, Emma had managed to glean the story of the young girl's escape, often needing to consult her pocket dictionary to translate words and phrases that were beyond her vocabulary. Mutesi spoke a little French, which was easier to understand than the local language, but it was still a challenge for her and the dreadful story she learned in dribs and drabs from the girl made her want to go out and commit murder herself. She knew every one of the women and girls in the building had a similar story to tell, but she hadn't yet learned to suppress her feelings of disgust and helplessness at the pain and suffering that these poor innocent victims had born.

"*Voilà! Il arrive.* Here he is." She gently manoeuvred the baby's shoulders until it slid free and she could take the tiny body into her hands. "It's a boy, Mutesi. A beautiful little boy." She tied and snipped the umbilical cord then bathed the child and laid him, wrapped in a piece of clean towelling, alongside Mutesi's breast, helping to put her arms around the screaming infant. She wasn't strong enough to hold him safely and Emma sat beside her, holding the baby in position.

Mutesi's hair was soaked with sweat, her eyes were dark and sunken, her face was drained of colour. She looked at the baby in her arms and tears poured from her eyes. "*Mon fils.* He's beautiful. *Son nom est Léopold,*" she breathed, her voice barely discernible. "Thank you, Emma, *milles mercis.*"

She lay back onto the soaked sheet, breathing raggedly. "Emma?"

"*Oui,* Mutesi."

"*Si quelque chose m'arrive, veille sur lui. Promets le moi.* If anything happens to me, look after him, Promise me."

"Of course I will. But nothing will happen. Just rest and you'll feel much better soon."

Her eyes closed and she fell into an exhausted sleep.

SEVENTEEN

April, 1995
Bumbogo, outside Kigali, Rwanda

Emma ignored the noise and mayhem around them in the makeshift ward and sat by the bed for a while watching Mutesi sleep. Then she gently removed the baby from her grasp, wrapped him in a cotton blanket and laid him in the plastic cot at the side of the bed. As she gently rocked the cot, she thought about Mutesi's story. The story that the young girl had relived as she lay, exhausted and emotionally drained, waiting to give birth to a baby that had been conceived by a man she didn't even know.

Mutesi hadn't been touched by the *Interahamwe* who had raped and murdered her family and friends in July the previous year. She was grabbed and taken aside by two of the Hutu men as soon as they arrived and tied to a post by her hands and feet. The next few hours of savagery were a nightmare that would scar her mind forever. She tried to ignore the bestiality that took place in front of her, but had to live through the horror of seeing her mother and three sisters raped repeatedly then slaughtered with her father and brothers by the blood-drunk Hutu murderers. By this time she was in a hysterical state, unable to stand, hanging dizzily from the ropes that bound her to the post.

When the *Interahamwe* had finally slaked their bloodthirsty appetites, the same two men dragged her outside and bundled her into a jeep, her hands and feet still bound. The jeep drove north-west for about sixty kilometres, arriving at the lake of Ruhondo, just outside of Ruhengeri, the stronghold of the Hutu rulers. They pulled into the driveway of a large property situated on a hillside overlooking the lake with large, well-lit gardens running down to the lakefront. Mutesi was taken to the basement of the house and pushed into a small, room with barred windows high up on the wall, containing only a bed, a small table and a tin bucket. The door locked shut and the thirteen year old girl who had just witnessed the deaths of all of her family members from the worst atrocities imaginable was left alone in the total darkness.

Ruhondo, outside Ruhengeri, Rwanda

The next morning, Sunday, Mutesi was lying curled up on the bed in a foetal position, having finally fallen into a troubled sleep, when she was woken by a skinny Hutu woman. She pulled away and pressed against the corner of the wall, shivering in fear, her eyes closed, trying to avoid contact with her. The woman spoke softly and said her name was Irene, the housekeeper, and she was to look after her. Gently but forcefully, she got Mutesi down from the bed, undressed her and took her to a washroom along the corridor. Irene stood her in the bath and washed her body and hair with great care, using a scented soap, then dried her with a soft cotton towel which smelled of lemons.

"Has your monthly bleeding started?" she asked.

Mutesi couldn't speak, she just nodded. The woman smiled and finished drying the girl's hair. With her she had a white shift decorated with red and yellow designs and she pulled it over her head. She left the girl in her room then returned with some breakfast, a dish of manioc and beans, fruit and milk. She waited until Irene had gone again then ate the meal ravenously, wondering fearfully what was in store for her.

Irene came back a little later and asked her if she could swim. Mutesi nodded, she had learned a primitive form of swimming in the lake near her village. She took her upstairs and out into the garden. The girl was overcome by the ostentatious opulence that surrounded her. Sculptures, fountains, streams, bridges, there was even a summer house built from white stone blocks and red tiles. It was a paradise on earth. Behind her, she saw the house was as big as a castle, like the ones in the French fairy story book she had seen in the village church. Irene took her to a large swimming pool, water cascading into it from a rocky cliff and running out over a small precipice into a stream that meandered down to the lake.

"*Viens.*" She said and helped her to take off the shift. "*Vas y, la piscine est à toi.* In you go, it's all yours."

Mutesi walked nervously forward then turned at the poolside, still suspicious of everyone and everything.

"Jump in", said Irene, encouraging her with a wave of the hand."

The girl jumped into the warm, clear water, staying under the surface as long as she could, trying to cleanse her naked body, trying to escape from the terrible events she'd suffered. Then she resurfaced and threw herself across the pool like an animal, swimming with a clumsy paddle stroke.

A man was standing at the window of a room on the third floor of the mansion. He was naked. He was looking through binoculars, held in his left hand. He watched Irene pull Mutesi's shift over her head and reveal her shapely nubile body. His eyes followed her as she walked to the pool. He stared as she came to the surface and swam across the pool. With his other hand, he began to masturbate.

Mutesi had just eaten another light meal, served by Irene. She was curled up once more on the bed, crying and wishing she had perished with her family instead of surviving to be brought to this place. Wondering who had saved her from the horrors that had befallen her family and friends, and why. Frightened and fearful that the nightmare wasn't yet over.

The door opened and a man entered the room. He wore spectacles but didn't look very old, a little older than her father. He was tall and slim, with a moustache and he was dressed in a black bath robe. "*Bonjour,* Mutesi," he said. "My name is Jean-Bousquet. This is my home; I hope you are comfortable here." He came to sit on the bed beside her. He smelled of perfume, like a sweet smelling flower.

Mutesi shivered and moved away into the corner of the wall. "*Oui, Monsieur.*" she stammered.

Jean-Bousquet placed his hand on her leg. "Tell me Mutesi, have you ever been with a man?"

She shook her head and looked away, trembling.

"*Bien.*" He stood up, placed his spectacles on the table and unloosened the sash of his robe and shook it off. She saw he was aroused, like the Hutu men who had raped her mother and sisters. She turned her head away again and cowered against the wall, shaking with fear, sobbing silently.

He stretched out his hand and pulled her towards him by the arm. "Come Mutesi, I want to be your friend," he said.

EIGHTEEN

July - December, 1994
Ruhondo, outside Ruhengeri, Rwanda

Irene came to Mutesi's room the next morning, Monday. There were bloodstains on the bed and she was curled up again in the corner, crying with fear and pain. The woman had brought creams and oils with her and she turned the girl onto her back so she could minister to her.

"The master has gone to Kigali," she said. "He is only here at weekends, sometimes he doesn't come for two weeks. I will look after you so you don't suffer." She gently applied the cream and massaged the girl's body with the fragrant oil until Mutesi began to feel a little better. Irene fetched some breakfast and sat at the bedside as she ate it, slowly getting Mutesi to talk about her village, herself and eventually, her family, and what had happened to them. Little by little the girl began to trust her, began to believe that she had a friend in this house.

The woman said she'd worked at the house for seven years and spoke of Jean-Bousquet in reverential tones, telling her, "He is a very important man. A big politician in Rwanda, doing good things for the people. He is head of a radio station. A very well-known man. If you do what he wants you will be safe, but you must not upset him. He can be very cruel if he gets angry. Just do what he wants and I will look after you. After a while you won't even feel anything at all."

Jean-Bousquet came back on Friday night and that weekend he came to Mutesi's room several times, at all hours of the day and night. Irene had shown her how to use a little of the cream to reduce the pain of the visits without arousing his suspicions. He wasn't cruel or sadistic, speaking kindly to relax her for his own comfort. But she waited for his visits with ever increasing dread. Afterwards, she lay curled up on her bed, shivering with the memories of her mother and sisters being ravished by the Hutu men, wondering whether it would have been better to have died with them rather than to have lived only to be brought to this house and this man.

The following weekend Jean-Bousquet didn't return from Kigali. Irene now permitted her to walk around the gardens and swim in the pool when he was away. She also met Auguste who was his major domo, valet, butler and bodyguard all rolled into one massive, muscular frame. He was gentle and kind to Mutesi and she would seek him out to talk when Jean-Bousquet was away. There were several other employees working in the house and grounds, but she was too frightened to communicate with them.

The killing in the country came to an end that month, but the girl didn't know. It was never spoken of by Irene and she was not ready to bring the subject up herself. The Hutu government was removed on July 18th by the Tutsi Rwandan Patriotic Front and a Tutsi regime began under the new President, Pasteur Bizimungu. Paul Kagame, the leader of the RPF, became Vice President; the power behind the throne.

For the next two months, Jean-Bousquet came to the house every other weekend. With Irene's help Mutesi was able to withstand his frequent visits to her room. By now, he hardly spoke at all, just came in and took her without a word. She sensed he was losing interest in her body and wondered what might happen if he became angry with her. She decided to ask Irene what she had meant by her warning.

"There have been other girls." Irene was walking in the garden with Mutesi. "After a while, he loses interest and wants to get rid of them. Usually, he gets angry for no reason then hands them over to his *Interahamwe* comrades."

"What happens to them?" Mutesi shivered, memories of her family's ordeal flooding back into her mind.

"I don't know. They're taken away and we never see them again. You might be luckier because he has been to the house much less and hasn't had time to get tired of you."

By this time Mutesi had lost all interest in her life. She couldn't decide which fate would be better, to remain in this palace-like prison or be taken away and murdered by Jean-Bousquet's *Interahamwe.*

In October, Irene became certain that Mutesi was pregnant. The girl had missed her period in September and then suffered a couple of weeks of morning sickness. Jean-Bousquet was away at the time and when he returned Irene said nothing to him and he didn't guess the truth. But by November, she knew it couldn't be hidden any longer. She took Mutesi aside and told her she was to have a baby, but she must not tell Jean-Bousquet. She had grown fond of the young girl and was afraid he would get rid of her like the others.

Mutesi was thrown into total confusion. She had lost both parents and her siblings in the most appalling circumstances and with their deaths, her own desire to live. And now, like a gift from God, she had conceived a baby. That evening, in her dark and lonely little room, she prayed, asking the Lord to help her carry her child safely. Her pregnancy was still too early to show but she held her hands around her stomach, praying that she could bring a new life into the world, to begin her own family to love and cherish. She decided to survive, somehow, whatever it took, for the sake of her unborn baby.

Irene and Auguste tried to devise a plan to help her escape but there was no way of getting her safely away from the house. There were few dwellings in the surrounding countryside and a lone girl in the forest would be vulnerable and easy to spot. And Mutesi had no transport to take her back to her home village. Rukara, in the most eastern part of the country was a hundred kilometres away. She worried over the problem until a few days later it was resolved by outside events.

In mid-November, Jean-Bousquet came back to the house after spending ten days in Kigali. He seemed shaken and panicky when he called Irene and Auguste into his office.

"I have to leave for a while," he told them. "There's a few things I need to sort out and I can't get it done here. I'll need my bags packed for a few weeks stay abroad. My flight is tomorrow evening. Get everything ready." He went to his office and didn't emerge until morning. Auguste came up to help him carry stacks of papers and recording tapes from his files and they burned them in a furnace in the basement. He spent the rest of the day throwing out more papers and making telephone calls. He never visited Mutesi.

"Don't worry," he told Irene and Auguste when his car came to take him to the airport. "I'll be away only a few weeks, so keep everything in good order and I'll see you soon." As he was getting into the car, he asked, "Is the girl still here?"

When they both nodded, he just said, "Get rid of her."

They never saw Jean-Bousquet again.

A month went by and the atmosphere in the house became more relaxed. The two servants had decided to ignore their employer's orders and wait to see what happened. Mutesi was moved to a room on the ground floor, where she could walk out into the gardens. Irene helped to improve her reading and she assisted in the household duties. She told the girl that the killing was over, but there was still much danger outside. "The Tutsis are settling scores now. It's not safe for anyone to go out alone, Hutu or not. You're fine here. We'll decide what to do when we have news of Jean-Bousquet."

As she walked in the grounds, Mutesi wondered what would happen to her and her unborn child. She thought of escaping from the property but she knew she wasn't experienced or clever enough to make it on her own. She had no knowledge of the surrounding area, nor the long journey back to Rukara. But knowing that she was carrying a new life had changed her mind-set completely. Now she was determined to survive at all costs, to keep this baby from harm and bring it into the world, perhaps a world without killing. She followed Irene's instructions about eating and looking after herself and she waited patiently for something to happen. Her fourteenth birthday came and went without anyone knowing, she didn't want to draw unnecessary attention to herself. Her pregnancy was starting to show, but the two senior servants still insisted she should stay at the house until they were advised of Jean-Bousquet's return plans. However, they never received any news.

One evening in mid-December, an army jeep came to the house, carrying a Tutsi officer and three soldiers. Mutesi hid down in the basement room with the door locked. Auguste went to meet them at the door.

"We're here to take possession of this house," the officer announced, waving some documents in his face. "The property has been expropriated on the orders of the government. I am Major Obasanjo and I will stay here until the new owner is announced. Show me round the house now."

Auguste was terrified. He knew that one wrong word would be his death warrant. He bowed low to the soldier. "Welcome Major. You must be tired after your trip. Please come in and we'll prepare supper for you before looking around the property."

Irene went down to the basement room where Mutesi was hiding. "You have to leave now, tonight. You're no longer safe. These Tutsi soldiers are filthy murderers. They slit open the bellies of pregnant women and eat the unborn children. We'll keep them occupied while you get away. I'll help you pack a few things and give you some food then you can slip out in the dark. You're in good health and you can make it to a safe place if you take care."

Mutesi was shaking with fear. She knew Irene had been indoctrinated into believing the Tutsis were capable of any atrocity, but it seemed to her that everybody in her country had been converted into a murderer, Hutu or Tutsi. Whatever the truth, she and her child were in mortal peril. She nodded her thanks and collected the few belongings she'd been given during her stay.

Just before midnight, the housekeeper took her to the woods at the edge of the property and gave her a bag with food in it. She had also brought a loose smock and a cardigan for her. The smock would help to hide her pregnant state and the cardigan would keep her warm. She helped Mutesi to put them on.

"This is the route to your home," she said, pointing it out on a small hand drawn map. "You see the main village names on the way? In each village you'll see signs for the nearby places and you just have to follow the names on the map. If you get lost, wait for a woman to pass and ask the way to the next village, but stay away from the men, any men. If you have to go on the roads, mix in with a group of women and don't talk about being pregnant. Go along this path until you come to the Kigali Road then follow the directions. Goodbye, Mutesi. God be with you and your child."

The girl couldn't speak. She kissed the Hutu woman and walked away. Fourteen years old and four months pregnant, Mutesi walked out into the darkness alone.

NINETEEN

December, 1994
Ruhondo, outside Ruhengeri, Rwanda

Leaving the property, Mutesi followed the path in the dark for a couple of kilometres. The forest was deserted and she encountered no one until she came to the main road, where she stopped in astonishment. The road was overflowing on each side with a massive wave of people trudging slowly up towards her, in the direction of Butaro, away from Kigali. She had never seen so many people in her life, old people, children, cripples, not many men but a lot of women, many with babes in arms. It was a frightening sight. *Where are they all going?* She asked herself.

It was impossible to walk through them and stay on the tarmac, so she sat at the side of the road, waiting for a gap in the tide of people. A large group of Tutsi women passed near her and she asked one of them what was happening.

"We're leaving Rwanda," the woman replied. "Everyone says the killing has stopped, but we don't believe them. Before, it was the Hutus and now it's the Tustsis. But you can't trust anyone any more, they're killing their own people now. Everyone's gone mad in this country. We want to get out."

"We're heading for Zaïre," another woman said. "They're taking in refugees. We'll be safe there. We just want to get away from the slaughter. Come with us. There's nothing any more in Rwanda for a young girl like you."

Mutesi turned away, unsettled by the women's talk, suddenly undecided in her mind. She sat at the roadside for a while longer, trying to work out what to do. Zaïre, a new life in a new country. Maybe a better place for her and her baby. But a country she didn't know, people she didn't know. She thought about it for a long while, but knew she couldn't face another challenge in her life while pregnant with her child. Rukara was her village, her home, the only place she had ever lived; the only people she had ever known. The only place she had ever felt safe.

She carefully got back to her feet and fought her way slowly through the mass of humanity, down the road towards Kigali.

It took Mutesi twelve days to cover the hundred kilometres to her home village. She walked in the very early morning and late afternoon and evening. It was the dry season and there was no rain, but the sun was still hot during the day and it exhausted her. Following the Ruhengeri - Kigali road south east, near Tumba she branched off and took the road to Mugambazi, about fifty kilometres from Ruhondo and half way to Rukara. With the help of the map and the women she passed on the road she found her way without too much difficulty. The mass of refugees moving towards her forced her to walk parallel with the main roads and she took small trails and paths, always fearful that she'd be seen and apprehended. The atrocities she'd witnessed and the months with Jean-Bousquet had made her frightened and suspicious of everyone, man or woman.

At Mugambazi, she left the road and struck across country to the east, in the direction of Rutare and its hilly, forested slopes. She saw fewer people now, small groups of women and occasionally men. Many of them seemed to be camped out temporarily, as if they didn't believe the killing was over and were afraid to return to their villages. Her progress was slow and tiring and her pace dropped significantly with each day. She fashioned a crude walking pole from a tree branch to help keep her balance on the untracked terrain. Fearful of falling and injuring herself and the baby she skirted steep climbs and descents as best she could, often having to make a wide circuit to get back to her original line of direction.

Three days later, after struggling through the forest and around the steep and dangerous hillsides Mutesi managed to find the north side of the Muhazi River. Although she had consumed it sparingly, the food and water Irene had provided had almost run out and she foraged for nuts and berries and edible plants that she recognised, like wild cucumbers and yams, putting whatever was left into her bag as a reserve for the next day. She drank river water and found safe hideaways to sleep in at night, out of sight or smell of any wild creatures that might be roaming nearby. The evenings were cool, but the smock and cardigan provided by the housekeeper were sufficient.

She walked alongside the river for two days, becoming more and more tired and less careful, narrowly avoiding injuring herself in the inhospitable terrain. Small groups of people, bedraggled, dirty and listless, passed her from time to time, seeming dazed and walking aimlessly along, sometimes not even speaking a word.

From time to time she would see wild creatures, bands of wild dogs or jackals, and once, she saw a leopard drinking from the river at sunset. But she was able to stay downwind of the animals and was never threatened by any of them. She had little sleep, being disturbed by the many animal noises in the night, lying tired and hungry in whatever sheltered spot she could find.

Ten days after leaving Ruhonda she saw the sheen of Lake Muhazi up ahead, near her home village. The sight energised her and she began to walk faster and with more abandon. Her mind went back to the tranquil life with her family, before the killings. It was a comfortable, safe feeling. Familiar voices, sounds, odours, began to resonate through her. The smell of cooking, the laughter of her sisters and brothers, the sound of her father and mother talking. She was reliving her past life, she was safe at last, safe in the comfort of her family. Mutesi was hallucinating.

As she hurried towards the lake, she stepped down from a rock and the ground gave way beneath her foot. She had stepped into a moss covered ditch. The slope she was on was only a gentle decline, but steep enough to carry her down the hillside. Helplessly she rolled down the shale covered slope, more than ten metres to the bottom. Mutesi lay for a while, breathless and bruised, fearfully holding her hands around her stomach. Then the baby kicked. She breathed again deeply and gave thanks to God.

Painfully she climbed back to her feet. And fell again. Her left ankle was swollen badly, it was sprained. She managed to crawl to the riverside and dangled her leg in the cool water until the stinging of the sprain diminished and the swelling dissipated a little. Mutesi remembered the healing plants taught to her by her mother. Looking around she saw a group of pineapple lilies growing nearby. The leaves of the plant had healing qualities for bruising and fractures. She crawled over and collected some of the leaves to wrap around her ankle. Then she placed a thick coating of mud from the river bank over the leaves to form a primitive poultice. A wide strip of cloth torn from her smock served as a bandage and the strap from the bag given to her by Irene fastened around her ankle held it in place.

Mutesi sat back against a tree trunk and rested until the pain in her ankle eased. Exhausted with her efforts she fell asleep for several hours, her body recuperating while she slept. When she awoke it was early evening, the star-filled sky above her like a magic sparkling carpet. A balmy, soft moment in her journey. She ate the last of the food from her bag and drank some water from the river. Her ankle was much improved and she managed to fashion a cushion around the top of the walking pole with the rest of Irene's bag so she could use it as a crutch. She climbed carefully back to her feet and limped towards the lake. Heading towards Rukara. Heading towards her home.

The last part of her journey, as she skirted Lake Muhazi, was a place of rocky terrain, lazy streams and lakes, surrounded by marshy, treacherous land. She spent many hours retracing her tracks to find a way through the hostile environment. The pain in her ankle was a constant reminder of how close she was to failing in her task but she somehow found the strength to carry on. Now she walked and rested in equal measure, for her own and the baby's sake. Mutesi had no strength left to wash herself, and she ate whatever plant or flower came to hand, with water from the streams. In a constant daze by now, she would fall into an exhausted sleep then climb back to her feet, again and again, to stagger forward, determined to carry herself and her baby back to their home.

It took two more days for her to cover the last twenty kilometres and at long last, almost two weeks after leaving Ruhonda, she reached the outskirts of Rukara. Mutesi knelt down on the dirt path and thanked God for her deliverance. She had made it home alive, with her baby safe. Clambering painfully back to her feet she limped wearily past the line of shacks towards her parent's home. The village seemed deserted, she could see no one around, until she came to the church building in the centre. She heard singing and went up to the door.

The tiny building was filled with people, singing their hearts out, praising Jesus and the Lord. Thanking the heavens for their miraculous survival; against all odds they were still alive. She looked around at the decorations in the church and realised it was Christmas Day. She had lost count of time and hadn't realised the date. Now she saw a few familiar faces, women and girls, friends from the past. She stepped inside and sat by the door, filthy and exhausted, sobbing quietly, hardly believing she'd returned home again, but knowing that no member of her family was there to welcome her back.

Some of the women turned and came over. "It's Mutesi. Look, Mutesi's come back. God be praised. Mutesi is back with us."

Mutesi wrapped her arms around her stomach, around her unborn child, and she fell asleep, surrounded by what remained of her village friends, lulled by the musical voices in the church, finally feeling safe, finally realising that the killing was over.

TWENTY

April, 1995
Bumbogo, outside Kigali, Rwanda

Mutesi limped slowly towards the temporary clinic in Bumbogo, forty kilometres from Rukara. Emma was getting some fresh air outside and saw her stagger into the encampment, helped by another young woman. Between them, they helped the girl into the clinic. One of the beds had been vacated that morning and they lifted her onto it. Emma could see she was due to give birth soon; she looked exhausted and frail, at the limit of her strength. She bathed Mutesi gently with warm water then let her rest. Doctor Constance, the only doctor in the clinic, would examine her later, when his impossible schedule permitted the time.

Going outside, she sat with Marianne, the woman who had accompanied her, who chattered in voluble French, which she tried desperately to understand. From what she could make out, the young woman, who Emma learned was about seventeen years old, told her that Mutesi had stayed with her in her home since she had returned to their village in December. Marianne's husband had been murdered last July, in the same final mad wave of violence that Mutesi's family had fled and which had spread as far as the lakes on the eastern border with Tanzania. She had taken the young, pregnant girl into her home to help her regain some strength, but even now she was still fragile and weak. Mutesi was only eight months pregnant but because of her frail condition she feared the baby would come prematurely.

In Rukara, the Hutu had slaughtered anyone who could bring children into the world, including the wise woman, the village midwife. The village was reduced to mainly old women and children, with the few men who had escaped death returning one by one to their decimated families. Mutesi had fought so hard to survive that she was fearful of putting herself and her baby in the hands of an unqualified person. Marianne also knew she was at the limit of her strength. She would need all the expert help they could find to bring the baby into the world.

Euphrasie, another woman who had survived to return to the village from Kigali told them she'd heard of a family clinic which had been set up in Bumbogo, about forty kilometres away, just outside the capital. It was run by French people and helped women who had lost their families. Despite the atrocious manner in which so many Rwandan women and girls had been impregnated, it was still too shameful to admit to being a rape victim. The clinic was called a Family Assistance Clinic, although almost all the patients were pregnant women in desperate need of care and attention.

Mutesi knew that she could lose her own life and her baby's without expert assistance and facilities, but there were none in Rukara. There was no midwife, no electricity, no tap water, no facilities of any kind to help her if anything went wrong. She told Marianne that she was determined to get to the clinic in Bumbogo to have her child in a safe place.

At first Marianne tried to dissuade her, she was too weak to make the journey. But Mutesi was adamant. If this was the last thing she could do for her baby, she had to do it. She had to get to the clinic in Bumbogo. Marianne saw that she couldn't win the argument, so she insisted on going with her, she couldn't let her attempt it alone. She found out there was a bus to Kibali that they could pick up at Kayonza, about ten kilometres walk from the village The bus would take them to the outskirts of Kigali, just a couple of kilometres from the clinic. Euphrasie explained to them how to find their way, but both she and Marianne were concerned that Mutesi wasn't strong enough to undertake the journey. It would challenge any woman, but for a full-term pregnant teenager, it could be fatal.

The two women prepared themselves as best they could with their limited resources and set off towards Kayonza. It took them a day and a half to get to the clinic.

Emma requested permission to look after Mutesi herself. She wanted to be the one who made a difference to the girl's life.

Mutesi went into labour the next day.

TWENTY-ONE

April, 1995
Bumbogo, outside Kigali, Rwanda

Emma woke up, aroused by the baby's cries. It was evening and he was hungry. Mutesi was still sleeping. She fetched a bottle of warm milk from the kitchen and picked up the baby.

"Mutesi, it's time for Leopold's first meal", she said. When the girl didn't respond, she shook her gently, still to no effect. Emma suddenly had a terrible premonition. "Mutesi! Wake up Mutesi!" she cried, shaking her more urgently, her heart racing.

The young girl lay still, her eyes closed and a peaceful expression on her face. "No! No!" Emma sobbed. "Not after everything you've been through. Your son is safely delivered into the world. Mutesi! You've got everything to live for. You can't give up now." She replaced the screaming baby in the cot and raced through the clinic to find Dr Constance.

He checked Mutesi's vital signs then shook his head. "I'm sorry, Emma. There's nothing we can do."

"This is all my fault." Emma grabbed the doctor's arm. "If I hadn't fallen asleep she would still be alive. I should have realised she wasn't just sleeping, that she wasn't well. I should have called you before."

He shook her hand away. "I don't think it would have made any difference. I was afraid this would happen."

"What do you mean?"

"When I examined her, I noticed an irregularity in her heartbeat. It was fairly weak, which doesn't always mean trouble but it was quite inconsistent, which means there's a fault somewhere. Maybe a faulty valve, which causes the heart to work harder on one side than the other. Extra stress, like childbirth, added to the severe exhaustion she was suffering can place too much pressure on the heart and it can fail. I'm sure that's what happened."

"But why didn't you say anything? Maybe I could have done something. Don't we have anything that could have helped the condition?"

"Emma, you know what limited facilities we have here. We're not equipped to deal with complex issues like heart problems. We don't even have equipment to diagnose the problem. And she was about to go into labour. If we'd given her anything we might have jeopardised the baby's birth."

He took Emma by the shoulders and looked into her eyes. "We have saved one life today. Without our help, Mutesi and her son might have both been lost. You must think of the positive aspect of our work."

"But, I fell asleep. It was wrong of me. I should have been alert to her condition, her weakness. I should have been extra vigilant when she was sleeping. I should never have dozed off."

"What time did you start this morning?"

"I was called at four o'clock to help with a caesarean and I've been on ever since."

"That's fourteen hours without a break. Be reasonable, Emma. Everyone needs time to recuperate. We're not machines, without sleep we'll make even worse mistakes. But the point is, you didn't make a mistake. Mutesi had a weak heart and we've got nothing that would have helped her. Her heart failed after the exertions of the birth, but she leaves a beautiful healthy little boy."

"But she died on my watch. How can I rationalise that?

How can I cope with her death on my conscience?"

"Emma, please stop blaming yourself for this. If anyone is to blame, it's me. I should have prescribed something for her immediately after the delivery, but I didn't expect it to come so soon and I was trying to do a thousand things at the same time." He looked down, disconsolately, "And I was half asleep myself. I haven't been to bed since the night before last. We're all overwhelmed here. We've got a team of six to look after seventy women and the chances are we're going to see some accidents. After what they've been through, these girls are so weak, so traumatised, so….vulnerable. Sometimes they just don't have the strength to carry on. Especially if they have a condition like Mutesi's.

"I understand you're grieving for Mutesi, we both are. She was a sweet girl and she didn't deserve this wretched end to her life. But the chances are she wouldn't have made it whatever we did. She obviously had a very severe heart problem and she succumbed to it. We did our best and we can't do more than that. But you must put incidents like this into perspective, admit that we can't win every time, however hard we try to beat the odds, and we're going to have a few failures alongside the many successes. If you can't, then I'm afraid you need to evaluate your suitability to this work. I'll tell you frankly it's not the job I signed up for, but it's what we've got to cope with. It's not easy, nobody said it would be, but if we don't do it then it will be a whole lot harder for these poor people.

"Now, I want you to go and take a break. Have something to eat then sleep until tomorrow morning. "I'll look after Mutesi. And I'll talk to Marianne. Trust me."

"Then I'll take the baby and feed him. He can spend the night with me, there's nobody else available to look after an orphan." 'Orphan'. The very word rang out in her own ears. Leopold was now an orphan. Who in Rwanda would care for a one day old orphan?

"Please let me look after the child." She implored. "You have to let me do this for Mutesi. I promised her and I can't break my promise."

Emma finally wore down the doctor until he agreed and she took the tiny baby to her quarters, changed and fed him, then made up a comfortable cot for him in a drawer in the room. Then she fell onto the bed in an exhausted sleep.

MARBELLA
TUESDAY, JULY 13, 2010

TWENTY-TWO

Marbella, Spain

Emma sat quietly sobbing, the vivid memories of Leo's birth and now his abduction overcoming her again. Jenny went over and put her arms around her and soothed her for a moment.

"No wonder you're distressed after dredging up those fifteen year old memories. My God, that's the most appalling story I've ever heard. You must have been heartbroken when that poor girl died. And she was only one of hundreds of thousands who perished in that dreadful genocide." She paused, "Leticia's parents have a similar story to tell about Angola, if ever we could get them to tell it. We never learn, do we? Humans. We never learn."

She shook her head and pulled Emma to her feet and they walked into the kitchen. "You can tell me the rest over lunch, but now at least I know where Leo came from. It's not at all what I imagined."

"I know. You thought I'd had an affair with someone in Rwanda. Well, that's also partly true, but that comes later."

Jenny gave her a quizzical look, but said nothing. They still had plenty of time to finish the story.

Encarni served them lunch on the terrace. The sun was burning hot and a wide awning protected them from the direct sunlight.

It seemed to Emma that it was as hot as Rwanda, but a lot more civilised. They chatted about inconsequential things, getting to know each other again after many years of little contact.

The housekeeper brought them coffee and Jenny said, "I'd better explain the situation here. It's a bit complicated. When Charlie, Ron's father died, he left his estate, including this house, to me and a young Angolan woman called Leticia da Costa. She became his companion after he lost his wife. She used to be his housekeeper then they fell in love and had a son together, a lovely boy called Emilio. Leticia actually owns half the estate in trust for him, but that doesn't really change anything.

"Encarni is Leticia's mother and she offered to become housekeeper so Leticia could spend more time with Emilio. He's only four, so he still needs his mother with him. They're on a two week holiday in France right now, with her fiancé, Patrice. He's a banker, here in Marbella, a Frenchman. Very French, if you know what I mean."

"Don't you like him?"

"It's not that. He seems like a sweet guy, but it's just the way he dresses and talks, very 'in your face continental'." She grimaced then laughed. "Listen to me. I'm getting to be a bitchy old widow. They're getting married in October and I'm probably just jealous. Anyway, the point is we've got the house to ourselves for another couple of weeks, so we can stay here to sort out this business about Leo. It's an enormous place with everything we could possibly need; six telephone lines, speaker phone, cinema screen, Internet, Fax, you name it. Charlie ran his business from here. And it's a lot closer to Africa than Newcastle." She pointed across the swimming pool at the distant mountains vaguely discernible in the heat mist. "You can get a ferry to Morocco from just along the road. Not that we'll need to, but that's how close we are."

"It's a marvellous place Jenny and you were right to get me out of Johannesburg. I'm feeling more positive and relaxed and starting to think better already."

"Good. So before you go and settle in and have a bath and a sleep or whatever you need to do, finish telling me about Leo."

Emma took up her story again. "You were right about the affair, but it didn't start in Rwanda, it started in London. It was a man who worked with *SOS Médicale*, Tony Forrester was his name. I met him before he joined them, when I was with the Red Cross. He was an assistant administrator at University College Hospital. I was renting a little studio flat in Marylebone then. That was before it became fashionable and impossibly expensive.

"We met at a fund raising event for *SOSM* at the Langham Hilton in Portland Place. He was mad keen on joining them and working somewhere exciting, but he hadn't had the chance until the Rwandan atrocity occurred. Then, later on when he heard they were sending in five teams, he applied to go down as local administrator and got the job. He could speak three or four languages, he was very clever. That's how I got the job too. We were going out then and he introduced me as an experienced nurse and they hired me, so we were able to go together.

"After Mutesi's death, Dr Constance suspended me from maternity work. He thought I was too emotionally involved and would go to pieces if there was another death on my watch." Emma sighed. "I hate to admit it, but he was probably right. I just couldn't stand seeing these poor girls suffering because of what had been done to them by the genociders. If I'd had a machete I think I'd have run amok and killed half of Kigali. So, I was left in charge of Leopold until they could arrange to fly me back to London."

"And that suited you perfectly?"

"I loved it. I felt so fulfilled and I believed I was keeping my promise to Mutesi. And Tony was a great comfort in helping me get over her death. He was based in Kigali, but we saw a lot of each other and he was fantastic with me after my spat with Dr Constance. We were very much in love and by this time, we were talking about getting married."

"What was Tony doing in Rwanda? What was his job?"

"He was in charge of all the administration; travel, security, buying equipment, managing the budget, reporting to Head Office in

Paris, all that administrative stuff. And, crucially, he was responsible for registering births and deaths at the clinic and making contact with the orphanages when it was necessary. But everything was delayed and complicated because the whole system was in chaos. The hospitals, morgues, schools, orphanages, nothing was working, so Leopold's birth and Mutesi's death hadn't yet been registered.

"Then after a couple of weeks, I began to feel quite maternal towards Leopold. He was beautiful, the loveliest baby I've ever seen. He hardly ever cried and he seemed very contented when I held him, as if I was his mother. Tony loved him too. He was made to be a father. A very soft and loving man and he was happy that I had the baby to look after because of Mutesi. So, I started to imagine he was my son, that I could keep him. That Tony and I could begin our married life with a gorgeous baby boy.

"I couldn't bear the thought that he'd have to go to an orphanage. Can you imagine, a tiny baby in a Rwandan…." She suddenly looked at her sister. "Oh my God, Jenny, I'm so sorry. I wasn't thinking. I'm rattling on about the baby and I just wasn't thinking. Please forgive me, I feel terrible."

"It's fine, Emma. That was a long time ago. I hardly think about it anymore." Jenny tried to bluff her way around the subject, but her sister had seen the tears that had come to her eyes as she remembered the pain of losing her baby and never being able to have another. The beautiful, helpless children she'd seen when she visited the Bulgarian orphanage, lost in a vortex of despair and desperate for love and affection, from anyone. "Don't worry, I'm fine. And this is not about me, it's about Leo. Tell me how you got him out of Rwanda and into the UK."

"Well it was really Tony who did it. First, he had to arrange for Leo not to appear in the system."

"So he somehow managed to register Mutesi's death without registering Leo's birth?"

"That's right. But he didn't tell me all the details. He just said we had to find a way to get Leo out of the country and nobody would ever catch on."

"And that was difficult, I suppose?"

"Yes. Getting him out of Rwanda was the main problem. Kigali airport was hardly functioning and was under military control, so we couldn't just turn up with an African child and fly off without a qualm. We'd have been slapped in prison and neither of us would have been heard of again and I don't know what would have become of Leo. So, Tony came up with a plan, which actually turned out to be fairly easy. Although I was terrified something would go wrong.

"He was in charge of transport, so he could arrange the flights to make it work. He booked me on a flight to Nairobi, then to London, to send me home. His thinking was that it's only two and a half hours to Nairobi, so if the baby's asleep, he won't be heard or spotted and he can't come to any harm in such a short time. Then he organised to send some medical samples for testing in Paris on the same flight. They were in big, insulated cases, a lot bigger than a little baby."

"And I suppose they treat these samples cases with extreme care?"

"Exactly. Leo couldn't have been safer than in one of those well-padded boxes with lots of air vents. They're marked all over with stickers like, 'Handle with Care', 'Right Way Up' and 'Do NOT Damage'."

"But I don't understand the Paris bit when you were going to London?"

"We couldn't send the boxes to London, because the *SOSM* testing clinic is in Paris. And we couldn't send Leo all the way to London, it would have been too dangerous for him. So when we put Leo in the case, just before he supervised the loading, Tony changed the cargo manifest and marked that box, 'Unload in Nairobi'."

"And he didn't wake up and give the game away?"

"We gave him the tiniest dose of sedative, just in case, and he slept for almost five hours. Right until I got on the plane to London."

"So, you took him out of the case in Nairobi and I suppose the controls there were pretty non-existent, so you just carried him onto the flight?"

Emma nodded. "That's right. They took the case out and I told them I needed a room to check the samples. I had a big carry-on bag with me, like a carpet bag, with a small box with tissue samples in it, the same weight as Leo. I took him out, he was still fast asleep, and I laid him in the bag and put the samples box into the case, to compensate the weight. Then I told them to put the case on the flight to Paris with the others, so the right number of cases would arrive in Paris and avoid any suspicion. Then I just carried Leo onto the plane in the bag."

"How ingenious. You're right, Tony was very clever. But then how did you get him through immigration into England?"

"That part was down to me. Luckily, I still had my Red Cross passport. It's a kind of ID card that shows you're a trusted employee and you deserve protection, respect and all that. I was shaking like a leaf, but the immigration people are trained to trust us and they did. I told them I'd had the baby in Nairobi and he wasn't yet on my passport. We chatted for a while then they wished me well and sent me through into London. I was so relieved that I sat on a seat in the arrivals hall with Leo on my knee and cried and cried my eyes out."

"I'm not surprised. You must have been absolutely terrified. I don't think I could have carried it off." Jenny thought for a moment, "Let me see Leo's passport. Have you still got it with you?"

Emma reached for her handbag. "Here. I've had it with me since we left England."

"His birth place is registered as London. How did you manage that?"

Her sister took a deep breath. "I hope you're not going to despise me for this, but it's the only part of the plan which was really illegal. That's why I've never talked about it before."

Jenny shrugged and said nothing, so she continued, "Tony came back to Paris on *SOSM* business after I'd returned and he arranged a meeting in London so he could fly over to see me. We talked about the problem of registering Leo's birth, because we didn't want any mention of Rwanda, for obvious reasons. The next day, he had to go out for his meeting and when he came back, he just said, "Problem solved."

"He gave me a photocopy of an entry in the birth's register at University College Hospital Maternity Ward, confirming the birth of a boy to Emma Stewart on April 23rd, 1995. It was an absolutely genuine copy of a real entry, signed by Dr A. Forrester. I have no idea how he did it, but when I read it I almost fell over with happiness.

"I went along to the registry office in Marylebone Road and registered Leo's birth, with parents as myself, single mother, and father unknown. It was a bit mortifying, but they just gave me a knowing look and stamped the form and gave me a copy and that was that. I doubt we could have got away with it now. They'd have asked for DNA tests or some kind of paperwork introduced by Brussels to prove I was the mother, but it really was that simple at the time. I had a beautiful son, all legal and proper and I was over the moon."

"And that's why you didn't want to give any information to the Foreign Office in South Africa. I don't blame you. They might have dug deep into Leo's dossier and put two and two together."

"Are you upset with me, Jenny? I know what Tony and I did wasn't legal, but it wasn't like robbing a bank, or killing someone. For us it was the opposite. We were saving a life, a life that might be lost if we didn't do something. And we were keeping faith with Mutesi. We were looking after her son, just as she asked me."

Jenny put her arm around her sister. "I think what you did was marvellous and I'm delighted you got away with it. You saved a life and now you have a wonderful son, so how can that be illegal? Well done you and Tony!"

Emma breathed deeply again and said, "Now, before you ask, I have to finish the story. The part about Tony. It's not a story with only happy parts."

She steeled herself. "Tony went back to Paris, then down to Kigali again. He had another four months to do on his contract before his first break. We were going to get married when he came back. He had two weeks off, so we'd do it in a registry office then take a week's honeymoon in Ireland. It would be July, the weather would be nice and Leo would be three months old, so we'd be able to do a lot of things together. We'd found a flat in Marylebone with two bedrooms so I rented it and moved in with Leo the week after Tony went back down.

"We didn't have mobile telephones then and in any case the phone system in Rwanda was terrible. He sent letters to me almost every day through the *SOSM* London office and I would go in and collect them. After about a month, the letters came less frequently, every week, then every other week. I knew there was something wrong, but I couldn't afford to go down and see him. Besides, I couldn't leave Leo, there wasn't anyone I could trust to leave him with. I remember you were on a project in France for the LSE then, and Mum was living in that dreadful council flat in Sunderland. Anyway, you know I couldn't have left him with her in the state she was in, so I just sat there and replied to his letters until I got the last one."

"The one you'd dreaded?"

"Yes. He told me it was over. He'd been offered a job with the Flying Doctors, in Australia, based out of Sydney. I remembered he'd always been going on about Australia, 'Opportunities as vast as the country'. But he didn't think it would work, taking me and Leo there. It would be 'too disruptive', was his phrase, and it was best to call the whole thing off. He was happy that he'd helped me get to England with the baby, but he couldn't foresee any future for us.

"Of course, I was sure he'd met someone else and I wrote and asked him. For the sake of honesty in our relationship I wanted to know the truth, and I was right. He told me a French girl had come down to take my place in the clinic. I remember her name, Nicole Charpentier. He'd fallen in love with her, just like he did with me and they were getting married and going together to Sydney. Afterwards I found out that she worked at *SOSM* in Paris, so I'm sure they were having an affair and he arranged for her to go to Rwanda to be with him.

"So, that was that. Leo and I were on our own and I just had to get used to it. Fortunately, I was still on salary from *SOSM* for another two months and I'd saved a little money, so I had time to find a job. It wasn't as if I was condemned to the poor house. But it broke my heart at the time. I was in a terrible state.

"You know that feeling, Jenny. You know what it's like. It's just so final, so out of your control. You want to blame someone, to fight against it, to change what's happened and get on with the life you'd planned. But there's nothing you can do, is there? Except get on with the life that's left to you. But I had Leo and that was worth more than anything to me."

Jenny's mind was back in Ipswich, after the death of Ron, her husband, killed by a pathological murderer and made to look like a hit and run accident. She did know how Emma had felt, losing the man she loved, under any circumstances. Starting life again, making the most of what's left for you to enjoy. Although she had no child to share her life and love with.

She pushed the thoughts aside. "I'm sorry, Emma. I had no idea you'd had such a disaster in your life. You could have confided in me, it might have helped, but I understand why you didn't. You couldn't take the chance that the truth about Leo's birth and his British nationality would get out.

"But the main thing is that you managed to save him and you've loved and looked after him for the last fifteen years and he's a son to be proud of. Now we've got to get through this latest episode and get him back. We've got to dissect your story about Mutesi and look for clues that will lead us to Leo. I'm sure his abduction is directly connected to your story and we've got to work out why."

She led Emma into the office, opened her laptop and went online. "Are you up to it now, or do you need to lie down and rest while I start looking up stuff from my notes? Emma?"

Her sister grasped her by the shoulders, tears pouring down her face. "Oh, Jenny. You have to help me get Leo back. He's my entire world. He's all I've got. Since I lost Tony, I've built my life around him. The only reason I write those dreadful books is to make enough money to look after him, educate him and see him do well. I miss him desperately and I'm so frightened when I imagine where he might be. Who he's with. What's happening to him. Why he's been taken. Please tell me we can find him and bring him back safe and sound."

"Emma. I promise we'll get Leo back. I promise you we will." She tried to make her tone sound convincing, but she had no idea of what lay before them.

It was forty-two hours since Leo had been taken.

TWENTY-THREE

Johannesburg, South Africa

He was swimming. Swimming underwater. The water was thick and treacly *and he couldn't make any progress. He struggled against the weight of the water trying to drag him down but it got heavier and heavier and he slowly sank deeper and deeper, threshing around like a drowning shark. It became dark; pitch black. The pressure of the water on him was unbearable. He couldn't breathe, his lungs empty of air, he was pulled down into the thick, watery bottom of something, something evil, a deathly place.*

Then he felt hands on his shoulders helping him, pulling him away from the deep. Faintly, he could see a light. He swam more strongly. It got brighter as he struggled to swim up towards it, brighter and brighter until...

Leo opened his eyes. He tried to focus, but his vision was blurred. In front of him was someone, leaning into his face and shaking him gently by the shoulders. "Wake up, Leo. That's it. It's time to wake up now. You've had a very long sleep, but you must wake up now. Here, drink this, you must be thirsty." A glass was pushed against his lips and he swallowed instinctively.

Water, he registered and coughed as it ran down his throat. He rubbed his eyes and gradually his vision cleared. He saw a young black woman, quite pretty, with a white cap. He squinted again.

She was wearing a nurse's outfit and holding the glass of water. He nodded and she placed it at his lips again. He grabbed it and drank the contents thirstily. He had a raging thirst, his mouth was parched.

"More water please," he said.

"Not just now, Leo. In a moment you can have some more. Just take it easy and do everything very slowly. You've been asleep for a while, so please just take your time until you feel better."

He moved his head from side to side, taking in his surroundings. It was a small square room, impersonal, with bare walls and no furniture except for a table in the corner with some equipment on it. "Is this a hospital," he asked the woman.

"More or less," she replied. "We have everything we need here to look after you, so don't worry."

The nurse took his wrist and felt his pulse, looking at her watch. She put a thermometer in his ear and he heard a click and she checked his temperature. She opened his mouth and looked down his throat with a polished spoon as a mirror. Then she brought a blood pressure monitor and slipped the band around his upper arm. It tightened on his bare arm and he realised he was not wearing a pyjama jacket. She noted the results from the machine on a notebook.

"Why am I here? Have I had an accident? Where's my Mum?" He tried to sit up, but the nurse gently held him on his back. He realised she was very strong and he was very weak. He decided not to fight. She wrapped another rubber band around his arm, tight.

"I need to take a little blood for testing", she said. "Lie still. Just for a minute."

She found the vein and swabbed it with antiseptic. "Now." He hardly felt the needle slip into his arm and a moment later, she said, "Well done. That's all we need." She put the phial onto a table near the bed. "Now you can have a little more water. Just one small glass until later."

He drank it down thirstily. "Have I been sick? Why is my Mum not here? What's happening?"

"Don't worry, I'll be back in a while," she said and taking her notebook and the phial of blood, she left the room.

Leo waited for a moment after he heard the door close then he tried to sit up in the bed. His head swam and he fell back onto the pillow. After a minute or two, he tried again, very slowly and carefully. This time he managed to get himself into a sitting position, his arms around his knees. He waited until his head cleared again and turned to sit with his legs hanging over the bedside. Absently, he saw that he was wearing a pair of jockey shorts, not his.

Gingerly, he pushed himself up until he was standing, holding onto the bedframe. It felt cool and was made of metal. There was another door on the right that he hadn't seen. Still holding on, he took a step towards the door, then another. He realised he had to leave hold of the bedframe to reach the door. Preparing himself, he lunged at the door and caught the handle to stay upright. His legs didn't seem to want to follow him, but he dragged them along until he was standing at the door, holding onto the handle. He turned it and almost fell into the room but managed to keep himself up. It was a small bathroom with a shower, wash basin and a toilet. It looked very clean. There was no window. *No way out,* he registered.

Using the wall to hold himself upright, he managed to reach the door the nurse had gone through. He hung onto the handle and tried to turn it each way, but the door was implacably locked. He looked over at the windows, they were closed up with blinds. Grabbing the bedframe again, he lurched across and reached the windows, but the story was the same, neither the windows nor the blinds could be opened.

"Shit!" He looked all around the room again. There was no other possible exit, or even view out of the room. Staggering back, he collapsed onto the bed and rolled over onto his back, looking up at the ceiling in frustration. Within a minute he was asleep again.

TWENTY-FOUR

Johannesburg, South Africa

Coetzee was looking at a CCTV screen in the manager's office at the Packard Hotel in Mayfair, Johannesburg. He saw Leo collapse onto the bed and fall asleep.

"He looks OK to me."

"We'll be sure when I've done the blood analysis," Doctor Blethin, the man beside him, replied in his accented English, "but he doesn't seem to have suffered any lasting damage. I didn't expect he would, he's a healthy, well-nourished boy of fifteen. They don't come much stronger than that. I'll get on with it right now." He left Coetzee alone in the office.

The security chief was in a foul mood. He and Nwosu had received their regular call from the Voice that morning, Tuesday. It was a very disagreeable call. After they'd summarised the catastrophic events of yesterday, there had been a very long and menacing silence.

Finally, the Voice said, "So, you have not only managed to lose Mrs Stewart, the boy's mother, you have somehow contrived to let her join her sister, Mrs Jenny Bishop, in her home in Marbella. I sincerely hope that you have not mislaid the boy too?"

"He's still safe and sound and healthy, under our control."

Once again they heard the sound of someone speaking quietly in the background, then the Voice continued, "Why would Mrs Stewart leave South Africa when her son is missing?"

Before Coetzee could reply, Nwosu said, "We have no idea. It came right out of the blue. She was supposed to come back here but she ran away to her sister's in Spain. Women do strange things." He looked at the security chief, wondering if he'd recognise the quotation.

"Could she have learned of the plan from someone, another of your incompetent employees?"

Coetzee interrupted. "No chance. She's never been in contact with anyone except Lambert and he's smart enough not to implicate himself in this business. There's no way she could have found out." He looked at Nwosu as if to say, *I've got you off the hook. You owe me!*

Again there was that faint sound then the Voice asked, "Do you have any knowledge of Mrs Stewart's sister?"

"Why should we have?" Coetzee was cursing the day he'd got involved in this pathetic farce. "Who the hell is this Jenny Bishop anyway, Wonder Woman?"

"Some people might say so. Let me advise you only that Mrs Jenny Bishop is not a woman to be trifled with and now she is involved in our little scenario. I am very unhappy with this turn of events."

"Funny you should say that," said Coetzee. "We're not too happy ourselves, actually."

"And what exactly is that supposed to mean?"

"We think you're underestimating our value in this transaction. The fact is our task was to abduct the boy and that's what we've done. You've told us nothing more about the reasons for the kidnapping, we've taken all the risks and you've done bugger all except give us shit about what a mess we've made of it. We think we deserve a little more respect, maybe a little more reward. We think it's time you let us into your confidence, after all, we have the boy under our control and you wouldn't want anything to happen to him, would you?"

Once again the silence was deafening. Nwosu looked at him as if to say, *now you've gone too far!* Coetzee shrugged and lit another cheroot.

Finally, the Voice continued, "Very well, let's put that matter aside for further consideration and we'll discuss it after the next phase of the operation. Agreed?"

"What do you mean, the next phase? What's that?"

"The boy must be moved. He is still in close proximity to the abduction scene and now that the Bishop woman is involved it's likely that exhaustive enquiries will be made. We will make arrangements to house him in a new location and you will deliver him there. Do you think you can manage that?"

"If you can manage to revise our remuneration, I think we can manage to relocate him safely." Coetzee was trying to play the Voice at his own game, but his vocabulary wasn't up to it.

"Good, then we are in agreement. I will call back tomorrow with the appropriate instructions and will give your request further consideration in the meantime. This is rather an important operation and we wouldn't want to jeopardise it for the sake of a little money."

The phone went dead and Nwosu said, "You've got a lot of balls, Marius. Well done! But it better be more than 'a little money'. You were right, we've got the upper hand now. Let's see how much the kid is worth."

Coetzee said nothing. He didn't trust anyone. Nwosu had never called him Marius before and the Voice had been too easy to persuade. This was a messy business and he didn't like it one bit.

Now, in the hotel, he picked up the phone. "Barry, come down here, will you?"

A few minutes later the hotel manager came in. "What's up? Is the kid OK?"

"He's fine, but we're going to have to move him. It's not safe here. Make sure everything's ready to move him tomorrow."

"You want him still sedated?"

"Wait until the doc does his blood analysis and then we'll see. Leave him for now to sleep normally. I'll call you in the morning when I've decided what to do."

Coetzee stood up from the desk and walked out of the hotel, only fifty metres from the room where the fifteen year old boy was sleeping. He was worried.

TWENTY-FIVE

Marbella, Spain

Jenny took her sister upstairs to a generous-sized suite with spectacular views over the Mediterranean. "This is where you're staying. You should be comfortable here. Whatever is going on, I want you to follow your normal routine whenever you can. I know you need to keep up with your work. It's important that you do."

"I certainly don't feel like it right now. And I do need a bath and a change of clothes. The only problem is, I haven't got anything to change into."

Jenny opened the door to a walk-in wardrobe off the bedroom. "I've hung a few things here that'll probably fit you. Just try anything you like, they've hardly been worn at all." Before Emma could say anything, she went on, "And please stop thanking me. You're my sister and if I can't help you out when you need it, what's the point in having a sister?

"Now, I want your permission," she went on, "to contact someone I know and trust and who saved my life a couple of years ago. He's a very clever man, used to be Chief Inspector of the Malaga Homicide Squad and now he's reinvented himself as a private detective. The main thing is that he's a very nice person and he'll treat everything with absolute discretion. Can I call him over to tell him the story? I firmly believe that he can help us."

"If you trust him and think he can help, that's good enough for me. But you know that I don't have the money to pay a detective. And there's something else worrying me. We haven't received any message or demand for a ransom. There's been absolutely no contact at all from these people."

"First of all, stop going on about money. This is about bringing your son back to you. If it makes you feel any better, I'm comfortably off and I'm not spending more than I can afford. As to the ransom message, they've probably just realised that you've escaped from South Africa and are trying to find out where you are. They'll be in touch as soon as they work out what's happened."

When Emma didn't reply, she went on, "Now, take a bath and have a nap or whatever you want to do and I'll see you downstairs when you're ready. I'm going to do some research and then I've got a few calls to make, so I'll leave you to it." She gave her a peck on the cheek and left the room.

Sitting in the shade on the terrace, Jenny started her research on her iPad. She found there were over two million items on the Rwandan genocide and opened up the first one that looked relevant. She started reading.

After two hours of researching she had filled three pages of notes with extracts copied from the various items. The sites were a mine of information. She checked on her sister a couple of times. Emma was out to the world, recuperating from her lack of sleep and emotional exhaustion. When she had finished her work she called a number from her Favourites list and had a short conversation. Then she ended the call and rang a mobile number in Malaga

After a couple of rings, a voice answered, "*Si, diga me.*"

"Chief Inspector Espinoza, this is Jenny Bishop. How are you?" She said.

There was a pause and an intake of breath, then, "Señora Bishop, How nice to hear from you again. But perhaps you don't know I'm no longer a Chief Inspector, just a humble detective, trying to make a living. May I ask how you discovered my telephone number?"

"José Luis has just told me all about your new career. Congratulations, I hope you're happy in your retirement."

"More importantly, my wife is much happier. What can I do for you, Señora?"

"First of all, please call me Jenny. I think we know each other well enough to be on first name terms."

"As you say, Jenny, I think we know each other well enough. So what's the reason for your call?"

"I want to hire you for an assignment, if you agree. It's complicated and potentially dangerous. Are you available at short notice?"

"When do you want me to start? I am, as they say, in between engagements and can be there in an hour."

"Perfect. *Gracias y hasta pronto, Pedro.*"

Malaga, Spain

Pedro Espinoza replaced his iPhone on the table beside his empty coffee cup. He was sitting at his favourite tapas bar, just down the street from the Comisaría. It was one of the old habits he'd maintained since his retirement and reconciliation with his wife, Soledad. She was shopping for groceries at SuperSol, something that he wasn't yet prepared to assist with. His mind slipped back to the business of Charlie Bishop's death two years ago and the subsequent murder hunt for Ray d'Almeida aka Francisco García Luna, fake lawyer. *Just in time,* he remembered. *Thanks to Sra Bishop I was just in time, but it was too close for comfort.*

After this high profile case, Espinoza had reconsidered his life choices. He was working too hard and earning too little and he no longer had any home life at all. With the help of his daughter, Laura, and his old lawyer friend, José Luis Garcia Ramirez, he had managed to convince his estranged wife Soledad to come back to their family home. Being in one house together reduced their monthly costs so they could enjoy life again. Early retirement from the force provided a basic income that covered the essentials and he had enough contacts to sell his services as a consultant or private detective which enabled them to enjoy a few luxuries. He had regained his equilibrium and his family and he had never been more content.

He paid the bill and went across to his car for the drive to Marbella. If the traffic was bad it could easily take an hour and he knew that Sra Bishop was very keen on punctuality.

TWENTY-SIX

Johannesburg, South Africa

Coetzee was trawling through Emma's website. It was crafted in two main colours, crimson and black. He supposed this was to give a subliminal dual message of blood and villainy. There was a photo of her, looking a lot happier than when she'd been with him and Nwosu. *She's a very good looking woman,* he mused. Emma had eleven books to her credit, the most recent, *An Extravagant Death,* having been published the previous year. It had earned four stars from the several readers who had posted their reviews. From the blurb and the preview pages he saw that her two main characters were *Angus Skelton,* an acerbic Scottish ex-policeman and *Victoria (Tory) West,* a wealthy widow turned private detective. He paid seven pounds ninety-five with his Visa card and downloaded the book onto his Kindle. *It might give me an insight into her mind,* he reasoned, subconsciously hiding his real motivation in wanting to read what Emma had written.

Next, he looked at her Facebook profile. There was nothing of any real importance, mainly photos and articles about her latest book. No information which could help him in his research. The latest posting was a photo of her and Leo at the airport, with the status change; *Off on holiday with my BRILLIANT son. Might get some ideas for my latest book. Happy Holidays everyone.*

He turned his attention to the problem of Leo's birth and the identity of his father. The Voice was very insistent on this point, so it was obviously a valuable piece of information. He took the copy of the boy's passport that he'd retained. It said Leo had been born on April 23rd, 1995, in London. He went to the 'Family Tree' site on the Internet. It cost him thirty pounds to get the birth records of Leopold Stewart; *Born at University College Hospital Maternity Ward, London, Mother: Emma Stewart, Father: Unknown.*

"Shit!" He was no further forward. For some reason Emma hadn't disclosed the father's name. She had also managed to evade every question about him during their extremely unproductive interrogation. *But why?* What was so important or damaging that she wouldn't reveal the name of her boyfriend or lover, or whoever the guy was? It was unlikely that she'd been artificially inseminated from an African source, especially given the hysteria around AIDS at the time. So, who was this mystery man and where was he now?

Also, the information had to be so important or potentially damaging that she hadn't contacted the authorities, at least as far as they knew. There had been no official contact from the British Embassy nor from any police or other investigative body. She had simply run away and left her son behind without making any public outcry. *There's some reason that she can't divulge what's happened to Leo,* he realised. *But what is it?*

Since he had no real information to provide, he decided to share it with Nwosu. "I know," the sergeant replied. "I got the same answer from my contacts in London. Nobody has a clue who the father is, so I'm wondering how we can up the ante with the Voice."

Coetzee was thinking quickly. "I'll go in to see the boy in the morning and get it out of him. He'll be groggy and I'll say his father is concerned about him and maybe he'll talk. We'll be in an even stronger position with that bloody dictionary quoter. This is going to cost him big time."

"Will you need any help with the removal?"

"Not necessary. There's Lambert and the doc, and in any case you shouldn't be seen down there. Keep that polished pate of yours out of the way and I'll fill you in afterwards."

"OK, so we won't mention it, just get the moving instructions and keep our powder dry. I'll see you tomorrow."

London, England

The man they called the Voice was sitting in an elegant sitting room with two other people. They were having afternoon tea. There were finger sandwiches, éclairs and scones on a cake stand and several small silver dishes with jams, sugar and cream on the table. The china was by Villeroy and Boch, in a pale lemon flowered design.

"So, the Stewart woman has fled to Spain and she's with her sister in Marbella. That could be very good news for us. But why do you suppose she ran off, when her son is still in Johannesburg?" The person sitting opposite asked. He was a good looking man, well built with dark hair and a healthy sun tan, obviously not acquired in the English climate.

"We have no way of knowing of course, but as you say, this is rather an interesting development. It corroborates our premise, if there was ever any doubt about it. Mrs Stewart was most uncomfortable in the police interviews and stubbornly refused to answer any questions about Leo's father. It would only have been a matter of time before she broke down and she couldn't risk revealing the truth. She must have decided that she could achieve more from afar than by continuing to be subjected to the police sergeant's charms."

"And her first reaction was to ask her sister for help. Jenny Bishop is the only person she could turn to. This is exactly what we hoped to achieve and she has done it without any prompting from us. It actually removes one stage from the education process we planned."

The Voice nodded, "I agree, Mr Slater. Everything seems to point in that direction."

"The fact remains that she has escaped and we have no control over her. And we know that the Bishop woman is very practical and inventive and has substantial resources, so we have to be careful."

"True," the Voice replied, "But the important point is that it is she, Jenny Bishop, who has the funds that we are targeting. Ms Stewart has lost her only son and wants him back. Whatever her relationship with her sister, such a moral dilemma involving a young boy cannot be ignored. In any event, from a pragmatic point of view there is very little they can do from Spain. They obviously won't go the authorities, so their options are virtually non-existent. To hire private investigators, instruct them and put them in place will take time and time is not their friend. I'm sure that she's already worked out that we know the truth, or at least the most important part of the truth, so she and her sister must be preparing for a demand of some kind. We must be patient for a short while until they are ready to respond as we desire."

"I'm being very patient. If I wasn't, I'd already be making other arrangements. I'm not impressed with the results to date."

The third person intervened, "I think we agree that events are moving in our favour. Let's not waste time on squabbling. Tell Mr Slater about the new safe house."

"Of course. As a simple precaution, since we are aware of Mrs Bishop's reputation and her financial status, we would feel more comfortable if the boy was moved away from Johannesburg. In fact it would be much safer to move him across at least one border to obstruct any enquiries she may instigate locally. We've been in contact with our friends in Zimbabwe and they have offered us their hospitality. The country is not a member of Interpol and we have good connections there. For a modest fee we've agreed terms on the transfer. The boy will be taken by car and handed over in Beitbridge, just over the border and held safely nearby."

"And Coetzee and the policeman? What's the plan with them?"

"Nwosu is his name. They're both expendable. As a matter of fact, they are foolishly trying to increase their reward. Silly men. When they get the boy to Beitbridge we'll ensure that they don't cause any further nuisance. The same applies to the hotel manager and the doctor. The guard has already been dealt with. It's not something to concern yourself with."

"And what about the nurse?"

"She knows nothing about our involvement, nor the reasons for the abduction. She'll be back in Cape Town tomorrow with enough money to keep her drugged and happy for a month or two. Long enough for our plan to run its course."

"Just remember, we don't want any trail, no tracks that could lead back to us. We can't risk exposure of any kind."

"Indubitably. It is our primary concern, you have our word. Once the boy is handed over in Zimbabwe and the South African people are removed, the trail will be completely cold." The Voice took a sip of his tepid cup of tea. "However, there is one further matter which requires your approval."

"What is it?"

The Voice coughed apologetically. "It's a financial matter. I'm afraid that we're about to run a little over budget. Although we will imminently rid ourselves of Coetzee and the policeman, it was necessary to temporarily increase their rewards in order to gain their continued allegiance. The Zimbabwe arrangement has also had an effect on our resources. We're obliged to request a modest increase in the operating budget."

"And how much is a 'modest increase'?"

"In order to guarantee full and complete execution of the plan, we think it would be wise to provide access to a further hundred thousand dollars. We are being rather conservative here and the actual requirement will probably be less. But it's better to be over financed than to run short once again."

"A hundred thousand! That's twenty five percent more. Our profit is shrinking while our risk is increasing." He stood up and began pacing the room, a worried look on his face. "You're sure you can't complete this business with less?"

"I regret, but I am unable to provide such an assurance. As you know, I have been involved in several sensitive transactions, some of a somewhat similar nature and there are always some, let's say, non-recurring, unexpected costs. This is one of those occasions and I will endeavour to ensure that there will not be another."

"Very well," Slater said finally. "I'll get the money, but we'll share this extra cost pro rata from our participations. You're in charge of the budget, not me. You need to pay more attention to how my money is spent."

The other two exchanged glances and the Voice said. "We agree. Please transfer the funds to the usual account and we will manage it in the most parsimonious fashion possible."

"I'll look after that tomorrow, but this additional investment means we have to begin the completion phase of the programme immediately. We can't afford to have such large amounts invested for a long period of time. In any case I don't think we need wait any longer. If she wants her son back she has to face the facts of life and act accordingly."

"What are your instructions?"

Slater continued to pace the room while the others waited silently. Finally, he said, "My decision is that we have to go public tomorrow morning, while time is still on our side. It's almost forty-eight hours since we took him. That's the key time period in a disappearance or kidnapping and I'm sure they know that by now, so let's strike while the iron is hot."

"I agree," said the Voice. "We don't actually know who the boy's father was, but they have no way of finding out what we know or don't know. In any event, it's most likely that it was one of the Akazu. We'll obtain a photograph of the boy and send it with the message that he is well and in a safe place and we'll make further contact shortly. I'll confirm as soon as it has been carried out. We'll communicate as agreed, by email. I have the address."

"Right. That's all for today. I'm staying in London for a few days so I can come over if necessary." Slater went to the door. "Call me on my mobile when you have further news."

When the door had closed behind him the Voice said, "Unfortunately, our friend is perfectly justified in his complaint.

This business is becoming very expensive, both in funding and potentially in bodies. It's just as well he doesn't know precisely what's happening down there."

"We knew there would be some collateral damage. But the prize is worth it."

"If the plan actually works, of course I concur. But that still remains to be seen. In the meantime, no more expensive mistakes or bodies left lying around or he's liable to withdraw his support."

"The plan will work, don't worry. Once we're out of SA it will be different. The trail will be cold and we'll be half way home."

"I hope you're right. Now we have a little over an hour to prepare for our call to Nwosu. It's an important call so let's have a brief rehearsal and you can make your comments ahead of time."

TWENTY-SEVEN

Marbella, Spain

"Hola, Pedro, Que tal?" Jenny shook hands with Espinoza and he greeted her warmly.

"You look wonderful, Jenny. You haven't changed at all in the last couple of years. Younger, if anything."

"If you remember, I was under a bit of stress at the time. But thank you for the compliment. How is your renewed family life?"

"As you English say, 'so far so good'. I suppose it was José Luis who told you all my family secrets. He talks far too much, even for a retired lawyer."

"If he didn't, you might never have managed to save Leticia's and my life, so you shouldn't complain."

He nodded modestly, "And how is Leticia? And Emilio, of course, he must be…., four years old now."

"They're both away on holiday with Patrice, I suppose you know they're going to be married? Come into the living room and have a coffee and we'll catch up."

Over coffee they talked about some of the people who had been involved in the Angolan diamond affair. She hadn't seen José Luis, her previous lawyer since he had retired the year before, but

Espinoza told her that they lunched together occasionally. "I think he's regretting his retirement," he confided to her, "He seems bored. How are you getting on with Javier, his replacement?"

"José Luis finished up everything to do with the will and the properties before he retired, so we haven't needed a lawyer, except for trivial things like permits and other Spanish paperwork. Patrice helps us as well. He's a banker, quite knowledgeable about financial and legal matters. So, we're managing just fine."

Espinoza finished his coffee and pushed away the cup and saucer. "Well, Jenny. I think it's time to tell me why I have the pleasure of seeing you again."

It took Jenny a half hour to summarise the events of the last few days in her precise, unemotional manner. Espinoza asked few questions. He was used to adding two and two to get five or six. On hearing of Leo's extraction from Kigali to London, he said nothing, just raised his eyebrows and gave an admiring nod. He did the same when she described Emma's escape from South Africa.

After looking at all the evidence Emma had compiled, he commented, "It's likely that one of the gang is a doctor. Even a very experienced nurse wouldn't necessarily have the proper training to administer drugs. It's quite complicated to put people out for a specific time, depending on their age, weight and other factors. They wouldn't want their victim to succumb just when they were at the moment of maximum risk."

He thought for a moment. "Has there been any contact from the abductors? Any ransom note or message?"

"Nothing. But I suppose it's because they're still investigating what happened to Emma."

"Nwosu can find that out quite easily. It won't be long before we hear something from them. So, when can I meet Emma?"

"Right now. She's had a bath and a sleep and she's busy answering emails upstairs. I want her to keep occupied as much as possible to stop her from dwelling too much on what happened. She's holding up well, but you can imagine the worry and distress she's feeling. Leo is her only child, in fact her only relative, apart from me.

She's emotionally shattered, so please go easy on her."

"I promise to be less of a policeman, more of a friend."

Once the introductions had been accomplished, Espinoza said, "Jenny has told me the whole story and it seems certain your son has been abducted. I'm sorry. But I know something of your sister's strength of mind and I'm sure we can work together and bring Leo back. My limited abilities are at your service if you think I can help.

Emma just nodded and he went on, "Tell us what you've discovered, Jenny."

"Well, I'm pretty sure that Rwanda is the key to this whole episode," she said. "I don't know why yet, but I think I've found the origin of the problem."

"But I was only in Rwanda for about two months, I'm sure nobody even knows that except for you and a few friends. It was almost sixteen years ago and I was an insignificant nurse who adopted an unknown baby from some poor unimportant girl who died. I don't see the connection."

"Wrong, Emma. I don't think Mutesi was an unimportant girl, or I should say, Leo was not an unimportant baby. I'll tell you my thesis and then we'll talk about it. You remembered that Mutesi was in the house of a man called Jean-Bousquet, right?"

Emma nodded, "I think that was the name."

"The housekeeper had said he was an important, wealthy politician involved with a radio station. And the house was in Ruhondo, which is just outside of Ruhengeri, in the north western part of Rwanda. That's where President Habiyarimana and all of the Akazu leaders lived. They were the Hutu people who ran Rwanda and who wanted to get rid of the Tutsis. I don't know whether the genocide was really a deliberate political strategy, but it certainly seems to have been motivated by hatred and a desire to eliminate the Tutsis and it was instigated by the Akazu."

"So you think this man, Jean-Bousquet was a member of the Akazu?" Espinoza was making notes.

"Well, there's a wrinkle, but I think I've sorted it. Let me show you exactly how I did the research." She took her iPad and opened

Google. "I'll put in *Akazu, Radio Station, Rwanda.* Look, the radio station was called *Radio-Télévision Libres des Mille Collines.* Now, watch this." She highlighted the link. "See, *Individuals associated with the station,* third one down, *Jean-Bosco Galaganza.* See what they say about him? *He was a Rwandan diplomat and the chairman of the executive committee of the radio station.* Not Jean-Bousquet, I admit, but very close.

"Now I'll put in *Rwandan genocide, Jean-Bousquet.* There's no one at all of that name, but it shows René Bousquet, who was indicted for war crimes committed when he was a senior member of the police during the Vichy government in France. He was a friend of Mitterand and that's the only connection, because of Mitterand's support of Habiyarimana and France's refusal to acknowledge the genocide.

"Now I'll cross check with the name *Jean-Bosco, Rwandan genocide.* There are two names, *Jean-Bosco Uwinkindi* and *Jean-Bosco Galaganza,* both involved in the Rwandan genocide. Uwinkindi was Pastor of the Pentecostal Church in Kanzenze, which is in Kigali, so I think we can rule him out. Strangely enough," she added, "After all these years, he's apparently just been arrested on genocide charges. You wonder what goes on in these international courts. Not much, by the look of things." She shrugged her shoulders.

"Galaganza, however, is once again described as a Rwandan diplomat and the chairman of the executive committee of *Radio-Télévision Libres des Mille Collines.* Look at his photo, tall, slim, with a moustache and glasses.

"In 2003 he was sent to prison for thirty-five years by the International Criminal Tribunal for Rwanda. I printed out the sentence of the court, listen; '*Galaganza and the other heads of the radio station conspired to exterminate the civilian Tutsi population and eliminate members of the opposition. The components of their plan included the broadcasting of messages of ethnic hatred and incitements to violence, the training of militias and distribution of weapons to militiamen, and the preparation and diffusion of lists of people to be killed.*'"

She shuddered. "He was not a nice person and he was definitely a member of the Akazu, it's well documented everywhere you look. And we know that all the Akazu members came from Ruhengeri, which is near Ruhongo, where Mutesi was held. I can't actually find evidence that Galaganza lived there, but there isn't another man called Jean-Bosco, member of the Akazu, politician and head of a radio station, so it has to be him. And the clincher is in the records of the trial. It says he fled Rwanda in 1995 and was brought to justice in 2000. That's what Mutesi said, he left in November 1995. I'm absolutely sure he's our man. He ticks all the boxes. I've copied out all the relevant extracts here." She opened up her notes.

"Impressive research. If I was still in the force, I'd hire you immediately, Jenny." Espinoza reached for the iPad and read the items one by one while the two women talked.

"What do you think, Emma? Might you have got the name wrong after all this time? Could you have confused it with René Bousquet?"

"You're right. I learned in school about Bousquet's deportation of Jews and the name has stuck in my memory. I've got the ending of the name wrong. Jean-Bosco rings a bell now that I think back to Mutesi's story. And there's a clear resemblance to Leo, tall and slim and fine boned. I'm sure you're right.

"So he was the man who raped Mutesi, a mass murderer. And she survived all that, only to die in bearing his child. He was Leo's father. My God!" She covered her face with her hands.

"Emma, that was a lifetime ago. Don't dwell on it now. Just look at Leo. Whoever his father was, he's a fine, clever, intelligent boy. We must look forward, not back, or we won't make any progress."

Espinoza looked up from his reading. "I see Galaganza died in April in Benin, of hepatitis. Quite a coincidence that Leo was abducted in July, just three months later, no?"

"Exactly, Pedro." Jenny said. "You know I don't believe in coincidences. The two events must be connected in some way. But I have no idea how or why."

"A political abduction? Something to do with the Hutus trying to re-establish their power against the Tutsi government?"

"I don't think there's much chance of that happening. I've been reading about Paul Kagame, the President. He's been in power for ten years, sixteen if you count the previous six when he was the power behind the throne from 1994. He's the leader of the Rwandese Patriotic Front. They're the refugees from Uganda who came back and took power from the Hutus and put an end to the atrocities. There's speculation that he actually masterminded the assassination of Habiyarimana and sparked off the massacre of most of his countrymen. I suppose that's one way to make your point, but we'll not dwell on that."

"He's highly regarded by the international community. They're throwing money at the country for development and agricultural aid. The usual, 'Spend now, don't repay later' funding that produces nothing except rich dictators." Espinoza sounded irritated. "However, if we assume that the reason for Leo's abduction is his Hutu genocider father, how did the perpetrators find out?"

"Exactly. If we want to find out who took Leo, we have to find out who knew about him in the first place."

"I have never spoken about Mutesi, about Leo's birth or his entry into the UK, not a word to anybody." Emma said. "Today's the first time I've talked about it and it was to you, Jenny, I would never have trusted anyone else."

"We must take some decisions here." Espinoza put aside the iPad and sat facing the women. "Is the reason for Leo's abduction something to do with his father, and was it instigated by his death a few months ago? If that's our working hypothesis, then we have a starting point."

"I have no idea why that would be the case, but I can't think of any other possible explanation." Emma looked anxiously at the others. Was this the right trail to follow?

"That's my vote too, Pedro. There are too many coincidences involved. They have to be connected, so we have to start joining up some dots."

"Very well, I agree it's the only apparent reason, but we don't yet know the motive because we've received no communication from the abductors. It could be political or financial or something totally unexpected." Espinoza's mantra was that there can often be motive without crime, but seldom crime without motive.

His whole approach to solving crimes was to identify a motive and let nothing divert him from exploring that path. "Let's put that aside for now. My second point is more delicate. Should we involve the police, or not?"

"Which police are you talking about?"

"We would have to use the British police as a starting point, because of Leo's nationality. But I would hope to escalate it immediately to an Interpol investigation. Then we could circulate information between countries and act through a higher level of police authority than Nwosu's level. I don't advise starting with the South African police, since we have no idea of the extent of this conspiracy. If we fall onto the wrong person, it could compromise Leo's safety. The South African police are not renowned for their honesty, especially if the stakes are high, as seems to be the case.

"I was a Spanish liaison officer with Interpol and South Africa is a member nation, so I could push in that direction from the UK to speed up the process. But it will be slow and complicated to get the machine moving and I'm concerned about time. Leo has been missing for two days now, so time is of the essence."

Emma caught her breath. "You mean the time between the kidnap and the murder, the forty-eight hour window as they call it?"

"OK, Emma," Jenny interrupted. "Let's explore that possibility, because I know that's weighing on your mind. I don't think Leo was taken in order to murder him. It would have been just as easy to kill him instead of doping him if that was the reason. I think this is about value, money."

"That's also my opinion," Espinoza spoke with quiet authority. "All the signs point to a well organised conspiracy. We know of five people involved so far, Lambert plus the two who pushed Leo out, plus Coetzee and Nwosu. You don't need five people to kill a fifteen year old boy. In addition, you haven't heard from the police since you left, no calls on your mobile?"

"None at all."

"So I think that confirms our theory. Nwosu is involved outside of his official capacity and he's part of a larger group of organised people. That rules out murder but it means we can't trust the normal police channels. It also means there are big stakes to play for. Life in South Africa is cheap, but they've got a large investment so they'll want a big reward.

"That brings us back to motive. Emma, I don't believe you have the kind of money that would warrant this crime and if the kidnappers are as well organised as I think, they would know that. But we won't know until they contact you. We just have to assume that it's going to be a cat and mouse game with a bargaining match at the end. The more we can find out, the stronger our hand will be when we have to bargain, so this work we're doing now is vital and valuable."

"Yes, I understand."

"So, what's the decision? Police or no police?"

"Pedro, first, please tell me if you condemn what I did in getting Leo out of Rwanda and into the UK. Tell me truthfully."

"On the contrary. I think you saved a helpless infant from a terrible future and gave him a loving life in a civilised country. Even if I was still a policeman that would be my opinion."

"But the authorities would have a totally different opinion. Leo's birth certificate, his passport, it's all illegal and would cause terrible problems in the UK." Emma paused, a sob in her throat. "I've thought about nothing else since he was taken. Leo's still a minor. They would prosecute me in a family court and he'd be taken from me as an unsuitable mother and put into care, or sent to foster parents. He might even be sent back to Rwanda because he has no right to stay in the UK. He'd become a refugee and I would end up in prison. I can't let that happen. I just can't.

"In any case, if you have the contacts and experience you seem to have, then you will be faster and more flexible than the authorities. We have to try to find Leo ourselves and bring him safely back. There's no other way."

Espinoza frowned. "I'm not sure it's as clear cut as you describe but I agree that you can't take that risk. We're going to mount our own investigation, but it will cost some money, maybe a lot."

Jenny said. "I can't think of a better way to spend some of my money than in getting my nephew back. So let's get on with it."

Espinoza took the iPad and pointed at the photo of the genocider. "Galaganza's our starting point and that immediately brings us to another question. If this was planned after his death and then Leo was abducted in Johannesburg, the perpetrators must have known about your plans to take Leo to the match."

"And if we cross reference those points," Jenny added, "we have to identify a person or persons who knew both things; Leo's connection with Galaganza and your trip to South Africa. In fact, they even knew which hotel you were staying in."

"I don't know why you asked me to come over, Jenny. It seems you've worked everything out without my assistance."

"Nonsense. I'll soon have to hand it over to you, because there's a point beyond which amateurs can't go but professionals can. Emma, I know it's difficult, but can you remember who knew you were going to Joburg and where you were staying?"

Jenny and Espinoza took notes as Emma ran through the persons who might have been aware both of Leo's birth and their plan to attend the match. The cross examination continued until Espinoza said, "I think that's enough for today. Emma must be exhausted. And I must call Soledad to tell her I'm on my way home for dinner. He pulled out his iPhone. He wasn't about to incur his wife's wrath once again, even for Sra Jenny Bishop.

London, England

Slater was on a call to someone in Nice, in the South of France. He uneasily related the result of his earlier meeting with the Voice. "I told them we can find the hundred thousand, but no more." he ended.

"This had better work," was the reply. The speaker had a noticeable French accent. "It means our investment will be half a million dollars. We're supposed to be partners but it's me who's putting up almost all the money. How long do you think we can continue like this?" A few moments of silence followed this rhetorical question, then, "Today's Tuesday. I can make the transfer in the morning, but that's the last time. If it's not enough, they can find some other idiot to provide it."

"I've told them the same thing. They're sending the first message tomorrow morning, so things should go faster now."

"Just make sure nothing goes wrong. We have too much invested to mess it up at this stage. Follow it up in the morning without fail." The speaker rang off.

Diepkloof, Gauteng, South Africa

Nwosu received a call from the Voice at six thirty on Tuesday evening, just before he quit for the day. He told the man they still had no information about Leo's birth or father, not so subtly trying to pin the blame on Coetzee for having let Emma escape. He waited nervously for his reaction.

After the normal pause, the Voice said, "Very well. Let's leave that for now, we may have more success tomorrow or when we get the boy into his new location. Now please pay close attention, Sergeant Nwosu."

He listened intently without taking notes. The policeman didn't believe in writing things down, it could be dangerous. When the Voice had finished his instructions, he said, "All right, I'll follow your orders, but I want to see the first payment in the bank before I do anything."

"Please repeat the number I gave you."

The policeman repeated it from memory. It was a Belgian number, +322, Brussels, but he was certain that the Voice was not in that country.

"Good. The funds will be in your account tomorrow morning," the Voice said. "Don't fail us."

It was forty-five hours since Leo had been taken.

DAY FOUR

WEDNESDAY, JULY 14, 2010

TWENTY-EIGHT

Johannesburg, South Africa

It was eight o'clock on Wednesday morning and Coetzee was in Lambert's office with Dr Blethin, looking at the live relay from Leo's room. He'd gone there early to try to prise some information out of the boy before the nine thirty call from the Voice was due. Leo was in a room in the manager's bungalow behind the main building. The house had a separate entrance so that any movement in or out wouldn't be seen. The CCTV system he'd set up was a miniature military camera on a flexible lead which sent the images to the manager's office by WiFi, so the staff would think he was discussing the boy's disappearance with Lambert when he was actually watching the relay.

"Looks like he's in good shape, Doc," he said. "Having some breakfast, no less."

"Physically he's in perfect shape as a matter of fact. Blood pressure, heart, pulse, eyesight, everything as per normal and the blood analysis is clean; no damage done to the kidneys or the liver. We took some urine early this morning and that's clean as well. He's ready to run a marathon."

"So I can quiz him now?"

"Just go easy, because he doesn't know what's happened to him and he keeps asking about his mother. It's the emotional aspect we have to watch out for."

"I'll be like a long lost father to him, OK?" He walked across to the bungalow and the nurse opened the door for him.

"Good morning, Leo. How are you feeling?"

"Who are you? Where's my mum? What am I doing here? There's nothing wrong with me." Leo pushed aside the empty tray and sat on the edge of the bed, staring at the security chief suspiciously. The nurse had brought his case with his clothing and other belongings that morning and he was now wearing his own black tee shirt and shorts.

"No need to be annoyed with me. I'm the guy who saved your bacon when you fainted. You should be thanking me."

"What do you mean, I fainted? I've never fainted in my life."

"The doctor said it was some kind of a fit, an epileptic fit or something similar. That's probably why you have no memory of it. You were out to the world, tongue sticking out, trying to choke yourself. I've got training and I got you under control until they could get a medic and a wheelchair and ambulance there. You're welcome!" He added sarcastically.

Leo struggled to recollect what had happened on Sunday night. He remembered going to the toilet at half-time, then his mind was a blank. *Did I faint,* he asked himself. *I can't even remember the end of the game.* "Who won the match?" he finally said.

"Spain won in extra time, but you didn't miss much. It was a lousy match, rough and dirty."

"So, who are you and what's this place?"

"I'm Marius Coetzee, the head of the security firm that manages the stadium. You were lucky I was nearby when it happened, or we might not be having this talk. This place is a private clinic near the stadium. We have an arrangement with them in case we have accidents or incidents during the matches and we certainly have a lot of them. Their response time is much shorter than the big hospitals and clinics."

"That's a camera lens up on the wall. Why is it there? Are you watching me all the time?"

"You're very observant. It's there for your own good, we've had to keep you under surveillance. Another attack like that could have left you in bad shape. We can't afford not to keep an eye on you."

"But where's my mother? Why isn't she here with me? What's happened to her?"

"Your mother's fine. She's been here with you all night and day since the accident. She was so exhausted that she's still sleeping at the hotel. I'm going to fetch her over in a short while."

"How long have I been here?"

"It's Wednesday morning, so you've been out for two and a half days."

"Shit, I don't believe it! And my mum's been sitting beside me all the time?"

"She's totally devoted to you. It's nice to see. She'll be happy when she comes in this morning."

"And we can leave as soon as she gets here?"

"We'll see. The doctor wants to make some more tests this afternoon and we may need to wait until tomorrow before giving you the all clear. That's actually why I came over to see you."

What do you mean?"

"Your mother told me the flight tickets you have for today are non-flexible and non-refundable and she doesn't have money to pay for new ones. So, I want to contact your father to see if he can help, but I don't have the details. I thought you could tell me how to get in touch with him."

Leo thought for a second. "If my mother wouldn't tell you, then I'm certainly not going to."

"No, I haven't asked her yet. She was too tired and I didn't think of it until this morning."

"Well let's wait until she gets here and you can ask her yourself."

Coetzee realised that Leo was a very smart boy. He was going to have to be more subtle. "When we were talking about your accident, it seemed she didn't much like your father. Are they divorced?"

"Ask my mother. I just told you."

"It's a question of time, Leo. I'm trying to get things sorted so you can leave tomorrow. The longer we wait, the longer you might have to stay. The flights are very full, but I could pull some weight and get you seats tomorrow if we move it along. Try to give me a break here."

Leo thought again for a moment. "Well, I'll tell you what I know and that is absolutely nothing. I've never met my father, I don't know who or where he is and I doubt very much that he'll help you even if you find him. So I suppose that means we have to produce the money for the tickets in some other way. You'll have to ask my mother. That's all I'm saying."

"You mean she's never said anything at all about your father? That's strange, isn't it?"

"We have an agreement that she'll tell me about it when I'm eighteen and that's fine with me. Until then, I can't help you, so stop asking questions."

Coetzee looked at his watch. Even if he knew something, which seemed doubtful, Leo was obviously not going to say anything further and he had to get to Diepkloof in time for the call from the Voice. He went to the door. "I'm going to get your mother; we'll be here asap."

Driving across to the police station, he went over his conversation with the boy. *Strange,* he thought, *she won't say anything and he doesn't know anything. What the hell is she hiding? What's behind this whole operation?*

In Diepkloof, Nwosu was checking his bank account online. The money still wasn't there. It was nine fifteen and Coetzee would be there in a moment. He rehearsed his lines again. It wasn't a good time to get it wrong.

TWENTY-NINE

Malaga, Spain

It was nine-thirty in the morning in Spain and five-thirty pm in Sydney, Australia. Espinoza was on the telephone to an old police colleague, an Australian liaison officer for Interpol. "This is informal, Mac," he said. "Just some enquiries for a friend. I'm not involved in police business any more, although I do miss our get-togethers around the world."

"Those were the days, Pedro, not anymore. Austerity is the watchword now. Can't take a shit without reporting how much toilet paper you use. Give me the full name and any details you've got and I'll get back to you like a berserk boomerang."

After giving as complete a description as he dared, Espinoza then called his previous opposite number at the National Police in Paris with a similar question. "*Aucun problème, Pedro.*" The Spaniard's French was as good as his English, the response was the same. The wheels were in motion.

Although he was an old fashioned policeman, Espinoza had a grudging respect for certain modern technologies. He opened up Google on his laptop and typed in a name. After trawling through several news items, he exclaimed, "*Bueno!*" He printed out the page and placed it with his notes.

Next, he checked two more sites and printed out several more pages with a sense of satisfaction. He was starting to get a feel for the people and the plan, putting himself into the criminal's minds. He would do some more research before going over to York House.

Diepkloof, Gauteng, South Africa

"Zimbabwe! You must be joking." Coetzee had just heard the Voice's latest instructions. He'd expected that they'd move Leo to another nearby town in SA. Now he was told they'd have to drive over five hundred kilometres and cross an inhospitable frontier into a country controlled through corruption, chaos and fear. Depending on the state of the roads and traffic conditions it would take him the best part of a day. He looked at Nwosu. The police sergeant seemed unperturbed and said nothing, a slightly smug look on his face. *Almost as if he knew already,* he thought to himself.

"You will be paid accordingly, of course," the Voice continued. "We have decided to agree to your request for improved remuneration. What would you say to a fifty per cent increase, retrospectively, of course?"

"In the bank before I go?"

The Voice laughed quietly, the laugh distorted by the acoustic effect. "Since you must leave today, I'm afraid that's impossible. But we have not yet failed to keep our word, it will be there by the time you reach Beitbridge. That's where you will hand over the boy." He gave instructions for the handover, a small hotel in the border town.

Coetzee looked at Nwosu again. He shrugged, as if to say, "why not?"

The two men hadn't admitted that they'd failed to obtain any more information on Leo's father, but for some reason the Voice hadn't mentioned it. Coetzee was becoming more and more suspicious, and nervous. He weighed up his options. He was in this business up to his neck and there were too many witnesses who could put him away. The fees he'd already received and the additional money on offer was enough to get him to a civilised place, where he could put this behind him and start anew with what was left of the modest nest egg he'd received from the army.

Images of Emma and Leo flashed through his mind. *If I deliver the kid in good health to Beitbridge there's nothing more I can do,* he reasoned. Whatever deal was on the table it would be bartered, she'd have her son back and he'd be on his way to a new life. He couldn't be expected to do more; he was just a cog in the machine. *But he's my responsibility.* He realised he was trying to justify his decision. *I'll go along with it to get paid and I'll make sure nothing happens to him while he's in my hands.*

He finally decided. "If you send the funds now by Internet and I get the confirmation, I'll do it. But I'm going with the Doc and the boy. I don't need any more company." His paranoia about Nwosu was increasing by the minute. The man was an untrustworthy, homicidal maniac and he didn't want to be trapped in the middle of nowhere with him at any cost.

"That's fine with me." Nwosu said. "I'm not desperate to drive to Zimbabwe. I'll clean up here."

All Coetzee heard was 'clean up'. He had no doubt that Nwosu meant Lambert, maybe Blethin, the doctor. *Where does the clean-up stop?* He thought. *We're all expendable. Once we get to Zimbabwe, the trail in South Africa will be cold. They can get rid of us and there's nobody left to tell the tale. If I stay in Joburg I'm dead meat, but if I take the job, I have a chance of making it into the Kruger and getting away from these bastards.* A voice inside him kept whispering, *What about the boy?*

"Unfortunately," the Voice replied, in an implacable tone, "the agreement with the border control requires Sergeant Nwosu's presence. We couldn't arrange it any other way."

"Can't I send on instructions from here?" Nwosu sounded like he really didn't want to go. "I can produce whatever official papers are required, anything that's needed."

Why is he pleading to stay? Coetzee couldn't work out what was going on. Whatever it was, he decided, he would take precautions to watch his back.

"Sergeant Nwosu," the Voice replied. "You are forgetting that you told me the boy has no passport with him. Only a police officer has the power to accompany him through the border control. And in respect of the payment, Mr Coetzee, the increase is only payable upon completion of the task. You must understand our position on this. Neither of us can afford to take any risks. We are obliged to trust each other in these circumstances."

The only guarantee of trust is for me to keep control of the boy. If I refuse to go, it probably spells curtains for both of us. "I'll take Leo to a hotel in Beitbridge and he'll stay in my custody until I see the money in my account," he said. His suspicions were even more aroused when Nwosu readily agreed to his conditions. *This all sounds very scripted,* he thought. *But what's the punch line? It's not going to be me, nor the kid.*

"There's one more thing," the Voice continued. "You must take a photograph of the boy and transmit it to the email address you have for us. You should do this before you leave for Beitbridge. That's all for now." The phone went dead.

"Why in Hell do they want to ship Leo to Zimbabwe?" Coetzee tried to find out what Nwosu was holding back from him. "It's a shithole infested by corrupt, murdering vermin. Have you ever been?"

Nwosu ignored the question. "It has to be to do with money. They want the kid somewhere he can't possibly be taken from them until they get paid a ransom. He must be worth a fucking fortune." Nwosu was cursing himself that he hadn't insisted on even more money, the stakes were clearly very high.

"Listen, Nwosu. I signed up to hold the boy until a ransom was paid then to deliver him safe and sound. No one said anything about handing him over to a bunch of murderous thugs in a lawless country. What happens to him there?"

"Get real, Coetzee. You think they ship young kids to Zimbabwe to work as waiters? I'm telling you he's a valuable commodity and he'll be handed over for a king's ransom and the deal will be done and dusted. And it's a bit fucking late to be changing your mind. We're stuck in the middle of this transaction and there's no way out except forward. We deliver the kid, get paid and live to enjoy it. If we don't, then neither of those things happens. You choose."

Coetzee was assessing the options one last time, as he'd done so many times in the army. If he refused to take Leo he would lose control of him and then who knew what might happen. The only way he could prevent that was to execute the plan.

"Right," he said. "I'll get you all up there and then I'll decide what happens next." They agreed he would pick up Leo and the doctor and meet Nwosu at twelve o'clock outside the hotel Packard. With any luck they'd get to Beitbridge by nightfall. He left Nwosu and as he went out he called Lambert.

"Barry, there's been some developments. We're taking the kid off your hands. We're moving him."

"That's great news!" Lambert sounded relieved. He'd done his job. All he wanted was to get rid of Leo, be paid and get on with his life. That probably included leaving South Africa. He had gone into the arrangement without thinking too much about the consequences, but the sight of Leo, drugged and helpless, had jolted him back to reality. Kidnapping wasn't for him, he'd decided.

"First, I want you to take a picture of Leo from the CCTV film and email it to me. Make sure he looks happy. Then pack his belongings, ready to leave. You can pay the nurse and send her home. I'll be over at midday to take the kid." He thought for a moment. "Get the Doc to fix a needle to keep him quiet for a couple of hours just in case. He's going to be very upset that his mother isn't there."

Coetzee had closed his office in Joburg when he was awarded the contract for the soccer stadium. He had moved into Soccer City when the refurbishment work was being finished in late 2009 and it was one of the few good commercial decisions he'd taken. He had much more space at a fraction of the cost and his permanent staff, all seven of them, loved being in the sports environment. Their first contract included eight World Cup matches, including the final, plus the SA v New Zealand Tri-Nations rugby match which was to be played in August. He called his PA to tell her he was taking a couple of days off. They had, for once, enough money in the bank to pay the salaries and suppliers and were well staffed with temporary workers during the anticlimactic run down after the big match. He'd managed to make enough to pay his staff for the last two years, but he'd never been able to take a salary for himself. Now, he knew he never would, but it didn't matter anymore.

He went back to his apartment in Parktown, in north Joburg, to pack for the trip. For a single man his bedroom was exceptionally tidy, a discipline drilled into him in the army. It took just a couple of minutes to throw a few articles of clothing and toilet items into a duffle bag. An envelope under the mattress containing his cash reserve went into the money belt under his shirt. On the bedside cabinet was a silver photograph frame. He picked it up and looked at the picture. A younger Marius Coetzee in dress uniform was smiling into the eyes of his pretty blonde wife, their young daughter standing between them. A Christmas tree in the room behind them was covered in decorations and lights. It was a happy scene. He looked contented and fulfilled. *It's a long time since I felt that good,* he mused. He removed the photo from the frame. The hand-written inscription on the back read, *I promise to love you forever. xxx Karen.* Taking a book from the cabinet he slid the photo inside and shoved it into his bag.

He took one last look around the flat, picking up a few odds and ends of interest or with good memories. There weren't many. He didn't intend to come back to Johannesburg. It was too dangerous and there was nothing of value to come back for. After Karen had walked out and taken Abby with her he'd moved into this cheap rental apartment with nothing to remind him of them except the photograph.

The conversation with the Voice was still running through his mind. His intention had been to deliver Leo to his family when he saw the money on his account. The move to Zimbabwe was another spanner in the works and now, he didn't know what he was going to do. *At least I'll have him under my control until I work it out,* he told himself.

It was easy to arrange the interior of the eight-seater vehicle to accommodate Leo. The third row of seats had been removed and the back area was long enough to accommodate a sleeping boy, even a six foot boy, curled up. It was a dull, cloudy day so it wouldn't be insufferably hot in the car. The photo arrived from Lambert as he was sorting the car out. Leo didn't look very happy, but he was sitting on the edge of his bed in a tee shirt and shorts, eating a banana. *He certainly looks alive and hungry,* Coetzee thought. He forwarded the snap to the email address in Azerbaijan without comment then drove to a nearby mall to buy sandwiches and drinks and withdrew as much cash as he could from the ATM. On the way to the Packard he filled up the car and got a couple of jerry cans of diesel fuel. He didn't want to take any chances.

Nwosu checked his account on his office PC for the tenth time that morning. His eyes gleamed and he hid his delight with difficulty. The payment had finally arrived at his bank account in the Maldives, a long way from prying eyes in his home country. Many years of looking the other way, or subtly assisting criminal activities, backhanders on drug deals, some highly profitable smuggling, removing obstacles of all kinds, a little blackmail from time to time, all of these side-lines had earned him substantial payments from grateful villains. His bank balance had built up steadily and now this transfer and the last amount he'd been promised would pave the way to a new life.

He salivated at the thought of it. Although homosexuality in South Africa was not illegal, it wasn't for the faint of heart. Quite apart from the very real risk of AIDS, regular violent riots and 'gay bashing' were now the norm and it was looking like it may even become outlawed, as it already was in many African countries, including the neighbouring states of Lesotho, Namibia, Botswana and Zimbabwe. Also, it somehow didn't go with his image as a tough, ruthless cop, ready to beat the crap out of anyone who got in his way. He was living proof that being gay was no barrier to also being tough and ruthless.

This last job and I'm out of here, he thought to himself. *Jamie and me on a beach in Mozambique, close enough to Maputo airport and far away from problems in Joburg. What a formula for a happy life!* Mozambique was a haven of peace for people of his kind and the Maldives was a haven of financial privacy. *The best of all is that the Voice is paying me to go to Zimbabwe, only two hour's drive from the Mozambique border through the Kruger. I'll get rid of the other two and deliver the kid and then who gives a shit what happens to him. It's not my problem.*

He announced to the duty officer that he was going on a two day trip and would call in regularly to check on things. Then he went home to pack a bag and call Jamie, trying to keep the smile off his face.

It was sixty-two hours since Leo had been taken.

THIRTY

Marbella, Spain

"I've never asked you how you became a best-selling author. I hate to say it but I was a bit jealous every time I saw a new book come out. I always wanted to do something glamorous in my life and become well-known, but I don't have any talent at all."

The two women were waiting for Espinoza to arrive to review their respective progress. Jenny was attempting to divert her sister's mind from Leo's predicament. She came downstairs for breakfast with dark shadows under her eyes, obviously not having slept well and then eaten almost nothing. Jenny insisted she had two cups of coffee, they needed to have their minds clear for Espinoza's visit. She was determined to make some progress this morning.

"Glamorous?" Emma grimaced. "You must be joking. I barely scrape by and everyone passes me in the street without a second glance. And the work! You have no idea how hard it is to find more and more plots that haven't already been done twenty times. Every book is another year of my life and I'm running out of them fast."

"So how did you get into it?"

"Well, after Tony, I never seemed to find the right man. He was, or at least I thought he was, special, and I kept looking for that man again, but I never found him. I had to face the reality of life as a single mother and get a job. Then I had a bit of luck. I replied to an advertisement from a publishing agency and, amazingly, they hired me. It's lucky I enjoy reading because all I did was read manuscripts from would-be writers, all day long. If I liked the story, the partners would take a look and sometimes we'd publish them, not very often, I must say."

She laughed out loud, much to Jenny's surprise and pleasure. "You can't believe the rubbish people write, most people, anyway. I could tell you some plots that you wouldn't even begin to understand, never mind enjoy, really obscure, twisted mind stuff. Hilarious, some of it. And some so-called 'erotic writing' that was just an excuse to write down someone's bedroom fantasies. But once in a while you get something really good, that grabs you, and I did see a few of them.

"I started jotting some ideas down, a lot of it plagiarised from stories I'd read. Then the big break though came when I invented these two characters, 'Angus and Tory'. Somehow they took on a life of their own and it became easier. The first book was actually quite good and it was taken up by an independent publisher, almost a one man band, in Edinburgh. Alan Bridges, the owner, helped me to get it into shape and it sold brilliantly, the next couple as well. But then you start to become stylised and formulaic and it's hard work to think of something new. That's more or less where I am now, looking for a new twist to reinvent myself. It's also why I'm broke. They're not selling so well these days. Time for new characters or a new career."

"And you've still never met the right man?"

"The nearest thing is Alan, Alan Bridges. We started going out a few years ago after he was divorced and we've worked out quite a good arrangement. He's got two kids and lives in Scotland, so we only see each other from time to time. I'll go up there to talk about my books and we might do a dinner or a show and he comes down sometimes for the weekend. It's very nice actually, no ties, and if I don't feel like it I just make an excuse and wait until the next occasion. I don't want to complicate Leo's life with a new father when he doesn't even know what happened to the last one."

Wanting to avoid becoming emotional about Leo again, she asked, "And you, anybody in your life?"

Jenny hesitated. She had never been one to bare her soul to the world, but it was her sister and there wasn't much to tell. "I'm not sure," she said with a wry frown. "Two years ago, Leticia and I went through a dreadful experience and it just about put me off people all together, men and women. After losing Ron and then that awful business I didn't want to see anyone at all and I became a veritable hermit for over a year. I'm lucky that I don't have to work, but there were still a lot of things I needed to sort out, legal matters and complications to do with Charlie's business, so it all began to get on top of me.

"Then Leticia talked me round and I came down here for a couple of weeks. She was a real tonic for me. She's lovely, clever and very good company and I started to get it back together again. Since then I come more or less every two months for a few weeks and it's done me the world of good."

"And the man?"

"Well, a few months ago I met someone here in Marbella. It was at a charity dinner at the Puente Romano Hotel, very posh. He was one of the sponsors in aid of a cancer charity. He used to be quite a well-known sportsman and was in the Olympic rifle team. He won a silver medal actually, at the Barcelona Olympics in 1992. There's a big memorabilia room in his house with all the family's cups, medals, awards and historical documents. He comes from a very good family in Agadir, you know, in Morocco. Some connection with the royal family, It's a really ancient family, goes back to biblical days apparently."

"He sounds too good to be true. Does he have a name?"

"Everyone calls him Sam. His actual name is a dozen words long and unpronounceable. He lives about fifteen minutes along the road, up in the Marbella gated community where the old ruler of Saudi Arabia built his palace in the seventies. Lots of Arab royalty and highly placed diplomats have homes there, there's even a mosque on the property. It's a fabulous house and very private, acres of land around it.

"Anyway, Patrice, Leticia's fiancé, introduced us at the dinner and we hit it off really well. He's very smart and sensitive with a great sense of humour and fascinating stories about his sporting career and his life here and there around the world. It made me realise how little I've done in my UK centric existence."

"I hate to ask and you don't have to answer, but have you slept with him?"

"Not yet, but I think we're getting closer, cross fingers. I'm not that keen on jumping into bed with men I don't really know, even after two and a half years of celibacy. So I'm still an occasional customer at Anne Summers." She laughed self-consciously but felt the familiar pang of unfulfilled emotion. Since her husband Ron's death in December of 2007 and the events of 2008, she had forced herself to keep busy. Busy enough to put aside thoughts of missing companionship, sex and possibly marriage, but at thirty-seven she knew that her chances of attracting a partner were not improving.

Emma saw the emotion in her face. "Am I going to get the chance to meet him?"

"He's supposed to be coming here tomorrow for lunch. But in the circumstances I'm not sure if it's a good idea."

"You mean because of me? Nonsense! I'd love to meet him. It'll take my mind off our problems. Anyway, he sounds like a good catch."

"Don't start marrying me off just yet. But he is rather nice."

"Well, you've given me a tremendous amount of good advice so can I give you one piece of my own?"

"Go ahead, I'm listening."

"Ron's been gone now for two and a half years, so you can't keep hiding away from men. This might sound brutal, but you have to get on with your life again and the best way to do that is with a new partner. My arrangement with Allen isn't ideal, but the point is it works for both of us. It keeps us sane and healthy in mind and body and free to get on with our lives. We get together when we feel the need or desire. It suits us both and that's what counts."

She's right. It's time I moved on. Past Ron, past the Angolan Clan and past the last year of stress and aggravation. Maybe Sam's the answer. Jenny's reverie was broken by the sound of the gate bell. "Sounds like Pedro's here. Time to get back to work."

Espinoza was bustled into the office by Encarni. He was a small man and she towered over him. He accepted her offer of a coffee, then sat facing the women. "Are we still agreed on last night's decisions?"

They nodded. "Bueno." He settled himself down. "I've set a few wheels in motion, so we should start to get feedback this afternoon. Meanwhile, I think I've validated one of Jenny's theories."

He handed them a printout of a newsletter from the Packard Hotel chain. "Look at the 'Management' section, on page three. Lambert took over at the Packard in Mayfair only two months ago."

"That was just a month after Galaganza's death. So he was put in place by the kidnappers in May to execute the plan in July. They didn't waste any time, did they?"

"When did you book your trip to South Africa, Emma?"

"It was last September, when we got the results of Leo's GCSEs. I splurged out on the tickets while they were still reasonably priced and gave them to him for his Christmas present. I made the hotel bookings at the same time. It was his reward for working so hard and finishing while still only fourteen." She shuddered. "What a reward it's turned out to be."

Espinoza ignored the remark. "We're narrowing this down. There were probably more people than you think who knew about your trip with Leo, but the plan to abduct him was only put in place in May. And it must have been planned by a person or persons who had followed the Rwandan story and heard about Galaganza dying in Benin immediately after it happened and who connected it to Leo."

"I want you to look at these also." He handed over two more printouts from his morning's research. "He's a very interesting man, Mr Coetzee, as you'll see."

Under the heading, ***Coetzee Security Services,*** there was a photo of the security chief wearing a safari jacket and a pith helmet, seated on a beautiful grey stallion. The introduction read, *Place your Trust in a Team run by an Ex-Officer of the South African Special Forces. We understand Security and we understand your Concerns.*

"He looks a lot nicer there than when I met him."

"That's normal. It's his publicity face. But there's a lot more to him than just a handsome picture."

Jenny was reading the BIO page. "I see what you mean. He was the youngest Major in the Special Forces and was with them for fifteen years. And in 2007 he was awarded the *Honoris Crux Decoration. One of very few soldiers to receive such recognition,* it says here."

"What was that for?"

"That's just the enigma." Espinoza frowned. "It's awarded, and I quote from the source, *for exceptional acts of bravery while in great danger.* I did some more research and learned that Coetzee saved the lives of a classroom full of schoolchildren who were being held hostage by pro-apartheid militants. He was entirely on his own because the local police had refused to back him up. It was a tragic affair, apparently, but not as tragic as it could have been. The school teacher was killed together with two parents, but Coetzee overcame eight gunmen to save the lives of twelve children and four parents."

"My God. He's a veritable hero. It can't be the same man who's abducted Leo."

"People do things for many reasons, Emma, but the more we know about what makes them tick and how they think, the more chance we have of finding out what it's all about and how to resolve it."

"And Nwosu, anything about him?"

"Nothing, apart from his address in Diepkloof. But he's a policeman so he'll be easy to find out about if it becomes necessary."

"I'm not sure, but I think he may be gay. Just something about him. He's definitely not a tough guy like Coetzee."

"Really? That's a surprise." Jenny slipped back into her school teacher role. "Right. Back to the detective work. Let's look at those names again." She had printed out several pages of her notes and read out the disappointingly few names of suspects on the first list.

> ***"People who know about Mutesi / Leo:***
> *Dr Antoine Constance,*
> *Dr Tony Forrester,*
> *Marianne, Mutesi's friend,*
> *Irene and Auguste, the two servants.*

"I think we can rule out the servants. They wouldn't even have known if Mutesi had survived and had her baby. They had their own problems, poor souls."

"Agreed, Jenny. And it's stretching things to imagine that Marianne could be involved in this plot. So we rule her out also. Which leaves us with only two suspects. Constance and Forrester, both doctors, both aware of Mutesi's death and Leo's birth.

"Emma," he went on. "You've told us a lot about Tony, but do you know much about Dr Constance?"

"Only what I was told by Tony. Dr Constance never told me anything about himself but I could see that he considered maternity work beneath him. He was a rather supercilious person, quite aloof when he wasn't working. Apparently he's a reconstructive surgeon and that's why he went down there. To help the victims who had been hacked to pieces but had somehow survived."

"You mean a kind of plastic surgeon?"

"A very advanced kind. There were thousands of innocent victims who were left dreadfully disfigured and he wanted to help them to lead a normal life again. Tony was quite cynical about him. He thought he was looking for personal fame and celebrity status. You know, '*French Doctor Helps Genocide Victims Find a New Face and a New Life.*' It would have furthered his chance of becoming a top plastic surgeon in Paris or London."

"So why was he working at the maternity clinic?"

"Because there were no other hospital facilities of any kind open. The whole national infrastructure was in a complete shambles. There was a hospital operating in Kigali, but it was closed to the public. Hutu government officials and those who had some kind of authority were admitted but only for very basic treatment, so it was really a private clinic where normal citizens couldn't go. There was literally no hospital in Rwanda where any kind of advanced surgery could be performed. That's why there are so many thousands of survivors with terrible disfigurements and scars, still today."

"So he ended up helping rape victims give birth to their illegitimate children?"

"And he did a wonderful job," Emma said defensively. "He managed to run that shed that we called a clinic in the most awful circumstances and he helped to save many lives. I don't know what he did before or since, but I will always remember his dedication to the people of Rwanda."

"The fact remains that it's highly probable that Constance asked Forrester about Leo after you disappeared and he learned the circumstances of his UK passport, so I conclude that we have two people of similar background with similar knowledge of what happened in Rwanda."

"But how could they have learned about our trip to South Africa? We've been out of touch for fifteen years."

"I think that information was easier to come across than Leo's parenthood."

"Maybe, but how do we find either of them? So many years have passed since we knew where they were." Emma was beginning to think that all this deduction was leading nowhere.

"I've already put feelers out to try to find them, Emma. My old police contacts are still useful. We should soon have some further information. Meanwhile, let's look at the people who knew about the South Africa trip."

He read out the names on the second list.

"People who knew about SA trip:
Jenny,
Leo's school friends and teachers,
Alan Bridges, Emma's publisher,
A couple of friends,
Travel agent,
Emma's bank."

Emma sighed in frustration. "None of these people are on the first list and I simply don't believe any of them could have known about Mutesi and Leo. There's absolutely no connection and I haven't said a word about it until I told Jenny yesterday."

"Emma, I must tell you that I share Jenny's mistrust of coincidences, especially in this matter. There are two separate events almost sixteen years apart, the birth of Leo, in Rwanda and the death of his probable father, Galaganza the genocider, in Benin. Then Leo is abducted in South Africa three months later. These events cannot be coincidences, there is a pattern and patterns never lie. The names on the lists are different, no name appears on both lists, therefore someone on one of those lists must have known or learned of both events and that is where the answer lies.

"We have to do old fashioned police work to unravel this mystery and it can take a long time. Let's go through the story again in case there's something we missed."

They started following the trail again, a fifteen year old trail that somehow had to lead them to Leo Stewart.

THIRTY-ONE

Johannesburg, South Africa

Coetzee arrived at the Packard at midday, his Land Cruiser was stocked with drinks and gasoline and there were blankets in the back for Leo. He went into the bungalow where the doctor was waiting. "How is he?"

"He's perfectly well, but getting very restless because he hasn't seen his mother. Maybe you shouldn't have promised so much."

"He'll get over it. Right, have you got a two hour fix ready?"

They went into the room together. Leo was dressed in a safari shirt and jeans and his bag was placed ready at the door. He was sitting on the bed looking very unhappy. "What's going on? You told me you'd come back this morning with my mother. Where is she?"

"She'll be coming here any minute. She's packing up ready to move to a hotel near the airport because I managed to wangle seats on a flight first thing tomorrow morning using the same tickets. It's going to save her almost a thousand pounds, so she's really happy. She'll be even happier when she sees you."

Leo's anger was momentarily abated. "I'm sorry. Thank you. You said I had to have some tests before we can go."

"That's why the Doc's here with me. He's going to take a little blood and analyse it before this evening, but he doesn't think there's anything to worry about."

"That's right Leo. I'm Doctor Blethin. Everything seems to be fine, but you did have quite a bad turn, so I just want to take one last look before I sign you off to go home. Can't be too careful." He spoke with an accent that seemed familiar to Leo.

The doctor came towards him with the hypodermic and Leo suddenly pulled back, his memory finally kicking in. "I know you. You're that foreigner who injected me in the toilet. Barry Lambert held me and you stuck a needle in me. Get away from me. You're not a doctor. You're not sticking another needle in me, you fucking weirdo." He lashed out at the doctor, punching and kicking.

Coetzee stepped up and grabbed Leo, restraining him while the doctor injected the needle into his arm. "Don't worry, Leo. This is for your own good. I promise we won't harm you."

"Fuck off, you bastard!" Leo struggled madly for a few moments then his body went limp and he fell back on the bed.

"He'll be out for about three to four hours." The doctor said. "I didn't want to give him more; it might be dangerous after the last few days."

"OK. That should get us half way to Beitbridge with a bit of luck."

Lambert took Leo's suitcase and put it in the back of the car. As they were preparing to carry him out, Coetzee's mobile rang. It was Nwosu.

"I need to sort out a few things before I leave the station. Don't want to leave any unanswered questions here that could cause us problems. It'll take me an hour or so then I'll join you. I can be there at one thirty, where will I meet you?"

They agreed on the pick-up point and he rang off. Coetzee's paranoia was increasing. *Nwosu would never go out of his way to meet me. He'd insist I come down for him. What the hell's he up to?*

Nwosu was sitting in the window of a café opposite the Packard Hotel. He saw Coetzee's Land Cruiser pull away from the bungalow with the doctor sitting in the passenger seat. After fifteen minutes he put on his sunglasses and walked across to the reception, his cap pulled low over his forehead.

"I'm Sergeant Bongani from Forbsburg Central precinct. I need to talk to the manager." As the receptionist called Lambert he moved away from her, pretending to make a call on his mobile, his back turned to the woman.

A moment later Lambert came towards him. Still with his back to the reception desk, Nwosu flicked his badge at him quickly so he couldn't read it. "Sergeant Bongani," he announced.

"Barry Lambert, hotel manager. What can I do for you?"

"We've received a report that a teenage boy has gone missing in the area. Apparently he was staying with his mother in this hotel."

Lambert thought quickly. *They know about Leo, but they're too late, thank God. Better be helpful and get it over with.* Aloud, he said, "That's right. I heard about it, but he hasn't been back and his mother left yesterday, so I don't think there's anything I can do to help."

"I need to check both their rooms, see if there's anything to explain their disappearance."

"I'll get the keys. They were in adjacent rooms on the seventh floor."

Lambert returned with the keys and they went to the elevator, Nwosu still looking away from the reception desk.

"Do you need me to show you the rooms?"

"Let's go up together in case I have a question. It won't take long."

Fifteen minutes later, Nwosu emerged from the elevator and walked unobtrusively out of the hotel. He went across to the bus station to collect his bag from the storage locker then hailed a passing taxi, "Take me to the intersection of Smit Street and the M1 north." On the way he called a number in Brussels.

Marbella, Spain

Espinoza checked his watch. It was one thirty. "I'm going to try to accelerate things," he said. "Let's give Mr Lambert a call and see what he has to say. Sometimes shock tactics can produce results."

"Don't you think he's likely to run for the hills?"

"Not yet. It's too early, they must be organising themselves for the next phase of the operation. I suggest that Jenny calls and makes it fairly innocuous, just a worried call from her in the UK about her missing nephew. He doesn't know that we've started unravelling their plot and it's less threatening if it's a woman. If we're lucky he might let his guard down.

"Do you have your UK mobile, Jenny?" He took it from her, dialled a number from his note pad and handed the phone back.

"Packard Hotel, Mayfair. How can I help?"

"Can you pass me Mr Lambert, the manager? This is Mrs Bishop. I'm calling from England."

"Just a moment please." After several minutes the woman came back on the line. "I'm sorry, but there's been an incident and I can't talk now. Can you please call back later?" The phone clicked and went dead.

Johannesburg, South Africa

The Land Cruiser set off for Beitbridge at a quarter to two. Coetzee's paranoia had caused a heated discussion about who should sit where in the car. Finally, the sitting arrangement was Nwosu in the passenger seat next to Coetzee with Doctor Blethin behind Coetzee and Leo lying on blankets with his legs stretched out across the back of the car. They drove onto the N1, direction Pretoria, five hundred and twenty-two kilometres of hot, dusty trouble ahead of them.

It was sixty-four and a half hours since Leo had been taken.

THIRTY-TWO

Marbella, Spain

"I don't like the sound of that." Jenny said. "I wonder what kind of incident she meant."

"I have a feeling something might have happened to Mr Lambert."

"I hope it was nothing trivial. That odious, hypocritical man." Emma frowned with distaste then turned as a 'ping' emitted from her laptop.

"Oh my God!" She suddenly started laughing and crying simultaneously, floods of tears running down her face. After studying the screen for a few moments she picked it up, kissing it and hugging it to her breast. She placed it back on the table so they could all see the screen. They saw a picture of Leo sitting on a bedside, eating a banana. Underneath the picture was the message; *Leo is healthy and in safe hands. Do not inform the authorities or take any untoward action as you will endanger him unnecessarily. We will be in contact again tomorrow.*

She looked wildly at Espinoza. "What does it mean? Leo's alive, thank God, but they're not saying anything at all. No demand of any kind. Nothing that can help us."

Jenny took her hands. "One thing at a time, Emma. Leo is alive and well. Our theory was right. They're after money, so they'll be making sure that nothing happens to him. I promise you this is really good news, right Pedro?"

"You're right, it's excellent news, the best we could hope for. It proves we are on the right track." He placed the machine in the centre of the table where they could all see the screen. "Right. Now let's study the message carefully. It's the first real clue we've come across and we need to extract every bit of information we can from it."

He started making notes. "First of all the photograph. Leo looks very well. They seem to be looking after him. He's got an appetite, which is a good sign. That's not his hotel room, of course?"

"No, his room was quite cosy. Wallpaper and an upholstered bedhead. That bed has an iron frame and the walls are completely bare."

"It looks like a hospital room, but there's something not quite right." Jenny squinted at the screen. "There's no pulley handle to lift yourself up and there's no knobs or levers on the side of the bed. It's like an army bed, just an iron frame and blankets, nothing else at all."

"So it seems he's in a room specially prepared to accommodate him, without any equipment or items which could identify it, either by him or by us. Very professional. There's a window behind Leo's head. See? It's got closed blinds so you can't look outside. Hmm." He put on his spectacles and looked closely at the screen. "Look carefully at the window and tell me what you see."

"There's a reflection in the window, because the blinds outside are closed, so the glass reflects. There's a door, partly open. Maybe a bathroom or toilet. What else?" Jenny's keen eyes spotted the phenomenon. "I see it. There's a picture on the wall near the door. No, it's not a picture. I don't know what it is."

"See if I can enlarge it." Emma double clicked on the photo. "No good. It's been pasted onto the message and you can't get to it. Wait. I'll zoom it up. Right, zoom to double size. See? It's a calendar with a photo of a pride of lions and a company name on top. Backwards of course." She read out the letters, "C, L, I, N, I. It's a clinic. P, R, I, V. Private. N, E, W , T. It's the Newtown Private Clinic. Just along the road from our hotel."

"I don't think it is in a clinic, but if there were a doctor and a nurse involved maybe that's where they came from?"

Jenny looked more closely at the screen. "I think there's something else. Can you make it even larger? "That's good. See? On the wall above the picture, a nozzle or a tube of some kind,"

"You're right. It looks like a CCTV camera lens. The flexible tube type they use for indoor surveillance. Just a wide angle lens poking through the wall on the end of a tube that's linked to a monitor. That's what they've taken the photograph with and it's reflected the image from the window."

"So that means he's been under constant surveillance from someone outside the room?"

"I think it means three things. Firstly, the calendar tells us Leo is still in the Mayfair area and there's some connection with the Newtown Private Clinic. Probably they have a doctor or nurse to keep an eye on him in case the drugs have a bad effect. Next, he's in a building where they've installed a CCTV monitor. Thirdly, now I understand why Coetzee is involved. This military type surveillance is costly and complicated. He obviously has experience in installing it and he probably supplied it. Can you see any properties on the photo file, Emma? Anything that could lead us to the originators?"

"There's nothing. When a photo is pasted like that, there are no properties until you copy or save it and then your own computer creates the file. No more clues I'm afraid. But wait, I'm looking up the Newtown Private Clinic. See what it tells us."

The website for the clinic was very understated, rather poorly done, in Emma's professional opinion. She went through the various services they offered then looked up the page labelled 'Consultants and Medical Staff'. There were twelve short bios of doctors and consultants and she scrolled down the page, looking at each one.

"Fairly normal services," She commented. "From Dermatology to Obstetrics. Nothing special that I can see."

"But we know the clinic is close to the hotel and their calendar is in the room where Leo is being held." The detective's mind was now fully in gear. He had some evidence to work with. They now knew for sure who had carried out the abduction and had a good idea of where Leo was being held and who was looking after him.

"Thanks to this small mistake on their part, we've already found out a lot more than they expected us to. Now let's see if the message itself reveals as much information."

They read through the message again. "That's strange. It came to my personal address and not my publishing one. Look, *emma@emmastewart.com*. I only use that website for personal affairs, my friends and family, never for anything public."

"Did you give Nwosu this address when you were being interrogated?"

"No. I always give my publishing address. It's the one that's on my visiting cards and website, everything. My private address is my only refuge from the publicity of being a writer."

"So, the abductors know a website address that's not public knowledge. That could mean that they have some connection with you, or some way of finding this personal address."

"Actually, it's not uncommon to have an address like that, first and last name only. I have one myself, *jenny@jennybishop.com.* You certainly wouldn't expect them to send such a message to Emma's publishing address, it's too risky for them, considering the subject matter."

"Perhaps. But I still think there may be a connection there somewhere. Look, the message was sent from an account called *args@ipsend.ph.* That's the Philippines if I'm not mistaken."

"The Philippines?" Emma gasped in incredulity.

"Don't worry, it doesn't really mean anything. It's just a very difficult place to find out who or where the actual users of the site are. It's like the old fashioned Mailbox addresses, the user could be anywhere in the world, just using it as a communication base without giving away their true location. The Internet isn't just a tool for innocent users like you, it's very valuable to fraudsters and criminals of all kinds."

"But it does tell us that the people involved are sophisticated enough to set up a CCTV monitoring system and this anonymous message service. They also seem to have expert medical staff looking after Leo."

"Yes, it's more professional than amateur, but we are still far from understanding what's going on. I'll check the ISP but I don't think it will tell us anything." He looked up *International ISPs* and chose a site then narrowed the list down to the Philippines. "There's no site called *ipsend.* It's a private address using a Philippine provider but we can't tell where it originated."

"It probably wouldn't help if we did, just another link in a long chain I suppose."

"Exactly. A needle in a haystack."

"And who are *ARGS*? It sounds like a company or an organisation of some kind."

"What about a group? If our theory is right the *R* could be for *Rwanda* or *Rwandan,* and then *Group* and so on. It could actually mean anything." Jenny racked her brain, trying to guess the acronym.

"I'm sure we'll find out in due course." Espinoza was still writing his notes. "What about the message itself?"

"Well, it was written by someone with a very good command of English. Look at this phrase; *Do not inform the authorities or take any untoward action as you will endanger him unnecessarily.*"

"Not many people write like that anymore." Emma intervened. "*Inform,* rather than contact, *untoward,* a very old fashioned word and *endanger,* rather than harm or hurt. It's almost as if it was written by a foreigner with a very good command of English."

"Since we have no idea of the identity of the sender, you could be right. It's certainly not the average message you get by email." He pointed at the 'Sent' panel. "The time tells us something, too. It was sent at one thirty-eight pm, Spanish time. It's the middle of the night in Asia and Australia and only seven-thirty in the morning in the US, so the message was probably sent from Europe or Africa, where it's daytime. I'm not sure that tells us very much, but it probably confirms that the Philippine address is a subterfuge."

"So it could have been sent from South Africa?"

"I don't know, Emma, but my instinct tells me it probably wasn't. Even though we have a lot of evidence pointing to an African motive, it just seems to me to be a red herring, as you would say."

"In what way?"

"Perhaps you didn't notice in the announcement of Lambert's appointment, that it mentioned he was English and came from the Sheraton in London. He was hired by someone in the UK, in my opinion."

"You mean that the Packard is an English hotel?"

"Not the hotel itself, but the management company is. Packard Hotels Ltd, in London. It may just be a coincidence, but ..."

"We don't believe in coincidences," Jenny completed the phrase for him.

Espinoza nodded in agreement then continued. "And the style of writing of the message is definitely not South African, they just don't talk or write like that. It's very European."

"Shouldn't we reply to the message? We might discover more information. I think we should do something."

"Normally in this situation, I'd agree with you Emma. We'd send a reply and ask for what's called 'proof of life'."

Jenny saw her sister's reaction and took her hand. "It's alright, Emma. It only means that we need a photo to prove that Leo is still there and in good health."

"Yes. A photo of Leo taken with evidence of the date, so we can see he is alive and well and possibly discover more, as we did here."

"But in this case we already have a photo, so that wouldn't be a convincing line of enquiry."

"Exactly. I know you're feeling helpless and desperate to do something, but what is needed now is patience. Let them make the moves, we keep up the detective work and wait for them to make mistakes. They will send another message within a short time and then we must decide how to react to their demands."

Before either woman could reply, Espinoza's mobile rang. He looked at the number and responded in French, "*Bonjour Marcel, quelles nouvelles?* What news?"

He listened for a while, making notes in his neat handwriting, interjecting questions from time to time. "*Bien, merci Marcel. Je te tiendrai au courant. Salut.* Thanks a million, I'll keep you posted."

"*Bueno.*" He addressed the two women. "We are starting to catch up on those sixteen years. This is what we know about Dr Constance.

"Apparently he left Rwanda in 1997, rather hurriedly. It seems there was some kind of incident and he left without ceremony and returned to France, where he got a job with a hospital in Toulouse, *l'Hôpital des Sœurs de Miséricorde.* He was there for three years as a Senior Consultant in Aesthetic Surgery."

"So it's true that he was a reconstructive surgeon and he returned to his original speciality?"

"Apparently. But then in 2001 he was fired from the hospital."

"Do you know why?"

"I don't have that information, but with doctors it's often negligence or inappropriate behaviour, in my experience."

"I find that hard to believe. He was a very competent doctor and never showed any signs of behaviour of that kind. Where did he go from there?"

"After that he had two more positions with smaller hospitals and ended up in 2007 at the *Clinique Saint Christophe* in the South of France, as Senior Consultant in Reconstructive Surgery. It's a very expensive private hospital in Nice."

"Is he still there?"

"Bad news, I'm afraid. He left France again in September last year and my source tells me that there was an ongoing enquiry at the clinic but it was abandoned when he left France. And that's where the trail goes cold. He is reported as leaving on a flight for the UK, but there's no record of his arrival. European passports have not been stamped at UK immigration for many years and the open border system means that we have no idea of where he might be now. He could have been in transit, either to a European destination, or elsewhere in the world."

"But if Tony talked to him about Leo, he could be involved in the kidnapping?"

"We keep coming up against the same problem, Emma. How could Constance know about your trip to South Africa? How could anyone who knew about Mutesi and Leo also know about your trip and organise this abduction in time? Who could plan and fund what is obviously a major conspiracy. Certainly not a French doctor who's been in and out of four jobs in the last ten years.

"And I still can't understand the motive. I suppose it has to be money in the end, it always is. But it's puzzling, because you've made it clear that you're not a wealthy woman." Espinoza sighed. "I find it all very confusing for the moment."

London, England

"I can confirm that the first message was sent off to Ms Stewart at twelve thirty this afternoon." The Voice sounded pleased with himself.

"Good. You sent a photograph with it"

"Of course. He's a very good looking boy, expressive and intelligent features. It's a rather amusing photograph. He is eating a banana. I thought it was quite a nice touch, after having been abducted in South Africa."

"This isn't a game. Just concentrate on moving him to a safer place and executing the rest of the programme."

"They're already on their way to Beitbridge, hopefully arriving this evening. The remaining connection with Johannesburg has been neutralised. Everything is proceeding according to plan."

"I'll feel a lot more comfortable when they've left South African soil. There's going to be a hue and cry there now that the Bishop woman is involved. She's a very determined person. Don't underestimate her."

Slater rang off then selected his partner's name from his Favourites list and relayed the message in a few brief words.

"When do we make the next contact?"

"Tomorrow morning. Things will be moving quickly now."

"About time. Are you sure the banking arrangements are in order?"

"Everything's in place. The accounts and standing instructions have been tested. The funds flow in series from Dubai to Nassau in six easy steps. After tomorrow's message it just depends on the negotiations, but she lives for that boy and she knows where to find the money. It won't take long."

"Call me tomorrow when it's started." The speaker put the phone aside and lay back on the sunbed by the hotel pool in Nice. A waiter came over with a whiskey. A single malt on ice.

In London the Voice called a number in Marseille. "*Tout va bien?* Everything's OK?" His French was more than adequate, but he usually preferred to keep that detail to himself. He listened for a moment then said, "So Sunday the 18th is confirmed? Right, please make the call to Geneva as agreed tomorrow afternoon. Call me if there is any other news."

THIRTY-THREE

Pretoria, South Africa

The trip wasn't going well. There had been a nasty accident on the NI to Pretoria, just south of Centurion. Two lorries had collided, with several cars joining the smash, causing a massive pile up on the northbound carriageway. It was almost four o'clock before they got to the Pretoria Eastern Bypass, leading to the NI toll road to Beitbridge.

By now, Nwosu and Coetzee were on very bad terms. The policeman blamed him for the delay. He should have been on the R101, the Old Pretoria Main Road, and not the M1. "There's always accidents on the M1," he said. "Everyone knows you should take the R101 up to Centurion. There's much less traffic and there's no tolls either. It's a complete waste of time and money.

"We've got at least five hours more driving and it gets dark in just over an hour. We're going to have to stop somewhere if we don't want to drive all night. And we'll have trouble with the kid if we're not careful. He's going to wake up and I don't want to be ferrying him around in the dark, he's too valuable."

"Let me worry about the driving and the kid, he's in my hands. I'll decide when and where we stop, or if we do. Just shut up and sit there and be ready to be useful at the border crossing." Coetzee's patience was already wearing thin, since he'd been forbidden to smoke his cheroots by both Blethin and Nwosu and he became more and more aware of how much he'd come to depend on the nicotine fix. He bit into a spearmint Chiclet and drove towards the first toll booth at Stormvoël.

Marbella, Spain

Espinoza seemed preoccupied. He turned to Jenny. "Could we have a word in private?"

Emma said, "I need to go upstairs anyway. You can talk as much as you like. I hope it's nothing bad."

Espinoza smiled. "Don't worry, Emma. I'm a little confused and I need to ask Jenny something."

When she had left the room, he said, "Jenny, as you know, my skill in detection is in identifying the motive and then working from that to find the culprit or culprits. It's the only way I know how to work. On this occasion, I'm faced with conflicting facts which are confusing the motive. Let me explain." He began pacing the room, his spectacles in his hand, a frown of concentration on his face.

"Firstly, we know, or at least we believe, that the threat of publicising the details of Leo's birth is the kidnapper's prime stock in trade. It means that Emma can't go to the authorities and will be obliged to negotiate his return. It's a very clever trap.

"We also know that only someone who had knowledge of that fact and also knew about the football trip could have planned and carried out the abduction.

"Because of the number of participants, the complex arrangements needed to kidnap Leo and the sophisticated communications set-up, the perpetrators must have invested a considerable amount and will expect a large return on that investment. That's where the motive doesn't stand up. Emma isn't in a position to pay any kind of reward and she can't go to anyone to find the money, because she can't disclose the reason.

"Finally, we are very short of suspects. In fact, I have really no confidence in progressing in that direction until I clarify the motive clearly in my mind."

He stopped walking and faced her. "Do you agree with my précis of the facts?"

"Of course, but I don't know how to help you clarify the motive if that's what you expect. I'm just as confused as you are."

"Then you're going to have to trust me completely. Can I ask you a very personal question?"

"If it helps to get Leo back, of course you can."

He paused, trying to find the best way to phrase his interrogation. "When we met two years ago, I believe you and Leticia had inherited a very large amount of money, some of which was stolen from you by the murderer, d'Almeida."

Jenny just nodded and he continued. "Are you still a very wealthy woman?"

She reflected a moment. "By most people's standards, I suppose I am."

"So, can you see what I am getting at? The reason for this abduction?"

When she still didn't respond, he said, "We know that Emma is, what do you call it? 'A starving writer'. At any rate she doesn't have a fortune that could be targeted by criminals of this kind. Criminals who have obviously done their homework and discovered an interesting combination."

"What combination?"

"That Emma has a secret that must be kept silent, the truth about Leo's birth. And that she has a sister who has a fortune that could pay for that silence."

Jenny sat up in shock. "You mean you think Leo was kidnapped to blackmail Emma so I would pay a ransom to get him back?"

This time it was Espinoza who said nothing. He looked intently at Jenny, waiting for her to join together the dots, as he had done.

"But that would mean there's someone who knows about Leo's birth, their trip to South Africa, that she's my sister and about my inheritance. It's absurd."

"Why is it absurd, Jenny?"

"Because we've got precisely two suspects and neither of them could possibly have known I even exist."

"Not necessarily, but that's a different question, opportunity. What we're trying to identify right now is motive and there's no doubt in my mind that the motive is money, a lot of money. And the only person who has a lot of money is you."

He waited while Jenny sat quietly, putting together his jigsaw puzzle in her mind, finally coming to the same conclusion as him. Then he asked, "Has anything occurred recently that has affected your fortune, Jenny? Any change of circumstances or event that would change your wealth or bring it to the knowledge of a wider group? A new person or persons?"

Her thoughts jumped back to January and her trip to Geneva; The twelve million dollar settlement with Klein Fellay, her visit to Ramseyer, Haldemann for the first time in two years, the new accounts with the Banque de Commerce. She moved nervously in her chair.

"So there is something. Do you want to tell me about it?"

She explained the year-long lawsuit and the eventual settlement, without giving any further details. Leticia had signed the documents for the Trust account, a little reluctantly, it had appeared to her, and their new individual accounts with Mme Aeschiman were also now operative. She didn't mention the diamonds, although she had fleetingly thought about them when she read the first message confirming Leo's abduction. But it was fleeting, because the diamonds were not hers to sell or barter and would never be disclosed unless some kind of disaster struck Leticia's family. She merely said, "You're right. There's a lot of money involved and it has already caused us many problems."

"And I'm afraid it will cause further problems, to Emma and Leo and yourself, until we resolve this matter."

Jenny frowned. *Silly woman,* she berated herself. *It should have been obvious to me. Those cursed Angolan diamonds. This inheritance has already caused deaths and tragedy for so many people and now it's caused the abduction of my nephew. Poor Emma. Leo was taken just because I came into a fortune.*

Aloud, she said, "You're right. I should have seen it before and I didn't, but it's the only explanation that makes sense. Pedro, I have to resolve this. We have to resolve it. It's my responsibility and you've got to help me get Leo back for Emma. Whatever it takes."

"And we will, Jenny. Between us we'll get Leo back, preferably without making a pauper of you in the process."

"So, what's the next step?"

"We've got to explain this to Emma and see if it throws up any other possible suspects. Let's call her back down."

THIRTY-FOUR

Mpumalanga, South Africa

Leo was awakened by the sound of a car door being banged shut. He didn't know it, but they were at the Kranskop toll plaza, about one hundred thirty-five kilometres north of Pretoria. Coetzee had dropped the coins for the toll machine onto the road and had to climb out to retrieve them. He blamed the nicotine withdrawal for giving him the shakes and making his fingers feel like sausages. He'd driven for the last two hours from Pretoria without saying a single word, the toll road through Mpumalanga slipping by in the darkening evening at one hundred twenty kilometres an hour. He didn't want to get pulled over for speeding with an unconscious boy in the back of the car.

He was feeling more and more isolated the further from Joburg they drove as he worried about the situation he was in. Nwosu had brought his most charming personality with him, chatting away in a friendly, sarcastic manner with Blethin, making a new best friend. Coetzee knew he was being set up and he just had to wait it out. He wound the window up and pushed the gear lever into drive.

Now Leo could hear car klaxons hooting from behind and someone say, "Get a fucking move on Coetzee! You'll have a mob of road-ragers after us if you don't get moving." Nwosu was enjoying the security chief's discomfort. He was in no hurry, biding his time until the right moment came. Then he would execute the Voice's instructions and ensure they wouldn't come looking for him when he went AWOL.

The car pulled away and Leo lay still, assessing his surroundings. He was lying on and under a blanket, obviously in the back of the car. It smelled clean, but there was a faint aroma of petrol fumes. He carefully pulled the blanket from over his head and looked around. It was pitch black, but he worked out that his body was in the boot and his legs were bent back and up around a flat seat. He was wearing a safari shirt and jeans, they fitted him, so probably his own clothes, he figured, but no socks or shoes. He could feel his bare feet against each other. His head was much clearer than the last time he'd been drugged and he wondered what time it was. He felt his wrist. *Good!* They'd replaced his watch. He put it right in front of his eyes, but couldn't see the face. It had to be after five thirty, because he knew it got dark then.

He heard another voice, it was Coetzee, the security man, if that's what he really was. "I'm going to come off the highway in Polokwane. That's about another hour, so we should get there by seven. We can get something to eat then decide if we continue tonight or stay in a motel. I'm not keen on arriving at the Zimbabwe border at midnight."

"Check on the boy, Blethin. He should be awake by now, unless you've killed the poor bastard. You'd better not have. His mother will be well pissed off with you if you do." It was the first man's voice again, laughing softly.

"I've been checking him regularly, Sergeant. I check the pulse on his ankle, since I can't easily reach his wrist. It's called the posterior tibial artery, if you want to know." Leo recognised the doctor's voice with its accent. He pulled the blanket over his head again and lay still. Blethin's fingers pressed against the back of his bare ankle. "He's got a perfectly regular pulse, you'll be happy to learn. I must have given him a bigger dose than I thought though.

I expected him to be awake by now."

"Take the blanket off his face. He'll suffocate if you don't." Blethin had placed the blanket over the boy's head at each poll booth, in case the attendant looked into the car.

Leo lay still as the doctor leaned over the back seat and moved the blanket. His mind was reeling from what he'd overheard. He was on his way to Zimbabwe, which he knew was a vicious dictatorship to the north of South Africa and there was an officer of some kind in the car. *A soldier, or a policeman?* He wondered. Coetzee must be driving and the other man was the fake doctor who'd drugged him. From their voices he knew the first two were definitely South African but the doctor was European. Not English, but with an English way of speaking. What the hell was going on? Where was his mother? *What's happened to her?* Why had these men kidnapped him to take him to Zimbabwe?

He tried to piece together the events of the last few days, struggling to understand the reason for this far-fetched scenario. The incident in the toilet was now clear in his memory. Lambert and Blethin had come over to speak to him as he waited for a free stall. The manager took him by the arms as he spoke to him about the game then Blethin pushed a needle into his upper arm. He was wearing only a tee shirt and the needle went straight into his triceps. Lambert held him as he struggled and the 'doctor' put his hand over his mouth. That was Sunday. He had a vague memory of the nurse waking him up in the hospital room. That must have been yesterday. Then before the last injection, Coetzee had said it was Wednesday morning and since then he'd probably slept for a few hours, so it must be Wednesday evening.

Now he was on the way to Zimbabwe and he had no idea how far it was or why they were taking him. He had to get away from them, get to a police station or a hospital. Some place where they could help him to get back to Johannesburg, back to his mother. *She must be frantic with worry. That's if nothing has happened to her.* But from what the sergeant had said, she was OK. *But where is she? The plane tickets were for today. She couldn't have gone and left me behind.* He felt a surge of anger at these bastards who had interrupted his holiday with her, a fabulous holiday that he knew had cost all her savings.

Strangely, he felt no fear of the men, only anger. They had taken a lot of care to keep him quiet and alive and there was a doctor to make sure he stayed that way. *They haven't even tied my hands or feet,* he realised. *I'm just a school kid who presents no danger to them. Well, we'll see about that. They don't seem to be the best of friends. Arguing all the time. I need to exploit that. Let's see if there's anything useful here.*

It was dark and noisy in the back of the vehicle and he risked moving his left arm to search the space immediately around him. There were some bags and cases between his body and the tailgate door and two jerry cans against the rear wheel arch, which was where the smell of fuel came from. Stretching his arm behind his head he felt along the area between the wheel arch and the second row seat, the one he knew Blethin was in. His hand was obstructed by something on the side panel behind Blethin's seat. He felt around it delicately with his fingers. It was a torch, fastened on clips onto the side panel. Carefully detaching it from the clips he brought his hand back in front of him under the blanket. The torch was quite large and heavy. He hefted it, gauging its use as a potential weapon. *Feels good. Now I'm not just angry. I'm angry and armed.*

He lay quietly and waited for the next stop, preparing his escape plan.

THIRTY-FIVE

Marbella, Spain

Espinoza was studying the list of possible suspects. The problem was that there were only two names on it:

Dr Antoine Constance,

Dr Tony Forrester.

It seemed they were the only people who could have known the circumstances of Leo's birth. They knew that Constance had disappeared from view after leaving the *Clinique Saint Christophe* in Nice and flying to London. Espinoza had contacted the Home Office, but there was no trace of him in the UK. He had vanished and they had no idea of his whereabouts.

Emma had been shocked at Espinoza's theory for the reason behind Leo's abduction. Although she had called her sister out of desperation, she had no idea of the extent of her wealth and that it had to be the motive for the crime. She sat looking at the other two, a dazed expression on her face.

"How could anyone possibly know all these facts? Mutesi's death and Leo's birth, Galaganza's death, our trip to South Africa and Jenny's fortune. There's no one who could have known all of this. It's just not feasible."

"We don't know that, Emma. There are basically three events, or key facts, and what we are looking for is a link between them. This is like any other sequence of events, there are links that lead from one to the next. As a writer you know that however strange the links you invent appear to be, the truth will always be stranger. In this case I think it has to be people; a person who knew one thing happened to meet someone who knew the next fact and so on."

"But why kidnap Leo in the first place? Why didn't they just kidnap me and blackmail Jenny? She's the one with the money. Or they could have blackmailed me with a threat to reveal Leo's illegal birth and I would have been just as desperate to pay for their silence."

"We are dealing with clever people here. This was a much more sophisticated undertaking than a simple kidnapping. They used the knowledge they had to create a double threat to you. Both Leo's life and your continued future together were threatened. Whichever way you turned the only solution was your sister. They knew this, but you didn't. It was an inspired idea to contact her for help."

"You're forgetting another thing, Emma." Jenny interjected. They might know a lot about us, but that can't include our feelings for each other. We've hardly seen each other for years and for all they know I might not have agreed to help you. But by abducting Leo they made sure that I would, however dysfunctional our relationship might be. And you didn't contact me to ask me for money. You had no idea of my situation until today. It confirms Pedro's theory about the combination of factors being known to someone. Somehow they knew I had money and by taking Leo they forced you to ask for my help because you were stranded in South Africa with no one else to turn to."

"My God, they really did their homework. They followed us into an inhospitable place then took my son away and forced me to look for the only solution that was available. I'm so sorry, Jenny. I got you involved in this whole horrible mess because there was no one else I could turn to."

"Let's concentrate on trying to find whoever knew all the facts and was in a position to exploit them with a fairly substantial investment. It's just a business proposition; the reward is potentially large and someone has funded the business accordingly."

"But I have no idea who could tick all those boxes. No idea at all."

After another hour of fruitless discussion, Espinoza said, "I have to get back to Malaga now, but I'll be here first thing in the morning. We must revisit everyone concerned in this business from the beginning. We know the motive now. We just have to work out the sequence of events, to see the plan, the opportunity, the execution. The link is there, hidden from us, but only until we find it."

He was preparing to leave when his mobile rang again. He saw the number on the screen and looked at his watch. "It's my Australian friend from Interpol," he told them. "Hello, Mac. What are you doing up at this time of night? At your age you should be in bed by now." He laughed at the response, then said, "Thanks for getting back so quickly." He took his notebook and pen. "Fire away, I'm listening."

After a few minutes, he looked at the women with a resigned expression. "Thanks, Mac. It's not good news, but thanks anyway. Now get yourself to bed and sleep well."

Espinoza put his phone back in his pocket. "I'm afraid it's bad news. We are down to one suspect!"

"Why? What's happened?" Emma looked at him apprehensively.

"I've just learned that Tony Forrester was killed in an aeroplane accident two years ago in Australia!"

Polokwane, Limpopo, South Africa

"There's a drive-thru McDonalds on the corner of Grimm and Thabo Mbeki. I'm going to pull in there, get some food and we'll talk about what we want to do." As Coetzee announced his decision, Leo felt the car swing off the exit from the N1 onto Pi-6 Main

Route to go through the Southern Gateway on the approach road into Polokwane Central. He had lain without moving for the last hour and was feeling stiff and sore. It was time to make a move. He stretched his body out and gave a loud yawn, waiting for a reaction.

"The kid's awake. Put the light on." Coetzee switched on the interior light and Blethin looked over the back seat. "How you feeling Leo?"

"I'm feeling like shit. What do you think? Where are we?"

"Here, take a drink." Leo grabbed the bottle of water from his hand and swallowed thirstily. His mouth felt as dry as sandpaper.

"How does he look?" It was the sergeant's voice.

"As well as can be expected. No signs of permanent damage that I can see."

Leo noted how they talked about him in the third person. *Just a harmless kid,* he thought. *Just wait.* "I asked where we are."

"We're driving through South Africa. Near Polokwane." Coetzee didn't want to mention Zimbabwe, the kid might go berserk if he knew that was their destination.

"Why the hell are we driving through South Africa? Where's my mother? She was supposed to meet me hours ago. Where is she?"

"There was a misunderstanding, Leo. She left first and we're going to join her. We'll be there shortly." Coetzee wondered how long he could continue with the same bullshit, but he didn't have a choice.

"There's three of you in the car. Who's the other guy?"

"I'm a police officer, Leo. I'm here for your safety and protection. To make sure nothing happens to you until we get you back to your mother." Nwosu put on his most charming and convincing tone. "Don't worry, you're quite safe and everything is under my control."

A police sergeant? Why the hell would a police sergeant be travelling with a couple of crooks who stick needles into people to drug and kidnap them? Leo didn't reply. He knew the men were lying but he just had to bide his time until the right moment.

"Are you hungry?" Blethin asked. "We're going to stop for Big Macs. You want one?"

Leo's juices started flowing at the thought. He was ravenous. "OK. With double cheese, fries and a Coke."

"We'll be there in two minutes. Just take it easy and you can get out and stretch your legs."

The men talked quietly amongst themselves so that he couldn't hear what was being said. He squeezed the torch in his hand.

Marbella, Spain

"Apparently Forrester was with the Flying Doctors for three years then left them to start his own charter airline in Perth."

It had taken Emma a lot of tears and some comforting from her sister to get over the shock of her ex-fiancé's death and now the two women were sitting listening to the rest of Espinoza's news.

"He built up a good operation, with three small jets flying business executives all over the country. It was called *N-Jet,* after his wife's name, Nicole. She was the business manager and handled the administration and ran the office. In July 2008 his own aircraft was lost in a storm in the Indian Ocean on a flight from Perth to Hobart, in Tasmania. There was a co-pilot and a cabin attendant with two passengers on board, both senior executives in a major oil company. So there was an extensive search which went on for weeks but they never found the plane, nor any survivors.

Mac, my Interpol friend, tells me that the Indian Ocean at that point is an unpredictable stretch of water and a light plane coming down there would be quickly destroyed and swept away by the waves and currents. It's also very deep, so it would be impossible to search for victims.

"Nicole Forrester closed down the business a few months later and petitioned the court to declare him dead. This is normal practice after such a high profile accident where the victims are quite clearly deceased. Tony was declared dead six months after the crash." Espinoza sighed deeply. "This news means that his name disappears from our list and we need to seriously look for any other possible suspects." He shook his head at the frustrating news.

"Do you know what happened to Nicole?" Emma asked.

"I have no idea, he didn't say. I suppose she just got through it then started a new life as people do after such a tragedy."

Jenny accompanied him to the door, trying to hide her disappointment. "I suppose there's no question about Tony's death?"

"I'm afraid not. Not just his death, but the four other occupants of the plane as well. In accidents like this, especially where executives of a large corporation are involved there are huge insurance implications, so the search would be well financed and well organised. Mac didn't give me many details, but in such a tragedy there would be no chance of survivors.

"In any case I can't reconcile him or anyone who could remotely be a possible suspect with the opportunity. There is a missing link, so it's still very confusing. But at least I think we've got the motive established, as well as the local perpetrators, so tomorrow we just have to dig deeper." He embraced her. "Good night, Jenny. *Hasta mañana.*"

It was seventy hours since Leo had been taken.

THIRTY-SIX

Polokwane, Limpopo, South Africa

"Feeling any better, Leo? Coetzee had ordered five hamburgers, figuring that the boy could probably eat two. It was eight thirty and he hadn't eaten since breakfast. *Maybe I can curry a little favour with him,* he thought. *I'm going to need it.*

"I'm still feeling like shit. Not hungry any more, but I feel awfully tired." Leo had decided to wait before making a move until after he'd eaten. He remembered what an ex-army officer had said in a survival lecture to his class at Newcastle Royal Grammar School. *Eat whenever you get the chance. It may be the last chance you get.* If he somehow managed to get away it was better to do it on a full stomach. He felt much better, but he wasn't about to show it.

He was sitting on the tailgate of the Land Cruiser eating the last of the fries. The car was parked on the outskirts of the town in a large field of sandy hardpan surrounded by a boxwood hedge. Blethin was sitting alongside him and the other two in the front. It was pitch black outside, the only light coming from the open doors of the vehicle. There was a steady hum of traffic from the nearby highway, but the car was virtually invisible from every side. The engine was running and the heater was on to cut the cool evening air. Coetzee and Nwosu were arguing about whether to find a motel for the night or drive on. Nwosu wanted to continue to Beitbridge, which Leo now knew was on the Zimbabwean border. Coetzee was dead set against it, he didn't trust the Zimbabwe immigration and he obviously didn't trust the policeman. They weren't paying attention to him. It was time to make a move.

He reached behind him and took hold of the torch under the blanket and said to Blethin. "I'm feeling light headed and my thighs are hurting and I've got no sensation in my feet," he said, in a quiet, pained voice.

The doctor got down from the tailgate and took one of Leo's feet in his hands. "Where's the pain in your thighs?" He squeezed the foot. "Can you feel that?"

"No but you'll feel this!" Leo smashed the torch into the side of Blethin's head. The man went down without a sound and lay sprawled on the hardpan. Leo looked back into the car. The other two were still arguing. They'd seen and heard nothing. He climbed quietly down and felt through Blethin's pockets, found his mobile phone and pushed it into his trouser pocket. The doctor was wearing sandals, but they looked to be several sizes too small. He was going to have to run barefoot across the field. From Coetzee's previous remarks he knew they were about two hundred metres north of Grobler Street, the main road leading back to the N1. He'd seen the occasional lights of cars moving along in both directions. If he could reach the road and run a hundred metres to the right, he'd be back where they'd bought the burgers, in a populous part of town where he could find help.

He moved quietly away from the Land Cruiser and stepped into a slow run into the pitch black night. After a few steps he shone the torch beam dimly through his fingers onto the ground. He didn't want to alert Coetzee and Nwosu, but he couldn't afford to injure his bare feet.

London, England

"We've had no news from Nwosu since they set off for Beitbridge this afternoon. He called at one o'clock Johannesburg time to inform me that he had neutralised Lambert, the hotel manager. He watched Coetzee and Blethin leave the hotel with the boy and he was going to meet them imminently at the departure point."

It was seven thirty in the evening in London and the Voice was on the telephone. He had heard nothing from Johannesburg nor Marbella and was feeling a little apprehensive. The operation was entering its most sensitive phase and they couldn't afford anything to go wrong.

"You should call him to see how things are going." Slater sounded uneasy too.

"He's presently driving on the highway with Blethin, Coetzee and the boy. I don't want to cause an unnecessary interruption. It's a long drive and I'm sure the good sergeant will call me just as soon as he is able. I believe patience is the best virtue to employ for the moment."

"Then call him first thing in the morning. Let me know immediately if you hear anything. Do you have the next message ready?"

"I do." The Voice read out a short text, written and read as always in impeccable English grammar. "Are you content with that?"

"I won't be content until we see the funds arrive, but it's OK. Send it first thing tomorrow after you call Nwosu. The sooner she receives it the sooner we can move into the last phase.

The caller rang off and the Voice said, "He sounds more nervous than us."

"He has more to lose than us." His companion took a sip of Sancerre and lit a cigarette. "In fact, exactly five times more. That's a considerable fortune."

"Hmm. You're becoming rather avaricious aren't you? Don't forget that he has financed this whole business. We are simply facilitators, paid to put the pieces together, with no accountability. I rather prefer being low profile. If the reward is less generous, the risk is similarly reduced."

"I think you're underestimating our contribution. No, I mean my contribution."

"Let me explain something to you, since you have no previous experience of this type of arrangement. Being a part of a conspiracy is rather like being a member of a vocal group or a band, or even a football team. It's composed of talented individuals who each imagine that their success depends on only one member, themselves. They don't understand the notion of, '*United we stand, Divided we fall*'. So, they usually decide to go off on their own and, of course, they generally fail miserably. The success comes from being together, not from being apart. You understand?"

"You sound like that talent scout on the 'X Factor'. My point is we shouldn't minimise the value of our services. Just think. I happened to put together a lot of valuable facts and told you about them. You then made the right contacts and set up this whole complicated money-making machine. Without you and me this operation wouldn't have been possible. I think that's worth more than twenty percent."

"Very well. I'll bear your point of view in mind and if the opportunity to enhance our position presents itself, I shall not fail to pursue it. Is that good enough?"

"If that's a yes, then I agree."

Slater thought about the telephone conversation. He decided not to call his partner, he didn't have any good news, or in fact any news at all. He'd wait until the morning.

THIRTY-SEVEN

Polokwane, Limpopo, South Africa

"Jesus Christ!" Coetzee had registered a movement from the corner of his eye. He turned and saw the torchlight as Leo broke into a run across the field. Throwing the car into gear, he turned it and sped towards the main road, headlights full on. Nwosu almost fell out of the vehicle then slammed the passenger door shut. The car raced across the hardpan to cut off the boy's escape angle, leaving a trail of items strewn around behind them from the open tailgate.

The policeman took his Vektor from its holster. "What the hell happened to Blethin? Bunch of useless pricks you managed to hire. Where's that bloody kid, I'll teach him a lesson."

"You'll teach him nothing, Nwosu. Wouldn't you try to escape in his position? He's showing spunk, like he should. And you seem to forget how valuable he is. We'll get him back in the car, that's all."

Leo looked behind him as the headlights caught him up, casting a long shadow on the ground ahead. He tried to make a turn to the right to get outside of Coetzee's flanking approach. "Ouch!" He started hopping. Something, a sharp stone or thorn had penetrated the sole of his foot. "Shit!" He staggered forward and dropped the torch then fell clumsily, holding his injured foot, helplessly watching the car's approach.

Nwosu jumped out and hauled Leo to his feet. "You'll fucking dead if you try that again." He waved the pistol in his face.

"Oh, you think so?" Leo grabbed him by the upper arms. The policeman was two inches shorter than him. He took his head back and butted him hard in the nose. There was a satisfying crunch of cartilage as the sergeant fell away with a cry, instinctively putting both hands to his face. Leo wrested the Vektor from his right hand and pushed him back. "Now who's going to be fucking dead?" He pointed the gun at Nwosu's head.

"Calm down, Leo. Let me have the gun" Coetzee came round the vehicle, his own M9 Beretta pistol in his hand. He had watched the scene in the car headlights, relishing the sight of Nwosu's mauling at the hands of a schoolboy. And he was delighted to see the policeman disarmed. *He's done half my job for me,* he thought. Now he had to make sure the kid didn't do anything dangerous with the weapon.

"I'll shoot the bastard if you come any closer." Leo said, waving the pistol between the two men. "Get away from the car. I'm taking it so just stay out of my way."

"I don't think so, Leo." Coetzee dangled the keys in his hand. "First, you're not the type to shoot anyone. Second, you've got a bleeding foot and no shoes and third, I doubt you could drive this monster. You may have managed to rearrange the sergeant's face, but you're not even old enough to have a driver's licence. Now give me that pistol, it's loaded."

"I'll take my own fucking gun. And then I'll blow away your balls, you vicious little prick." Nwosu pushed Leo over onto his damaged foot and made to grab the Vektor from his hand. Off balance, Leo tried to pull the gun away and there was a sharp crack as the double action trigger mechanism was released in the struggle. Nwosu screamed and fell to the ground, holding his left shoulder, an agonised expression on his face.

Leo dropped the gun as if it was red hot. He stood stock still, staring at the policeman on the ground, blood soaking through his shirt, his mind trying to register what had just happened. *I've just shot a police sergeant,* he realised. *Holy shit! I'll end up in prison in South Africa. What the hell have I done?* Aloud, he said, "I'm sorry. It was an accident. I didn't mean the gun to go off. I've never shot a gun in my life."

Nwosu said nothing. He was in too much pain to utter any more obscenities. He was holding his bleeding shoulder and groaning in agony. He knew the bone was smashed, he could feel it moving in his hand and his nose felt like it had been set on fire.

Coetzee bent down and picked up the Vektor. "That wasn't smart, Leo," he said. "Shooting cops never is." His mind was working overtime, trying to weigh up the situation. "Here, help me get him into the back of the car."

Between them they helped Nwosu into the open back of the Land Cruiser. Coetzee put the other seat flat to make enough room for the policeman to lie in a semi-foetal position, his shoulder on the folded blanket. He took a whisky flask from the glove compartment and poured out a stiff dose which Nwosu gulped down, still not speaking, just moaning in pain. Leo was silent too. He was trying to sort out in his mind everything that had happened over the last few days. Trying to reconcile what he had done to Blethin and Nwosu with what had been done to him. He was terrified at the thought of what might happen to him next.

Coetzee cut away the policeman's shirt with his knife. The shoulder was a mess. It looked to him like the bullet had gone right through the flesh and out the back. It had probably damaged the muscle and the tendons, but there was no sign of any broken bones and no intense arterial bleeding. "Can you lift your arm?" He asked.

Nwosu tried to raise his arm but gave a gasp of pain and dropped it again. "There's something broken. I can't lift it. The muscles won't work. That little shit! We should never have got involved in this game. It's not worth any amount of money. Just kill the bastard and let's get out of here."

"Shut up, you idiot. You'll frighten the kid. He's still a valuable commodity, so just shut your mouth."

They've kidnapped me for money. Why do they think we've got money? My mother's spent everything on this holiday. I know she's broke.

Coetzee opened up Blethin's medical bag and cleaned the wound with disinfectant, enjoying Nwosu's reaction to the sharp liquid. Like most bullies in authority, the policeman was a coward at heart. He padded some cotton gauze around the wound and bound it up around the arm and shoulder to support it, quietly considering the situation. *He won't be shooting anyone any time soon,* he thought. *And I've got Leo. He doesn't know it but he's just done me a great favour. He's the asset and I've got him and Nwosu's neutralised.* He finished the bandaging. "You're lucky, Jonathon. A bit of sticky tape and a sling and you'll be as right as rain."

He cleaned Leo's cut foot and bandaged it up too so he could walk without pain. They got into the vehicle and he drove slowly back across the field with the headlights on, picking up the torch and as much as they could of the stuff that had fallen out the tailgate. Fortunately the two jerry cans had been too heavy to fall out. He had a feeling he would need that extra gasoline the way things were going.

They made their way back to Blethin, who was still lying motionless on the ground where they'd left him. Coetzee climbed down to examine the doctor, feeling the pulse in his neck and opening his eyes. He looked closely at the side of his head, just above the ear. Leo was too frightened to get out of the vehicle. He sat silently, waiting for the security chief to return.

He came slowly back to the open window. "We've got a problem, Leo. Blethin's copped it. You smashed the side of his head in. What did you hit him with?"

Leo gasped. He felt as though Coetzee had pronounced a verdict of murder on him. "With that torch I found in the back. But I never meant to kill him. I just wanted to knock him down so I could get away. What's going on, Mr Coetzee? Why are you people holding me like this? What's happened to my mother? Where is she?" At this last plea, Leo started crying, a soft little boy's cry from deep inside him, tears running down his face. "What's happened to my mum?" He asked again in a strangled voice.

Coetzee didn't reply, just opened the tailgate again to check on Nwosu. He was lying groaning and nursing his shoulder, the blood from his nose making a ghastly mask across his face in the dim light. The nose was bent sideways, giving him a crazed look.

"You have to get me to a hospital. My nose is killing me and my fucking shoulder is busted to pieces. I need a doctor." Nwosu's voice came out with a nasal whine. It was no longer arrogant or charming. He sounded weak and exhausted from fighting the pain.

He rummaged in the medical bag. "Here, chew these." Handing the sergeant two five hundred milligram paracetamol tablets and the flask of whisky. "Take a swig to wash them down. Then shut up. I'll get you somewhere safe as soon as I work out what to do next." He leaned over and found the policeman's mobile and pushed it into his shirt pocket. "You won't be needing this for now." He slammed the tailgate shut again and climbed back into the cab alongside Leo.

"Please tell me what's going on, Mr Coetzee. Has something happened to my mom?" Leo asked in an anguished voice.

"Let me think for a minute, Leo. Your mom's fine and I promise you nothing bad will happen, but things have changed and I need to think this through. Just sit and be quiet for a while." Coetzee sat in the driver's seat, trying to work out a plan of action. It was difficult to concentrate over Leo's sobbing and the pained moans from Nwosu.

THIRTY-EIGHT

Polokwane, Limpopo, South Africa

Coetzee was examining Nwosu's phone. His suspicious mind wondered who he had been calling and when. Leo was lying back in the passenger seat in a deep sleep, snoring gently with his mouth slightly open. There was no sound from Nwosu in the back. *He's probably finished the whiskey and passed out. In any case, he's no threat. At least not for the moment.*

He knew the password, it was twelve zero nine, his boyfriend Jamie's birth date. It had been easy enough to notice and remember. The mobile lit up and he looked up the call register. The last outgoing call was at five past one that afternoon to a city code he'd never heard of, 32 2. He couldn't know that it was a number in Brussels, Belgium, which, via the miracle of modern telecommunications ended up as a 44 207 number in London. *That was just about when Nwosu was coming to meet us for the trip.* Not wishing to cause even more problems than they already had, he decided not to recall the number but it provoked his curiosity.

He went through the phone agenda and found '*Recordings*'. Knowing the sergeant's paranoia was second only to his own, he was sure to have recorded his calls, or at least those that might provide food for blackmail.

The call at 13.05 wasn't on the list. The last recorded conversation was at six-thirty on Tuesday evening, an incoming call from a '*not possible*' number. *The night before they told us about Beitbridge,* he registered. He walked away from the car and listened to the recording.

Marbella, Spain

Jenny and Emma were sitting in the kitchen. Encarni and Espinoza had both left and the women had the house to themselves. Emma was looking dejected and miserable.

Jenny tried to deflect her sister's thoughts. "I don't know about you, but I'm shattered and starving. Let's see what we've got for supper." She went to open the fridge door just as the telephone rang.

"Jenny? I'm glad you're at home. I was worried there'd be nobody there."

"Leticia? Where are you calling from?" Jenny put her hand over the mouthpiece and whispered to her sister, "It's my co-owner, Leticia."

"I'm still in Nice with Emilio, but Patrice had to go back to Marbella on Monday for an important transaction at the bank, so we're coming home in the morning. I hope you don't mind."

"That's alright, but you should know that my sister is staying for a while. She just arrived yesterday, quite unexpectedly."

"Emma's there? That's nice for you, but are you sure I should come? I don't want to spoil the party."

"Don't be silly, it's about time you two met. You'll like her. When are you arriving?"

"We'll get into Malaga at twelve-thirty so I should be home before two in the afternoon. You're certain I won't be in the way?"

"Not at all. And I can't wait to see Emilio again. As a matter of fact, Sam's also coming for lunch, so we can all get to know each other. I'll send Juan to pick you up. See you tomorrow."

She put the phone down and sat beside her sister. "You'll have noticed I don't try to speak to Leticia in Spanish. Her English is almost better than mine now. Thanks to Charlie, she's quite fluent. She's very clever and easy to get along with."

"How do we prevent her from finding out what's going on with Leo? I don't think I'm up to pretending everything's alright at the moment."

"You're going to have to, because we can't risk anyone suspecting something's wrong. We have to behave normally, as if everything's fine. We'll manage, don't worry. And she won't be with us all the time, she'll be in her own apartment. Last year we converted the other end of the house for her and Emilio. They need their space and they don't want to spend every waking moment with Auntie Jenny. She usually prepares her son's meals there and it works out very well. In any case she's very discreet and always in a good mood. And Emilio is adorable and really funny. He's destined to become a stand-up comedian. I'm sure it will do us both good to have them around. Now, what about supper?"

"I couldn't eat anything now. I'm going to have an early night if you don't mind. I feel exhausted and I need a good night's sleep."

"Right. I'll make you a hot drink and you're going to take one of my sleeping pills. You'll get six or eight hours of complete rest and you'll be ready for anything in the morning. No arguments." She sent her sister up to her bedroom and put on the kettle. *It's good having family around,* she mused. *Even in these circumstances.*

Polokwane, Limpopo, South Africa

Coetzee listened to the five minute recording twice. The second time he put the volume up to maximum. When he heard the second person whispering in the background he replayed the part several times until he was sure he'd heard correctly. *It's definitely a woman,* he thought to himself. *Don't tell me this whole business is being run by a woman?* He switched off the phone and stood quietly thinking for several minutes. Then he went back to the car and gently shook Leo awake.

The recent memories flooded back into the boy's mind. "What is it? What are you going to do? Please just let me go, I promise I'll say nothing. Let me call my mother and somehow we'll get out of his shitty country. Please let me go."

"I'm going to get you out, but we have some cleaning up to do first. Come on, give me a hand."

They climbed down from the Land Cruiser and went over to Blethin's body. Leo was shaking with fear. He'd never seen a dead person before and this man was dead because of him. He was terrified.

Coetzee started emptying the doctor's pockets. "We can't leave anything which might identify him. It'll take them at least a day to do it with DNA, so we'll have time to make a head start." He found his wallet with a passport inside. It was French, in the name of Ernest Blethin. *That explains the accent,* he realised. He passed everything to Leo then turned the body over and completed the search. "Funny. His mobile is missing. He must have had a phone on him."

Leo's heart was in his mouth. He'd forgotten he had Blethin's phone in his pocket. "I stole it from him," he blurted out. "I've still got it. Here."

"Good, one less problem to worry about. Although we don't know the password, so we can't check on who he's been calling." He spoke in a conspiratorial tone, as if confiding in Leo. He needed to get along with him until he decided what to do next. "Shove it in the glove compartment with the other stuff."

Leo opened the passenger door and reached across to the driver's side. He pressed the button and the compartment door sprang open. Coetzee was still kneeling beside Blethin. He pushed in the wallet and other items then banged the door closed again, slipped the phone back in his pocket and went back to the dead body.

"Help me sit him up. I'm moving him to a less obvious place." Leo gingerly took the dead man's arm and they pulled him to a sitting position. Coetzee picked him up and threw him over his shoulder as if he weighed nothing. He carried the corpse over to the edge of the field and laid it under the bordering hedge. Gathered some branches and shrubs and threw them over the body.

Leo went back to the front of the car, trembling at the thought of the dead doctor lying alone under a hedge in the middle of nowhere, dead by his hand. He climbed into the passenger seat and took Blethin's phone from his pocket. It was an old Nokia shell phone. He pressed the 'On' switch and it lit up, no password required. The battery was down to one cell. He didn't try to make a call, there was no time. He went to Messages, entered his mother's mobile number, quickly typed a few words, his fingers still shaking from the emotion, and pressed Send. He put the phone in the glove compartment and turned as he heard Coetzee open the tailgate and shake the sergeant awake.

"Are we at the hospital?" Nwosu's breath stunk of whisky and his voice was slurred. "I thought you were taking me to the hospital. I'm badly injured, I need urgent attention. You know the penalty for wounding a policeman. If you get me to the hospital I'll forget the whole thing. You and the kid just disappear and that's the end of it. " Although his mind was dulled by the booze, Nwosu could still spin a convincing yarn.

"So I disappear without a penny and you and Jamie piss off with another hundred grand, eh?"

Nwosu blinked his eyes rapidly. *How did Coetzee know that?*

"You should be more careful when you record conversations, Nwosu. Agreeing to murder three people might not be considered ethically acceptable in some quarters, even in Joburg. The penalty could be even worse than wounding a homosexual psychopath dressed in a cop's uniform."

"I don't know what the f ..."

"No? I suppose you're going to deny calling them back just before we left? Bullshit! It was probably to confirm that poor old Lambert was a goner. One down, two to go, right? And your clever plan got fucked up by the fifteen year old kid you were supposed to be hijacking. Ironic doesn't do it justice." He spat on the ground. "You're a piece of filth, you depraved maniac." Coetzee didn't mention his other discovery, that the second voice was a woman's. Nwosu seemed unaware of it and right now knowledge was power. Or at least it might be.

Leo was in a state of shock. Nwosu had killed Lambert and had agreed to kill Coetzee and Blethin. *He's a policeman and he's a murderer.* He shivered with fear. *What the hell is going on here? Who's organising all this?*

And why? What's going to happen to me?

"Get out the car!" Coetzee continued, his Beretta in his hand.

Nwosu sat up slowly, holding his bandaged shoulder. "You have to take me somewhere to get treatment, you can't just leave me here. I could die of exposure or get mugged or attacked by animals. You owe it to me to get me to a hospital or a doctor. We're partners."

"Partners!" Coetzee laughed mirthlessly. "Partners are people who work together and help each other, not plot to murder each other as soon as they turn their back. Just consider yourself lucky I'm not as pathologically motivated to kill as you are. Get out the car." He grabbed the sergeant's legs and swung them over the tailboard. "On your feet and walk!"

Nwosu stepped clumsily down onto the hardpan, swaying dizzily from the pain of his shoulder and the effects of the whisky. "Give me my phone. You can't leave me with no gun and no phone. This is a dangerous place. You don't want to be responsible for leaving me with nothing that can help me. I'm begging you to leave me my phone, Marius. "

"I'm leaving you with your life, Nwosu. It's more than you'd have done for me. Now piss off before I change my mind." He slammed the tailboard shut and got into the driver's seat. "Come on Leo. Our police escort has been dismissed."

Leo sat back in the passenger seat, thinking about what had happened in the last hour. Thinking about what he'd done. He didn't dare say anything in case Coetzee saw how terrified he was. *I have to stay alert. My mother will have seen the message. She'll be taking action. I need to be ready to escape if I get the chance.* He fastened his seat belt and tried to show no emotion.

Leaving Sergeant Nwosu standing in the middle of the hardpan, Coetzee started up the Land Cruiser and headed back to Grobler Street. He had a plan. Now he had to execute it.

It was seventy-two and a half hours since Leo had been taken.

DAY FIVE

THURSDAY, JULY 15, 2010

THIRTY-NINE

Malaga, Spain

It was seven am and Espinoza was reading the South African Broadcasting Corporation online news page. One of the headlines caught his attention;

'Hotel Manager in Suspicious Fall from 7th Floor'.

The article related how Barry Lambert, an Englishman, who had been manager of the Packard Hotel in Johannesburg for only two months had been found dead in the car park after apparently falling from a seventh floor balcony. An enquiry had been opened into the death, under the direction of the Johannesburg Central Police Station.

His mind went back to an affair he'd been involved with almost twenty years before, in 1992. A suspect in a Malaga murder he was investigating, a black South African, had managed to flee to Johannesburg to escape justice. Unfortunately for the man, he was wrongly identified at immigration as an anti-apartheid terrorist and was imprisoned in the police station building. At the time it was named 'John Vorster Square' and was the Headquarters of the infamous South African Security Branch, where countless innocent people were held and tortured and afterwards died in custody. Espinoza didn't know what had become of the man, he had never heard anything more about him. Subsequent enquiries proved that he couldn't have committed the murder, but by then it was too late.

He snapped out of his reverie, printed out the news page, kissed Soledad goodbye and went out to his car for the drive to Marbella. It was a sunny morning and he decided to take the Autopista del Sol, the pay road, where there was always less traffic. The reason was simple; it was far too expensive; the toll fare was over seven Euros for the thirty kilometre stretch between Mijas and Marbella.

The news article worried him. If Lambert had been killed by the conspirators, which seemed more than likely, it meant two things. Firstly, they had no compunction in killing anyone who might be considered a weak link or a source of danger. Secondly, they were already cleaning up behind them, which might signal a change or an acceleration of their plan. Although he was still convinced that Leo was in no danger until some financial negotiation had occurred, he knew that Emma would not have the same attitude. It was going to be a difficult morning.

Then another thought occurred to him. He pulled off to the side at the Calahonda toll station and made several phone calls. Fifteen minutes later he continued on to Marbella, a plan forming in his mind.

Polokwane, Limpopo, South Africa

Blethin's body was found at seven-thirty by a labourer crossing the field from Grobler Street to the farm where he worked. The corpse was lying under the hedge where he stopped to relieve himself. The body had been badly savaged about the head by some creature, probably a large rodent. Most of the lips, nose and ears were missing, the throat had been ripped out and the eyes were just black holes. The man vomited at the horrific sight then ran to the farm and delivered the news in a hysterical panic. Human nature being what it is, his employer went to look for himself. He too spewed up then ran back to dial the emergency number with trembling fingers.

By eight-fifteen the police had ascertained that the deceased had been killed by a blow to the head. Blood and tyre tracks were found on the sandy hardpan about fifty metres away. A quickly organised search showed up signs of a struggle and more blood nearer to Grobler Street. No papers or identification of any kind were found on the body and without a recognisable face it was likely that identification would be difficult and time consuming. The corpse was taken by ambulance to one of the morgues in Polokwane Central. By ten o' clock the mysterious death in Polokwane was a headline in the online news reports.

Phalaborwa, Limpopo, South Africa

"How you feeling, Leo?"

"Much better, Mr Coetzee." Last night he had lain awake for hours, reliving the events in Polokwane, unable to get the sight of Blethin's dead body, lying under the hedge, out of his mind. Wondering what would happen to him, how he would get out of this nightmare and back to his mother. Finally he fell into an exhausted sleep until Coetzee woke him at eight and he was now devouring a breakfast of pastries and fruit. His foot wasn't hurting and he'd placed a band aid over the small cut.

"It'll be easier if you call me Marius, or just Coetzee if you like. Nobody calls me Mr Coetzee, OK?"

"OK, I'll call you Marius. Why did you kidnap me, Marius?"

They were having breakfast on the terrace of the Riverside Self-Catering Safari House that Coetzee had booked in the Olifantsrivier Lodge, about twelve kilometres south of Phalaborwa. It had taken him just under three hours the previous night to drive there from Polokwane. The lodge was the largest place around, with accommodation for over two hundred guests. He had stayed there several times and knew they'd have space available when he'd called from the car. It was costing him over a hundred Euros per night for the two bedroom house but he figured they could go unnoticed in a place that size. In any event he wasn't counting on staying long. He had other plans.

Leo was mesmerised by the surrounding panoply of tropical bush, water features and wild life. The house was situated on the Olifantsrivier, a majestic waterway on the western edge of the Kruger Park, about fifty metres from a massive lake, created by a cleverly constructed wooden dam. He could see two other buildings around the curve of the river, but there was no sign of human life anywhere. The area around the lodge was effectively a bird sanctuary for hundreds of brightly coloured winged creatures, swooping and hovering over the water and calling from the leafy branches of the dense groups of trees on the banks of the lake. Some of the less timid birds flew down to the terrace and tried to steal food from the table. He threw some bread on the ground for a couple of red-breasted birds with blue heads and tails, more beautiful than he had imagined a bird could be.

"Those are called Southern Carmine Bee-eaters. They come down from Zimbabwe at this time of year." Coetzee put on a friendly and relaxed tone, which didn't reflect how he was feeling.

Despite it being winter time, the temperature was a balmy twenty-five degrees under a cloudless, clear blue sky. Leo was having a hard time reconciling his enjoyment of the location and the weather with his present predicament. His attention was caught by a family of black faced monkeys playing in the branches of an immense tree, at least twenty metres high, the pinkish-brown leaves being reflected by the morning sun.

Again, Coetzee observed his gaze. "It's a Jackalberry tree and they're called Vervet Monkeys. You'll find them all over the Cape. You want to watch out. They'll bite your hand off if you get too friendly."

After installing Leo in one of the bedrooms, Coetzee had grabbed a whisky from the mini bar and sat out on the terrace. It was well past midnight, but after the stress of the day he needed to relax and clear his mind. He lit a cheroot, switched on his Kindle and pulled up Emma's story, *An Extravagant Death*. It was two thirty and two whiskeys later before he went to bed, fascinated by her inventive narrative and already feeling a bond with the two detectives, *Angus Skelton* and *Tory West*. They argued and bickered like an old married couple, somehow managing to stumble onto clues, motives and clever deductions, seemingly by pure chance. He enjoyed the banter and the witty repartee. *Typically British*, he thought. *Inimitable*. They were actually falling in love with each other and just didn't realise it. It reminded him of the early years of his marriage. But then Karen had fallen out of love with him and he hadn't realised that until too late.

He had gone to bed in a maudlin mood, the whisky, lack of nicotine and the day's traumatic events taking their toll. But Coetzee was a military man. Military men didn't suffer from broken hearts. He had now slept for six hours and was fully focused on the problem in hand. He had to win Leo's confidence to get out of this mess, not just alive, but in good shape and able to start again. And that meant money. He needed money and he knew the deal with the Voice was now down the pan. In any case he was never going to put Leo's life in danger again. He had some cards in his hand and he had to play them well, better than he'd ever done, otherwise it would all have been in vain. Lambert, Blethin, Nwosu, Leo; it was a recipe for life incarceration. He was in deep shit and only money would get him out of it.

Now, he responded to Leo's question. "I did it for money, Leo. Just for money. No other reason. I didn't know you or your mother, it was just a job. I got paid and I helped to organise your abduction and get you to the safe house on the promise of more money and that's all. I will never hurt you or your mother, believe me. I don't even know why you've been abducted. It's all being manipulated from a distance by people I've never even met. I know it's not much compensation but I'm sorry for what I did. I swear I would never have let you get hurt.

He looked straight at Leo, trying to gain his confidence. "Just think. Now that I've taken you out of their clutches, my chance of getting another penny from them is zilch. On the contrary, they'll try to get it back out of my skin, so I've thrown away a chance of being paid and put myself in harm's way by helping you."

"Well Marius, if you did it only for money, I've got really bad news for you. We're skint! My mum spent all her savings on this holiday and I've got about thirty quid in my savings account. Will that do?" He tore up a bread roll and threw some more pieces for the birds. "And while we're at it, why don't you tell me where my mum is? You've been lying to me for two days now. What's happened to her? Where is she?"

Coetzee lit up a cheroot and blew the smoke away from the table. "I told you part of the truth. Your mum is fine, nothing's happened to her and nothing is going to happen to her."

"So why can't I see her?"

"Your mother has left South Africa, Leo. She became very frightened and managed to get away. And I don't blame her. Between you and me, her life was worth much less than yours. You're valuable, therefore safe, but she wasn't. Simple mathematics. There are some dangerous people involved in this game. Sergeant Nwosu was only one of them."

Leo thought about Coetzee's reply for several moments. *He must be lying. My Mom would never leave me behind in a foreign country.* "When did she leave?" He asked.

"On Tuesday afternoon. One of the cleverest escapes I've seen. She had everybody fooled. You'd have been proud of her."

Leo was taken aback. "She's at home in England?"

Coetzee was careful not to give too much away. "I'm not sure where she is, but she's out of danger, I promise you that."

"Where did she get the money to buy another ticket? I know she didn't have any."

"I have absolutely no idea. I have my suspicions, but I honestly don't know."

Leo decided he'd find out nothing further about his mother. If Coetzee knew, he wasn't telling for now, he'd have to bide his time. He changed tack. "So what's the point of kidnapping me if we've got no money? It kind of defeats the purpose doesn't it?"

"You're forgetting about your father. Your mother refused to say anything about him, so he has to be the one with the money. It's the only explanation that makes sense." Leo looked at him incredulously as he continued, "Anyway, I know there's money about somewhere. A lot of it. And I don't really care who's got it."

"So you kidnapped me without even knowing who had the money to pay a ransom? Pretty dumb move, don't you think?"

Coetzee took another drag and moved uncomfortably on his seat. *This kid is really smart.* Aloud, he said, "It wasn't me who planned this abduction. I was just a facilitator, a helping hand. I told you, I don't know who's behind it, but they're ruthless people and now it's gone too far and I'm out. It's not what I signed up for."

"So this is your way of getting out, to abduct me again?"

"You've got it all wrong, son. The way I look at it, I've rescued you. I've saved your ass. Look where you are. You're in a safari park, costing a fortune a night, free as one of those birds, within reason, and I'll make sure you get safely home when this is over."

"When what's over? I thought you said you've saved my ass. I've got no money, no shoes, no passport and no air ticket and I don't know where we are. I may even be wanted for murder. 'Free as a bird' I don't think. What's the plan now?"

"I'm talking about a reward, Leo. A very reasonable reward that I've earned." Coetzee dumped the end of his cheroot and tried to find the right words. "The kidnappers must have been after millions of dollars ransom money. I know this because of the costs of the operation. It was a very expensive job, so they'd be expecting a big return on their investment. Now I've got you out of their control I'll make sure that you get home safely just as soon as I see a reward for my intervention."

"But I keep telling you we've got no money. And my father, whoever he was, I doubt he even knows about me, never mind throwing away money that you're guessing he's got just to save my ass."

The security chief moved nervously again. This was all pure conjecture. He had no idea who had the money in this business, but he knew there had to be someone, someone very wealthy. "Leo, for Christ's sake stop arguing! I'm offering to return you safely for a small reward. You and your mother should be happy about that. I'll look after you and deliver you without harm for a fraction of the ransom that the perpetrators would be demanding. It's a good deal for everyone."

Leo was frightened and worried. He'd sent a message to his mother at about nine thirty last night. Twelve hours ago. Now he was no longer in Polokwane and he had no idea where she was. He knew she must be crazy with worry and he had no way of contacting her. With all the luck in the world he wouldn't last long on his own outside the lodge. This was a tough and violent country and they seemed to be in the middle of a massive jungle, *probably the Kruger,* he imagined. His only chance of escaping was by finding out where he was and getting a message to someone, so they could contact his mother. He was trying to put out of his mind that he'd committed murder and assaulted and shot a police sergeant. He couldn't make a move without the risk of being arrested.

Maybe she's answered my text. It's the only contact she's got. I have to get hold of Blethin's mobile again. He sat looking out at the river and said nothing more.

FORTY

Diepkloof, Gauteng, South Africa

Sergeant Nwosu was sitting at a table in his boyfriend's flat. He was working on his laptop. His shoulder was still aching and painful but Jamie had examined it and declared it was unbroken and would fix itself, given time and rest. He worked as a trainee nurse at the Lesedi Private Hospital, near Diepkloof, so his diagnosis comforted the policeman. After dressing the wound properly he had put a sling around the wrist to take the weight off the shoulder. Nwosu's nose wasn't broken, just badly bruised and he had a magnificent black eye to go with it. After another paracetamol he was feeling more comfortable but still harbouring homicidal thoughts about Coetzee and Leo as he opened up his laptop.

He had been neither as drunk nor as dozy as he had appeared the previous night and had watched as Coetzee carried Blethin's body across the field. He didn't know how the doctor had died but he couldn't risk being found with a wounded shoulder near an unidentified corpse in Polokwane, three hundred kilometres from his station. After watching the Land Cruiser drive off into the darkness he had managed to make it across the field to Grobler Street without incident. At the beginning of the urbanised area he passed a public drinking fountain and washed the blood from his face.

Further along the road he came to the Southern Star Motel, 'Open for Business'. He managed to remove the remains of his shirt, and draping it over his shoulder to hide the bandage he walked into the reception in his T-shirt and asked for a room. Any suspicions the night clerk might have had about a lone visitor at ten o'clock at night with a bloody nose, no luggage, no car and wearing a T-shirt and sunglasses were dispelled by the sight of five hundred Rand, in notes, on the counter. Nwosu entered cabin twenty, the furthest away from the office, picked up the phone and called a Johannesburg number.

He slept for a couple of hours while waiting for Jamie to drive from Diepkloof to pick him up then napped during the trip back. They arrived at the flat at four in the morning and he managed to get a few more hours sleep. He was feeling a lot better and his mind was working fast. The Voice mustn't know he'd lost Leo. He had to get him back and claim the big money. They were ruthless people and he was afraid of them, they had ordered the deaths of Lambert, Blethin and Coetzee without a qualm. He couldn't afford to let them down or he'd be on the same list, if he wasn't already.

Nwosu needed to reassure himself and went to his online banking link. He was relieved to see the same balance on his account. One more payment and he was on his way. This was his chance to get out of South Africa and he wasn't going to let it slip by. Coetzee was clever but too sentimental and he had to play on that. He went back through his conversations with the security man to recall exactly what he had told him.

He took a swig of coffee and concentrated on his laptop. Jamie had gone to work as usual to avoid suspicion so he was on his own in the apartment. He laboriously typed in names and places with just his right hand and googled them. It would take a while, but he would find what he was looking for in the end. Then, payback time!

Marbella, Spain

Espinoza and the two women were in the office at York House. His instinct had been right. Emma didn't take the news about Lambert's death very well.

"Why has he been killed? You keep saying you don't believe in coincidences and in this case I'm sure you're right. It must be murder and it must be Coetzee and Nwosu who are responsible. What's going to become of Leo now?" She sat with her head in her hands.

"Emma, please listen to me carefully." Espinoza put on his most convincing tone. "I know it doesn't seem like it to you for the moment, but this development is very beneficial to our investigation." Both women looked blankly at him. "There is now a criminal enquiry into a murder which has nothing to do with Leo's abduction. In other words, we know about the connection, but the Johannesburg police don't, so we can take advantage of that. Let me explain.

"This morning I spoke to a Chief Superintendent Hendricks, he's Head of the Homicide Division in the Johannesburg Central Police Station. I was introduced by an old colleague in Interpol. I told him that Lambert was involved with a criminal gang I'm investigating and I'd like to come down and consult with them in their enquiry. He agreed to meet me since it might throw up something which could help their investigation."

"You mean you want to go to Johannesburg?"

"Yes, Jenny. I don't think I can accomplish anything more here and you can probably achieve just as much. It makes more sense for us to split up. I'll go where the crimes were actually committed and take advantage of the enquiry into Lambert's murder to try to follow Leo's traces. You stay here with Emma and monitor the communications with the abductors. There's bound to be a lot of chatter now. Things are heating up, so they'll be moving into the last phase, the negotiations phase. And people and facts might emerge that point us to the link between the key events. I think you'll be better than me at that particular job."

"But we agreed not to involve the police. Not to risk revealing Leo's background." Emma looked anxiously from one to the other, her fear confusing her logic.

"I don't need to tell them anything about Leo. I'm simply helping them with a murder enquiry. This way we don't have to advertise his abduction and there's no chance of his background coming out. It's an excellent camouflage. And I don't see any other way of making further progress."

"Pedro's right. It's a clever idea. He can use the police resources to investigate Leo's disappearance while helping them to find Lambert's killers. Don't forget that if we find Coetzee and Nwosu, then we'll find Leo."

"And what happens when you find them? Leo's story will come out and the police might take some action."

"Leave that to me. I'm sure the perpetrators won't want to have child abduction added to their list of crimes and the Johannesburg police will be happy to solve the murder. I'll get Leo away without any further enquiry, I promise you."

He consulted his notebook. "We need to decide on this plan right away, so I've already checked the flight possibilities. The quickest flight to Johannesburg is with SAA/Lufthansa at five ten this afternoon. It goes via Frankfurt to Joburg and gets in at ten thirty tomorrow morning. May I request tickets and a travel budget, Jenny?"

Phalaborwa, Limpopo, South Africa

"I have to make a call." It was almost nine thirty and Coetzee was expecting the Voice's usual morning call on Nwosu's phone. He couldn't risk Leo hearing the conversation. It would give the whole game away. "Just stay on the terrace and look at the wild life for five minutes. I'll be in the car, in front of the lodge. Don't do anything silly."

"There's not a lot I can do, Marius. Even though I'm apparently as free as a bird, I doubt I'd be able to fly very far at the moment."

Coetzee nodded absently and went through the lodge to the Land Cruiser in front. It was nine thirty precisely and the mobile rang the moment he climbed into the car.

"Good morning, Coetzee here."

There was a pause, then the slightly distorted voice said, "Mr Coetzee, it's a pleasure to speak to you. Are you safely in Beitbridge?"

"No, not yet. We had a terrible journey yesterday with traffic delays and accidents, so we spent the night in Polokwane. We'll be continuing on as soon as Sergeant Nwosu gets back."

"The sergeant is not with you?"

"He went off with Doctor Blethin before light. Said he had some business to attend to. He left his phone so I could take your call. I expect he'll be back shortly."

Another pause, then, "How is the boy?"

"He's perfectly fine and eating well. Don't worry about him, he's as strong as a horse."

"How long do you estimate it will take you to reach Beitbridge? How far is it?"

"A bit over two hundred Ks, so we should make it in three to four hours, barring accidents. We should be there by mid-afternoon if Nwosu doesn't keep us waiting. Do you want us to call when we arrive?"

"Very well. Please ask the sergeant to call me when you have crossed the border."

"I didn't know he had your number?" Coetzee smiled at this slip-up. The Voice wasn't quite as clever as he thought he was.

"Of course. How foolish of me. Tell him I will call back at three pm, expecting that you'll have finally arrived at your destination. Travel safely." He rang off.

Coetzee walked back through the lodge to the terrace. Leo was still watching the monkeys. *So far, so good, he thought.*

Diepkloof, Gauteng, South Africa

"That's it!" Sergeant Nwosu banged his good hand on the desk in triumph. He'd been trawling telephone directories for over an hour, but it was his access to old police files that had finally provided the breakthrough. He pulled up a map of the town and found the street name. There were five houses on the street, on the outskirts in open countryside. The one he wanted looked like a farmhouse. With no neighbours. *Perfect.*

He printed out the names and address and the map of the area. It was a place he'd never visited, about eighty kilometres from Diepkloof, a small farming town to the east of Joburg. An easy hour's drive if the traffic wasn't as bad as yesterday. If he had any difficulty locating the property in the dark the SatNav would resolve that problem. *The wonders of modern technology,* he reflected, then went to prepare some lunch for his boyfriend. Jamie would bring back the spare Vektor with some belongings from his apartment and buy a new prepaid mobile for him. It wasn't the time to leave unnecessary tracks. Taken several paracetamol tablets and his shoulder was causing him much less pain. *I'll be able to drive by this evening.* Things were looking up.

Marbella, Spain

"I'd better have your mobile number, Pedro." Emma looked around for her phone. "Hang on," she said. "Sorry. I put it on charge last night and forgot to bring it down." She went out to the staircase.

Espinoza turned to Jenny. "How do you think she's coping?" He had dealt with many family dramas in his time as a policeman and knew how devastating the effect could be on loved ones.

"As long as she knows that Leo is alive and well and that we're working to get him back safely, I think she'll manage. But she's really at her limit."

"Here we are." Emma came in with her mobile and switched it on. "There's a message!" She announced excitedly. "Oh my God! Leo. It's from Leo!" She cried out with relief and happiness and showed the mobile to the others.

The message read, *Kidnapped. Cotzee secutry, Nosoo cop, Blethin doctr in Polkwane. Please come 4 me. Leo xxx*

Jenny looked at it in amazement. "Well done Leo. He's with Nwosu and Coetzee and this third man, Blethin, must be the doctor. Brilliant!"

Espinoza took the phone. "Polokwane?" He said, his mind digesting this new event. "Where's Polokwane?"

"It's in the north part of the country, in Limpopo province. They had one of the soccer matches there. It's a big town." The World Cup was still fresh in Emma's memory. "He's stolen a mobile to text us their location."

"You're right. This is a South African number, country code 027. It must belong to one of the kidnappers. They're moving him to another safe house and he's telling us the way. He's a very bright boy."

"Look. Here's Polokwane." Jenny showed him the map on her laptop.

"I see. It's about three hundred kilometres north of Johannesburg with an airport, so there may be a connecting flight." He looked at the phone screen again. "Unfortunately, Leo's message was sent last night, so he's probably no longer there, but Polokwane could be a starting point."

Emma took the mobile from his hand. "I'll call him back. He might still have the phone."

"No, don't, Emma. You might alert them and we don't know what could happen. We now have a unique advantage. Leo's in touch with us without their knowledge. We know which way they're going and I can start following the trail when I get to South Africa."

Espinoza didn't mention something he'd seen on the map. Polokwane was half way to the Zimbabwe border. But it was also en route for Mozambique and Botswana. He hoped against hope that they were heading to either of those countries and not to Mugabe's brutal dictatorship.

He put the thought aside. "Can you bring up the website again for the Newtown Clinic? Look for a Doctor Blethin."

Emma took her iPad and searched the list of Consultants

and Medical Staff on the website. "You're right. He's here, Dr Ernest Blethin, Senior Consultant in Psychology and Aesthetic Procedures." She sat down on the settee, a smile on her face for the first time since she had arrived.

Espinoza looked just as pleased. The plot was falling into place in his mind. Emma had been right about Nwosu and Coetzee and his hunch about Blethin and the clinic was confirmed. "This is an incredible breakthrough. We've now confirmed the identity of the abductors and where they are. We're making great progress and we haven't even left the house."

His mind was now sifting through the possibilities. If Leo was in Polokwane when he sent the message, they must be heading further north. It made no sense to stay in Johannesburg if they had already gone. He said, "Jenny, can you look up the flights from Johannesburg to Polokwane? I get in at ten thirty tomorrow morning."

Jenny quickly found an efficient booking site for South Africa. "There's a South African Airways flight at twelve fifty. You can be there by early afternoon. I'll book it now."

"Good. Now I really feel we're getting close to recovering Leo. I have a starting point and definite names to track down. With Superintendent Hendricks' resources I'm sure I can get to them and to Leo. I'll call him in the morning from the airport before leaving for Polokwane."

He turned to Emma. "I've just remembered something. You said you have Leo's passport. Can you get it for me? I'm going to need it to bring him home with me."

Emma ran upstairs to fetch the passport and Espinoza said to Jenny, "The problem is that we still have no idea what the connecting point between these various events is. Somewhere there's a crossover of information about Leo's birth, the trip to South Africa and your fortune. If we find that connection we'll have solved the whole conspiracy and identified the perpetrators."

"One step at a time, Pedro. As you keep repeating, detective work is one step at a time. We're counting on you to keep taking those steps."

He looked at her, a wry smile on his lips. "As they say in your country; *No pressure there!*"

London, England

"What did he say?" The Voice's companion blew a smoke ring across the room, appearing unconcerned at the latest conversation.

"Very little. Our Mr Coetzee is not the most talkative of personages. Only that they have managed to get no further than Polokwane, which as you know is approximately two-thirds of the way to Beitbridge. It seems the good sergeant may be out executing, (a most appropriate verb), our latest instructions. I'm talking about Doctor Blethin of course. After which they intend to pursue their itinerary. I'll call again after lunch when they should be in Beitbridge with our friends. Once the boy is safely there, neither Coetzee nor Nwosu will survive their visit."

"I'm not surprised. I hear it's a very dangerous country."

"Indeed. I sometimes wonder how many of these leaders manage to hang on to power, considering the strife and discontent they create amongst their subjects."

"Do you think Leo Stewart will be safe there? He's just a boy."

"I have no idea and it's really beyond our mandate to worry about it. From the moment Leo fell into our hands he became an item of merchandise. A very valuable item of merchandise, but merchandise all the same, nothing more, nothing less."

"That's a very heartless way to look at the situation. You're suggesting he might not be returned to his mother when the ransom is paid?"

"I'm not suggesting anything of the sort. I am simply stating that it's not our business, that's all. By the way, speaking of payments, were you able to call back the last transfer?"

"Of course. I haven't forgotten what I learned in my previous profession. I told the bank I'd duplicated the previous order by mistake and they required only an email confirmation from me. It will be reversed with tomorrow's value date. They always hang on to the funds for a day or so. Sticky fingers, bankers. Oh, and the further hundred thousand arrived in the account just a moment ago. We have a little over quarter of a million available now."

"Excellent! We may be able to make an additional profit for ourselves, as you so often request. Now, it's time to send the second message. Let's see what reaction that will provoke."

The Voice opened up his laptop. "Very beautifully written, even if I say so myself," he said as he read it aloud for the twentieth time. "Off it goes," he announced and pressed Send.

FORTY-ONE

Marbella, Spain

Jenny was reserving the flight to Polokwane when Emma's laptop pinged. Espinoza saw the blood drain from her face as she read the message. She turned the screen towards them without a word then sat with her elbows on the desk, her head in her hands.

The email was from the same Filipino address as the previous one, *args@ipsend.* He adjusted his spectacles and read it aloud.

> *Over one million Rwandan Tutsis were slaughtered in 1994 in a bloodthirsty genocide orchestrated by the Hutu government, aided and abetted by the Hutu press and media. Retribution by the courts has been slow and ineffective and has brought no recompense to the Tutsi people. We, the descendants of hundreds of Tutsi families who were decimated by the slaughter demand that amends be made by the instigators, families and descendants of those who committed the atrocities. To that end we have formed the* ***ALLIANCE OF RWANDAN GENOCIDE SURVIVORS*** *to find those people and to seek retribution for our suffering.*

*We have proof that your son, **LEOPOLD STEWART**, who is in our custody, is the illegitimate son of a member of the Hutu Akazu, a murderer, coward and instigator of hatred and genocide toward the Rwandan Tutsis whose actions contributed to the slaughter of our people. You are amongst those who must make amends.*

*In return for the safe return of your son we hereby demand the sum of **TEN MILLION US DOLLARS** as your contribution to the ARGS which will be used to alleviate the suffering and impoverishment of many Tutsis in our community. We will provide instructions for the transfer of this amount by tomorrow evening, Friday 16th July. Leo will be released and delivered to a safe place within one hour of funds being received. If funds are not received by close of business on Wednesday 21st July, or if you attempt to make any contact with the authorities, they will be informed of your son's illegal status and you will have no further news of him.*

ALLIANCE OF RWANDAN GENOCIDE SURVIVORS.

London, England

"I can confirm that the second message has been sent as agreed a few minutes ago."

"Good. Have you spoken to the policeman?" Slater sounded even more nervous than previously.

"I will speak with him this afternoon. He has been dealing with unfinished business it seems."

"In Beitbridge?"

"No, in Polokwane, on the way. I spoke with Mr Coetzee."

"So the boy's not there yet. Why not."

"The boy is fine but they have been delayed due to traffic problems. A mundane excuse I agree, but unfortunately we have no way of influencing the world around us. They expect to arrive in a few hours and I have advised our Zimbabwean friends accordingly."

And the unfinished business?"

"I believe we may have mislaid the good doctor."

"So there's only two remaining witnesses?"

"Exactly, until that is, later this evening. To quote my favourite plot maker, Agatha Christie, *And then there were none.*"

"Call me when everything is sorted out in Beitbridge."

Slater called his partner's number. "The boy will arrive in Beitbridge this afternoon and there are only two remaining witnesses. The second message has gone."

"Good." So everything's back on track. You'd better make sure it stays that way. When are you coming back?"

"I'll stay until we get some two way communication. Somebody needs to be on top of them, so it'll have to be me."

"Agreed. Call me when there's anything to report."

Slater sat back in his chair feeling a sense of relief he hadn't enjoyed for some time. He couldn't imagine they had just demanded a ransom for a hostage they no longer held.

Phalaborwa, Limpopo, South Africa

Do you have a family, Marius?" Coetzee had ordered ice cream. It was very warm on the terrace.

"Everybody's got a family, Leo."

"OK. I mean a wife, kids, that kind of family." Leo was looking for a chink in the security man's armour, a weakness he might be able to exploit.

Coetzee pushed the empty dish away, wiped his mouth, took out a cheroot, lit it, took a deep drag and pondered the question. "I have a wife and daughter, but they don't live with me."

"Shame. There's a lot of kids like that in school, no dad. Me, for example. In fact there might even be more without a father than with."

"It's the way of the world. The number of people getting married goes down as fast as the number of divorces goes up."

"How old is your daughter? If you don't mind me asking."

"I don't mind. She's the exact same age as you, fifteen. Her name's Abby. She's football mad as well." Coetzee took another drag on his cheroot, trying to look indifferent to the discussion.

"So why would you kidnap a kid the same age as your own daughter?"

"I told you already, I did it just for money, it's that simple." He stared angrily at Leo. "Do you realise I could take you to the authorities and testify that you shot a police sergeant and killed a doctor and your life would be over. Instead, I'm looking after you like a son and asking for a very reasonable reward to return you to your mother."

"Maybe, but maybe not." Leo tried to sound confident and assertive. "I'm pretty sure Sergeant Nwosu would say it was you who did it all. He hates your guts and wants to get his hands on me. He's a cop and as far as Blethin is concerned, it's my word against yours and you're a kidnapper. So I don't really buy your story."

"OK, Leo, I agree we're both in a tight spot. But one thing's for sure. If you try to make a run for it or somehow manage to escape, you'll be a target for Nwosu and me both and I'd strongly advise against that."

"Have you already asked for a ransom? Sorry, reward. Was that what the phone call was about?"

"Stop quizzing me. You'll know soon enough what's going on." Coetzee got up and walked into the lodge. *This kid is going to drive me insane,* he thought. He sat at his laptop and began to prepare an email to Emma. He wasn't happy about it, but it was the only way.

Marbella, Spain

"I'll make you a cup of tea. That'll sort you out." Jenny took refuge in the oldest restorative mechanism in the UK, the teapot. Despite her own astonishment at the ransom message, she had spent the last fifteen minutes trying to console her sister. She and Espinoza had explained that this was a negotiating stance by the abductors. There was no way in the world they would expect to receive the amount they asked for.

"Statistics show that ransoms paid, if at all, usually constitute a fraction of the original demand. It takes time, but it always works that way." Espinoza was making facts up as he went along, hoping that both women would be reassured. He himself had been thunderstruck by the amount. *Not even Mme Bishop can raise so much money,* he said to himself. *The sooner I get down to Polokwane the more I can find out about this business and the better positioned we are to negotiate.* He didn't want Jenny to start thinking about any kind of settlement. There was vital investigative work to be done before any negotiation.

He tried to calm Emma down. "You must understand that Leo is presently the safest he can be in the circumstances. The abductors have now made their demand, so we know what this is about – money, so they are not about to kill the golden goose. I'm sorry, that was a bad analogy," he added as she looked at him in distress.

"We must play for time. We've found out a lot but now it's essential I go to Polokwane to start my investigation in the place where he's been taken."

"We were absolutely right about Galaganza, weren't we?" Jenny brought the tea and joined in the discussion. "Pedro's right, without even moving out of this house we have found out an enormous amount. When he gets down there, he has the advantage of that knowledge and police resources to work with."

"But it's already four days since he was taken. I can't bear it, not knowing where he is, what's being done to him. He's only fifteen, he's still a child. Every single minute without him seems like an eternity. And now this demand for a ridiculous amount of money."

"Emma. I've told you to leave the problem of money to me. I'm quite sure that we can negotiate them down to an amount I can manage. They're bound to have demanded much more than they expect to get. And Pedro's right about investigating what's going on in South Africa. At the same time we have to open negotiations and try to discover the link that leads us to the brains behind this plot.

"Let's examine the message itself." Espinoza moved the discussion to a more pragmatic point. He placed the laptop where they could all see the screen. "It was sent to your personal address just a few minutes ago, which reinforces our theory that the sender is on European time. Let me read the text again slowly."

Jenny was the first to comment. "I don't believe this ARGS group even exists." She took her iPad and typed the initials into Google.

"Look! It's an acronym for *Alternate Reality Game*. That's a kind of Internet game where people can enter whatever input they want to change a story to influence the events or the ending. It's just a made up name. I'm certain it has nothing to do with Rwandan retribution, just a gang of kidnappers trying to blackmail us into handing over a fortune of money. "

Espinoza interjected, "They say they have proof of Leo's birth. Is that possible, Emma?"

"Unless it's written by Tony or Dr Constance, it's impossible. Only you and Jenny have heard this story. I wouldn't dare tell it to anyone else."

"They may be bluffing, but they must have some knowledge of what happened in Rwanda. However, if they divulge whatever they have discovered they lose one of their bargaining points, so I don't think that's likely. What else can you read from the message?"

"I'm pretty sure it's been written by the same person," she said.

"You mean the elaborate English?"

"Exactly." She forced herself to concentrate on the message again, even though reading the words made her feel physically sick. "Phrases like, *make amends* and words like *decimated, instigator* and *impoverishment.* This is very English. Really old school vocabulary. With texting and Twitter and the ineffective school system, the modern generation don't use words like this anymore."

"So, you're suggesting it was written by an older, English person?"

"Yes. Someone who enjoys writing beautifully. Even though the content is untruthful, horrible and villainous, they want it to read like Charles Dickens."

"It sounds like someone with a high regard for themselves."

"Probably. Someone who feels superior to others. An academically qualified person, or someone born into money or power. Possibly a member of the aristocracy?"

Jenny said, "Now I suppose we have to ask for what they call, 'proof of life'."

"That's right. It's more or less a formality, but we have to let them know that we understand the rules of the game. And we may glean some additional information, as we did from the first photograph." Espinoza looked at his watch. "It's now after noon. I must get home to prepare for my trip and be at the airport on time. First, I have to take my dear wife out for lunch since she's going to lose me for a while."

"And we have visitors for lunch." Jenny said. "We'll reply to the email this evening when we've had time to think about it."

They went to the door. "Oh!" Jenny added, "I forgot to tell you, Leticia's coming home today."

"Please give her my best regards. I hope to see her on my return. Goodbye, ladies."

Emma squeezed his hand. "Please bring Leo home soon, Pedro. I'm putting all my trust in you."

"Try to keep your morale up. Have confidence and I promise we'll continue to move forward. I'll be in touch as soon as I arrive in South Africa." He embraced them both and went out to his car.

It was eighty-six and a half hours since Leo had been taken.

FORTY-TWO

Phalaborwa, Limpopo, South Africa

At his hostage's request, Coetzee had ordered pizzas for lunch. Leo had decided to make the most of this enforced prolongation to his vacation. It might be years before his mother could afford another holiday. They were both in swimming trunk, sitting on the terrace under a canopy, having had a dip in a cordoned off area of the river in front of the lodge. He was thrilled to have swum in a river that Coetzee told him was infested with six foot crocodiles, although they hadn't seen one.

Coetzee was studying the *Mail & Guardian* morning newspaper that had been delivered to the lodge. He stiffened noticeably and folded it up. "Leo, get me a beer from the minibar, will you?" He waited until the boy was inside then shoved the folded paper under the cushion of his chair.

The local news headline still burned in his mind. *Suspicious Death in Mayfair. Packard Hotel Manager in 7th Floor Death Plunge.*

Poor old Barry Lambert, he thoght. *Nwosu got him before he left, just as I thought.* It wasn't the kind of item he wanted Leo to read, even though he had probably already worked it out. And the police sergeant would be looking for them as soon as he was fit to shoot a gun again. He thought back over the last twenty-four hours. There was no way they could be traced to the lodge. He'd paid for everything with cash, given a false name and bribed the desk clerk to forget the passport requirements. *The guy probably thinks I'm a paedophile,* he reflected. *I've got two days, max., then we'll move and keep moving until I see some money arrive.*

Leo brought his beer. "Thanks," he said. "I can't eat all this, do you want a slice?"

He transferred half his pizza onto Leo's plate and took a swig of beer. They continued their lunch in silence, both thinking about their situation. Both making plans.

Malaga, Spain

"Why are you off to South Africa, Papa?" Espinoza was lunching with his wife and daughter at his favourite tapas bar. It was a very hot day and they sat inside to avoid the burning sun, as most Spanish people did.

"It's quite an interesting job, Laura. An abduction, a young boy. But I can't tell you more than that, it's rather complicated and confidential."

"But it happened in South Africa?"

Espinoza said nothing, just gave his daughter a look and took a bite from his *croqueta de jamon.*

His wife interrupted, "Isn't it to do with the nice English lady who was almost killed two years ago? Snra Bishop, in Marbella?"

"Please Soledad! How can I earn a reputation as an irreproachably discreet private detective if you keep guessing the names of my clients? Anyway," he added, "it is not Mme Bishop, it's another person entirely."

"I was just thinking that it would be typical if the poor woman hadn't seen the last of that business. There were some nasty people involved, I remember. And you should know better than I do that people like that have a way of turning up again, just like bad pennies."

His wife and daughter continued to chatter on while Espinoza's mind turned to a new track. Soledad was extremely inquisitive and intuitive and had a woman's knack of sometimes seeing things that he missed. He reflected back to the cast of characters involved in the d'Almeida murder spree. Sadly, most of them were dead, but apart from poor Adam Peterson, not on his watch. He tried to remember anyone who had survived, anyone involved with the murderer. He dredged a name from the back of his memory, d'Almeida's French girlfriend. *Ellen,no , Ethel, no. Esther, Esther Rousseau, that's it!* He recalled with satisfaction. The woman who had never been found. The bank employee who had provided d'Almeida with information that permitted him to transfer the Angolan Clan fortune from the Swiss bank to no one knew where. The fortune that Jenny had recovered just a few months ago. Unfortunately there was no clear proof that she was involved in the Internet robbery and he had been unable to obtain an Interpol warrant for her arrest. Once the hue and cry had died down he knew that the national police and immigration personnel would have quickly lost interest in her and she could be anywhere in the world.

I wonder what happened to her? He asked himself. *She knew all about the bank accounts, the diamonds and the keys. Did she know about Emma and Leo? Could she be the missing link?*

Then another name from the past came to him. *Vogel, Kurt Vogel. The accountant who stole a million dollars. He had an intimate knowledge of the Angolan Clan bank accounts and probably knew about the diamonds too. I always considered him to be a small time crook. An opportunist embezzler who took what he could then ran off before he was found out. Maybe I was wrong?*

Espinoza leaned across the table and kissed his wife on the cheek. "*Gracias amor mio.* Thank you my love."

"Is that so she'll miss you when you're away?" Laura laughed.

"It won't work. We're going to shop and spend his money until he gets back," responded her mother. "That will stop him rushing about the world like Hercule Poirot."

Espinoza poured some of the cold, delicious Navarra rosé. "Salud!" he said, "Enjoy the shopping."

Marbella, Spain

"I've just had a good idea." Jenny gave her sister a mischievous smile.

"What's that? I could do with a good idea."

"Since Leticia and Sam are joining us for lunch, why don't I invite Patrice, her fiancé, as well."

"No way. I've told you I'm really not up to seeing anyone. I'm likely to get upset and make a mistake. Just count me out, I'll stay in my room with a migraine."

"Nonsense. This way you'll get to meet the whole group in one go, give the performance of your life and get it over with. You can't put it off forever. Agreed?"

"Very well, Miss Schoolteacher Jenny, if you insist."

"If we're lucky, Fuente might join us too."

"Ah, Fuente, the famous, but as yet, invisible cat! Obviously a TS Eliot mystery cat, like Macavity. *When a crime's discovered then Fuente's not there.*"

"Rather, *when a crime's prevented*! But that's another story. I'll call Patrice now."

Jenny called the bank and was put through to Patrice's extension. "This is Victoria, M de Moncrieff's assistant. Who's calling please?"

"Hello Victoria, it's Sra Bishop, I'm calling Patrice on behalf of Leticia, his fiancée."

"I'm sorry Sra Bishop, he's travelling on business out of the country today."

"I thought he was in Marbella today. Maybe I misunderstood. I'll call his mobile. Thank you."

She turned to Emma, a puzzled look on her face. That's funny, I'm positive she told me he had to return to Marbella for an important deal at the bank."

"Well that's one less encounter for me to worry about today. Let's go and give Encarni a hand."

She went with her to the kitchen, going back over last night's conversation with Leticia. *Why would Patrice say he was coming back to Marbella if he wasn't?*

Phalaborwa, Limpopo, South Africa

Leo took the dishes into the kitchen and came back eating an apple. Coetzee was still sitting at the table looking pensive. He sat across from him and said, "Why did you split up from your wife and daughter, Marius?"

"What? Oh, it wasn't my idea, it was Karen's."

"So what was the problem? People don't usually split up without a reason."

"It's actually none of your business, Leo, but the answer is, I have no idea. Two years ago she just said she was fed up with the whole marriage bit and wanted to leave me and take Abby with her"

"Just like that?"

"Exactly like that, she moved out within a week and that was it."

"Did she have a boyfriend?"

"Not as far as I know. She found a job and a place to live and went off with her daughter and her belongings."

"Why do you say her daughter? Isn't Abby your daughter too?"

"It's more complicated than that and I told you it's none of your business. Why don't you tell me about yourself instead?"

"I thought you knew all about me and my mom. Isn't it part of the *Abduction for Dummies* manual, *Get to Know your Prey*?"

"Very funny. I mean, for example, do you have a girlfriend?"

"There's a girl I go to the cinema with sometimes. Not a girlfriend, but she's good company. We like the same kinds of things."

"What kind of things?"

"You know, stuff like computer programming and thinking up new applications and ideas. We like science fiction films, space stories, like Matrix, Lord of the Rings, that kind of thing. She's the only girl I know who likes football and she's got nine 'A' passes, one more than me."

He's smitten, thought Coetzee. "What's her name?"

"Alice, but don't start spreading rumours." Leo laughed self-consciously.

"Sounds like a real catch and I promise not to say a word."

He picked up his mobile phone. "Time to be a film star. Come and sit here."

"This for the reward message?"

"Yes it is. I want to show your mother you're OK. I don't want her to worry about you."

"You mean any more than she already is?" Leo sat in front of the lodge wall as directed.

"Say cheese." Coetzee took a couple of snaps. "Right, keep yourself busy for a minute or two. I've got stuff to do." He went into the lodge.

At the desk, he opened up his laptop and transferred the photos from his mobile. He chose one and attached it to his draft message. After making a couple of changes, he read the message one last time, then taking a deep breath, pressed Send.

Leo waited until he was busy preparing the reward message then quietly extracted the newspaper from under the cushion and retired out of view of his abductor.

It took him only a moment to find the news item. It was true! Lambert was dead, undoubtedly murdered by Nwosu. Coetzee was right, the policeman was a vicious killer. *I wounded him but we let him go free.* His blood ran cold. *And I made it worse by killing Blethin. Shit! What's going to happen to us if we get caught?"*

"You weren't supposed to read that." Coetzee was standing at the patio door, holding out his hand.

Leo folded the paper again and handed it to him. "You told me last night, remember? When you accused the sergeant of murdering him? It didn't register with me then. Reading it like that in the paper, it's different. It's a really fucked up situation." Tears came to his eyes, but he was determined not to blab, not to show weakness.

"We live in a fucked up world, Leo. Get used to it." Although the South African tried to sound hard, Leo sensed a lot of emotion beneath the surface.

He lay back in the recliner, wondering how to get hold of Blethin's mobile again to send another message to his mother.

Now he knew where they were. Not the town or area, but the name of the safari lodge where they were staying. It was written on the top of the newspaper for the delivery boy, *Olifantsrivier Lodge.* Now he had the advantage. He had to use it.

FORTY-THREE

Marbella, Spain

Emilio was delighted to see his Aunt Jenny again. "Hola Jenny!" He cried, reaching up so she could hoist him into her embrace.

"You're becoming far too heavy for me. It's all that French food. We'll have to put you on a diet," she laughed.

"*Je parle Francais,*" he said proudly.

"Well, I don't, so you'll have to talk to me in English." She turned towards Emma. "This is your other English auntie, my sister, Emma."

He put his hand out politely. "How do you do, Auntie Emma."

"Hello Emilio, it's lovely to meet you." She took the little boy's hand and gave him a kiss. "You must be very clever, speaking lots of languages."

"Don't be fooled, Emma. He speaks very good Spanish, but only a dozen words of English and French. I'm Leticia. I'm so happy to finally meet Jenny's big sister."

"We're helping Encarni with the lunch, so go and sort yourselves out and we'll see you when you're ready," Jenny instructed. Lunch was the first priority. Sam would be arriving from the airport at three o'clock.

Leticia took her son along the hall to their apartment. "What a beautiful woman!" Emma admired Leticia's graceful figure as she walked away. "She's even lovelier than you described. Makes me feel quite dowdy, especially at the moment."

"Well, she's just as nice as she looks, so you'll get on well together. Now, into the kitchen, pronto!"

"So, how was your trip to South Africa, Emma? Did Leo enjoy the World Cup?" Lunch was under control and Emilio was already in the swimming pool, under Encarni's supervision. Sam was due in fifteen minutes and the three women were sitting on the terrace, enjoying a glass of *Fino* and getting to know each other. Suddenly there was an air of tension around them. Leticia was immediately aware that she'd struck a raw nerve.

Emma looked worriedly at Jenny. How did she know about South Africa? She wasn't on the list and Jenny hadn't mentioned it to Espinoza.

"Did I tell you she was going to the football? I can't remember doing so." Jenny racked her brain, she had no recollection of such a conversation.

"We heard you talking about it on the phone last time you were down here. You invited Emma to stay while I was away with Patrice and she told you she would be at the game with Leo. Have I said something wrong? I didn't mean to overhear. I'm sorry." Leticia looked mortified. Jenny was her idol and she bathed in her approbation.

"Of course not, I had just forgotten all about it, that's all." Jenny looked at Emma and shrugged, *just one of those things.*

"It was a very eventful trip," Emma replied carefully.

"Where is Leo? We can't wait to meet him. Jenny says he's a keen footballer, he can teach Emilio to play."

"Leo's staying just along the road in Estepona,." Jenny said quickly, before Emma could react to the question. "His friend Nigel's parents have rented a house there, down near the beach."
"It's a nice coincidence both of them being here on holiday at the same time. You'll see him before they go back."

"Patrice keeps telling me we should go down to South Africa," Leticia went on, "he says we should go while Mandela is still alive, because you don't know what might happen afterwards. Was it quiet? Did you see any signs of trouble?"

Jenny saw her sister struggling and interjected again, "From what Emma told me they saw no signs of trouble in Cape Town, but Johannesburg has quite a different reputation. Is that right, Emma?"

"Yes. There's a lot of problems in Joburg, but Cape Town is lovely and quiet. The football was a bit of a disappointment, but it was a very memorable holiday." She took a deep breath. "And how was Nice? I'd love to visit the Côte d'Azur sometime, when I save up for another holiday."

The moment passed, apparently without provoking any suspicions in Leticia, who started rattling on about the weather in the South of France, the luxury hotels and wonderful restaurants, first class service and beautiful shops. She sounded as if she was reading from a travel brochure. "Patrice loves it down there and so do I. We've decided we're going to buy a place near Nice, it's so beautiful along that coast. My French is quite good now and I'd love to spend more time in the country." She saw Jenny's frown and added, "Just a small place. I couldn't afford anything big now."

Jenny was thinking, *she's obsessed with all things French. I just hope she doesn't throw away her money on some chateau in the middle of nowhere.* Aloud, she said, "I phoned to invite Patrice for lunch, but apparently he's travelling."

"*Presupuesto.* Of course. He told me he was coming back to Marbella but when he arrived he was called away again on some big transaction the bank's involved in. He's travelling an awful lot these days. It's rather stressful."

"Do you hear that, Emma? Leticia could hardly speak a word of English when I first met her a few years ago. Now she speaks fluently and is mastering the Latin languages one after the other."

"I'll invite him for the weekend when he gets back, so Emma can meet him. How long are you staying?"

Once again Jenny stepped in. "Probably about a week or so. It depends when Leo gets back from his friend's."

Leticia again failed to notice Emma's unease at the mention of her son. "Of course. Stay as long as you like. I suppose writers can work from anywhere?"

Gradually the atmosphere became less tense and they settled down to swapping stories about their activities. Jenny encouraging Leticia to tell them about her travels with Patrice, to keep Emma out of difficulty. It was not the easiest of conversations.

Malaga Airport, Spain

Laura drove Espinoza directly from the restaurant to the airport. He was travelling in economy to Frankfurt and wanted to get through check-in and security without any stress. He had only a carry-on bag and his laptop case to save time when he arrived. During his time as Chief Inspector of the Homicide Squad of the National Police Department in Malaga, he had been spoiled. When he travelled for the force, he had a privileged parking spot and a fast track route through to departures and business class. Now, he was just one of the millions of low fare passengers who had to queue to claim their uncomfortable, tightly spaced seat in the back of the plane. Sometimes he pined for the old times.

He sat in the departure lounge near to gate D 53 and settled down for his sixty minute wait. Taking out his mobile he called Marcel Colombey, his friend at the French National Police. "*Salut, Marcel.* I've another little job for you, if you don't mind." Although Esther Rousseau hadn't been heard of for two years, there might be a trail he could follow. Even if it just meant eliminating her as a suspect.

Next, he called Inspector Andréas Blaser in Geneva, one of his Interpol contacts who had followed Vogel's trail two years ago. The search had been fruitless, but it might be worth opening up the investigation again. At this point he had to follow up every possible link, however unlikely.

He made a couple more calls then looked at the South African Broadcasting Corporation website again. The front page had a new item which jumped out at him.

Latest News: Murdered White Man's Corpse Discovered in Polokwane.

Another death. This time a definite murder. And in Polokwane! This is not a coincidence. Espinoza's mind was whirling. *But who is the unknown victim? And who is in charge of cleaning up?* He decided that he was obliged to share this information with his employer before he left, in case she changed her mind about his trip. He called Marbella.

Jenny saw Espinoza's number appear on her phone and walked away from the others. She listened in silence as he related his latest report, her mind numbed by the announcement of another death.

"What do you think? Should I change my plans? I'll do whatever you decide."

Jenny tried to think clearly. She took a deep breath. "You have to go down, Pedro. It's even more important now. We don't know who this victim is and we have to find out immediately. It's clearly not Nwosu, but what if it's Coetzee? It would mean that Leo is in the hands of that despicable police sergeant. My God! I just can't tell Emma about this. She'll fall apart completely."

"Agreed. Now we have two murders to help us in our investigation and that could be of vital use to us. Let's see what I find there before we tell her. We'll talk tomorrow evening. I'm going to call back CS Hendricks. He'll be keen to get me involved if I can show the two deaths were connected. His resources will be valuable to my investigation."

Jenny mumbled her agreement, her brain still trying to cope with this latest revelation. In the back of her mind she was blaming herself again.

Espinoza was still speaking. "There's another thing, Jenny. Can you bring to mind anything about Esther Rousseau or Kurt Vogel? They knew all about the money and diamonds and they disappeared off the radar when d'Almeida was killed. There could possibly be a slender thread there, perhaps?"

A shiver ran down her spine. *Schneider's assistant at Klein Fellay, d'Almeida's lover. And Vogel, Charlie's crooked accountant. More links to*

Charlie's fortune and to the diamonds! It was like a poison to her. That's why the diamonds were hidden away in Geneva, where they could do no further harm. No one, including Espinoza, knew she had both keys so she avoided the subject. "What do you mean, Pedro? Has something happened to implicate them?"

"Not as far as I know. Someone reminded me that bad pennies tend to turn up again and I've lived that experience before."

"I've heard nothing more about Esther since the night d'Almeida died. From what he said, they were going to meet, but I don't know where. She just disappeared. And so did Vogel, I have no idea what happened to him after he embezzled the Angolan Clan's funds. I agree they knew all about the Angolan fortune, but I can't believe they somehow managed to find out about Emma and Leo and their history. It's too far-fetched."

"Well, I've put out some feelers just in case. We don't have many suspects, so we need to examine them all with a microscope."

This remark jogged her memory. "Pedro, there's been another unexpected development. We just found out that Leticia knew about Emma's trip with Leo. I hate to say it of Leticia, but your list of suspects has now doubled!"

"Or perhaps trebled or quadrupled," he replied.

Phalaborwa, Limpopo, South Africa

"Ah, Mr Coetzee again. Good afternoon" The Voice tried to sound friendly and relaxed but he didn't quite succeed, especially with the acoustic distortion. "The good sergeant still isn't available?"

"I'm glad you've called. We've got a problem here." Coetzee smiled to himself. *Now the boot's on the other foot.* He had left Leo on the terrace and gone to the car so he wouldn't hear the conversation.

"And what might that be. Has something untoward occurred?"

"You could say that. The fact is that we're stuck here in Polokwane because Nwosu is in hospital having surgery on his shoulder. He's been shot!"

A longer pause than usual, then, "How did Sergeant Nwosu manage to get shot?"

"It seems that Blethin was a tougher cookie than he imagined, He shot him with his own gun apparently. But he's been, what's the word, neutralised"

"So, at present only yourself and the boy remain unscathed?"

"That's about the size of it. The boy is fine, but he's shaken up by the recent events, naturally."

"Where are you staying in Polokwane?"

"In the circumstances, with people getting shot and murdered all over the place, I'd rather not say on the phone. You'll understand my position."

Another pause. "Yes, I understand, of course. In which hospital is the sergeant being treated?"

"Same thing. I'd rather not say on the phone."

An even longer pause. "Do you know how long he will have to remain in the hospital?"

"The bullet went through his shoulder. It looked like a clean wound to me, but if there's muscular or ligament damage they might have to operate and it could be a while before they let him out. There's no chance he'll be able to travel today, that's for sure."

"Mr Coetzee. I understand your predicament and I sympathise with it. With your permission, I will spend some time considering the optimum solution to the problem and I shall call you back again later this afternoon without fail." The phone went dead.

FORTY-FOUR

Marbella, Spain

Sam turned out to be just as pleasant as Jenny had described. *Maybe a little too pleasant,* Emma thought to herself. He came across as very entertaining and rather seductive but she sensed he was trying hard to impress them. He was a few years older than she and Jenny, tall and chisel-featured, excellent English with a soft, seductive French accent and an apparently totally relaxed self-deprecating attitude. *He was obviously brought up by a very good English nanny,* she mused.

He was charming with all three women, but she noticed his attention never wavered far from her sister. He also made a great fuss of Emilio and their attempted conversations in three different languages made them laugh. Encarni served a delicious lunch and Jenny was delighted to see Emma enjoying herself and apparently putting her worries on hold, at least for a little while.

Sam wanted to learn all about Emma, her childhood and travels to Africa, her writing career and her son. With Jenny's help, she managed to fend off his questions without raising any suspicions. Leticia unwittingly helped, by continually interposing comments about her parent's flight from Angola and their new life in Spain.

As they reached the end of the meal, Jenny announced, "Fuente has arrived. I told you he would turn up. He can smell grilled fish at a hundred paces. Here you are, Fuente." A beautiful, black, long haired cat padded across to rub itself against her legs then bent over the dish she placed in front of him, gobbling up the remains of the fish.

"He's magnificent." Emma stooped over to stroke him.

"He's a woman's cat," said Sam. "He doesn't let me touch him. If I get near him he hisses and backs away."

"Don't complain, Sam," Jenny laughed, "he's done much worse than that in the past."

"Fortunately for us," added Leticia.

Neither woman expanded on the story and the cat padded quietly off into the garden. At Jenny's insistence, Sam told a few amusing anecdotes from his days in the Moroccan Olympic rifle team and they finished lunch in a pleasant ambience, relaxed in each other's company.

"I'd better check my messages. I'm on holiday, so there's probably nothing." Emma gave Jenny a knowing look and went up to her room. There was nothing on her phone but she checked her laptop in case there was any further news.

"Jenny, come quickly!" Emma's voice echoed from her bedroom window down to the terrace.

Sam jumped to his feet, "I'll go. Something's happened. Where is she?"

"No, please don't worry. She gets these panic attacks," Jenny invented quickly. I'll go up. She'll be fine."

She ran upstairs, her heart thumping. Emma was sitting at the desk staring at her laptop screen, hand at her mouth, tears running down her cheeks.

London, England

"We'll have to inform them of this. It will inevitably become known and I have no desire to be accused of concealing material facts." The Voice and his companion had been checking the online news reports for Johannesburg and Polokwane. The two deaths were reported. It seemed that Coetzee's story was correct, but the situation was worrying.

"You're right of course, but they'll be bloody furious with the news. I don't know how we managed to end up with so many idiots on this job, it's not exactly rocket science."

"Calm down, it's merely a minor impediment. Our job is to provide solutions so that's what we'll do. I'm going to call Harare first. We'll send a couple of our friends to pick up the boy and neutralise the remaining intermediaries."

"Tell them to be quick about it!"

Ten minutes later the Voice called Slater's mobile number.

The man listened in silence, his heart pounding as he registered these latest events. *This is all just hearsay from Coetzee.* Aloud he said, "How do you know he's telling the truth? It could be a purely fictitious story. Nwosu may even be there and he doesn't want to talk to us. Maybe they've worked out a different agenda. This whole plan is falling apart. Isn't there anybody there you can trust? Fucking Hell! How could you let things get so out of hand?" His voice trembled as he thought, *How I am I going to relay this news?*

"Please remain calm, Mr Slater. I believe our South African colleague is telling the truth. We have some independent verification of the local situation. There are reports of two murdered white men in South Africa in the news today. The first is Lambert, the hotel manager, in Johannesburg and the second is an unknown man in Polokwane. That must be Blethin, the doctor. This corresponds exactly with what he has told us. I will instigate a means of locating the others and report back to you this afternoon.

"In my view, things are still under control. We know where they are and that they still have the boy. Why would they change their plan when they are to receive a substantial amount of money from adhering to ours? It is not so easy to suddenly become an independent agent in an abduction. Just think how long it took us to organise what has been so far a successful enterprise, despite one or two unforeseen events."

Slater took a deep breath. "So what are you going to do?"

"I have already dispatched two of our Zimbabwe friends to intercept them in Polokwane. It is not such a large town that we can't find Nwosu in a hospital or Coetzee and the boy wherever they are. We cannot assume they do not wish to be found. When Coetzee knows that help is at hand I am certain he will reveal his whereabouts. If Nwosu is unavailable to escort the boy to Beitbridge my people will do so and the matter will be resolved."

"When will they arrive in Polokwane?"

"In three hours, no more than that. They will be back over the border later tonight, all being well."

"Call me as soon as you have definite news." He rang off then with trembling fingers he called his partner's number. He was terrified to report the news but he had no option.

The listener waited for the end of his abbreviated version of the story without speaking, then said, "I can't talk now, I'll call you back," and rang off.

Slater put the phone down and went to pour himself a whisky. *What have I got myself into?* He asked himself as he slumped into the hotel chair.

Geneva, Switzerland

At Ramseyer, Haldemann the director, Claude Jolidon, had received a call from Marseille. It was a disagreeable conversation and he shifted uncomfortably as he listened to the bad news.

"*Putin de merde.* Shit!" He slammed his phone down on the desk in anger then calmed himself down, made some notes and called a number in Brussels on his mobile.

The voice that replied sounded slightly deformed, as if the speaker had a handkerchief over his mouth. "One minute please, I will go to another room." A moment later he came back on the line, this time speaking French in a clear voice. "What is it, M. Jolidon?" He listened to the news and said, "You'll have to call our client immediately. He may be able to remedy the situation. It's always a matter of money, you know."

"Very well, but remember, I'm not responsible for this. He's my client but it was you who set up the transaction." Jolidon finished the call and took a deep breath. He called another number and waited anxiously as it rang. "Bonjour, Monsieur," he said in French. "I have some news on our transaction. Are you free to talk for a few minutes?"

Marbella Spain

Jenny went across to her sister. "What is it?"

"Look at this. I can't believe it. What's going on?"

She turned the laptop towards her. The email message was from *m.coetzee@css.com.*

It read;

Hello Emma, I have good news for you. I have managed to rescue Leo from his abductors and we are in a safe place where no one can locate us. As you can see, he is in good health and has suffered no ill effects from his experience. I am certain you will want to reward me for saving your son and I don't want to be greedy after the anguish you've gone through. I hope you agree that the amount of ***$1,000,000-*** *would be a fair recompense for the trouble and danger I have faced to be able to reunite you with Leo.*

Your son is a fine boy and I have no wish to harm him, so this is not a trap of any kind. I need these funds to remake my life elsewhere, because I will be in danger if I stay here in SA. Please confirm your agreement as soon as possible and I will send you instructions for the payment and for Leo's return to his home.

Thank you for your understanding and a positive response.

Marius Coetzee

Jenny looked at the photo attached to the message. Leo was sitting in a wicker chair against the wall of a wooden building, like a cabin or a garden pavilion. He appeared calm and composed, not frightened or angry. Her mind went back to Espinoza's call. *It looks like it must have been the doctor, Blethin, who was killed. He said it was a white man so if it wasn't Coetzee I don't see any other candidates. But where is Nwosu in all this?*

She noticed it was sent to Emma's publishing address, *emma@emmastewartwriter.com. Not her private address, the one used by the other senders, but the one that's in the public domain.*

"How can I be getting messages from two sources, both claiming to have Leo? I don't understand what's going on" She sat on the side of the bed, tears falling down her face.

When her sister didn't reply, she stifled her sobbing and asked, "What is it, Jenny? What are you thinking?"

"I'm thinking this could be very good news. It could be genuine."

"Why would you doubt it? It was sent by Coetzee from his own email account."

"Emma, we don't actually know if this message came from Coetzee. All we know is that it came from his email address."

"So we don't actually know if Leo is with him or not, if this message is genuine?"

"Not for sure, but I'm inclined to believe it for several reasons. First, because it was sent to your publishing address, which implies he doesn't know your private one, so he may not be close to the main perpetrators. Second, from the way he writes I don't think he suspects that you know he was involved. You seem to have got away without them catching on that you were onto their deception. Third, the photo is not pasted onto the message. It's attached separately so we can see the properties."

Emma opened up the photo file. "You're right. Look, it was created by Marius Coetzee and loaded onto his computer on July 15th at 15:15. That was just half an hour ago, so it must be genuine."

"And then there's the amount he's asking for, it's a fraction of the other demand."

"What should we do? Shall I reply immediately"

Jenny thought back to her conversation with Espinoza, considering whether she wanted to divulge the last piece of evidence unearthed by him.

"What is it? There's something you're not telling me."

"It's something I learned from Espinoza today. Something that happened yesterday."

"Don't leave me in suspense, tell me what it is. If Leo's safe and we can get him back then I can take any news now, good or bad."

"First, I need to get rid of Sam and send Leticia out to the pool with Emilio. Then we can talk about this. We don't want them to think there's anything wrong."

She went to the door, "Stay here and I'll tell them you're not feeling well and need a rest. I'll be back in a moment."

Sam was on his mobile at the other end of the terrace with his back to the others. He put the phone away and came over to her. He seemed suddenly to be distracted. "Is anything wrong?" She asked.

"I'm afraid I have to leave. Is Emma alright? Can I help?"

"She just needs to rest. I think her trip to South Africa was more tiring than she realised. She's sleeping now, so we'll leave her in peace."

Leticia stood up from the table. "If Emma's sleeping I'll take Emilio up to the lake to feed the fish so we don't disturb her. Say *au revoir* to everyone, *chéri*." The little boy kissed them all goodbye and went off happily with his mother.

Sam took Jenny in his arms. "I hate to rush off, darling, but there's a problem I need to deal with immediately."

"I'm sorry to hear that. Is there anything I can do?"

"It's a business matter that I need to take over myself. You know what it's like, the buck ends here." He laughed. "Don't worry. I'll sort it out. But I don't like to leave you after such a short visit."

"That's alright. I have to look after my sister anyway. She seems very tired and she's missing Leo."

"Yes, I was wondering where her son is. It's strange that he's not here when they just returned from Joburg, don't you think?" He looked intently into her eyes, awaiting her reply.

"She wants him to be with other young people, Sam. It's his summer holidays and he's been with her for the last two weeks, wouldn't you feel the same?"

"Of course, you're right. I wasn't thinking. I was just a little worried that something might be wrong. I'm glad that's not the case. How long will Emma be staying?"

"Probably another week or so. And Leo will be coming next week, so you can meet him. If you're staying around that is. Are you? Am I going to see you again soon?"

"It depends on this latest development. I may have to take a trip. I'll call you tomorrow when I've made my plans."

She walked with him to his convertible sports car and they kissed for a long moment. "Give my kind regards to Emma. I hope she feels better soon." He climbed into the car and waved as he drove out of the gate.

Jenny breathed a sigh of relief when he disappeared from view. *Oh, Dear God, please let Espinoza find Leo,* she prayed as she walked back to the house. *Emma can't take much more of this. And neither can I.*

FORTY-FIVE

London, England

The Voice was speaking to someone in Cambridge, a university city about sixty miles north of London. The town is at the heart of one of the UK's Hi-Tech research areas, known as *Silicon Fen,* England's answer to *Silicon Valley* in California. Thousands of innovative inventions and discoveries have been incubated in the business start-ups that populate the area, a lot of them directly linked to the thirty-one colleges which constitute the University.

Simon Pickford, one of the Voice's old pupils, was now a celebrated pioneer of satellite and terrestrial tracking, of vehicles, equipment, people, just about anything that moved. His company, *EzeTracker,* had recently been floated on the UK stock exchange, making him an extremely, not to say obscenely, wealthy young man, much to the Voice's chagrin, since he had taught the young man everything he knew for four years. However the valuable knowledge Simon had extracted from his old mentor was not unappreciated by the entrepreneur and he welcomed the opportunity to give assistance whenever he could. In addition, his experience in the cut-throat arena of hi-tech innovations had taught him to be discreet, very discreet, and the Voice usually required that quality.

"So, what is it this time, Sir? Are we looking for elephants in Cameroon, or black rhinos in Zambia?"

"Nothing so exotic, my dear boy. A very mundane request. For you and your team, technically undemanding in the extreme. Nevertheless, time is of the essence and I would appreciate your immediate collaboration."

"Right. Hang on and I'll get Louise to cancel my next appointment. I wasn't looking forward to the interview in any case."

He came back on the line. "My limited abilities are now at your disposal. What can I do for you, Professor?"

Marbella, Spain

"My God, yet another death. These people who've got Leo must be monsters."

Jenny had decided to tell her sister about the death in Polokwane and that she was convinced that it would help Espinoza in his investigation. Emma was white in the face, imagining her son in the hands of merciless murderers.

She's falling to pieces, thought Jenny. *We can't go on like this.* "Emma," she said, "it's time I spoke to you sensibly, so please don't get upset. I know this is an awful situation for you and Leo, but you can't take refuge from everything that occurs by bursting into tears. You're a clever woman and you've got to start using your brain in a more constructive way. We've made amazing progress already and I'm certain that we'll continue to do so when Pedro gets into Polokwane. But I can't think of every possible angle by myself and I need you to help me."

"But you have no idea what it's like to have your only child in the hands of faceless murderers in some far off place. I feel so helpless."

"Actually I think I know pretty well what it's like. I've been held hostage myself, with my family and a close friend, at gunpoint, on the brink of death at the hands of a pathological killer. But somehow we prevailed. Not all of us made it unfortunately, but the murderer died and I and Leticia and Emilio survived and I will never forget it as long as I live. I know that we can do the same here if we refuse to give up and work together to find Leo and bring these people to justice. I know we can do it, Emma. Please snap out of this mood of despair and help me."

Emma stared at her in astonishment. "So that's what happened when you came over here after Charlie's death?

Jenny nodded. "And Ron's death too. It's not something I care to talk about or even think about, Leticia neither." She paused, wondering how much to say. "It was a revenge attack by someone who thought Charlie and his friends had robbed his family in Angola. A man called d'Almeida, posing as a Spanish lawyer. He was abetted by a French woman called Esther Rousseau, a very clever accomplice. He was killed, but she subsequently disappeared.

"My point is that our experience is an example of how strength, resistance and planning can win the day. Not just in your novels, but in real life as well. With Pedro we're a team of three. Let's start acting like a team." She looked at her watch. "We can't advise Pedro about this message now, he must be just boarding his flight. I'll text him to call us when he gets to Frankfurt. In the meantime, let's look at it again and see if we can spot anything further."

Phalaborwa, Limpopo, South Africa

Nwosu's phone rang at just after four, it was the Voice again.

"Good afternoon, Mr Coetzee. Do you have any further information for me? Have any other events transpired?"

Coetzee was sitting on the deck, smoking a cheroot and reading page one hundred and eighty of *An Extravagant Death*. He had told Leo to stay in his bedroom because he had to take an important call.

He put aside the Kindle. "Things are still just the same. I called the hospital and they've stitched up Nwosu's shoulder and he'll be able to leave in the morning. So I'll keep the kid with me in this motel tonight then pick the sergeant up early and we'll be on our way."

"I see. Are you still unwilling to divulge the whereabouts of the hospital or your accommodation?"

"It's not that I'm unwilling. I just don't think it's safe for us to let on where Leo is. It seems to me there's far too many 'accidents' happening around us for me to give anything away."

"To what are you referring, Mr Coetzee?"

"I'm talking about Lambert and Blethin. And Masuku, the guard. I don't know what kind of cleaning up operation is going on, but me and Leo aren't going to be part of it."

"You seem to be very well informed about recent news. Polokwane must be a veritable mine of information."

Coetzee took a deep drag of his cheroot. "They have newspapers here. We're not exactly in the darkest jungle. And I have my sources, of course." He waited expectantly for a reaction to this last comment.

After the usual pause, the Voice continued, "Well, Mr. Coetzee, be that as it may, I give my assurance that you and the boy are in no danger, none at all. That is precisely why we have removed any possibility of this arrangement becoming known to a wider audience. It is in our own and indeed in your own interests that you should leave no traces behind when your task is accomplished. Which is why I am now speaking to you, to assist you in accomplishing just that. However in order to do so, I do need to know where you are, because I have made some arrangements which will facilitate your endeavours."

"I'm listening."

"Instead of you going to Zimbabwe, I have arranged for two of my friends there to drive to Polokwane to take the boy off your hands. You can then pick up Sergeant Nwosu from the hospital and return to Johannesburg without further ado. What do you think of that?"

"When is this supposed to happen?"

"In point of fact, my friends are already on their way. I expect they will be in Polokwane by nightfall, that is to say in about two hours. You will therefore understand that I do need an address since Polokwane is quite a large town."

"OK. Give them this number and tell them to call me when they get to Polokwane. I'll take the boy to them on one further condition, the money you promised me. I want it in my account before I hand over the boy. I've done my job and I want my reward. Otherwise the boy and I will disappear until I see the money. Is that understood?" The security man had no intention of handing Leo over to anyone. He held his breath, waiting for the inevitable explosion.

"I agree, Mr Coetzee. You have done your job and you must be rewarded accordingly. I will give immediate instructions for the transfer and it will be in your account shortly. In the meantime please be prepared for my friend's arrival and all will be well." The phone went dead.

Now Coetzee was really worried. He didn't believe for a moment that the Voice intended to fulfil their agreement. *Thank God we're not in Polokwane,* he reflected. *Looks like we'll need to move again tomorrow to keep ahead of them. They have more resources than I do.*

Cambridge, England

Simon Pickford received a call from his chief telecoms engineer at four fifteen. "Thanks Tom," he replied and made a note. After quickly checking the information online he called a London number.

"Simon, that was impressively efficient." The Voice sounded ebullient. "Do you have good news for me?"

"You haven't lost your touch, Sir. Just as you suspected, the phone is in South Africa, but not in Polokwane."

"Do you have an exact location?"

"Not precisely. We used triangulation because of the short time available, but it's accurate to less than a kilometre." Pickford had not enquired after the reason for the trace and he had no wish to know. He received regular and unusual requests from his old College Master and he was wary of becoming embroiled in any suspicious affair. He had a very large fortune to protect.

"And where might that specific kilometre be situated?"

"I've never heard of the place. Phalaborwa. I looked it up and it's in Limpopo province, right next to the Kruger."

"Phalaborwa? Can you spell it out for me? It's far beyond the geographical knowledge of a University Professor." He noted the name down from Pickford's spelling. "Do you have the coordinates of your triangulation?"

He wrote down the latitude and longitude cross references. "That's marvellous. Well done and thank you, young man. No wonder your company is so successful. I envy your propensity for technical competence. I can hardly operate a mobile phone, even less a computer."

"You taught me all the theoretical knowledge I needed to build my platform, Master. So it's at your disposal whenever you need my help."

"Thank you, Simon. Now, if I may make one further request?"

"The entire *EzeTracker* team is at your disposal."

The Voice explained his requirements in a few words. "Is that technically feasible?"

"It's more difficult if there isn't an open line, but still possible now that we have the IP address of the phone. As long as it remains switched on and on the same network, we can follow it to the nearest GSM mast. I need an hour or so to get it set up then we can report whenever you want."

"It's now four thirty. Can you start to give me positions from, say six o'clock, on the hour? You don't need to spoil your evening by calling. A text from your technical people will be more than adequate."

"Don't worry about me, I've got more meetings. I'll arrange the set up immediately and check it myself until I leave at eight-thirty. Then we can report until midnight. After that my support staff are on duty and I don't want to give them such a delicate task, so we'll be off the air until seven in the morning. I hope that'll be OK."

"Thank you Simon, that will be most acceptable. Please give my regards to your wife and family and I hope to see you all soon."

The Voice put down his phone and turned to the other person in the room. "Did you hear that? It seems our Mr Coetzee is trying to bamboozle us as to his whereabouts. Impertinent man! I can't believe he is insulting our intelligence in this fashion. He must pay for such prevarication."

"Here it is." His companion had already found the location. "The cross point is situated right on the Olifants River. Sounds like an ideal spot for a safari holiday, several hotels and lodges there, they must be in one of them. Do you want me to start enquiring?"

"No. You won't make any progress by phone from England to South Africa. It will be a waste of time and money and may come to Coetzee's attention. I'm sure he has protected his privacy with some ready cash. I know I would have taken that precaution. I shall inform our Zimbabwe team to head for Phalaborwa and they can scour the area when they arrive. It can't be too difficult to find a single man and a boy in a hotel. It's bound to be noticed. In addition, we now have a trace on him if he decides for some reason to relocate to another destination. But my attention is now directed to Sergeant Nwosu. Where is he? Has he really been injured? It's all very odd."

"Have you thought of the possibility that Coetzee doesn't have the boy? Perhaps it's Nwosu who has him and he's making plans of his own."

"I think we can be certain of just one thing. The boy can't have escaped or we would be aware of it. He would have sought help and there would be some sign of it in the news or in the behaviour of our 'targets'.

"So what do you suggest? We wait until the gorillas get to Phalaborwa and just hope for the best?"

"I suggest that you google Polokwane and look for hospitals and clinics? They can't be too numerous. Then you can feed your impetuous nature by calling to ask if they have a Police Sergeant who has just undergone shoulder surgery. That may complete our picture; Nwosu in hospital, Coetzee and Leo in Phalaborwa."

"Are you going to tell the others about this?"

"I think not. There have been too many anti-climaxes already. I have no wish to provoke another. I'm calling Harare now."

Masekwaspoort, Limpopo, South Africa

The 1995 black Mercedes long wheelbase S600 was driving through the Nzehelele Nature Reserve on the N1 South in the direction of Polokwane. Although the car was fifteen years old and had done almost two hundred thousand kilometres, it was in showroom condition, gleaming in the late afternoon sunlight. It approached the Boabab Plaza toll station through *Masekwaspoort*, a natural cleft in the *Soutpansberg*, the magnificent forested mountain range of northern South Africa, at one hundred sixty kilometres per hour as if it were coasting. Nightfall was still more than an hour away and there was a soft luminous light in the sky.

The driver was a grizzled black man in a worn black suit and shoes, a white shirt and a straw trilby. Sunshades hid his eyes, which was just as well, they weren't pleasant to look into. They'd seen too many dreadful things over the last fifty years, many of them at his own hands. He looked straight ahead at the road and hadn't spoken since they had set off from Beitbridge, in Matabeleland South, Zimbabwe, just over an hour earlier. He was by nature taciturn and didn't make friends easily, nor for long. One of his friends, or maybe an enemy, had once said of him, "Plato's a difficult man to forget, but it's well worth the effort."

The man sitting beside him was about thirty, with a huge explosion of frizzy black hair, wearing a tennis shirt, jeans and white, expensive sneakers with a red motif. On his wrist he sported a large, ostentatious two-tone gold watch. Despite the size of the car's spacious interior, big enough for eight persons, he was so tall and massive, his knees were almost up under his chin. He reached for a cigarette then remembered the driver's admonishment, "No smoking!" Instead, he placed a piece of gum in his mouth and rubbed the tattoo on the back of his neck in frustration. The incongruous drawing was of a lithe, elegantly beautiful gazelle done in brown and black.

Despite the frigid atmosphere that separated the two men, the darkened windows created an intimate ambience inside the limousine. The only faint sound was that of the V12 engine purring as quietly as a kitten, when the clamour of pop music suddenly invaded the silence. It was the raucous voice of Tina Turner, belting out, *You're the Best.*

The passenger pulled out his mobile. It looked like a toy phone in his huge hand. "Hello, this is Gregory," he said in a melodious bass voice. He listened for a moment then said, "Wait a minute," and held the phone aside. Turning to the driver, he announced, "We've got new instructions. You'd better pull over."

The car pulled across to the hard shoulder and the driver switched on the warning lights. "Give it here," he took the mobile from the younger man.

"Plato speaking," he said. "Who's this?"

He listened for a minute then said, "Hold on. Greg, write this down. OK, go ahead."

He repeated everything twice and the passenger scribbled it down on the back of a take away menu.

"Is that it? Alright, we'll call when we get there." He gave the phone back and started the car again. "We're going to visit the Kruger," he said and drove the enormous vehicle back onto the motorway.

London, England

"Hello?" Slater replied cautiously to the call on his mobile. He was still sitting in the chair in his hotel room. After downing a stiff whisky he had fallen asleep and the ring tone had rudely woken him. He was still drowsy.

"Yes, it's me." he said.

"Listen carefully." It was his partner, the funder of the transaction, calling back. "I can hardly credit what's going on. I've put a half a million dollars into this deal and it sounds like it's in the hands of a bunch of bloody incompetent arseholes."

The man listened in silence, dreading what might come next. He couldn't afford to lose this opportunity. His share of the profits would set him up for a new life, a life he desperately wanted and needed. There was no way he could continue much longer in the situation he was in. He was desperate.

"I'm flying to London to oversee the whole business myself, tomorrow! Book me into your hotel and arrange a meeting with the others. I'll sort things out. If I have to, I'll fly to Joburg and kick the shit out of those amateurs over there as well. Everybody is making money at the moment except me and it's going to change. You know how good I am at organising complicated solutions."

He breathed a sigh of relief. The deal was still alive. "I was going home tomorrow afternoon, but I'll stay and organise a meeting for when you get here. Send me your flight details and I'll arrange for someone to pick you up at Heathrow."

After agreeing on the arrangements, he said, rather feebly, "Have a safe flight."

When his partner rang off he called a London number. "Good afternoon," replied the mellifluous tone of the Voice.

FORTY-SIX

London, England

"Have you been able to ascertain the whereabouts of the good sergeant yet?" The Voice had been otherwise occupied in arranging a pick-up car and hotel accommodation for the funder and hadn't followed his companion's online search.

"I've established that there are two clinics in Polokwane and twenty-five in the whole of Limpopo. So, to live up to your perfectionist demands, I called all twenty-five of them."

"And with what result?"

"None whatsoever! If Sergeant Nwosu was treated by a hospital or clinic, it wasn't near Polokwane. No policeman has been seen by any of them since last year when four officers were injured in a drug bust at the airport. And there has been only one patient who came in for shoulder surgery this month and it was a sixty-five year old woman. Sorry to be the bearer of bad news."

The Voice's demeanour didn't change. "Not necessarily bad, but intriguing. If Nwosu isn't in the hospital, where is he? Why and how has Coetzee usurped both his telephone and the boy? And why is he in Phalaborwa with him? Or without him, since we actually have no proof that he has Leo in his custody."

"There must have been a falling out of the gang. Coetzee has overcome Nwosu and has both the phone and the boy. That's the only explanation."

"I agree, but the question I am posing to myself is, why has Sergeant Nwosu not contacted us? He has the Belgian number and could have called. He knows that we have resources nearby in Beitbridge, so why is he avoiding us?"

"We'd better have more accurate information when the funder arrives tomorrow morning or it could get nasty."

"I agree. We must make every effort to ascertain the whereabouts of Nwosu, Coetzee and Leo. Our paymaster will expect no less from us. We must avoid incurring a wrathful reaction at any cost, there is a tendency towards rather drastic remedies and it could be expensive in many ways."

"I don't see what we can do from here to locate them. That's the problem with this transaction, we've got no visibility on what's happening over there and it's running out of control." His companion lit a cigarette and started pacing the floor nervously. "We'll have to wait and see what the Zimbabweans find when they get to Phalaborwa. Coetzee doesn't know we have traced him there and as you said, there are only so many places he could be staying, with or without the boy."

The Voice looked pensive. "Perhaps. But I'm going to take one more precaution. I shall ask Mr Coetzee for a recent photograph of the boy. If we receive it, we'll have located two out of three of them, and most importantly, our most valuable asset, Leo Stewart."

Phalaborwa, Limpopo, South Africa

Coetzee was immersed in Emma's book again when he received the call from the Voice at six thirty. He walked away from Leo, who was still sitting on the deck. After the usual pleasantries and queries about Nwosu's health, the caller asked, "Would it be possible for you to provide me with a photograph of Leo, taken today?"

"I could do that. Why do you need it?"

"I'm sorry to say, but it's a matter of money, as are so many things these days. Our partners agree to make the additional payment to you, which is comforting, but being rather less naïve than myself, they would like to receive what is, I believe, known as *proof of life*, a photograph taken today."

Coetzee weighed up his options. He still needed to buy as much time as he could. This was one way of gaining some time and might even produce some money into the bargain. "I'll take one and send it to you now," he answered. "Give me the email address. I haven't got my laptop handy." He waited, hoping that the Voice might make another tiny error, but it didn't happen.

He wrote down the Azerbaijan address that they had always used. "Right. It'll be with you in five minutes."

"Thank you, Mr Coetzee." The Voice rang off.

He picked up the newspaper and went back outside. "Right, Leo. I need another photo. Put that chair back up against the wall. Things are starting to happen. It won't be long now." He tried to sound confident but inside he was feeling very anxious. He would have been more worried if he'd known that he was about to make a mistake. A very big mistake.

Marbella, Spain

At six forty-five, Leticia received a call on her mobile. "*Bonsoir chéri*," she answered then continued in Spanish. "Where are you? It's Patrice", she mouthed to Jenny and walked out of the kitchen to talk to her fiancé.

Encarni had gone home and Emilio was watching television in the living room. Emma was upstairs, resting from the ordeal of keeping up appearances for the whole afternoon.

"How is he?" Jenny asked when she returned.

"Very tired, I think. This big transaction he's working on is taking it out of him. He's coming home tomorrow, so you'll see him at the weekend."

"Where is he now?"

"In London, I think. I never know where he is when he's running around like this."

"They told me at the bank he was off on another trip. Was he only here for a day?"

"I suppose so, but it's very hard to keep up with his travelling."

Leticia's voice had a dejected note, unlike her usual bubbly self. Jenny decided to drop the subject. *Strange that he comes to Marbella then flies up to London,* she reflected. *It's not exactly the shortest route.*

Leticia said, "Do you think you could find the time to help me with something tomorrow? I mean with Emma being here and everything."

"Of course. What is it?"

"Well, you're so clever with money and banks and I'm not. There's some papers I'd like to ask you about, financial papers."

"We can look at them now if you like."

"Not tonight. I have to put Emilio to bed, he's tired with all the travelling. Perhaps in the morning?"

"Very well. I hope it's nothing to worry about."

"Probably not but I'd like your advice." Leticia brought her son to say goodnight and they went along to their apartment.

Jenny watched them disappear along the corridor, a worried frown on her face. She went upstairs to check on her sister.

London, England

The Voice's laptop pinged. It was the message from Coetzee. It simply said, *Photo attached, as per your request. I'll contact you again when we manage to meet up with your colleagues. MC.*

The attachment was a snap of Leo sitting against a wooden wall, looking very fed up. He was holding a copy of the *Mail and Guardian,* in front of him, folded so that the front page displayed that morning's headlines and date.

In between Leo's hands was the local news headline, *Suspicious Death in Mayfair.*

"It seems that our Mr Coetzee has a sense of humour. A gentle reminder of the increasing body count in this business."

"Here. Let me blow it up so we can take a good look at it." His companion zoomed the photo up to twice its size and moved the view to the top of the page. "That's better. *Thursday, July 15th 2010.* It's definitely today's paper, but we knew that from the headline. Wait. There's something scrawled in the top margin." A moment later the faint handwriting became legible. It read, *Olifantsrivier Lodge.*

"Well, well! It appears that our Mr Coetzee has been rather careless. He has the boy and now we know exactly where they are. I think it's time for another call to Harare," said the Voice. "Well done to your inquisitive nature."

Phalaborwa, Limpopo, South Africa

Leo had found a weapon. An unimpressive weapon, lighter than the torch that had cracked Blethin's skull and more difficult to wield, but a weapon no less. He held it tightly in his right hand as he came quietly out to the terrace. *I'm sorry, Marius,* he apologised silently, *but I have to get that mobile again.*

Coetzee was smoking a cheroot. Still in his bathing shorts, he was standing on the edge of the patio looking thoughtfully down into the river. He had put his Kindle away at a very critical moment in Emma's book. Tory West was perilously near to becoming the victim of a violent death and he wanted to enjoy the chapter later, when this mess was over and he could relax for a while.

Now, he was waiting. Just waiting for something to happen, as he had done so often in his life. Learning to master his impatient nature had been one of the benefits gained from his time in the Special Forces. Long periods of waiting, usually to no avail, listlessly smoking and playing cards with his mates, wondering why the hell he was doing this, suddenly interrupted by mad, frenetic, adrenaline-pumping mayhem; the only overriding motivation being to kill or be killed.

He had left all that behind and he didn't miss it at all. This was different, no mayhem involved, just a financial negotiation. As long as he could stave off the Voice's hounds, the ball was now in Emma's court and she had to respond. No point in sending another message until she reacted. It wouldn't take long; she was desperate to get her son back and there seemed to be money around. He was beginning to suspect it was her sister who had it.

A reflection in the water made him turn around, too late to prevent the heel of his own hiking boot smashing into the side of his head. Dazed by the blow, he fell backwards into the river.

Leo dropped the boot and ran into Coetzee's bedroom. Found the car key in the trousers lying on the bed and raced outside to the Land Cruiser. He knew the tank was full because he'd helped Coetzee empty two jerry cans of diesel fuel into it. First he took Blethin's mobile from the glove compartment and shoved it into his pocket. Then he put the key in the ignition and turned it. Nothing! He tried again. Still nothing! His mother didn't have an automatic car and he wasn't aware that the ignition wouldn't fire unless he pressed on the footbrake

"That was very unfriendly, Leo. I might have drowned if you'd knocked me unconscious." Coetzee had pulled open the door. He was dripping water from head to foot and holding his bruised temple.

"Kidnappers have to expect that kind of treatment, Marius. You should know that."

"Come on, give me the key and get out. I'll forgive you on this occasion but my patience is wearing very thin, so no more heroics or I might have to show you some tricks we learned in the Special Forces."

Leo climbed down from the vehicle. He hadn't really expected to be able to get away but it was a good cover for the recuperation of the phone. Coetzee seemed to have forgotten about it. He said, "Remember the war, Marius. Every prisoner had to attempt to escape and if they failed, to die in the attempt. Or try again whenever they had the chance. Don't count on me not trying every chance I get."

"Be careful what you wish for, Leo. Right now you're under my protection. You're safe, because you're valuable to me. The minute you leave you become vulnerable, to the villains who are looking for you and to the police. They may already have been advised about your tendency to kill and wound everyone you meet. Just think about your options. Apart from me, they're not great."

FORTY-SEVEN

Diepkloof, Gauteng, South Africa

Nwosu checked his Vektor pistol once more and shoved it into the holster on his right hip. He was wearing the spare uniform that his boyfriend had brought for him with the gun from his apartment and his left arm was supported by a sling, carefully made and arranged by Jamie. He tended to preen in front of the younger man when he was in uniform. His partner couldn't resist his authoritative appearance. He was a good looking, charismatic man, even with his bruised nose and half-closed black eye, and took advantage of it whenever he could, especially with his male friends.

Jamie was seventeen years old, tall, slender and olive-skinned, with Mediterranean rather than African features. Lying back on the couch in just his shorts, he had soft feminine skin and hardly any hair on his body. Nwosu could barely restrain himself.

He had also brought a new prepaid mobile. Nwosu stored Jaimie's number along with several others in it. "Give me your phone. I've got to get moving." He put the new mobile number into the boy's phone. "That's so you can recognise this number if I get into trouble."

"Are you expecting more trouble, Jonathon? You know I worry about you."

"Where I'm going? No chance. I'll call you to arrange our flights when everything's under control. It'll be either tomorrow or Saturday, I've got everything planned perfectly, so don't worry." He wasn't as confident as he sounded, but the truth was he didn't have a choice. The money was still in his bank account when he'd checked earlier, but he knew he wouldn't live to spend it if he failed to deliver the boy. *Either this plan works or I'm in really deep shit.*

It was seven o'clock and dark. The drive should take about an hour at that time of night. The chances of them being in the house at eight o'clock were also high. He hadn't called, it might have caused them to worry, but he would wait in the car if there was no one home. He had time.

He kissed Jamie goodbye and went out to his Ford Escort, small, reliable and, fortunately for his present handicapped condition, automatic. It was too risky to take his own police vehicle in case he came across a patrol or another official car and had to explain why he was injured and away from his station. The tank was full and a backpack with his spare clothing and toilet items was on the back seat, just in case. He pulled the gear shift into *Drive* with his right hand and drove off into the night.

Tzaneen, Limpopo, South Africa

The black Mercedes was about one hundred kilometres from Phalaborwa, on the R71, a secondary road leading from Polokwane. Plato had chosen to drive as far and fast as possible on the N1 then go east across country. In fact, the drive wasn't too bad at that hour. Traffic was light and he was able to drive at a hundred. He expected to get to his destination in an hour and a half.

Greg was listening to music on his earphones when his mobile vibrated just before seven o'clock. He listened then said, "Hang on," and turned to the driver. "Can you find the *Olifantsrivier Lodge?* It's a tourist hotel in Phalaborwa, right on the river."

"Sure. I've been there before; I can find any place if I know the name." He looked at his watch. "Tell them we'll be there by eight forty-five."

The younger man closed the phone and sat back, trying to get comfortable in the cramped space. He placed another piece of gum in his mouth. "So. Who's this guy, Marius Coetzee and the kid? What's the story?"

"I don't know and I care less. My Greek ancestor had a motto. He said, *the less you know about people the easier it is to kill them.*"

Greg looked impressed. That was the longest sentence he'd heard the old man speak. "Is that right? Did he really say that?"

"Don't be a fucking idiot! He died a million years ago. Who the fuck knows what he said?" He gave a contemptuous laugh and lapsed back into silence.

The big man looked at him in disgust. *Arrogant bastard. Old and past it. He should retire. Maybe I should retire him myself.* He shifted into a less uncomfortable position, replaced his earphones and chewed his gum.

Plato reached for a bottle of water and took a swig. It was warm in the car and he didn't want to get dehydrated before going into action. He wasn't as young as Gregory Capstick anymore.

Delmas, Mpumalanga, South Africa

"Time for supper!" The blonde woman called up the stairs. "Switch off for tonight, it's eight o'clock."

Five minutes later her daughter came running down to the kitchen. "What are you making? I'm starving."

"Pour some water and grab a couple of cokes from the fridge. I bought some pork sausages and bacon and I'm doing a fry-up. OK for you?"

"Hmm. Sounds great. I'll set the table."

At eight fifteen they were sitting eating their supper at the big oak table, chatting about the day's events. Mobile phones and other gadgets weren't allowed at meal times. The sun had gone down and it had become chilly, so she'd lit a fire in the wide fireplace. The sound of the crackling logs made a pleasant background noise and the flames threw shadows across the room. Old fashioned values reined in their small family and they both looked forward to this precious time together.

The farmhouse was a massive, sprawling building, or rather a collection of buildings, that had been her ancestor's working farm for several generations, until no one in the family wanted to farm anymore. It was situated on the south side of the R42, not far from the golf club in Delmas, a farming community of about seven thousand souls, seventy kilometres due east of downtown Johannesburg. She and her husband had spent every weekend for two years driving over from Joburg to convert it into a habitable residence. The living room consisted of three stables transformed into one vast space with crossover beams high above their heads and old fashioned wooden-framed windows on all four walls. Some of the outbuildings had been connected to the main house to form a quadrangle behind, where they'd built a swimming pool and sun deck for the children they hoped to have.

The woman worked at the nearby Pleasant View Grape Farm, helping to grow a fine selection of table grapes, harvested for the production of a variety of white, red and rosé wines. It could hardly have been more removed from her previous job as a high profile journalist for a top-selling daily newspaper in Johannesburg, but she loved her new vocation. The predictable and never ending seasonal changes gave her a sense of comfort and certainty and the gradual transformation of the vines from dirty looking weeds to luscious fruit-bearing greenery was a continual reminder of the renewal and vitality of life.

Above all, she relished every moment spent with her daughter, thankful every day for the divine intervention that had brought their lives together. Three years after the event, she tried not to reflect on the dreadful moments they had experienced in the township. Although through her unconscious self she re-lived the trauma too often in her dreams.

Her reverie was broken by the barking of their two black Labradors, who raced to the front door. Her daughter got up from the table. "That's the front door bell. Who could be calling at this time of night?"

"Wait!" She jumped up and caught the girl's arm. "I'll look through the spy hole. I've told you before not to open the door before checking."

She walked through the kitchen to the entrance hall and switched on the outside light. "*Oh no!*" she thought, seeing the uniform through the hole. *"Not another visit from the police. I thought they'd finally laid it all to rest."* She called out, "Who is it? What do you want?"

"Good evening," a man's voice answered. "I'm Sergeant Bongani from Johannesburg Police Department. I'm very sorry to trouble you, but it's about your husband. Can I please speak to you for a moment?"

The woman looked worriedly at her daughter. "Take the dogs upstairs and I'll bring him into the living room. It's probably nothing important." She sounded more confident than she felt. Why would a policeman from Johannesburg be knocking on their door at eight in the evening? *Has something happened to Marius?*

She pulled back the deadbolt and unlocked the door. "Good evening, Officer" she said nervously. "What's happened?"

It was ninety-four and a half hours since Leo had been taken.

FORTY-EIGHT

Phalaborwa, Limpopo, South Africa

Leo was in the toilet with the door locked, checking Blethin's phone. There was no text from his mother and the red warning light was on. The screen read, *Emergency calls only.*

He quickly typed, *at Olifantsrivier Lodge in Phalaborwa with Coetzee. Plse come for me. LXX*

As he pressed Send, the screen went dark and the phone died in his hand. "Shit." He put it back in his pocket then flushed the toilet, ran the tap in the wash basin and went out to the terrace, wiping his hands. Coetzee was preoccupied with his laptop and didn't pay any attention to him.

"Are we going to have anything to eat?"

The South African looked up and laughed. "I've never seen anyone or anything eat as much as you can, and that includes a twenty-ton elephant. Get the room service menu."

They were looking at the menu when Nwosu's mobile rang. It was a Joburg number that Coetzee didn't recognise. "Hang on," he said. "I'll see who this is." He walked into the living room. "Hello?"

Nwosu's voice said, "There's someone who wants to talk to you, Marius. Hold on."

A moment later a woman's voice said, "Coetzee, I'm so sorry." He heard a sob and nothing more.

"Karen?"

Nwosu came back on the phone. "That's right, Coetzee. I'm presently a guest in Karen and Abby's house. It's a very nice place as I'm sure you know."

"What the fuck do you want, Nwosu?"

"Don't get upset, Coetzee. Something precious might get broken. You know what a short temper I have. I've got a very simple transaction to propose. Would you like to hear it?"

The South African clenched and unclenched his fist. If Nwosu had been in the same room he'd be a dead man by now. *Take your time,* he told himself, *be patient. There'll be time for revenge. There always is.* He gritted his teeth, thinking frantically. "I'm listening," he said.

"Look, Marius. This couldn't be simpler. You have something I want; Leo, and I have something that you want; your wife and daughter. The easiest and safest thing to do is just swap them over and everyone will be safe and happy."

"And how do you propose to do that?"

"Well, we don't want to make a public spectacle of ourselves, so it has to be done in a nice, quiet, private place. As a matter of fact, this house is perfect. Bring Leo here and I leave with him and you stay with Karen and Abby. Job done!"

He missed out the bit about killing me, he reflected. "And what happens to Leo?"

"I take him to Beitbridge and he'll be released when the ransom gets paid. It's what we agreed to do, but for some reason you screwed it up and ran off with Leo. You've been paid for your work, so just give him up and get on with your life."

He doesn't know about the Zimbabweans, realised Coetzee. *Nor about the story I told the Voice. He hasn't spoken to him because he's lost the boy. What happens when he gets Leo and calls him back? Even if I survive I'm a dead man and probably so is Leo, that's what happens.*

"What do you say, Marius? You don't want to risk anything happening to your family, do you? I don't think they'd appreciate being put second to a kid you didn't even know a few days ago."

Nwosu put the phone to Karen's mouth again. Both she and Abby were sitting on a window bench, hands bound behind them. The dogs were upstairs, barking intermittently behind the locked bedroom door. "Please, Marius." She cried. "Please come to get us. Abby is frightened to death and you know why. She can't go through this again. You have to come to help us."

Coetzee's heart sank. Karen was right, there was no turning back. "Has he hurt you or Abby?"

"No. We're OK, but we can't take any more of this. Promise me you"ll do what he wants."

"Don't worry, Karen. I'll be there."

"I heard that, Marius. A very sensible decision if I may say so. Where are you? How long will it take you to get here?"

Coetzee quickly calculated distances and time.

"We're a long way away. It's about a six hour drive, so we'll be there in the early hours. Meanwhile, just remember, if you lay a finger on my family, you won't live long enough to regret it."

"Don't worry, Coetzee. I promise to treat them as I would my own loved ones. By the way," he added, "don't forget to bring Leo, will you?"

Coetzee sat for several minutes, thinking about the call. He blamed himself entirely for the crisis Karen and Abby were in. *If only I hadn't humiliated Nwosu and left him behind, if only I hadn't tried to cut him out of the deal, if only…*

He took the book he'd shoved into his bag and removed the photo of Karen and Abby. *I was an idiot to lose you last time. It's not going to happen again.*

Coetzee stopped thinking about the past and switched to the present, his military training taking over. Nwosu was probably armed but his shoulder couldn't have healed by now. The advantage would be with him, but he would be surrounded by three vulnerable people, his wife, daughter and Leo. He started to work out the strategy that had come to his mind a few moments ago. A strategy to turn the tables on Sergeant Jonathon Nwosu.

London, England

"Coetzee and the boy are still at the lodge in Phalaborwa." The Voice read the text from his mobile. "It seems they haven't moved at all. They're presumably staying there for the night, so I think we can rely on the Zimbabweans to take control of the situation very shortly."

"And what about Sergeant Nwosu. Are we just going to forget about him?"

"At the moment, I'm afraid there is absolutely nothing we can do about the good sergeant. Until Coetzee can be interrogated we won't know his whereabouts, nor the circumstances of their separation, although one can hardly imagine that it was an amicable divorce."

Delmas, Mpumalanga, South Africa

"There. That wasn't too dificult was it?" Nwosu laughed. "I see there's still some warm food left. It looks delicious. You don't mind if I help myself? I've been driving for quite a while and it's going to be a long night."

He brought a stacked plate and sat at the table, gobbling the food and ignoring them.

Karen sat close against her daughter, hoping to bring some comfort from the warmth of her body, whispering positive and reassuring messages, trying to help her forget the memories which she knew would be invading the girl's mind. Memories of her school in Alexandra, on a Thursday in March, three years ago.

ALEXANDRA
JOHANNESBURG, 2007

FORTY-NINE

March 2007
Alexandra, Johannesburg, South Africa

Alexandra is one of South Africa's poorest and most dangerous townships, about sixteen kilometres north east of central Johannesburg. Ironically, it is close to Sandton, one of the wealthiest suburbs of the city. It was 17th March 2007, a warm, sultry morning and a cloudy sky threatening rain and probably thunderstorms. Karen was visiting the school to interview students, parents and teachers as part of a report commissioned by her newspaper. A devastating exposé of the poverty gap and treatment of blacks in wealthy areas, which still continued despite the accession of the African National Congress government under Nelson Mandela. Several parents had agreed to attend the session and there were nineteen people sitting with her on the floor of the large, windowless room at the rear of the building that served as an assembly hall and gymnasium; twelve teenage children, their teacher and six parents.

Thirty minutes after the start of the interviews, the alarm bell rang. There was no other noise and thinking it was a fire drill the teacher led everyone out into the corridor to take them outside. The corridor was already thronged with screaming children, the staff attempting vainly to evacuate the building in an orderly fashion.

They tried to make their way to the main entrance, but couldn't fight through the crowd of panicking children. Karen's heart jumped when she heard a noise like thunder coming from outside. She suddenly had a premonition of trouble. The sound came closer and she realised with horror it was gunfire. *An armed attack.*

The teacher shouted, "This way," and they turned and ran back along the corridor towards the rear entrance, struggling through the chaotic melee that surrounded them. They turned right at a sign marked *Emergency Exit.* As the three leaders turned the corner the sound of a fusillade of shots rang out. They had run in the wrong direction. They were blown backwards, their lifeless bodies thrown into the path of the others, blood gushing from their gunshot wounds and running across the filthy wooden floor. Screams erupted from the remaining parents and children as they ran back around the corridor and flung themselves to the ground. They clung to each other, terrified, wailing, and huddling together on the unexposed side of the passage.

Karen made sure no one else was hurt. "Wait here and don't move. Don't try to run or they'll shoot again. Just stay still and quiet," she said. Then steeling herself, she walked slowly forward with her hands in the air, looking in disbelief at the lifeless corpses of the people she had been talking to only minutes before.

As she approached the corner, she called, "Don't shoot! We have children here. Show mercy, we can't hurt you." There was no reply and she walked forward with her hands in the air, alone and frightened to death. In front of her stood eight men carrying an assortment of rifles and hand guns. To her astonishment she saw they were all white men. They had no insignia of any kind on their clothing.

"Please." she called again, "We have children with us."

"Who are you?" A slim, fair haired man with a wispy beard stepped forward. She noticed he had a squint, one of his eyes was looking straight at her but the other looked to the side.

"My name is Karen Spellman." She gave her maiden name, somehow sensing it could be important.

He gestured with his pistol towards the passageway. "How many people with you?"

"Twelve children and four adults. There are three people dead in the corridor."

He gestured again with the gun. "Tell them to come forward."

Karen noticed that his bad eye twitched nervously from time to time. "Do you promise not to hurt them?"

"If they come forward quietly they won't be harmed." He said to the other gunmen, in Afrikaans, "Don't touch them. We need them alive. This is our lucky day."

Karen signaled to the others to come forward. They were shaking with fear, the parents herding the crying children between them.

The man looked at the terrified group and spat on the floor. "Why is a white woman co-mingling with this black trash?"

"I'm visiting the school to write a story about education in the townships." She didn't dare tell them the truth about her mission. Karen had already realised that these men were members of a right-wing pro-apartheid militia. She didn't know which, perhaps the *Boeremag*, the Farmer Force, or the *Afrikaner Weerstandsbeweging*, the Afrikaner Resistance Movement, but it didn't matter. She knew they would kill her along with the others without a second thought if they knew she was there to try to sway public opinion in favor of the blacks

"So you're a journalist? What paper?"

"The Johannesburg Sun. I live in Joburg, not Sandton." She wanted to dispel any impression of wealth that could make her a hostage target.

"That's your bad luck and our good luck," he replied. "You should have stayed where you were. You came to the wrong school on the wrong day. You're going to regret that."

There was no one else in the corridor and an eerie silence now pervaded the atmosphere. It seemed that the school had been successfully evacuated, apart from them. The man pointed to a classroom on the corner of the corridor. Like the rest of the classrooms, there was no glass in the windows. "In there!" He ordered.

The children went to the back and Karen and the four remaining parents sat in the front. A man was posted in the corridor at each end of the classroom, so they could cover both approaches. The other men took the mobile phones from those who were carrying them then pulled seats up by the teacher's desk and sat facing them. None of them spoke and two men with rifles held them at the ready, waiting for an order from the leader.

He sat on the teacher's desk with the pistol in his hand, smoking and looking over the bedraggled group of blacks. His eye twitched more frequently as though he was becoming angry.

Karen tried to defuse the mounting tension. "What's this about? Can you tell me what's happening?" Now she could hear sirens outside. The police response had been rapid, considering Alexandra's reputation. Often the authorities waited until any disturbance had been settled between the protagonists before arriving on the scene to sort out the dead and wounded.

The man looked at his watch and placed his mobile on the desk. "You're now officially hostages, that's what it's about. Sixteen niggers and a white nigger lover. Shut that row up," he shouted at the crying children, brandishing his rifle. They clung to each other, weeping quietly. The adults were afraid to turn and comfort them, the women also trying to stifle their sobbing.

Hostages? What do they expect to get in return for a group of black, penniless families? Karen's mind was whirling, trying to fathom the reason for the attack. "I don't think you're going to get much of a ransom for us," she said.

"You hear that, Jan?" The youngest of the group laughed. "She thinks we want money. Stupid bitch."

"Don't use names! I told you not to use names. Fucking arsehole. Shut the fuck up!"

"Shit! I fucked up there. It won't happen again." The man sat back on his chair, suitably chastised.

"So what is it you're after, Jan? If it's not money, what is it?" Karen was now convinced that they were not about to be killed, at least not yet. These men wanted them alive so they could barter them for something.

The man looked past her with his unsettling squint. "You'll find out soon enough. The police already know, that's why they got here so quick. We sent a message at eleven o'clock. It took them just ten minutes, so we've got their attention all right."

His mobile vibrated on the desk. After the third ring he picked it up. "Who's this?"

He listened for a while then said. "There are sixteen niggers and a white woman from Joburg. None of them are hurt. You've got until four o'clock to agree to our demands. If you don't, we'll start killing them one by one. Starting with the children," he finished menacingly. He hadn't mentioned the three dead blacks lying in the corridor. He closed the phone and sat back on the desk, looking pleased with himself.

"What did they say?" The same man asked, he must have been in his early twenties. *He seems nervous,* Karen thought. *That's why he's talking so much.*

"It was the police chief from Sandton. He said they're examining our demands. They'll get back within the hour."

Karen shivered. *That doesn't sound good,* she thought. *It's usually the precursor of an assault where the gunmen and most of the hostages get slaughtered.* She sat silent, looking the men over. Four of them were typical middle aged Afrikaans; two were bald, two had moustaches, one had a beard and they all carried comfortable paunches behind their belts. They looked as if they spent a lot of time watching television and drinking beer. The leader, Jan, carried himself with some panache, despite his affliction, whilst the sixth, the youngest was short, skinny and uncomfortable, nervously moving about the room and sniffing.

Trying to ignore the sound of the crying children and parents, she attempted to assess the situation pragmatically. Over the years she had covered a lot of stories about the white pro-apartheid movements. Three of the leaders of the *Boeremag,* Mike du Toit, Herman van Rooyen and Rudi Gouws, were amongst twenty-six men arrested in 2002 for the Soweto bombings and for plotting to assassinate Nelson Mandela and overthrow the National African Congress. They had been in prison in Pretoria since then and likely to remain there for the rest of their days.

But she didn't think these men were part of that organisation. More likely some crazy splinter group that was trying to turn the clock back against all the odds and world opinion. Karen wasn't optimistic about the chances of a happy ending to this nightmare unless there was some way she could intervene and affect the outcome. She forced herself to think laterally, outside the box. *Coetzee's in Joburg today. He can be here in thirty minutes. I need a pretext to get him here.*

"Can I ask a question?"

"Depends what it is." The man called Jan lit up a cigarette.

"Are you hoping to swap us for someone?"

"Smart! She's smart." It was the younger man again.

"Will you shut your fucking mouth up! What did I tell you?"

Karen waited a moment until the men quietened down. "Are you trying to get du Toit and the others released?"

Jan took a drag on his cigarette. "Why would that be of interest to you? You're a hostage now, we're the ones negotiating and we're the ones with the guns."

"I told you. I'm a well-known journalist. My paper is the second biggest in the country and I'm on TV regularly. I know a lot of people and I can reach them easier than you can." She paused to let her words sink in. "Maybe I can help you get what you want and get what I want at the same time."

"Which is?"

"It should be fairly obvious. I want to get out of this alive. I don't really care about the blacks, but I care about my own life."

There was a long, pregnant pause, the men looking at each other, at Jan and at her. The black families huddled even closer together, whimpering miserably. This white woman had just announced their death sentence.

Finally, Jan said, "We're not the *Boeremag.* They're a bunch of incompetent arseholes and they're all going to snuff it in jail. Their plans were completely insane. Fucking idiots, they deserved to get caught." He dropped his cigarette and ground it out on the floor with his silver-buckled boot. "We," he waved his hand around the group, "are members of the *Wit Heerskappy Vegters,* The White Supremacy Fighters." He stared expectantly at her with his good eye. Was this woman whom she claimed to be, a well-known journalist who would know about his organisation?

"So it's Julian Sumerschmidt that you want to get out?"

The men looked around at each other, impressed by her knowledge and by the extent of their reputation.

Now, Karen was very afraid. Sumerschmidt had been imprisoned the previous year for leading a frenzied attack on another school in Soweto. He and his followers had set the building on fire, causing the deaths of more than a dozen teachers and children. His extremist right-wing militia group had pledged to eradicate schools and education from the reach of the black population of the country. The man was a monster. If these apparently moderate group members were anything like him, no one would escape alive.

"You know your business." Jan nodded his agreement. "How come you're writing about educating niggers? Are you for it or one of the thousands who agree with our anti-education agenda?"

"My personal politics aren't important here. I want to save my life, that's my only agenda."

"What can you do for us that we can't do ourselves?"

"You need a bigger platform to get your message across than a crappy little school in Alexandra. This is just a little local upset, it won't get an inch of newspaper space or any of the TV exposure that you need for such a campaign. You have to be seen by those thousands of supporters that you're talking about. I can arrange that for you."

"Oh yeah?"

"I think I could arrange a TV interview. You could state your case and ask your supporters to help you in demanding Sumerschmidt's release against the liberation of me and the others here."

Now she had their attention. The other men looked at her with admiration. They would be on television, celebrities. This could be the start of a massive nationwide surge in support for their ideals. They were hooked.

"How'd you organise that?" Jan was clumsily trying to grasp the implications of the idea. The rewards were clear, it could be a personal triumph for him, for Julian, for their whole campaign against these filthy niggers, but he was trying to weigh up the risks. Was this really possible? Could she get what she said? Was it a realistic idea?

"The Sun has a permanent link into the South African Broadcasting Corporation. This would be a perfect piece for SABC2. You could make your statement in English and Afrikaans to get the maximum impact. It would probably be rebroadcast all over the world, on prime time television. I can even help you write the script if you want."

"How do we do it?" Jan was becoming more and more seduced by the idea. He could see himself on the screen, telling the world the truth about their group, about the need to cleanse the nation of the corrupt black government and to put a white man back in his proper position as President. A return to white supremacy with the blacks back in the chains they had weasled their way out of through the machinations of that lying bastard, Mandela. And Julian Sumerschmidt sitting in the Houses of Parliament in Cape Town.

"We can do it with a mobile phone. Mine has a video app on it. It's a cinch. We can post it on Youtube and Facebook. It's a great idea." The skinny young man was walking excitedly around the desk.

Karen gave him a disdainful look. "That's not such a great idea. Have you seen the crazy stuff that gets posted on social media? That's the kind of amateur thing the *Boeremag* would do. You'll be taken for just another band of maniacs like them. I thought you wanted to be taken seriously?" She spoke convincingly, desperately trying to persuade Jan to do it her way, otherwise there would be no escape.

"Shut up both of you!" Jan shouted. "I'm in charge here." Standing right in front of her, he said. "I know your plan, lady."

Karen's heart sank. She looked at him anxiously, trying to ignore his peculiar stare.

"You want to do this just to get a story on TV, don't you? You want to use us to get an exclusive. Just to get your face on TV."

She breathed a silent sigh of relief. "You're dead right. If we do this properly we'll both become big names. Now I have two agendas; to save my life and to become even more well-known. Is that a problem for you? You get your agenda at the same time, even better than you planned. In any case, what have you got to lose? You've still got the guns and the hostages." She faced him down, putting on a show of strength that she didn't feel. "And there's another thing we have to consider," she added, hoping it wouldn't backfire on her.

"What's that?"

"Why did you kill the three blacks? You're going to have to address that. Your supporters might approve but there's an awful lot of people who won't."

"It was just an accident. This kid, Rich, he just lost his rag and blasted them when they came round the corner."

"I thought we were being attacked. I just saw people running at us. I was protecting our group is all."

Jan lit up another cigarette. "We came in the back way expecting to find people like your group trying to escape. The whole plan was to take hostages, so you were our lucky charm, walking into our arms like that. And a white woman to up the stakes. That's a bonus. I don't give a shit about the dead niggers, but it was a mistake, I know it."

"Well, you've got to find a convincing explanation for that so it doesn't get in the way of your petition for Julian."

"I need to think about this." His eye twitched several times and he turned away to call the other men around him, all of them furiously offering their opinions in hushed tones.

After a couple of minutes, he sent them back to their seats and their guard posts. "So, what's your plan? Remember, any tricks and this place goes up in flames and you're all dead meat."

"You'll have to let me speak to the police chief who called you. I'll probably know him or one of his bosses. I told you, I know lots of people."

"Then what happens?"

"One of my friends is a cameraman at SABC2. If he's in Joburg I can get the police to ask for him and a sound technician to come immediately."

"Nobody except the cameraman. No assistants, no security, no other equipment, nothing. One guy with only a camera, that's all. And we frisk him before we let him in."

"Whatever you say. If he'll do it, I'm OK with that."

"I want you to write down what you're going to say and you'd better stick to that, word for word. Any tricks and you know what'll happen."

Coetzee never told Karen exactly what happened behind the scenes. When she recommended Marius Coetzee as her preferred cameraman, it took a while for the local police and the Sun to put two and two together. The police refused to back an intervention by an operative who was married to one of the hostages, but when he was apprised of the situation Coetzee fought tooth and nail to be permitted to save his wife. In the end his arguments and reputation won the day. But this would be a one man mission with no support. If it failed, the police would storm the school and God only knew what mayhem would ensue.

"Search him, head to toe." It was two hours later and Coetzee was standing at the classroom door, holding a JVC TV camera over his shoulder. He was wearing sunglasses, a tight-fitting shirt and jeans and sneakers and his unruly curly hair was slicked down with lotion. Not his chosen attire, but carefully advised by Karen's boss at the paper. She had also given him some quick instructions about the equipment but he didn't need much. He had to be able to do just one thing.

Jan had ordered the adult hostages to move the corpses along the corridor, so they couldn't be seen from the classroom. The members of his group wouldn't touch the black bodies, but they threw some water over the floor to make the blood stains less visible. Now everybody was back in position and he was rehearsing his speech in his head, hoping to be able to brush off that minor incident without jeopardising his TV performance. Karen had made several suggestions and he had taken notes.

Coetzee let Rich search him thoroughly and check his camera over then he sauntered into the classroom, as he imagined a media personality would do. He laid the camera on the desk, ignored the black families, and smiled at his wife. "How you doing?"

"I'm OK." She said casually and pointed at the boss man. "This is Jan. He's with the *Wit Heerskappy Vegters.* We're going to film him making an appeal for Julian Sumerschmidt."

Coetzee shrugged. "Whatever. Have you got a speech ready?" Jan nodded. "How long?"

"Five minutes or so."

"Where do you want to set up?"

"I think I should be standing in front of my guys and the hostages. In charge. What do you think, Karen?"

"Sounds good. Maximum effect, minimum explanations."

Coetzee stood behind the desk with his back to the wall while the others took their places. Karen was prominent in front of the hostages, and the militants stood to Jan's other side, toting their guns and trying to look tough. Jan was holding his crib sheet and his pistol was in its holster.

He hoisted the camera off the desk and pointed it towards Jan. It was a JVC HDV professional model, the microphone sitting on top of the lens. When he saw they were ready, he counted down from five, as he'd been told, then pressed the trigger. Nothing happened. "Sorry," he said. "Bad battery contact. It happens a lot. One second."

He opened up the battery compartment at the back of the JVC and removed something, then laid the camera on the desk again.

"What the fuck's going on?" Jan reached for his pistol.

"I wouldn't do that if I was you." Coetzee was holding a small object in his hand, about the size of a golf ball. He pulled a metal loop from it and held the ball firmly in his left hand. "This is a Dutch V40 fragmentation grenade and I just took the pin out," he announced calmly. "As long as I keep hold of the security grip nothing happens. If I let go, we all get blown to tiny pieces."

There was a long moment's pause while everyone registered what he had said then the hostages started wailing, crying and hugging each other again. If this was man was a rescuer, he was more lethal than the terrorists.

Jan raised his pistol. "If you do that you'll kill yourself and all the hostages and this white woman!"

"What do you care?" Asked Coetzee. "You'll all be dead as well. Do you really want to get blown apart for the sake of Julian Sumerschmidt?"

Jan looked round at Karen, a crazed expression on his face, his eye flickering madly. "You fucking bitch! You've set us up. Who is this guy?"

Karen ran to the desk and stood beside Coetzee. "He's my husband and he's a Special Forces Officer."

After the terrorists were led away by the police Karen sat with the remaining hostages, talking, praying and comforting them. Now they realised that her deceptive act had been to save them they cried even more than before, but now, tears of joy and relief. Coetzee had left with the police to do his debriefing so she had time to get to know them. She spent a long time talking to Abigail Wantusi, whose parents were killed in the first shooting. The ten year old was inexplicably calm, seeming not to have registered their deaths, not fully understanding that she had survived the tragedy only to become an orphan.

Finally Karen left them and went out to her car. She knew there would be no counselling for them, no compensation, no apologies from anyone, nothing to assuage their trauma. They would just have to get back on with their mean existence and be thankful they had survived, sometimes wishing they had not. She drove back to the Sun's offices in Johannesburg slowly, in a pensive mood, trying to put the incident into perspective, looking for a rational explanation for an otherwise meaningless attack which had taken three innocent lives, wondering if it would change anything. But deep inside she knew it wouldn't make any difference.

At the Sun, it seemed that every member of the staff wanted to greet and embrace her, voicing congratulations for her mental fortitude and the quick thinking that had resulted in the rescue of sixteen innocent blacks. In tomorrow's headlines she would become a celebrity, but even as she sat at her desk writing the article that would project her into the limelight, she was wondering if she really wanted to continue in this job. Trying to change things that couldn't be changed, trying to make sense of a state of affairs which could never be justified, trying to understand a status quo which could cause such chaos and human misery in such a brief moment of time.

Karen wrote her article then went home to prepare dinner for Marius. They both deserved to enjoy a quiet evening after today's events.

DELMAS

MPUMALANGA,
SOUTH AFRICA, 2010

FIFTY

Delmas, Mpumalanga, South Africa

Sitting on the floor of the living room alongside her daughter, Karen reflected that the episode in Alexandra was the catalyst that started the inevitable breakdown of her marriage.

That evening both she and Marius were in a sober mood. Although he was in a violent job she knew he didn't enjoy the violence and never spoke about the incidents he dealt with on an all too regular basis. He wasn't a man who shared his secrets or his life very easily. He had kissed and held her with relief after the gunmen had been disarmed, but had said no more about the matter when he returned home in the evening, apart from one remark.

When she asked him what he had felt when he was holding the grenade, with everyone's life in his hands, he laughed and said, "You didn't think it was armed, did you? I'm not that crazy. That grenade is about twenty years old and it's a bloody tricky little weapon. The fuse is only four seconds and the security grip is crap. It would probably have blown us all to kingdom come if it had been armed."

That was the night her nightmares began, recalling parts of the ordeal through her unconscious mind and senses, like scenes from a fragmented movie. The burst of gunfire out of nowhere, the dead bodies lying in a pool of blood in the corridor, the smell of sheer terror emanating from the hostages, the unbearable suspense of being at the mercy of a gang of bloodthirsty extremists. She relived the indescribably joyous feeling of confidence and relief at the sight of her husband, their rescuer and protector. Only to be assailed again by the sensations that returned to invade her senses, the stench of cordite, blood, urine and worse pervading her nostrils until she woke up feeling frightened and physically sick.

Somehow she couldn't separate Marius from these scenes of brutality. His insouciance in front of six armed murderers wasn't normal. He had taken a gamble with seventeen innocent lives, including his wife's and it had paid off, but what if he had been challenged? She realised that to him it was just another day in the life. That was what he did, perhaps that was what he was, deep down inside. She began to see her husband in a very different light. The terrorists hadn't harmed her physically but they had triggered a change in her mental attitude. A change that would lead to many more important and not necessarily good events.

The next morning Marius had to leave for Durban, to coordinate security measures in preparation of a signatory meeting for an international protocol on maritime terrorism, with the presence of many government leaders. He would be gone for several weeks. Karen called her boss at the Sun and obtained a month's sick leave on compassionate grounds. He readily agreed, on one condition; the article she had written after being released had boosted sales and sparked off a TV campaign which they would benefit from for quite a while, now he wanted a series of follow-up articles which she could write from home.

Karen accepted the assignment and over the next few weeks, she regularly drove out to Alexandra to visit Abigail at her aunt's home, a tiny, crowded shack, where she and her two younger brothers were now staying, sharing a bedroom, a bed, a cot and the floor with their two cousins. She took them out for walks and drives, gently helping them to push away the memories of the awful episode they had suffered. When she saw that the children couldn't yet cope with returning to school, she stayed in the evenings, tutoring them and coaxing them back to normality. She slept with Abby on the cot, alongside her brothers stretched out on a rug on the floor. After a while she started to bring the girl back to their flat in Kensington. It had a spare bedroom that they had always assumed would one day be occupied by their own child. Now it was sometimes Abby's.

Little by little, she was becoming the child Karen had never had, or rather had never had time to have. Coetzee had been twenty-seven and she twenty-five when they were married, still plenty of time to have kids, once she'd accomplished something worthwhile in her career. And she had accomplished a lot. She was now Senior Current Affairs journalist at the Sun, the largest daily newspaper in the Joburg area. A top job which gave her immense satisfaction, but at a price. Marius had never tried to persuade her to change her priorities, he respected her work and her success and was happy to see that she was happy. He had also been immensely successful in his army career. At age thirty-five he was promoted to Major in the Special Forces unit, requiring him to travel a lot, sometimes for weeks at a time. They were both immersed in their work but relished the time they could spend together when they were in Joburg for a while, quality time, just the two of them, happy and in love with the life they shared.

Somehow the time slipped by as she kept putting off becoming pregnant another year, another promotion, another step up the ladder. Then suddenly she was forty and they were still childless and when she finally decided to let it happen, it wouldn't. She had waited too long and her body clock had ticked away until it was no longer able to conceive a child. After two years of trying and then taking fertility drugs, she was still unable to conceive. She and Marius discussed *in vitro* fertilisation, but there had recently been a number of high profile 'accidents' involving such drugs, which Karen had actually reported on for her paper. For once, Coetzee put his foot down and refused to let her risk her health. They had each other and they were very involved in their respective careers and that was enough, in his opinion. If children were no longer an option then they would manage without them.

Marius was gone for more than a month after the events in Alexandra and she made the most of it, devoting herself to improving life for the victims and especially for Abby. She also fulfilled her promise to her employer, turning in a series of top-selling articles on the reality of post-apartheid life for the black community.

When Coetzee returned, they had both reached decisions that would change their lives forever, but neither was ready to discuss them. He had decided to leave the force and set up his own security company; she had decided that Abigail needed parents and they should adopt her. A year later they were divorced and she still couldn't understand why.

The day he had agreed to adopt Abby, as they now knew her, was probably the day she decided to divorce him. At the Sun, where she was plucking up her courage to call time on her journalistic career, one of her colleagues excitedly called her over. "Congratulations, Karen, that's a fabulous honour for Marius."

"What do you mean? What's happened?"

"You mean you don't know? He didn't tell you?" The woman pushed a draft text towards her. "It just came from the daily news desk."

Karen looked at the article in amazement. It read;

Honoris Crux Decoration for Special Services Major.

Capetown September 15th 2007
This morning in the Houses of Parliament, on behalf of the President, the Minister of Home Affairs bestowed one of the nation's most prestigious decorations on Major Marius Coetzee of the SA Special Forces Regiment. As reported in this newspaper on March 17th this year, Major Coetzee overcame a gang of eight members of the White Supremacy Fighters to save the lives of twelve children and four parents at the Alexandra Junior School. Major Coetzee's wife, Karen, was also saved by his single handed intervention, without any back up from police forces.

The white extremists are presently in jail awaiting trial for murder, abduction and plotting against the African National Congress government.

Speaking on behalf of President Mandela, the Minister of Home Affairs, Nosiviwe Mapisa-Nqakula, awarded Major Coetzee the Honoris Crux Decoration after paying tribute to his bravery and his notable contribution to the eradication of white extremist groups in our country. *Full story on page 7.*

Karen went back to their apartment and checked her husband's wardrobe. His dress uniform was missing. He had left early that morning without disturbing her and having said nothing about the ceremony or the award. She sat in their bedroom, asking herself what she really knew about the man she was married to. What reason could he have for not sharing this prestigious award with her? What kind of a man would overcome six terrorists, virtually unarmed, save seventeen lives without blinking an eye, refuse to talk about it afterwards then sneak off to Cape Town to receive a medal without letting her know. Marius was a hero, an extraordinary man, but he had no idea how to be a husband. She shook her head and went to shower and change for him coming home.

Marius had taken an afternoon flight from Cape Town and was back early. Karen had chilled a bottle of *Krone Borealis Cuvee Brut,* a South African champagne. She poured two glasses and took them out to the terrace. "Cheers, Marius," she said. "Did you have a busy day?"

"Oh, you know, same old same old. Nothing special."

"Really? I thought you were down in Cape Town?"

"Oh, that? Just some government business."

Karen tried to remain calm, but her emotions overcame her. "So you think that getting the *Honoris Crux* is just some government business. That's why you didn't even mention it to me. Just the 'same old same old'. Didn't it occur to you that I might have liked to be told about it before I read it in a newspaper column? Before my colleagues realised that you hadn't even mentioned it to me? Or that I might have been thrilled to accompany you to the ceremony?

"What's wrong, Marius, are you ashamed of receiving a medal for saving my life and sixteen others? Or is it of so little consequence that you can't even be bothered to speak to me about it? For your information, I'm immensely proud of what you did, but I just can't work out what goes on inside that shell of yours. After twenty years of marriage, I feel I still don't know you at all. And it's starting to get to me."

Coetzee said nothing for a moment then he raised his glass. "Cheers, Karen. I've been thinking about our talk the other night and I agree it's a great idea to adopt Abby. Let's drink to that."

In November, Karen learned that she had been awarded the runner-up prize in the Taco Kuiper award for her investigative Sun articles on post-apartheid conditions. She attended the ceremony alone, without even informing Marius of her achievement. He was still away from home frequently on emergency calls and an ever increasing number of government missions which he couldn't or wouldn't share with her. Abby's adoption came through in December and they all spent Christmas together in the old farmhouse in Delmas. She had never felt so happy and fulfilled in her entire life, but she knew that it had more to do with Abby than with Marius.

Six months after the adoption, Karen and Abby went to live in Delmas and Coetzee rented a small apartment in Diepkloof. She filed for divorce the following week. She demanded no alimony, she had a small pension and some savings and had already found a job at the winery. She was with her daughter and that was enough for her. He was left with his army salary and a bitter taste in his mouth. A month later, he resigned from the force and started Coetzee Security Services.

Every other weekend when he came to take Abby out for the afternoon, Karen was aware of something missing, something lost, an aching feeling of unfulfilled emotion, but she never said anything. He'd never understood what he'd done wrong.

Frankfurt Airport, Germany

Pedro Espinoza was in the Lufthansa lounge at Frankfurt airport waiting for his flight to Johannesburg. Jenny had booked him in business class for the eleven hour journey. He had received her text message as he got off the first flight but waited until he found a quiet corner to call her back.

Jenny was alone in her room and she answered immediately. "Pedro, are you safely in Frankfurt?" Without waiting for his reply, she immediately told him about Coetzee's message. "I haven't forwarded it to you because it's so sensitive. What do you want me to do?"

"Just read it slowly to me."

Jenny did as he asked then re-read it a second time. "What do you make of it?"

Espinoza asked, "Do you think it's genuine?"

"Emma and I have looked at it very carefully and we're convinced it is." She summarised the observations she'd made to her sister.

"Very good points as usual and I agree with you. So, this changes everything. If Coetzee has Leo, it means there's been a disagreement and the whole organisation may be in disarray. But we still don't know who is telling the truth. We need to reply to both of them and ask for proof of life from the ARGS people. If they are unable to provide it, Coetzee's message will be conclusive. Then we can decide exactly how to act."

"We'll do them both this evening. A more specific reply to Coetzee's demand?"

Exactly. And can you stop Emma from doing anything until I get there? She'll obviously want to transfer the money immediately and get Leo picked up by some trusted person, but it's not as easy as that. Whichever option is the right one, it still all comes down to money. Most kidnappings go wrong just at that moment and it's usually the hostage who pays the price. We can't afford to take that risk. It has to be a carefully planned operation, with no room for error."

"The good news is that you'll be there by midday tomorrow and you are that trusted person. But I don't have a bank account there so I don't know how I can get the funds to you. And cash, which is probably what he wants, is impossible. We need a friendly banker to help us. I'll make a few phone calls tomorrow morning."

"We also need to negotiate the amount. A million dollars is still a lot of money and I'm sure that Coetzee hopes to get only a half of that."

"Right. I can start that negotiation this evening by email. But there's another thing that's even more important, Pedro. There is some person, or perhaps more than one, who has organised this whole business to harm my family just to steal my money and two people have been murdered in the process. I don't believe it was Coetzee and Nwosu alone. We must catch all of those persons and make them pay for their crimes so they can never harm us or anyone else again.

"If we can get Leo back through Coetzee, that's a wonderful result, even if we have to pay him first then trap him later. But we have two objectives; first to get Leo safely back and then to bring the culprits to justice. Do you agree and can you do it?"

"That's why I'm going to South Africa, Jenny. I'll do my very best, trust me."

Marbella, Spain

After Leticia had taken Emilio to bed the sisters sat together on the terrace. There was no breeze and the slender croissant of a new moon floated over their heads.

"It really is paradise here," Emma sighed. "I just wish Leo could share it. The pool, the lakes, everything. I could have taken him to Tarifa to try paragliding. He's always wanted to do it but the Scottish climate isn't exactly ideal. Although we do get plenty of wind."

"I'm sure he'll be with us very soon and he's welcome to do anything he wants. After what he's been through he deserves no less."

"What are we going to do about Coetzee's message? Why would there be two groups trying to blackmail me and which one really has Leo? And then there's the money, it's such a fortune. Can you really afford to lend me so much?"

Jenny thought for a moment before replying. She could afford the money, but that was almost a secondary issue. She reflected on her conversation with Espinoza. Someone was responsible for this abduction plan and its dreadful consequences, but they were still no nearer to finding out who it was. She had to explain to Emma that the punishment of the kidnappers was just as important as the return of her son.

"First," she said, "I'm now convinced that Coetzee has taken Leo away from whatever group it was and is trying to help us, but for a price. As far as that demand goes, the answer is, yes I can afford to lend you the money, but I won't. I won't lend it to you because you'll spend your whole life working to pay me back and I would never impose such a burden on you. It will be a gift to you and Leo and I'll be delighted to give it, at the right moment.

"But secondly, we must find these people and bring them to justice. They've committed terrible crimes and we have to make sure they pay the price of their actions."

"Oh, Jenny, I've been having nightmares about finding the money and I don't know how I could ever pay it back. But I'll try to find a way. I have to. Leo's my son and I'll sacrifice everything I have for him. And you're right, we have to find these people and stop them from ever harming us again."

She paused for a moment. "It's going to be very complicated to arrange this with Coetzee. Tell me how you think we should proceed."

"That's the most delicate part of this whole sordid story. We have to set it up with the utmost attention to detail so that nothing can possibly go wrong. I'll speak to my bankers tomorrow morning. Pedro will be there by midday and we can work out the procedure with him. He's clever and resourceful; we couldn't have a better partner.

"But it will still take some time. We have to be absolutely certain of Leo's whereabouts and who he is with, so we need to maintain contact with both sources without raising their suspicions. I have to arrange for the cash to be available in Polokwane and Pedro has to set up the meeting and ensure that Leo is in a safe place where he can be picked up and flown home. I've told him I'll pay for a private jet to Mauritius, as I did for you. That way we don't have to worry about the immigration police." She said nothing about her other objective. *One thing at a time,* she told herself.

"Now come and help me write these emails. In Coetzee's case we need to haggle. If we don't negotiate he won't think we're serious." They took Emma's laptop up to the office and opened up his email.

FIFTY-ONE

Phalaborwa, Limpopo, South Africa

Coetzee had paid the hotel bill with cash, so no one could track his credit card payments. He knew he was becoming even more paranoid, but since Nwosu had somehow managed to find Karen in the middle of nowhere, he couldn't risk leaving a trail of any kind. He changed into a long sleeved shirt and cotton trousers and threw his remaining clothes into the travel bag. Leo helped him repack the Land Cruiser and put his own suitcase in, he was still biding his time hoping to get a chance to escape somewhere nearer to civilisation, where he could find help, or at least make contact with his mother.

The South African checked the bedroom once more and went to get his laptop from the desk. Out of habit, he looked for messages. There was an email and it was from Emma Stewart.

Mr Coetzee. Your message was such a relief to me. I have been incredibly worried about Leo and now I can see from the photo that you have been able to rescue him from his abductors and he is in good health. Thank you, I will never forget your help and I agree that you should be rewarded generously. The problem is the amount you are asking. I have very little money of my own and I cannot lay my hands on such a large sum, it is quite impossible, especially in *a short space of time. I have a friend who is able to lend me $300,000- and that is all I can raise at the moment. It seems heartless to be bargaining over the value of my son's life, but I have no choice. You say you like him and that you want us to be reunited. I promise that I or my friend can fly down immediately to pay you $300,000- if you can find it in your heart to return Leo to me and end this dreadful episode.*

Please confirm that you can do this for me.

Sincerely, Emma Stewart

"Don't you think that's a bit over the top?" Emma had asked, before they sent the message.

"We have laid it on a bit thick," answered Jenny, "but since he knows you're an author, he probably thinks you write like that all the time. In any event we should get his attention, three hundred thousand is a lot of dollars. Let's see what he says."

Coetzee closed the laptop and went out to the car. "I've got good news and bad news."

Leo looked at him and said nothing. He continued, "The bad news is that we've got a hell of a long drive ahead of us. The good news is I just got a message from your mum. We're on the right track to getting you home."

London, England

"There's an email." The Voice's companion went over to Dudley's laptop when she heard the 'ping'. "It's from Emma Stewart."

"Aha! And what does Ms Stewart have to say?"

"I'll read it to you. It's quite short. *I have received your messages concerning my son. I won't try to tell you how despicable your actions are, since you are obviously bereft of any human emotions or compassion. Your demands are quite beyond my financial capabilities, but I will make every effort to raise whatever funds I can. However, before I enter into any negotiations to get Leo back I need to see a photo of him showing today's date. I will then contact you again. If Leo is harmed in any way I promise that you will never escape justice.*

Emma Stewart.

"She appears to be suitably upset."

"And well informed of the normal procedure. She wants an up to date photograph."

"Naturally. The one we sent had no date on it, but fortunately we have the one we just received from Coetzee with today's local press headline. Are you able to remove the handwritten address on the top of the page?"

"Of course. But I'll need to take over your laptop for a few minutes."

"Very well. Please do so, but we won't send it yet. Let's wait until we have confirmation from the Zimbabweans before we do anything." The Voice tried to sound confident but he was beginning to worry. He prayed that the situation could be brought back under control. If not, he hated to consider the alternative.

Phalaborwa, Limpopo, South Africa

The Mercedes S600 pulled into the courtyard of the Olifantsrivier Lodge at eight fifty pm.

"Stay here and don't get noticed." Plato climbed out of the car, stretched his back then went through the reception door.

Greg watched him disappear into the building. *Fucking supercilious old shit.* He took the chewing gum from his mouth and wrapped it into a ball in a Kleenex tissue. Threw it out of the car then replaced it with a fresh piece and started chewing again. He was becoming increasingly irritated with the driver's behaviour. He either said nothing at all or made a sarcastic or patronising comment. *Who the hell does he think he is?*

He knew Plato was the oldest and most experienced man in the company, with a fearsome reputation. The story was that he'd been part of ZANU during the Rhodesian Bush War and when Mugabe was appointed prime minister after independence, like many of his close supporters, he became a part of the inner circle. The lessons he'd learned during the fifteen year civil war became even more useful in clearing the path for Mugabe to become president. Greg had been with them for only two years and this was his fifth job, all totally successful, but it was the first time he'd been paired with Plato and he wasn't enjoying it at all.

There was only one employee at the counter, a pretty young black girl who couldn't have been more than sixteen. She smiled at the Zimbabwean. "Good evening. Are you checking in?" Opening up what was presumably the guest list for the day.

He didn't smile in return. "I'm looking for a friend, name of Marius Coetzee. He's here with his nephew."

"You mean Mr Marius Ridgeway I think?"

"Right, he has a double barrelled name, I forgot."

The girl looked crestfallen. "I'm sorry. You've missed them by about ten minutes. They checked out and drove off just after eight."

"Did you see which way they went?"

"No. When you leave the drive you can turn east, west or south and they didn't say where they were headed, so I have no idea.

"He told me they were staying here tonight."

"They were booked for the night, but he said they'd changed their plans. They've been gone for literally ten minutes, if you know their mobile number you should be able to meet up. "

"Thanks." Plato turned and walked away.

"You're welcome." He heard as he went out the door.

He took off his jacket, carefully placed it on the back seat and climbed back into the car. "They're gone and I don't know where. Somebody's fucked up big time. I'll have to call the office."

Greg said nothing as they drove out of the driveway and parked on the side of the road. As the girl had told him, there were three possible choices; east, into the Kruger, south towards Joburg and west, the road they had come on from Polokwane, but they had no idea which to choose.

"Get them on the phone." Plato said.

Greg pulled out his mobile and called the number. He passed the phone to the driver without a word. He was becoming really sick and tired of this old man.

Cambridge, England

"Good evening, *EzeTracker*." Simon Pickford answered the phone himself. It was after eight o'clock in the UK and most of the staff had already left. "Oh hello, Master," he continued, cursing his luck that he was still in the office. He was tired and wanted to get home for a glass of wine and dinner.

"I'm sorry to bother you again, Simon, but I'm pleased you're still there."

"What's the problem this time?"

"It seems that our target has left Phalaborwa. He was in a lodge there and he's checked out. The problem is that I don't know where he has gone and I need to make contact with him." The Voice's companion gave him an amused look, mouthing *'make contact'*?

Simon breathed a sigh of exasperation. "Right. I'll ask for a trace immediately and get back to you." He terminated the call and rang the technician in charge of the monitoring with the new instructions.

He sat back in his chair, rubbing his eyes and wondering what his old college mentor was doing tracing someone in South Africa. His usual requests involved tracking animals or precious artefacts or other strange objects which he deliberately asked nothing about. If the Master was involved in smuggling or anything similar he preferred not to know about it. But this was a different kettle of fish. *Why would he be tracking someone via their mobile phone when he could just call them up directly? I can't think of any reason which wouldn't be illegal and I don't want to tick that particular box.* He decided he would become unavailable for any future requests from the man. It was becoming too risky for him and his company.

London, England

It was eight thirty before the Voice's telephone rang.

"Simon. Thank you for calling back. I see from the map that our target could be driving east, west or south. Which is it?"

"I have no idea. That's why I'm calling so late. We can't trace the phone at all."

A shiver ran down the Voice's spine. This was not the time to lose Coetzee and the boy. "How can that happen? Has he switched it off or thrown it away?"

"I don't know. We can't find it on the network. It probably just means that he's driving and there aren't any transmitter masts nearby. South Africa is a very big place and there are enormous areas where there isn't any mobile connectivity. I've been looking at the network coverage and whichever way he drives from Phalabarwa, there are very few masts, because there's hardly anyone or anything there."

"I see. So there's no way that we can trace him at the moment?"

"The problem is that if the masts are very far apart, he won't stay in contact for long enough for us to get a fix. We need a short period of continuity to be able to identify the address and match the signal to at least one mast. The maximum coverage for a GSM transmitter is four kilometres. If he's driving at a hundred an hour, that gives us about a two minute spot between the entry and exit of the transmitter range. I've given instructions to set up a search on an area of one hundred clicks around Phalabarwa in every direction. As soon as he passes an area with enough masts, I should be able to give you his whereabouts within a four kilometre range."

"Assuming of course, that he hasn't discarded the phone or switched it off."

"Exactly. If that's the case I'm afraid even our technology can't help."

"Well, thank you and I'll await your news." He closed the phone.

"You'll have to call Harare, I suppose." The Voice's companion lit up a cigarette. "Their men are sitting waiting in the middle of nowhere. They won't be very happy with us. It's been a long day and now a long night."

"Indeed. However, they are being remunerated. I'll call now and tell them to be patient. We unfortunately have no alternative."

"And what if we've lost them completely? If Coetzee has realised the danger of the phone and switched it off or thrown it away?"

"I feel that is highly unlikely. It is his only means of communication with us, he won't want to cut that thread until he is good and ready. After all, we are the channel to the money. He believes he is manipulating us, even though it is the contrary that is true, I am confident that we will find him again soon. Please pour me a glass of wine and try to be patient."

Over Germany, en route for Johannesburg, South Africa

"Can I get you a drink, sir? Champagne or something else?" The Lufthansa air hostess was rather pretty, about thirty, with a charming smile.

Why not? Thought Espinoza. *It's a shame to waste the business class privileges.* "A small glass of champagne would be welcome, thank you."

The hostess poured him a generous glass and placed a packet of savoury snacks on his table. He took a sip, *Hmm, cool and delicious.* Opening up his notebook, he started rereading everything from the beginning. He was looking forward to his meal and then to a good night's sleep. He wondered what was happening in Polokwane and Marbella. *We'll find out soon enough tomorrow.*

Marbella, Spain

"Don't worry about it, Sam. Emma and Leticia are still here so I wouldn't be able to spend much time with you for a few days anyway. Call as soon as you get back and we'll arrange dinner, just the two of us. " Jenny breathed a sigh of relief and after exchanging fond farewells she closed the phone.

The Moroccan had called as she was getting ready for bed to say that he had to leave early the next morning for a few days. Now she could forget the subterfuge around Leo until he returned and with luck the trauma might be resolved by then. *One less complication to worry about,* she thought. *But I am looking forward to some time with him when it's over. This week is hard work, even for my only sister.*

After sending the messages to Coetzee and ARGS, the two women had gone up to their bedrooms. They were both exhausted. Emma was trying to take her sister's advice; to focus her mind, think constructively and avoid becoming too distraught and overwhelmed by the ongoing situation. Jenny, pragmatic as always, was assessing the chances of arranging a large amount of money, in cash, to be available to Pedro, eight thousand kilometres away, within a few days. She climbed wearily into bed, wondering what tomorrow would bring, trying not to imagine all the things that could go wrong.

Gravelotte, Limpopo, South Africa

Coetzee drove past Gravelotte, on the R71, at a hundred and twenty kilometres an hour. It was just before ten o'clock, there was virtually no traffic on the road and he was ahead of his own tight schedule. Leo was snoring quietly beside him and his headlights were now pointing towards Polokwane. He calculated their arrival in Johannesburg in about five hours. That would give him the leeway he needed to execute his plan. He let the window down a little and lit a cheroot, holding it near the gap to carry the smoke away from the boy. He was momentarily surprised at his consideration. *Getting too fond of him,* he mused.

He had driven past two small townships so quickly that the Telkom GSM network hadn't even registered his presence, but the Land Cruiser had now been in range of the masts in Gravelotte for over two minutes. In Cambridge, the *EzeTracker* technician saw the IP address pop up on his screen. He quickly identified the transmitting mast then compared it with the next one to appear. He called Simon Pickford, who was now at home and enjoying his well-earned glass of wine. The target was going west towards Polokwane on the R71. Simon called his mentor and the Voice called Harare. The re-entry into cellular coverage also caused Blethin's battery-dead phone, which had been asleep, to awaken for a tiny moment, consigning Leo's text message to the Telkom spectrum, on its way to his mother's phone in Spain.

It was ninety-six hours since Leo had been taken.

FIFTY-TWO

Phalaborwa, Limpopo, South Africa

"Gravelotte? You're fucking joking! We came through there two hours ago in the opposite direction." Greg had answered the mobile since Plato was out of the car relieving himself. He hadn't accepted the younger man's suggestion of waiting in the lodge and getting something to eat. It was almost ten pm and after the long drive down from Beitbridge then waiting in the car for an hour in an icy silence Greg was tired, hungry and in a foul mood. "I'll tell Plato. If we don't call back then we're on our way. How often are you checking the direction?"

Plato listened without comment to Greg's report then they climbed back into the Mercedes. A moment later, the limousine was on the road again, driving at a hundred and twenty kilometres per hour towards Gravelotte, then Polokwane. They were sixty minutes behind Coetzee and Leo.

Delmas, Mpumalanga, South Africa

The woman and her daughter were lying on a settee curled up together, fast asleep. Nwosu looked at his watch. It was almost ten thirty, *time to get things moving*. He went to the corridor and called his own mobile number again.

"What is it, Nwosu?" Coetzee sounded irritated.

"Where are you, Marius? Are you on your way with Leo?"

"No, Nwosu. I'm driving through the Kruger with a chimpanzee. Don't be such a bloody idiot, of course we're on our way, approaching Polokwane, and the less you call me, the faster I'll get there, so piss off and leave me in peace."

"See you later, Marius." The policeman reflected for a moment then called the Brussels number he'd stored in the disposable phone.

"Who is this?" Although he hadn't recognised the number, despite the slightly distorted words the Voice sounded as calm and collected as always.

"It's Sergeant Nwosu. Is this a good time to talk?"

After the usual pause, the Voice replied, "Sergeant Nwosu, how pleasing to hear from you." Another pause. "Unfortunately I can't speak at the moment. Can I call you back in a minute or two on this number?"

London, England

The Voice and his companion had been watching Mathew Bourne's Swan Lake on the Sky Arts Channel. He pressed the 'Record' button and regretfully switched off the TV. "We'll finish watching that later. So, our missing sergeant has emerged from the twilight zone of Polokswane. Let's find out where he is calling from and if he tells us the truth, shall we?"

He called another number. "Simon, dear boy, I hope I'm not interrupting your evening too much but I'm afraid I need to ask one last favour."

Five minutes later he called Nwosu's number back, the connection now being followed by the EzeTracker network. "Sergeant, I apologise for keeping you waiting, but I'm rather busy as you may imagine. I understand from your colleague, Mr Coetzee, that you have been incapacitated. Are you fully recuperated now?"

He waited, wondering what pretext he would hear next.

"I'm fine. Just a shoulder problem that needed attention. It's fixed now and we can get on with the transaction."

"That is indeed good news. Is the boy with you?"

"He's arriving shortly with Coetzee. I just talked to them."

"Excellent. And may I enquire where you are awaiting them, Sergeant?"

"We're meeting here in Polokwane, then driving up to Beitbridge. We'll be there in the morning. This time nothing's going wrong."

"I see." The Voice smiled grimly. "Then let's leave it like that until Mr Coetzee and the boy arrive then you could perhaps kindly call me again."

His companion said, as he put down the phone, "I'll be very surprised if he's still in Polokswane."

"It's possible, because that's where Coetzee is headed with the boy. In any event, we'll know as soon as Simon calls back."

A few minutes later, Simon Pickford informed him that the second phone was in Delmas, Johannesburg.

"It's a small farming town in the east suburbs of Johannesburg," his companion showed him on the iPad.

"I see. So Nwosu and Coetzee are both lying to us, but it seems that neither knows that the other is in contact, nor what they are saying. It's possible that Coetzee could be heading there with the boy, since the fastest route from Phalaborwa is via Polokwane, down the N1. But I'm at a loss to decide which of their conflicting *histoires* is closest to the truth, if either."

"I'm trying to find the location in Delmas. If I put in the exact coordinates then look on the street map, there's only one property it can be. See?" The photograph showed a long empty road leading out of Delmas with one large house at the end, bordered by empty fields. "It looks like a farm, there are several buildings all grouped together."

"Can you find the exact address and discover who lives there?"

"It's on Groot Street, but I can't find the number. There are only four houses at the beginning of the street and this one right at the end. I'll pull up the street directory."

The Voice poured out two more glasses of Burgundy as the woman continued the search.

"Here we are. It can only be the first or last street number, so we've got a choice of number one, that's a Veterinary Office, or number five, Ms Karen Spellman. What do you think?"

"Is there any chance of finding her on the Internet?"

"I doubt it, considering there are six point nine billion people who aren't on it. But I'll look anyway." Her fingers travelled quickly over the iPad keyboard. "She is in here, lots of entries. She's a journalist in Johannesburg, quite well known, it seems. Let me open this one about an award she won."

The Voice turned in distaste at the exclamation that followed. "I don't believe it! You really are the luckiest man in the world. Look at this."

"You know I hate reading those screens. Please quote it to me without undue excitement."

"This is from November, 2007. Karen Spellman was awarded the runner up prize for the Taco Kuiper award. That's a journalistic award for investigative reporting, apparently. It says here that she wrote a series of articles on the challenges of post-apartheid hardships suffered by the blacks. The articles were instigated by her capture in the previous March by white supremist gunmen in a school in Alexandra, along with a group of black teachers, schoolchildren and their parents."

"I'm sorry, but I fail to understand how….."

"Please just wait. The kidnapping was foiled by a major in the Special Forces who captured the supremists single handed and saved the lives of all of the hostages. Would you like to know who he was?" This last question was issued in a smug tone.

"I can hardly control my excitement."

"Major Marius Coetzee! And, before you interrupt again, he is Ms Spellman's husband!"

Delmas, Mpumalanga, South Africa

Nwosu made himself comfortable in an armchair and closed his eyes. Everything was back on track and he could get a well-deserved rest. He let his mind drift to Jamie, the money and Mozambique.

R 71, near Gravelotte, Limpopo, South Africa

"New orders from Harare. Do you want to stop?" Greg stopped scribbling and held the phone away in case the driver exploded. He had driven in a state of silent rage for the last thirty minutes, the atmosphere in the car becoming more frigid by the kilometre.

"Where is it this time? Disneyworld? Just tell me where and if I don't have to turn around again, we'll go."

"It's a place called Delmas, east of Joburg. We've got the name, street and house number, everything. They'll all be there. Coetzee, the cop and the kid. There's a woman there as well, they said. It actually sounds right this time."

"How the fuck do you know whether it's right or wrong? Wait." He entered the destination into the Satnav. "I'm taking a left here and going down past Lydenburg to the N4. It cuts out Polokwane and Pretoria and it'll be faster than going through the toll stations. Tell them we'll be there in five hours or so. I'll give it this one last try and if it's crap, we're going home."

Greg relayed the message and sat back, trying to get comfortable. His stomach was aching with hunger and he was full of gas. He needed to ask for a pit stop, but it wasn't a good time. He hated this old man.

London, England

"Well that was almost as enjoyable as the original production at Sadler's Wells." The Voice switched off the TV. "Were you ever fortunate enough to see it?"

"No. You know I haven't been in England for very long. It's a controversial version. Was it a success?"

"You mean the prince and the male swan pairing? It was much more successful than the traditional production. It ran forever in London and New York and is still produced all over the world. I personally prefer the story like this. It's somehow much more nostalgic."

"I suppose that should tell me something about ballet lovers. But I'm not a highbrow, so I'll take your word for it."

The Voice laughed. "Touché," he said. "Now it's time to conclude our business for the day. Please send the edited photograph to Ms Stewart's email address without any comment whatsoever. If she's still awake she will worry about it all night. If she's already asleep I'd like it to be the first thing she sees tomorrow morning, by which time her son will be once more in our possession."

"I'm surprised to hear you talking so cruelly. It's not like you."

"I confess that I am becoming rather frustrated with this business. What seemed like a fairly simple plan has become all too complicated. I dislike complications and I dislike schoolboys and I shall be very glad when we terminate the programme successfully."

The woman registered this remark without comment. She pressed the Send button.

He heard the familiar 'whoosh' as the photo left the laptop, on its way via the Philippines address to Emma's mailbox. "Excellent, well done! Now, it's quite late so you are welcome to stay the night if it is more convenient for you."

"I'd rather not if you don't mind. Our funder is arriving tomorrow and I want to be presentable to give assurance as to how the funds are being spent."

He masked his disappointment and helped her into her jacket, carefully positioning himself for the most impressive view of her magnificent bosom. Lord Arthur Dudley was bisexual but he appreciated beauty in all its forms, especially in the male or female physique. Never having seen the woman's unclothed breasts was a constant source of disappointment and of future promise. He walked her to the apartment door. "Goodnight, Esther. I look forward to seeing you tomorrow morning."

"Goodnight, Arthur, sleep well." His companion gave him a peck on the cheek and walked up the street towards Bayswater.

Dudley watched her gently swaying hips until she disappeared from sight then came back into the apartment. He unlocked the door to his private office, a generously sized room which no one else, not even his Philippine cleaning lady, who spoke very little English, had ever entered. The walls above the height of his desk were papered around with newspaper articles and photographs of all kinds. There were many erotic images of young men and women, mostly theatrical looking adolescents, all with fair hair. The news articles were dedicated to various felonies involving contraband, trafficking and fraudulent or financial crimes, mostly in Europe, but some in more far flung places like Singapore, South America and Australia. There were reports of the events themselves and in many cases the results of trials and prosecutions. The earliest items were from 1998 and the latest in January of the current year.

On a beautifully restored Chippendale dining table in the corner was an eclectic display of memorabilia, each exhibit labelled with a date and description. An African elephant's foot stood next to a horn from a white rhino and the dried penis of a South China tiger. Several Egyptian relics from the Valley of the Kings were presented next to a collection of antique manuscripts and a Roman ivory diptych. A shelf above the table held a large collection of rare publications of erotica; a 1955 French edition of Nabokov's *Lolita, Ratirahasya,* Kokokka's Indian sex manual written in the eleventh century in Sanskrit, a Latin edition of *Ars Amatoria,* by Ovid and others of equally unique provenance. Tellingly, a copy in the original Mandarin, of Gao Lian's *On Abstinence in Sex,* from the XVI century was prominently displayed. There were many more priceless or unobtainable items, the epitome being a small, exquisite vase dating from the Ming dynasty placed on top of a beautiful Japanese lacquered cabinet from the 15th century. The table held a treasure trove of stolen antiquities and illegal hunting trophies collected over a period of almost twenty years.

Despite owning these objects from many parts of the world Dudley had never been beyond the borders of England and would not take a trip longer than a local taxi ride. He suffered from hodophobia, an irrational fear of travelling any further distance on transport of any kind. He didn't own a car and had never learned to drive. The very thought of setting out on a trip, even a holiday away from his apartment filled him with panic and caused sweating and often nausea. And so, since his relocation from Cambridge to his apartment in Westminster, seven years ago, he had never been further north than Regent's Park nor further south than Wandsworth Common. He relied entirely on the network of friends and colleagues he had managed to assemble during his years at Cambridge College of Digital Computing. Without travelling anywhere, Lord Arthur Dudley had virtually the whole world in his hands; to make money and to obtain what he wanted.

Looking around the study appreciatively he sat at his desk and pulled a file towards him. A diary was open at today's date and he flicked through to July 18th. The date had a red ring around it and a handwritten note, *Shipment from Marseille.* He opened the file and reviewed the email he had received that morning via his ISP in the Philippines. On the desk there were three prepaid mobile phones, each with a SIM from a different service provider; T-Mobile in Germany, Bouygues in France and AT&T in the US. All of them would show up as *Not Possible* on the recipients' screens, because they all transited the communication through Proximus in Belgium. He chose the phone with the AT&T connection and called a Geneva number.

"Oui, allo."

"*Bonsoir,* M Jolidon," he said. He could hear music in the background and assumed that the man was in the casino as he usually was in the evenings.

"*Ah, bonsoir Monsieur.* Just a minute, I'll find a quiet corner to speak. Right, that's better. What can I do for you, Monsieur?"

Dudley continued the conversation in fairly fluent French. He was at ease both in that language and Spanish but had never spoken

French to Esther. He preferred to keep such information to himself. It often proved useful to overhear a conversation that he wasn't intended to understand. "Do you have any positive news for me since our last conversation? I need to make certain arrangements, as you know. What is the latest situation?"

"It's still not clear. There is some confusion over the bids for the merchandise and as you pointed out to me, money talks."

"And what are you doing about it, if anything?"

The funder is flying over to see me in the morning. I'll see what we're able to salvage from the operation. It may only be a question of making a little less profit, but I need to speak to him personally."

"On the contrary. I strongly suggest that you induce your funder to increase the financial incentive. It's in everyone's interests, his own and ours too."

"I see what you mean. He can hardly walk away from his original investment, can he? I'll try that approach and see how it works. *Merci beaucoup, Monsieur.*"

"Please call me as soon as you have further news. I'll be awaiting your call."

Dudley rang off and sat reflecting on the conversation. *It's strange how small the world is.* He had been introduced to Esther by Jolidon and it promised to be a very profitable introduction. His position as Director of the Safe Keeping Department at Ramseyer, Haldemann brought him into contact with a large number of wealthy and often well-known personalities. It was only to be expected that some of that wealth would rub off on those around them.

Using the US phone again he called the number in Marseille from his contact list. "Thank you for your email message. So you've informed the other party that the merchandise is no longer available?"

"*Bien sûr, Monsieur*. Of course. I called him yesterday in accordance with your instructions. He is going to call me after he meets with his funder."

"That's excellent, well done. And it's confirmed that the shipment will be arriving on Sunday, the 18th?"

"*Oui Monsieur.* The ship left Latakia on the 13th and is arriving in Marseille early evening on Sunday. Unloading will commence first thing on Monday morning. Everything is going according to schedule. I am only waiting for your final instructions on who is actually going to collect the merchandise."

"You will have final and definite instructions by Saturday at the latest, together with details of the payment and collection procedure. Is that acceptable?"

"You have never failed me Monsieur, *merci*."

"*Très bien. Merci et bonne nuit.* Thanks and goodnight."

Dudley closed the file, locked the office door and went to pour himself a glass of Burgundy. *That's the problem with being an intermediary,* he smiled to himself. *You're never really sure what's going on elsewhere.*

DAY SIX

FRIDAY, JULY 16, 2010

FIFTY-THREE

Diepkloof, Gauteng, South Africa

Coetzee's Land Cruiser pulled up in front of the apartment in Diepkloof at two forty-five in the morning. He had smoked ten cheroots on the journey and drunk a litre of water and he was knackered and feeling queasy. He'd made a quick stop for petrol after leaving the toll road at Pretoria. Thankfully the car had an enormous capacity, over six hundred kilometres, but he was being ultra-careful. Leo had stayed awake from then on, trying to cross examine him on where they were going and why, but he had stayed tight lipped. He had a plan and he didn't want it second guessed by an inexperienced school kid, however bright he might be.

"Come on," he said as he got out the car. "We're going to pick up a friend."

They went up the stairs to the second floor and he pressed on a doorbell, three times. A moment later a light came on and a voice called, "Is that you, Jonathon?"

"It's the ambulance service," Coetzee called. "There's been an accident." He put his finger across his lips and held Leo to one side so they wouldn't be seen through the spy hole.

"What's happened?" The door opened a crack.

Coetzee smashed it open with his shoulder and pulled Leo inside with him then shut the door behind them. Jamie was standing in his underpants looking suitably terrified. "Who are you?" He asked in a trembling voice. "What do you want?"

"I'm Coetzee. Is anyone else here?" Jamie's eyes flickered towards a door in the hallway.

The security chief strode to the door and pushed it open. A teenage boy was sitting up in the bed, a mobile in his hand.

"Throw it here!" Coetzee put out his hand and the boy threw the phone to him. "Well, well, two-timing your boyfriend, Jamie. He'll be really upset when he finds out. You know he has a very short temper? Murderous I would call it." He turned to Leo. "Sorry, I forgot to make the introductions. This is Nwosu's devoted partner, Jamie and this is … who gives a shit? Get out!"

As the boy ran out the door, carrying his clothes, Coetzee said, "Get ready, Jamie. We're going to visit your boyfriend."

Delmas, Mpumalanga, South Africa

Plato parked the Mercedes about one hundred metres from the farmhouse and he and Greg walked along the road in the darkness. It was just after three in the morning and the moon was obscured by light cloud. They both carried Makarov PM semi-automatic pistols, provided by Russian intermediaries to the Zimbabwean gangster regime. Plato, who was a firearms fan and a renowned sharp shooter, held his pistol in his hand. Greg preferred to use his physical force and had never yet needed to resort to a pistol. It remained in his pocket, a decision he would come to regret.

He was feeling a lot better, since Plato had begrudgingly agreed to grab a take away from an all-night burger house in Lydenburg. Three cheeseburgers and fries and a large Coke had sorted out his stomach. He belched noisily as they walked and Plato gave him a disgusted look. *Who gives a shit what he thinks,* he told himself.

Light footed, they walked along the driveway to the entrance. The house looked enormous, a square building in the centre of a large plot of land. There were lights on downstairs but no sound to be heard. Inside the building every living creature, three humans and two dogs, was sound asleep. The house was silent and still until the sound of the doorbell rang out. Karen and her daughter awoke to the frenzied barking of the angry and frustrated dogs upstairs, fear and apprehension immediately returning to their minds.

Nwosu jumped up and took out his Vektor. "Get to the back of the room," he told Karen. She and Abby struggled to their feet and retreated to the far end of the living space and sat on a settee, holding each other close.

"Is that you, Coetzee?" Nwosu called. When there was no answer, he looked through the spy hole. He could see nothing because Greg's great thumb was in the way. He pressed the button in the front of the trigger guard to release the safety catch and held the weapon out in front of him in his right hand. "Get back, I'm opening up."

He pulled the door ajar, still on the security chain. "Step forward, Coetzee. Careful, I'm armed."

A huge black hand appeared through the gap, grabbed his hand, squeezed and turned it around. The pain was excruciating. Nwosu dropped the gun, but not before his wrist was broken by the strength of the unknown intruder. His hand was released and he stepped back, trying desperately to push the door closed with his unhurt right shoulder. The next moment he was lying on the floor in the open doorway after Greg had kicked the door and the chain bracket was torn off the wall.

Plato walked through with the Makarov in his hand, stepped over him and went directly across the room. "Where's Coetzee and the kid?" He snarled at Karen.

Trembling with fear, she placed herself between Abby and the Zimbabwean. "They haven't arrived yet."

"Who're you?"

"I'm his ex-wife and this is our daughter."

"Sit there and keep quiet." He walked back to where Greg was shoving Nwosu onto a chair near the door. He replaced his pistol in his pocket and picked the Vektor up off the floor, pointing it at the policeman's head. "Why isn't the kid with you?"

Nwosu's had taken his arm out of the sling and was cradling his broken right wrist in his left hand. He was taking deep breaths, tears streaming down his face, his mind churning with this latest development. He realised that these men must be the Zimbabweans, sent by the Voice, He had no idea what had happened while he was in radio silence in Diepkloof. He had to brazen it out. "I don't know what the fuck you're talking about," he blustered. "I'm a police officer interrogating a witness and you'll be in deep shit if you don't get out of here. There are other officers on the way."

He screamed in pain as the Vektor smashed into his injured shoulder.

"I said, where's the kid?"

"He's on his way here with Coetzee," he managed to gasp. "They overcame me and left me for dead. Just let me go and we'll forget the whole thing. I've got a car, I can just disappear."

"You can count on that. How come we got here before him from Phalaborwa? He left an hour before us."

"I don't know. I didn't know he was in Phalaborwa, he just said it was a long drive. I have no idea where the hell he's been since he attacked me."

Plato turned to Karen. "Is he telling the truth? What's your name, anyway?"

"It's Karen Coetzee and I don't know what you're talking about." She was determined not to say anything that could hurt Marius. "Will you tell me who you are?"

"No. But we won't hurt you or your daughter. We don't wage war on women or kids."

At this Nwosu started sobbing. He knew he'd never get out of this mess alive. He cursed the day he'd listened to the Voice, sold his soul for money he would never see.

Greg went into the kitchen and grabbed a handful of tomatoes. He was still hungry. He came back and sat on the couch by the TV, noisily chewing the fruit. He stretched his huge body out, trying to get rid of the stiffness after sitting for so long in the car. Plato sat by the dinner table, still set with plates of half-eaten food and tried to ignore Greg. He checked his pistol, ensuring the safety was engaged and the hammer not in the cocked position. He was religiously cautious about checking the side-mounted safety lever when the magazine was in and the slide had been pulled back. He'd seen too many accidents to be careless. Placing it on the table in front of him he sat back in the chair to wait.

Over Mali, en route for Johannesburg, South Africa

Pedro Espinoza switched off the video screen and folded it back into its slot at the side of his seat. His flight had been delayed by an hour but the pilot had announced that a favourable tail wind would get them to Johannesburg on time. He had enjoyed his supper then relaxed and watched a film; *Lethal Weapon 4*, a cop movie about the Chinese Triad in Los Angeles. He'd enjoyed it until the hero managed to escape from drowning by dislocating his own shoulder. Espinoza knew that such a self-inflicted injury could only make matters worse.

A cabin attendant came up and made his flat bed for him and left a bottle of water at hand. He settled down for a few hours of sleep. *Thank you, Jenny,* he said to himself. *I'm too old for an eleven hour flight in economy.* Within a few minutes he was fast asleep, on his way through the night sky to South Africa, to find Leo Stewart.

Delmas, Mpumalanga, South Africa

Coetzee cut his headlights and coasted quietly along towards the farmhouse. About half way along the street a large black car was parked at the side. He pulled in behind it so he could examine it without being seen from the house. It was a Mercedes S600 with a white registration plate and in black lettering, the number 259-TCE 59. A Zimbabwe diplomatic registration, obviously belonging to someone with connections at the highest level. Diplomatic plates didn't necessarily mean what they implied. TCE plates were issued to so-called *'Technical Co-operation Experts'*, which Coetzee knew covered a multitude of sins and often included friends and family of the government leaders. The African thugs were here. He hadn't expected this. The Voice had said he was sending two of his friends but how had they beaten him to Karen's house? He'd never divulged where he was nor where he was going and somehow they were here before him. *How did they manage to find Karen? Unless Nwosu informed them, which I doubt.* For a moment he was impressed with the investigative prowess of the opposition, as he now considered them.

He had to adapt his plan to these new circumstances. Facing two men didn't worry him, he'd faced greater opposition many times and he was still around. It was two years since he'd seen active service but he knew he hadn't lost the skills he'd learned during his years with the force. In addition, Coetzee was a fatalist, he'd do his best and to hell with the consequences. He knew that was the main reason his marriage had broken up. Karen was an idealist, striving for a better world, but in a cautious and thoughtful way. Although he had the same objective, he didn't spend a lot of time thinking about it. He made a plan then just got on with the job and so far he'd been lucky. Somehow that aspect of his character had been hard for her to understand and had driven her away. Now, once again he had to use that same approach to resolve this situation. There was no other way.

He sat for a few moments thinking about his options. He'd driven down with a plan of action and having Jamie in his hands had been the key to disarming Nwosu, although that wouldn't have been difficult anyway. But now there was an added complication, two Zimbabwean gangsters, presumably armed to the eyeballs, presented a challenge, especially with his wife and daughter in the house.

"What's up, Coetzee? Is Nwosu in the house? Is that what this is about, swapping me for your family?" Leo was adding two and two and he didn't like the result.

"Nwosu isn't the problem, Leo. There's two of the opposition in the house with my wife and daughter and they want you. I don't think it's a good idea for you to go with them so I'm going to have to stop it without you or my family getting hurt."

Leo took a moment to register this. *Coetzee wants to save his family and he also wants to save me.* "Can I help?"

"Come with me, keep your head down and do what they say. You're in no danger. They want you alive so they're not about to hurt you." He turned to Jamie in the back seat. "You're staying here. If you come with us you'll get yourself killed and I don't want that on my conscience. Stay in the car with the doors locked and wait for us to come back."

"Do you think anything's happened to Jonathon?" Jamie's voice was tremulous.

"I sincerely hope so. You need to get out of that relationship. Nwosu is a pathological murderer and the day he drops you it's likely to be in a grave."

He drew the Land Cruiser up until his front bumper touched the Mercedes. It was now disabled in one direction, reverse, and the street was a cul de sac. A slight advantage. "Come on, Leo. I'll introduce you to my wife and daughter, since you've been so inquisitive about them. Don't make any noise."

Leo climbed out of the car, his heart thumping and his mouth dry. He knew they were walking into an ambush, but Coetzee didn't even seem to be concerned. He mustered up all his courage. *This isn't the time to be a wimp,* he said to himself. *He's got enough to worry about without me.*

They walked softly through the dark towards the farmhouse. Coetzee knew that whatever else happened, Leo would be safe. *After all, he's the only valuable commodity worth saving.*

FIFTY-FOUR

Marbella, Spain

Jenny was on an easyJet flight. She was the only passenger in the plane. *On every one of the other one hundred and fifty-five seats there was a brown paper parcel measuring thirty-two by thirteen by fifteen centimetres. Jenny knew that each parcel contained five thousand one dollar bills, stacked in four piles of one thousand two hundred and fifty notes, a total of seven hundred and seventy-five thousand dollars. That was the final amount agreed with Coetzee for Leo's return. This flight was the only solution she had found to make the money available in cash to Pedro Espinoza in South Africa.*

A cabin attendant in a black outfit poured her a glass of champagne. A young woman with a slim figure wearing a tight sweater that accentuated her beautifully-formed breasts. Jenny sensed she knew her but she wore a shawl over her head so her features couldn't be seen. The champagne bottle carried the label 'Newtown Brut' and the wine spilled out into the glass as red as blood.

When the passenger door opened Jenny walked out with an oversize suitcase containing all the cash. Fortunately the case had wheels, since it was so large and heavy she couldn't lift it. She struggled along the concourse pulling the case behind her until she arrived at the top of a long flight of stairs. Scanning the crowded hall below she managed to pick out Pedro's form. He was dressed in a smart military uniform with a large medal pinned to the breast of his tunic and wore a cap on his head with the motif 'ARGS'. Standing next to him was a young woman in a black outfit, wearing a shawl. It was the cabin attendant, but Jenny still couldn't recognise her from that distance. Between Pedro and the woman stood a young dark-skinned boy. It was Leo Stewart. He was standing stock still, looking straight ahead and showing no expression at all.

Jenny somehow managed to carry the suitcase down the first of the stairs, until suddenly the handle came away in her hand. She watched helplessly as the case tumbled over and over down the staircase for what seemed like an age. Finally it landed, upright and undamaged at the bottom. The woman left the others and ran to the case as Jenny came down the stairs towards her. As she grabbed the now perfectly intact handle, she looked up the staircase and removed her shawl. Jenny gasped with shock. It was Leticia da Costa! She smiled at Jenny then turned and ran out of the hall with the bag rolling along behind her. Before Jenny could react, she had disappeared from view.

She walked across to Pedro and shook his hand. "Well, the money's gone," she said. "But we've got Leo back and that's all that counts. Well done Pedro."

"I'm afraid it isn't as simple as that." He turned to the boy. "Look."

Jenny stepped closer to Leo, only to realise it wasn't him at all. It was a life size waxwork. A perfect replica of Emma's son that had cost her seven hundred and seventy-five thousand dollars.

Jenny awoke in a sweat and looked at the illuminated clock on her bedside cabinet. It was four in the morning. She knew something had happened or was going to happen, but she didn't know what and Jenny didn't like not knowing things. Her dreams were often prescient but she never knew in exactly what way. She switched on the light, took her pad and scribbled down a few notes from her memory of the dream. A vague impression of something or someone else lingered at the edge of her subconscious but she couldn't bring it back to mind. Espinoza had to be called as soon as possible. There were some things that she now knew for certain, but how could she convince him of the source of her knowledge? She switched off the light and tried to get back to sleep.

Delmas, Mpumalanga, South Africa

Coetzee walked up the driveway to the farmhouse, ensuring that Leo kept behind him at a safe distance. The door was ajar, the security chain hanging down with its bracket still attached. He quietly pushed it open and strolled into the living room leaving Leo in the hallway. Quickly taking in the scene, he was relieved to see Karen and Abby at the far end of the room. They looked unhurt but terrified. Nwosu was sitting near the dining area. He was holding his arm as if it was damaged. A huge black man, virtually a giant, was relaxing on the couch near the fireplace and another, hard faced, older character in shirtsleeves was sitting at the table, his pistol in front of him. No one was speaking. Half-empty dishes of food lay on the table.

"Marius!" Karen shouted across the room. "Watch out, they're armed and they want Leo."

Plato grabbed his pistol from the table and disengaged the safety. The Makarov would now fire once with a long, strong squeeze of the trigger then in single action with short, light trigger squeezes. He held it with his elbows on the table to give himself more stability and a better aim. "Are you Coetzee?"

He walked past the table to the centre of the room and stood in front of the fireplace, where there was more space. "That's right. And I'm unarmed." Turning to face them he held his arms apart to show he wasn't carrying a gun. "Who are you?"

"Plato. I'm taking the kid to Zimbabwe." When Coetzee didn't respond, he went on, "Why have you got him? What's your job?"

Once again Coetzee said nothing, He was waiting for an opening. Being patient, biding his time. Out of the corner of his eye he saw Leo moving towards the fireplace. *Stay out of it, kid,* he willed him silently. *You're not the one who's in danger.*

He grimaced when Karen shouted out, "He's just an accountant. He doesn't have anything to do with this. He just came to collect the money." *She obviously knows the whole story,* he realised. *Nwosu's been spreading his poison.*

"Don't be fooled by her. He's a Special Forces guy. He was a major. He got a medal." Nwosu tried to inveigle some good will from the two Zimbabweans. "He set the entire operation up. He's the brains behind the whole abduction."

At this, Greg sat up and took notice. "Special Forces, eh? So you're a tough guy, a white gangster beating up on poor black folk?" He spat on the floor. "Put that Makarov away, Plato. I'll show you what I think of Special Services officers, bunch of fucking murdering cowards." It was time to show Plato what he could do, time to get a little respect. He stood up and advanced on Coetzee, punching him in the chest.

Plato said nothing. The feel of his index finger on the trigger gave him an exciting, almost sexual feeling of power. He didn't want Greg to master Coetzee, he wanted to shoot him to death. To shoot him in the feet and knees, in the legs and the arms, in the stomach and the chest until he begged for the last bullet that would put him out of his misery. He waited to see what would happen.

Coetzee fell away with the punch, turned and lashed out a kick at the Zimbabwean's crutch, which was almost at the height of his shoulder. Greg caught his foot and twisted it, sending him crashing to the ground. On his knees, he grabbed the giant's ankle and managed to bring him to the floor beside him, his arm around his neck, trying to get a head lock on his opponent to force him down to his height where he had some chance of inflicting damage to his eyes or throat.

Greg's great ham fist smashed down on Coetzee's head and knocked him flat out on his back on the floor, arms and legs akimbo. The huge Zimbabwean knelt beside him and took his head between his hands, ready to twist and break his neck like a chicken. Leo looked on in horror, fearful of what was about to happen. Karen held Abby close, turning her face away from the awful scene being played out in front of them.

"Do it slow and painful," Plato barked across the room.

Greg turned his head and looked at him scornfully. "Don't tell me how to do my job, old man."

Coetzee pulled the short, flat handled throwing knife from the sheath strapped to the inside of his left wrist and plunged the needle-sharp blade up into the back of the huge man's neck, exactly through the belly of the tattooed gazelle. The blade slid up alongside the spinal cord behind his ear and entered the cerebellum, the brain's movement regulator. Greg put his hands to his head and screamed, a primal, animal scream, and his eyes rolled around in his head. Then like a grotesque giant marionette he fell sideways towards Coetzee.

The South African hauled Greg's massive body over himself just as Plato loosed off a fusillade of shots, sending blood and flesh flying around the room from the now lifeless giant. Cartridge shells sprayed out behind him onto the floor. The full complement of eight shots spent, the Zimbabwean picked up a new magazine from the table in front of him.

Leo grabbed the iron poker standing beside the fireplace and smashed it across the gunman's back. He dropped the magazine onto the table and as he leaned forward to reach for it, in one swift, coordinated movement, Coetzee pushed Greg's body away and pulled the blade from the dead man's skull. He threw it with deadly aim straight into Plato's chest.

"Fuck!" The hit man looked down in amazement at the handle sticking from his shirt front and fell forward onto the table top.

It took Coetzee, Leo and Jamie a half hour to bring the Mercedes to the door and haul the two bodies out of the house and into the car. Greg must have weighed a hundred and fifty kilos. Nwosu was now locked in the upstairs bedroom with the dogs. His wrist was excruciatingly painful and he was a nervous wreck after witnessing Coetzee's one man killing-machine demonstration, wondering what might be in store for him. Karen and Abby, having seen him in action three years before, were remarkably calm after their ordeal, and set about cleaning the living room. The washing and scrubbing was a good form of therapy, but just being alive and together was enough.

Karen was desperately worried about Leo's abduction, but he seemed to be alright and Marius had saved the situation again, in such an infuriating fashion, so she didn't question him, for now.

He'd hugged them both and simply said. "I'm sorry, that was all my fault." She knew she'd have to worm the story out of him, as usual, but he wasn't ready for that yet. She'd have to bide her time. After what he'd accomplished he deserved some quiet.

Coetzee drove for about five kilometres east along the R50 and turned off onto an old beaten track leading to a disused slate quarry. Karen had shown him the spot when they were fixing up the farmhouse. She used to cycle there to fish with her grandparents as a child, but it hadn't improved with the years. It was now an unkempt wilderness with used syringes, condoms and even more disgusting rubbish littered around the flat, dirty plateau at the top of the cliff. He parked the Mercedes on the edge of a twenty metre slope going down to a wide stagnant pond at the bottom. He had removed all identification papers from the men and put their mobile phones in the boot, switched off. Finally ensuring there was nothing else except the two bodies inside the car or in the boot, he opened the windows slightly then put the gear shift into neutral and turned off the engine. He tied the steering wheel to the passenger door handle and released the hand brake, climbed out and pointed the remote at the car, locking the doors. With one push from his shoulder, the limousine rolled gently forward down the slope and into the pond. It floated out to the centre before slowly disappearing into the dank depths. It saddened Coetzee to see the beautiful machine meet such an end but there was no alternative. With any luck it wouldn't be discovered for years, if ever. Jamie, subdued and frightened, was waiting in his Ford and they drove back to the house in silence.

In the farmhouse Leo was helping to clean up and was getting to know Karen and Abby. His first reaction had been to ask for a mobile phone to call his mother, but it was the middle of the night and he was still worried about the incriminating events he'd been involved in. He decided to wait until morning, when he could talk quietly with Coetzee and agree on a mutual truce; a life for a life. He was still coping with the revelation of his Special Forces career and his deadly skills. In the space of just four days he'd been exposed to abduction, drugging, accidental death, police corruption, violent death and now an incredible demonstration of murderous expertise from a man whom he'd taken to be an unscrupulous stadium security guard, with not many redeeming qualities. There was a lot more to Marius Coetzee than met the eye, he now realised.

Karen didn't question him about the abduction. Nwosu had already bragged about it to her and she didn't know what to believe, except that the boy must have endured a very traumatic experience. Kidnapping was a serious criminal offence, far too important to be simply put aside by Marius, as she knew he did with so many things. It had to be discussed, examined and somehow resolved, but it wasn't the time for that yet. She kept the conversation as light as possible in the circumstances, talking about schooling and life in the UK and South Africa. Successfully engaging Leo with her and Abby and moving them both away from the horrific scene they had just experienced.

He would occasionally ask a question, trying to get to know more about them and about the man who had taken him away from his mother so brutally. Wondering why they were no longer together and what the story was behind their African child, Abby. And why would a highly decorated SA Special Services Officer kidnap him, an unknown, unimportant schoolboy from Newcastle? Trying to understand why that same man would risk his own life to save his. Despite his recent experiences, deep down he was beginning to admire Marius Coetzee.

It was one hundred and three hours since Leo had been taken.

FIFTY-FIVE

London, England

At six forty-five am Lord Arthur Dudley called his contact in Harare. Despite having heard nothing since the previous evening he had slept well, was trying to remain positive and enjoying his morning cup of tea. He was looking forward to some good news about the recapture of Leo Stewart. His frame of mind changed when he was informed that the field agents had not been in contact since they were instructed to drive to Delmas. The man agreed to contact them and find out what the situation was.

Dudley showered and dressed in a sombre mood. The funder was arriving in a couple of hours and he had absolutely no news of the whereabouts of Leo Stewart. He was sitting waiting anxiously by the phone and snatched it up on the first ring. His heart stopped at what he heard. The contact gave him the news that the field agents could no longer be contacted, their phones appeared to be switched off. He immediately called EzeTracker.

Cambridge, England

Simon Pickford was an early riser and in his office by seven in the morning. He grabbed a coffee from the machine in the hall and went into his inner sanctum. His phone rang as he walked into the office, it was Tom Owen, his chief technical officer.

Pickford replaced the phone. He had awoken with Lord Dudley's questions still foremost in his mind and he was concerned. Now he had just been informed that the two mobile phones were in Delmas, obviously because the person they had been tracking from Phalaborwa had driven there during the night. This whole scenario was looking more and more dubious. His ruminations were interrupted by the phone ringing again. Dudley was seeking an update and sounded less ebullient than usual.

He reported the latest news and waited for his mentor's reaction. Dudley seemed rather preoccupied and merely thanked him. Pickford opened up his laptop. He was asking himself again why the man would be secretly tracking two people in South Africa when he had their mobile phone numbers? And now they were both in the same locality. With a fortune in the bank and a public company to protect he couldn't afford to take the chance of being involved in anything compromising. He owed Dudley a lot, but there were limits.

He searched online for the name of a local newspaper in Phalaborwa. There was nothing. He checked for Polokwane and found the Observer and the Express. Both newspapers carried stories of a mysterious death the previous day, a murdered white man whose body had not yet been identified. A cold chill ran down his spine. What were the odds against the two events, his Master's initial request, to find someone in Polokwane, and a murder occurring there on the same day, being a coincidence? He was a mathematician and he knew the answer was, *not great.* He needed to cover his backside before anything happened that might implicate him. Looking up the contact list on his mobile he found the number of an old college friend in London, Detective Inspector Callum Dewar at Scotland Yard.

London, England

Lord Dudley was becomingly increasingly worried. From Pickford's report, it seemed that both Coetzee and Nwosu were now in Delmas, presumably with Leo Stewart. What was more, the two agents sent down to neutralise them and snatch the boy had disappeared off the face of the earth. *Why would they not be answering their phones,* he asked himself. It could only be because they didn't want to or weren't able to. Either explanation was very worrying and he had no way of finding out which it was. He thought of calling one or other of Nwosu's mobile numbers but decided it was too risky. If there was some plan being hatched between them, or if on the contrary there was a disagreement, his intervention might alert them and cause further disruption to the programme.

He called back the intermediary in Harare to ask if they had any resources available in Johannesburg in the event he might need assistance. After receiving so many instructions and counter-instructions and with two of his agents missing, the man was rather uninterested. He said his first priority was to locate them. If he had the time he would check and call back if they could offer any further help. Dudley sat waiting nervously.

Marbella, Spain

At seven thirty, Emma rushed into her sister's room. "It's a text from Leo!"

Jenny was at her desk. "Is it good news?"

"I don't know. He's in a different place, Phalaborwa. And he's with Coetzee."

"Phalaborwa. Where's that?"

"In the Kruger. That lodge is a safari destination on the river."

"So, Coetzee must have taken him to the Kruger to hide him from the others and wants to arrange his return. It seems he was telling the truth. That's good news, it means the others are lying."

"There's also an email from the ARGS people which confirms that as well." She showed her the email and photograph she'd received from the abductors. "It's similar to the photo Coetzee sent, the same chair and background, but Leo's holding the newspaper to show the date. We know the other one was genuine because of the properties but this one is pasted onto the message so we can't see where it came from. They might have obtained that photo from Coetzee to pretend they have Leo. I'm starting to believe he has reverted to type, as he was when he saved those children three years ago. If he really has Leo, it could bring this nightmare to an end."

Jenny said, "I'll text Pedro right away, he'll be arriving soon. We need to speak to him immediately he lands. There's no point in him flying to Polokwane if Leo's in the Kruger ..." She paused. "There's something else I have to tell him also."

"That sounds ominous. What is it?"

"I had one of my dreams last night."

"About Leo?" Emma was aware of her sixth sense. Jenny nodded her head. "What was it?"

"I'm not sure. There's one thing I can tell you. The text from Leo was received at nine last night and I don't think they're still in Phalaborwa. Wait until we speak to Pedro and you'll hear it at the same time. We'd better get ready now, we have a lot to do today."

Emma went back to her room and closed the door. She opened up Leo's message again and typed, *Hello Leo darling. I got your texts. Be strong and don't worry, I'm coming for you. I love you and I'll see you soon. MXXXX*. She hesitated for a moment then pressed Send.

Delmas, Mpumalanga, South Africa

Everyone in the house was up and about by eight thirty. Coetzee took a swig of the black coffee that Karen had prepared for them. The house had been more or less in order when they returned from the quarry and they had managed to get a few hours' sleep. She had taken a mug up to Nwosu, who, she said was remorseful and repentant, "He says he's learned his lesson and just wants to forget the whole affair and get back to Diepkloof with Jamie."

"He says lots of things, but very little that's true. Ignore him until I decide what to do." Coetzee was looking at the phone he had taken from the policeman in Polokwane and the one he'd confiscated from him that morning. There were only a few numbers stored in the second phone, including one beginning with the prefix 32, labelled, 'Voice, Belgium.' There were three numbers on the recent call list; two were to Nwosu's own phone which Coetzee now had and the third to the Belgian number. There was no recording App on the new phone so he couldn't check the conversations. He opened the calls list on Nwosu's first phone. The call made from Joburg on Wednesday was to the same Belgian number.

Leo and Abby had taken the dogs for a walk and now he could hear them setting the table for breakfast. The smell of toast and fried eggs made his juices run. Leo saw him with the two phones and came to sit by him. "What's up?" He was starting to feel a sense of complicity with the South African.

"I wondered how the opposition knew where we were and it's very simple. Nwosu called and told them we were coming here. He called their number last night." Coetzee's logic was faultless but his conclusion was wrong.

"Why would they beat him up if he invited them here? It doesn't make sense."

Karen came to call them to the table and Coetzee asked, "Did you see what happened when the thugs arrived?"

"Yes. Nwosu thought it was you. Then they broke the door down and smashed his wrist. They were asking where you and Leo were. They thought you were already here. He told them you were on the way with Leo."

"Sounds like you're right again, Leo. They didn't get the address from Nwosu 'cos he didn't know they were coming. Where the hell did they get it?"

"Breakfast is on the table. Come and sit down."

They all sat at one end of the dining table. Jamie had been sent upstairs with a tray for him and Nwosu. Coetzee knew he didn't have anything to fear from a man with a broken wrist and a busted shoulder and Jamie was no threat of any kind. He would work out what to do with them later.

"Do you remember anything else?"

"Yes. They said they'd come from Phalaborwa." Abby spoke up with confidence. "The old man said that they'd left after you and how come you weren't here yet."

"She's right. I remember now," Karen agreed.

"The phones! It has to be Nwosu's phones, Marius. They followed us to Phalaborwa and then to here. There's no other link to those two places except the phones. You used one to call someone about the abduction when we were in Phalaborwa, I know because I heard you. Then Nwosu called you in Phalaborwa from here on the other one. Somehow they've got the phones tapped and they're following our trail through the mobile signals."

Coetzee gave Leo a look. "Normally I'd give you shit for listening to my calls, but this time I'm glad you did. That's the only explanation that makes sense. Two gorillas from Harare drive down here and they know exactly where to go, even the lodge where we were staying. Then they leave an hour later to come here because they got new instructions. You're right! It has to be the phones."

"By the way, here's the phone I took off Blethin." Leo took the mobile from his pocket and gave it to the South African. "The battery's dead, but I was keeping it just in case."

"Speaking of phones, Marius, it's about time Leo called his mother, she'll be worried sick about him."

"I sent her a message last night, so she knows he's fine and he's with me. Can we wait until we get rid of Nwosu? I want to talk to all of you and set things straight before he speaks to her. Just a couple of hours?"

"It's OK." Leo said. He also wanted to get things clear before he spoke to Emma. He was well aware he was still in the country where he'd injured a police officer and accidentally killed a French doctor. "I managed to text her before the battery died, so we can wait a little while."

Coetzee gave him a begrudging look of admiration as Karen announced. "Very well, but you have to call this morning without fail. Now will you eat your breakfast? Abby and I have gone to some trouble and we'd appreciate you enjoying the meal before it gets cold."

They tucked into the toast and eggs, Coetzee's mind working overtime. *If the phones can bring them to the right place, they can also send them to the wrong place.*

London, England

"Oh, my God! Harder, harder. Don't stop." The man's voice was strained as he arched his back and pushed his hips upward.

Esther's magnificent breasts swayed and bounced as she gripped her knees tighter around his body and pushed herself up and down on him in an ever faster rhythm until with a scream she climaxed. Finally collapsing alongside him on the bed she kissed him passionately, her tongue thrusting into his mouth. They lay side by side, completely satiated.

He was drunk when she returned to the hotel the previous evening. Drunk and incapable of sex. Even the sight of her magnificent naked body failed to arouse him as she reluctantly helped him undress and fall onto the bed, immediately lost in a semi-comatose state. She lay down beside him, watching him snoring gently, aching with unspent passion until she finally fell asleep. Esther was a highly sexed woman and her first action on waking that morning had been to arouse him and this time he had been ready for her.

She cradled his face in her hands. "Chéri, I missed you so much yesterday. Being stuck with that pompous ass Dudley all day is too much. I couldn't believe it. We spent two bloody hours watching a ballet about homosexual swans. Then he invited me to stay the night. I thought he was into men, not women."

"I think it was students of both sexes, but he's too old for it these days. Come on, in the shower. We have to go to the hotel to prepare for this afternoon's meeting with my partner. I hope to God Dudley has found the boy, there'll be all hell to pay if he hasn't."

She noticed that his voice trembled when he said those words. *He's in bad shape,* she thought. *I wonder how he's going to fix it. It's not just money. It's never that easy.*

Slater watched her as she went to the bathroom. Her body was the most beautiful he had ever seen. When he wasn't with her he fantasised about it like a prurient adolescent and fretted until the next time he could feel her moving under him again. Even now he was becoming aroused for the third time. "What are you wearing for the meeting?" He called.

"Something suitably serious and business-like of course. Don't worry, I won't let you down. I'll play my part like a true professional." She came back into the room and removed a man's navy blue business suit from the wardrobe. "Here. Put this one on, it makes you look like an experienced conspirator." She laughed, her head thrown back and mouth open, white teeth against her pink tongue.

Slater resisted his overwhelming urge and picked up his mobile. It was time to make an important call before getting ready.

Delmas, Mpumalanga, South Africa

"Right, Nwosu. You're not looking great this morning. Jamie's taking you to the clinic to get your wrist fixed. You're booked in for ten o'clock."

Nwosu looked like a clown impersonating Admiral Lord Nelson. His nose was still red and blue, his eye was black and almost closed, his right wrist was in a sling and Jamie had pushed his left hand across his chest into his buttoned jacket to ease his shoulder. He hadn't slept all night and had a day's stubble on his face.

"This better not be a trick, Marius. I need urgent help or I'll lose the use of my right hand. Do you want that on your conscience? You didn't need to book me in, I can go to any clinic. Just let us go, Marius, I'm begging you as a friend. Just let us go and you'll never see us again."

Coetzee ignored the reference to 'friend.' "That's very ungrateful, Jonathon. I'm thinking of your wellbeing. You don't really want to go to a clinic near Diepkloof, do you? They'll question why the neighbourhood's star police officer looks as if he's been arm wrestling with a gorilla. You're going to a clinic to get special attention and no questions asked. It's the Newtown Private Clinic, in Mayfair. You know where it is, don't you?" Coetzee waited to see if the name rang a bell with the policeman.

"I've heard of it." The name hadn't registered. Nwosu didn't know where Blethin had come from. He looked at Jamie, who seemed relieved and pleased. "Is it true? Did you hear him book me in?"

"It's true, Jonathon, I heard him arrange it."

"I still don't trust you Coetzee. You'd never let me go in case I get in touch with the Voice again or go to the authorities about Leo."

"Once you're out of my sight I don't give a shit what you do, Nwosu. You're stupid, but not that stupid. Between Leo and me we've got a dossier that would put you away for a long time. I know where you live and where Jamie lives, don't I? But just to be sure you get to the clinic safely, I'm coming along. You obviously need a bodyguard, the number of enemies you create everywhere you go."

The two cars set off in convoy, Jamie driving the Ford with Nwosu and Coetzee and Karin driving the Land Cruiser with Abby and Leo. They had left the dogs in the quadrangle behind the house with enough food until the next day. The westbound traffic flow was light and they arrived at the clinic on time. Nwosu was escorted in by Jamie and Coetzee and an efficient looking black nurse checked the appointment book then took him straight through to the X-Ray department.

"Okay, Jamie, he's all yours now. I'll give you just one piece of advice. Get him to stay away from me and you stay away from him if he comes near me. Understood?" The young man nodded, looking very youthful and vulnerable.

He turned to go. "I almost forgot. Here are his two phones. I even charged them up." He handed them to Jamie, walked out of the clinic and climbed into the Land Cruiser. "We're going off to have a serious talk," he said to the others and pulled away from the clinic towards the N3 going south.

Jamie watched until the car disappeared into the distance then gave a long sigh of relief. He shoved the phones into his trouser pockets and settled down to wait for his boyfriend.

Marbella, Spain

The sun was already hot on the terrace when Emma went out. "*Buenos dias,*" she greeted Encarni who was setting breakfast. The woman laughed and answered in rapid Spanish which she didn't understand. She sat out of the sun, opened her iPad and found the Newtown Private Clinic again. Pulling up the bio of Dr Ernest Blethin she read the whole text, studying it more carefully. Jenny came out just in time to see her catch her breath.

"What is it?"

"I've been looking at Blethin's bio. It turns out that he's actually French and just look at this." Emma put the cursor over a paragraph at the bottom of the summary. '*Dr Blethin joined us after several years as a Senior Consultant at Saint Christopher's Clinic in Nice, France*'.

"We didn't notice it before because we didn't know where Dr Constance had worked and probably because the name was in French, but it's the same place. See?" She showed the clinic's website in English and French. There was no doubt. It was the same establishment.

Jenny laughed out loud. "Well done, Emma. So we've finally found a connection between what happened in Rwanda and Leo's abduction. Constance knew about Mutesi and Leo, they presumably worked together and Blethin was part of the abduction team.

"I should have spotted it. But we still don't know what the connection is with your trip to Joburg. I don't understand how they found out about that, especially in time to set up the whole complicated kidnap operation."

"I know. There has to be another link. Someone or something that connects Leo's birth, your fortune and our trip to South Africa."

"We'll tell Pedro when he calls. He can ask his contact in Paris to check on possible connections of Constance and Blethin and try to tie one of them to the South African trip, but I'm not very optimistic."

OR Tambo Airport, Johannesburg, South Africa

The flight from Frankfurt had made better time than expected. At just after ten o' clock Espinoza arrived at the carousel, collected his bag and hurried across to terminal B for his flight to Polokwane. After six hours sleep on the plane and a quick cold water spruce up he was freshened up for the day. He'd received Jenny's message and called her while he was waiting.

She replied immediately and switched the phone onto speaker. "Emma's beside me and can hear the conversation. We've received a text from Leo. He's not in Polokwane, so there's no point in going there. We've also received a photo from the so-called ARGS and it's almost identical to the one we got from Coetzee. It looks as if they have somehow got it from him and sent it to us to pretend they still have Leo."

Espinoza was confused. After a moment he said, "Where is Leo supposed to be now? I can go straight there and save time."

"It was sent from Phalaborwa, in the Kruger, but I don't think he's there now." When he started to interrupt with more questions, she went on, "Pedro, you have to trust what I tell you now. There is no rational explanation for it, but I have some information that we need to consider. First of all, I think your instincts were right. I suspect that Esther Rousseau is involved in the abduction."

This time he didn't respond and she went on, "Then there is something about air travel in the story. I don't know what, but there is some connection somewhere.

"And lastly, I think Coetzee is a good man, but Leo is not where we think he is. I don't know where he is but it's none of the places we've been looking at." Jenny said nothing about Leticia's face appearing in the dream. She took a deep breath, looking at her sister's amazed expression and squeezing her hand.

"I see. And where did this new information come from?"

"The same place that I learned about Vogel's embezzlement, you remember?"

"I remember very well and I have confidence in that source of information. Vague, but helpful in planning our next steps."

"And Emma has some important information for you too." Her sister quickly related Blethin's connection with Constance's last employer.

"So he's also French. That's interesting. It opens up a whole new area of investigation for me. I have to find the connecting point. It's there somewhere but we just can't see it yet." The line went quiet for a moment.

"Pedro, are you there?"

"Sorry, Emma. I was thinking about the various contradictory reports we're receiving. Was the number of the phone that sent the text the same 027 number from South Africa?"

She checked the text message with the previous one. "Yes it is. So Leo's still using the phone he got in Polokwane. Why? What's wrong?"

"I'm concerned that we have two versions of where Leo is and who he's with, but no verifiable confirmation."

"But what about this text from him? He says he's in Phalaborwa with Coetzee."

"You're probably right that the messages came from him, but I'm paid to be suspicious and at the moment I'm not sure who is telling the truth. A text message could be sent by anyone, that's the problem. We assumed he took the phone from someone in Polokwane but we actually don't know. And if it was someone else's phone, would he have been able to keep it all this time? Wouldn't they have noticed it was missing?

"And you say a similar photo was used for both messages. I find that strange, as if there is an attempt to mislead us. It's possible that Coetzee is still part of the original conspiracy and they are playing with our minds. Or he plans to take Leo away but hasn't yet, until he's sure that a payment has been made. We're not certain of anything at the moment. Nothing at all."

Emma suddenly realised that Leo hadn't replied to her text of that morning "I understand," she said. "So what do you suggest?"

"Firstly, I think you should send another email to the ARGS, acknowledging the photo and asking for some time to raise the funds. If they really do have Leo we have to keep in touch with them and buy as much time as we can."

"We'll do that right away," Jenny answered. "What else?"

"I think it's time I used the police resources available to me here in Johannesburg. I'm going to see CS Hendricks. I have some important information for him concerning his murder enquiries. I'll call you later when I have more news."

Espinoza rang off and walked out of the departure lounge. He found a café in the arrivals hall and sat pondering these latest developments. His years of working in the force had taught him that events surrounding a crime were seldom unconnected. In his last experience with Sra Bishop and the killer, d'Almeida, he had failed to find the common thread to the murders and it had almost cost her and her family's lives. He ran through the history of the abduction in his mind and, tearing a sheet from his notepad, he drew a kind of jigsaw puzzle, listing the possible connecting points that could lead him to the common denominator that must exist to link them together.

Several ideas came to him and he looked at his watch, it was now a quarter to eleven. He made some telephone calls then went to find a taxi into Johannesburg.

FIFTY-SIX

London, England

"You mean to say they have left Delmas and gone together to the same place?" Lord Dudley was speaking to Simon Pickford.

"Yes According to the trace, both phones are stationary in a place called Diepkloof. It's a suburb to the south of Johannesburg. They must have just arrived there. We had a technical glitch in the network, so we were late in checking." He gave Dudley the map coordinates. "It seems to be an apartment building, but I can't give you a more exact address." The EzeTracker boss had been instructed by DI Dewar to find out more about his search for the phone users. He agreed that the business looked very suspicious, but for the moment nothing illegal had occurred. While he studied Dudley's file, Pickford should pry discreetly into the matter.

"Perhaps if you tell me what it is you're looking for I can get more resources onto it," he suggested.

Dudley had already realised it must be Nwosu's apartment. He even remembered the address from the background check they'd made before their very first contact with the policeman. "It won't be necessary, dear boy. I'm confident that we can identify the location by other means. If you can just keep up the monitoring

I'll be quite happy. It's a rather sensitive investigation, a marital problem. Nothing of any concern to anyone but the couples involved. Thank you for the offer and I won't take up any more of your time."

Pickford rang off, wondering if he had involved Dewar unnecessarily. He considered calling the policeman back but decided to let him check out Dudley first. Now that the matter was in Dewar's hands he felt relieved. He could forget about it and get back to making money.

Dudley immediately called Harare again. This time he changed his approach. He told the intermediary he thought he might know how to locate the two missing operatives and asked him how much it would cost to send a 'colleague' to an address in the Johannesburg area.

"Hold on, let me check." The man came back on the line again. "We could get someone there fairly shortly." He quoted a fee, higher than usual, but Dudley knew he had no choice. If the two phones were there, the chances were that Leo Stewart was also there.

He agreed to the offer and gave him instructions about Leo, with the address and coordinates he'd just received from Pickford. "If it's in the name of Nwosu, you have the right place. And there will be at least two mobile phones in the apartment, please ensure they are retrieved. Call me as soon you have any further information." He rang off. *Things are starting to look up. Now we might see some results,* he reflected more confidently.

He went into the bathroom to clean his teeth again and sprinkle some after shave onto his neck. Esther would be waiting for him at the Park Lane Hotel and he was looking forward to his good morning kiss.

Geneva, Switzerland

"*Veuillez attendre ici Monsieur. M Jolidon arrive tout de suite.* Please wait here, sir. Mr Jolidon will be with you immediately." Gilles Simenon nodded politely and backed out of the room.

Prince 'Sam' Bensouda sat in an armchair in the small salon adjacent to the reception hall at Ramseyer, Haldemann and placed his briefcase on the floor beside him. He had flown in from Malaga the previous evening with Swiss International, who still offered an acceptable Business Class, and was staying at the Hotel Kempinski on the Quai du Mont-Blanc. Much to his self-satisfaction he had abstained from his usual visit to the casino in Divonne. Although he knew that Jolidon would be there, since that was where they had met, by chance, for the second time, he had decided to meet him on this occasion away from the temptation of the tables.

"Votre altesse. *Soyez le bienvenu à Genève.* Welcome to Geneva." Jolidon shook hands with him almost reverently and led him into his office, sitting across the desk from him, the bulky file between them. "Was your flight comfortable?"

After completing the formalities and accepting a coffee, Bensouda asked, "What is the problem you mentioned on the telephone?"

"It has to do with the valuable merchandise we acquired on your behalf, Monsieur. We have had some trouble holding onto it."

"I don't understand that phrase, 'holding onto it?"

"It seems there is someone else who has understood the value involved and is attempting to usurp the transaction."

"But the merchandise was safely in our hands just a few days ago. What happened to change that?"

"There has been a change of allegiance. One of the principal players has decided to strike out on his own. At the moment we are not sure what the situation is." Jolidon flinched as he said this. The Moroccan's temper was legendary and he had no desire to bear the brunt of it.

"And what about our prepayment of one million dollars? Where is that?"

"The operation has so far cost us eight hundred thousand, more or less. After we settle with the ship's captain and the local agent there will be nothing left to, how can I put this, sweeten the pill."

Bensouda said nothing for a few moments but his heart was pounding. He didn't believe a word of Jolidon's story, but he had to play along. His very life depended upon doing this deal. *These people are corrupt and only money will get things back on track. It's always money,* he thought. He quickly assessed the value of the remaining treasures in the family safety deposit box downstairs. *Another bribe won't make any difference in the grand scheme of things. If it's successful.* Finally, he said, "Perhaps we should discuss the commission arrangements."

"What did you have in mind, Monsieur?"

"I was thinking that we could make an effort and pay an additional commission of, let's say fifty thousand dollars, to ensure that there are no more complications or delays. Would that sort the matter out?"

Jolidon shrugged his shoulders. "You are probably on the right track, but I think the problem is a little more complicated than that."

A few minutes of discussion resulted in an agreement of an additional commission of one hundred thousand dollars. Jolidon tried to supress his reaction. *Another hundred thousand. How much of it could I divert my way?* "That's a very fair offer. I'm sure it could resolve the matter. I'll get in touch immediately and call you as soon as I know something. Are you at the Kempinski as usual?"

Bensouda nodded. "Let me know as quickly as possible so I can arrange the funds. The merchandise must be on the last leg of the journey and I don't want anything else to go wrong. Now I would like to retrieve something from my safety deposit box."

Jolidon called Gilles over and he accompanied the Moroccan down to the circular vault.

Ten minutes later Bensouda came back to the entrance hall, clutching his briefcase at his side. Jolidon was waiting for him by the door.

"I will call you the moment I have confirmation of the new arrangement. Goodbye, Monsieur le Prince."

The two men shook hands and Bensouda went out to his waiting limousine. Some habits he found hard to change.

Marbella, Spain

Emilio came running out to the terrace to greet Emma. "*Bonjour, Emilio. Comment ca va*? How are you?"

The little boy laughed infectiously. "*Vous parlez Francais*? You speak French?"

"That's all I can say, so now we have to speak English."

Leticia followed him out, glamorously dressed in an expensive looking pink casual dress. "His English is not bad, Emma, but maybe you can help him improve it while you're here. I wish mine was good enough to read your books, Jenny told me you're a famous author."

"That's what sisters are for. To brag on your behalf. The truth is I've written a few mediocre books and made very little money and no one knows who I am. That's what being a famous author means."

Emma looked nervously at her sister but she just winked and immediately started fussing Emilio. They had just composed a reply to the ARGS and sent it off after checking it with Espinoza and she was still a little on edge. However, breakfast was so relaxed and pleasant that she felt a pang of guilt to be enjoying herself while her son was still not out of danger.

"When is Patrice arriving?" Jenny was still wondering about his apparent propensity for travelling in circles instead of straight lines.

"He called me a little while ago. His flight arrives at two o'clock and he's coming straight here. Is that alright?"

When Jenny nodded agreeably, she went on, "He's been on so many aeroplanes recently I keep forgetting where he is. But it's definitely London and he'll be here in time for lunch."

Jenny had turned her mind to Leticia's appearance in her dream. She didn't know what it meant but maybe it was time to find out. She got up from the table. "Shall we look at those papers now?"

"Oh." Leticia gave a nervous laugh. "You don't need to bother about it. I'm sorry if I worried you, I was just a bit tired last night. I'll work it out with Patrice. Now I'm going to take Emilio for a walk and leave you with Emma. *Vienes, Emilio*." She walked off towards the swimming pool with the little boy.

Jenny went into the kitchen to collect her thoughts. *What's going on with Leticia? This is becoming very confusing.*

Scotland Yard, London, England

DI Dewar was at his desk, looking though a large, brown dossier, reading only the sheets marked with a red pen. The name on the dossier was *Lord Arthur Selwyn Savage Dudley.*

Underneath was written,

AKA: Sir Sydney Lynx-Scarborough,
The Right Honourable Harold Scott-Jamieson
Percival Livingstone-Smythe.

He hadn't expected such an abundance of information so quickly. Flicking through the pages Dewar couldn't believe the man hadn't been incarcerated on many occasions. Although using aliases wasn't strictly speaking a crime, using them for fraud, smuggling, confidence tricks and other nefarious activities certainly was. It seemed that Dudley was clever enough to be just beyond the 'reasonable proof" requirement in a great number of prosecutions and had never been amongst those jailed. Many of the convicted criminals were known to the policeman for various felonies, including trafficking of endangered creatures, smuggling contraband, sanctions busting, securities fraud and embezzlement and armed robbery. Somehow Dudley had remained at liberty while others paid for the crimes he had visibly helped to perpetrate.

Even his real name was a fraud. Arthur Dudley had been a technical college teacher until he had 'found' the money to acquire a title from a company that sold them on behalf of impecunious members of the aristocracy. According to the file he had paid five thousand pounds for the Lordship of Caistor, in Lincolnshire. Armed with this title, he changed his name by deed poll from Rex Thompson to Arthur Selwyn Savage Dudley and thence to Lord Arthur Selwyn Savage Dudley. Somehow an MBA in Computer Sciences became attached to his name in place of the modest BA in languages he had actually earned. It seemed the Board of Governors of Cambridge College of Digital Computing was duly impressed by his qualifications and pedigree and offered him the post of *Senior Lecturer in Telematics* in 1994.

On this occasion the Board had judged rightly. Dudley proved to be a visionary and a pioneer in the development of Machine to Machine, (M2M), Communications. Within a few years the College was on the front page of every industry magazine and many more far reaching esoteric publications devoted to the enablement of machines to talk to each other. A new industry was born and Dudley, now *Professor of Connected Machines Eco System Studies,* was one of the godfathers. Several start-ups were incubated in the College tech labs and one of these went on to be a dotcom darling in a billion dollar IPO. *EzeTracker,* a ubiquitous tracking system for labelling, following and finding anything that moved, won a multimillion dollar contract with the US Home Security Department in the post nine eleven anti-terrorist panic. Equipment, products and people could now be tracked from Spain to Singapore to China to New York by the insertion of a simple GPRS SIM into a plastic device attached to them or to a container. The markets loved it. After all, terrorism was a growth business.

The brain child of this technology, Dewar's student friend, Simon Pickford, had become, much to the policeman's chagrin, an exceptionally wealthy man and, as he knew, greatly indebted to Dudley, his College Master and mentor. Dewar was not in the same research stream and had hardly known the man, since he was unfortunate enough to be involved with *Personaliti,* a social media start-up which failed miserably years before Facebook became a global phenomenon and was discarded by its backers almost before it was launched, which was when he opted to follow in his father's footsteps in a career with the Metropolitan Police.

There but for the grace.... he regretted, as he looked at the photograph of Dudley's large smiling face and read the last paragraph of the bio. Apparently it was a badly concealed secret that the 'professor' had been asked to resign in 2003 after several complaints over a period of years in respect of his inappropriate relationships with both male and female students. It seemed the man was corrupt through and through.

Dewar's rapid rise to seniority in the force was due partly to his retired father's brilliant reputation but also to his own instincts. Instinct to spot a potential connection and instinct to act decisively and quickly. He looked up his International Contacts list and called Chief Superintendent Johannes Hendricks, Head of the Homicide Unit in Johannesburg.

London, England

Lord Arthur Dudley was in a taxi on his way to meet the others at the Park Lane Hotel when he received the call from his contact in Marseille. "*Cent mille de plus*? A hundred thousand more? That's about what I expected. It's not a bad offer."

It was Friday16th and the shipment was due in on Sunday 18th. That left very little time to haggle any further over the commission. *In any case,* he reflected, *a bird in the hand...* "*Très bien. Je suis d'accord.* Very well, with the same pro rata compensation then I agree. You can confirm it to them immediately. But I want the additional funds in a different account. I'll send you the details by email later today and you can forward them to Geneva."

Dudley ended the call and sat back in his seat, reflecting on the current situation. Even if the Leo Stewart business fell by the wayside, he would suffer no personal loss, in fact he had already appropriated a part of the funds budgeted for non-existent costs and he was insulated from any fall out. This morning's arrangement would bring an additional substantial commission into his account in the Bahamas and more than compensate him for his efforts in the abduction transaction.

Marbella, Spain

Jenny had spent the last half hour speaking to Valerie Aeschiman and Philippe Jaquelot at the *Banque de Commerce* in Geneva. As she had feared, sending hundreds of thousands of dollars to South Africa was a virtually impossible task in these days of compliance and money laundering avoidance. They didn't have a sister bank there and opening an account with a new bank would take weeks of complicated paperwork. Even then, making large withdrawals in cash would prove impossible. The only solution was to do what she had dreamt of last night; to take the money from Geneva to Johannesburg in cash. Mme Aeschiman was prepared to provide her with the cash but flying it down to South Africa would require hiring a private plane, to avoid the security checks. She put the matter aside for the moment. It was Friday and nothing could be done before Monday. *We don't even know for sure where Leo is. At least I have one option that works.*

She went back out to the terrace where Emma was typing away on her laptop. "What are you up to?"

"I'm actually writing. Alan just reminded me that I've got a book to deliver by November 30th so I can get my next advance, otherwise Leo's Christmas is going to be rather frugal."

"Alan Bridges, your publisher, *stroke,* on-off boyfriend?"

Emma laughed sheepishly. "He called a few minutes ago. He's feeling neglected and I don't blame him. We haven't spoken since I left for Johannesburg. I haven't been in the mood."

"But all's well on the Bridges Front?"

"He should be so lucky. While I've been stressing and worrying my head off down here, he's lapping up the sun in the South of France."

"You didn't say anything about our problem?"

"Not a word. Too dangerous. When I get Leo back I'll make sure he doesn't divulge anything either."

"Alan must be doing quite well to afford holidays on the Côte d'Azur."

Emma laughed. "He's not that well off and you're forgetting that he's Scottish. One of his authors is Mike Pringle, you've probably heard of him, much better known than me?"

Jenny shook her head and she continued, "Anyway, Mike has a hotel apartment near Nice and Alan gets invited down a couple of times a year. I was there two years ago. It's a fabulous place, restaurant, pool, everything at hand and right by the beach."

"That's something to aspire to, so you'd better keep on writing. What's the new book about?"

"Oh, nothing very original. It's called *Red Sky over Orkney*, with the same boring characters doing more or less the same boring things, just in a different place. I told you, I'm running out of fresh ideas, that's the problem. I just keep writing and hoping that something new and gripping will come out of it but so far it hasn't. I'm really not that good a writer."

"I like the title. Anyhow it's good to see you thinking positively and writing again."

"I was thinking about something else before he called, actually," Emma said. "How long have you known Leticia?"

"I first met her at Ellen and Charlie's house-warming party when she was working for them. That was seven years ago. The next time was the following year, at Ellen's funeral." She paused, unwelcome memories flooding back into her mind.

"Sorry. I didn't mean to upset you," Emma said.

"It's alright, just not something I like to dwell on. Anyway, I didn't get to know her until after Charlie's death, when I found out about her and Charlie and Emilio. That was a bit of a shock, but she was so honest and naïve that I couldn't imagine anything wrong about their relationship. And her son is such an adorable child, he thinks of me as his aunt, which makes me really happy.

"Then we had that awful business with d'Almeida that I told you about yesterday. That's when we became very close. I think I'm like an elder sister to her, the way you are to me. So I felt I had found a new part of my family, after losing Ron and both his parents." *Oh dear,* she thought. *That wasn't very tactful of me.*

Emma shook her head. "I don't think of myself as an older sister to you. On the contrary, I feel younger. You've experienced so much more than me and you have a way of getting things done, despite any obstacles or objections. But I know what you mean about family. We didn't see much of each other when Leo was young. I was writing every day when I wasn't rushing from one book shop to another to sign future priceless first editions. I was probably a bit obsessed with my own life and not looking in your direction." She paused, looking guilty. "I'm sorry, Jenny. It seems that it's taken some really serious problems for us to come together again."

"It's just the way things work out. You were living in the North and I married someone with a business in Ipswich. Life throws changes at you. You just have to take them in your stride and get on with it. The main thing is that we're back in touch and we've got a mutual objective to accomplish. Getting Leo back, with Coetzee's help!"

Emma nodded. "I just hope he's with him. Now that we've sent the others a holding message, I'm praying we'll get a reply from Coetzee this morning. At least something that proves Leo is with him. It will probably be in the form of a counter- offer. It's like an auction, you can't stop bidding until you're successful."

Jenny said, "Why did you ask me about Leticia?"

"Oh, I was just trying to think through the people involved in this awful business and her name popped into my head."

"In what connection?" Now Jenny was intrigued.

"Well, think about it. She's the only person who knows about your fortune and that I was taking Leo to the football. I was looking for a common denominator, as Pedro calls it, and I thought of her."

"It's certainly half a connection, but she couldn't have known about your story because you say that no one did. She knew I had a sister, but nothing personal about you, never mind that you have a Rwandan son, so I'm not sure about the common denominator."

Jenny remembered her conversation with Leticia word for word. It had only occurred yesterday. Emma had been upset by the event and she had shrugged it off. Leticia had said, '*I heard you talking about it*'.

Could she possibly have found out about Leo's birth? Could Leticia be the common denominator between past and present? She pushed the thought away, it wasn't conceivable. Then the last discussion she'd had with her came to her mind. Last night she had asked her to look at some financial papers, only to change her mind after she had spoken to Patrice that morning.

Uneasily she thought about their other conversations. Another memory came to her, another phrase that had sounded out of place, when she was talking about buying something in the South of France, 'I couldn't afford anything big now'. *Why did she say, 'now' and why had Patrice not wanted her to show me the papers?*

Once again she rejected the idea, only to be confronted by a vivid memory of her dream the previous night. The woman who had taken the money had Leticia's face. She shivered at the thought. It wasn't possible, or was it?

London, England

"Bensouda has offered one hundred thousand more and the Marseille people have accepted. They're sending me bank details for the transfer. Everything is back on course for Sunday."

Dudley supressed a laugh. He had just paid off the taxi and was entering the Park Lane Hotel. "Well done, M Jolidon. Our arrangement is becoming more profitable by the minute. I'm in rather a hurry at the moment, but I'll leave you to handle everything with your usual efficiency. Thank you for your call."

He put the US phone back in his pocket. *One intermediary in Geneva and the other in Marseille and never the twain shall meet.* Arthur Dudley was feeling quite pleased with the terms of the transaction and it was only going to get better.

FIFTY-SEVEN

Johannesburg, South Africa

Espinoza had taken a cab directly to Chief Superintendent Hendricks' office. He had caught him on his mobile and been invited to go over immediately. He was still mulling over his call with Jenny and Emma and the message they had now sent to ARGS. This investigation was becoming more and more complicated and he needed time to think about the various pieces of the jigsaw and how they fitted together. Maybe he would learn something from the policeman.

He saw on arriving that Hendricks was stressed out at having two suspicious deaths on his hands at the same time. As usual, the top brass were piling on the pressure for an announcement, any announcement. He was summarising what they'd learned to date when the call came from DI Dewar in London. Hendricks' eyes widened when he was told who was calling. Two European contacts in the same week as two mysterious deaths. What was this all about?

He listened to Dewar's information in silence, making notes with a cheap ball point pen on a pad of shoddy recycled lined paper. Espinoza's ears pricked up when he heard, "You say that the trace followed them from Polokwane to Phalaborwa then down here to Delmas? Is that where they are now?"

He listened again for a moment. "Good, please email the details and I'll follow it up. Here is my private email address." He dictated the information. "Thank you for your assistance, Detective Inspector."

"News about our investigation?" Espinoza asked ingenuously.

"Possibly, but I doubt it. Apparently someone in England has been tracing mobile phones in South Africa. I can't see why that would be connected. I'll wait for the email. Now, as I was saying, the death of the hotel manager, Lambert, seems definitely to be murder. The receptionist said he went upstairs with a Sergeant Bongani from Forsburg Central and next thing he was lying dead in the car park. The problem is that there is no policeman in Forsburg or even in South Africa with the name Bongani. The woman couldn't give a good description of him and there are no other witnesses, so we have no idea whether it was actually a police officer or an imposter."

Espinoza didn't comment, but he was certain it must have been Nwosu. "And the second death, in Polokwane?"

"We think it was also a murder, because of blood traces and tyre tracks on the nearby ground and there was no identification on the body. But we have nothing to go on. The corpse had been savaged by wild animals and the face was unrecognisable. We've done house to house visits in the area, but no one knows anything. Or if they do they're not saying."

"Have you done a DNA analysis?"

"I'm waiting for the result. It should be here this morning. But if it's not on our data base we'll still be in the dark."

Again the Spaniard made no comment. He was still putting two and two together from the snatches of speech he'd heard during the call. "Why do you think an English police inspector would be interested in a phone call trace in Polokwane?"

Hendricks seemed irritated with the logic employed by the other man. "I have no idea why he called. Something to do with a fellow called Lord Arthur Dudley. Can we please concentrate on my murders that's the priority right now."

An English Lord! Espinoza's curiosity was now really aroused. Emma had said the ARGS messages might have been written by a member of the aristocracy. He didn't believe in coincidences and he didn't believe that simultaneous events in South Africa and England were not somehow related. Both Emma and Lambert were English and he had suspected from the start that the epicentre of the conspiracy might be in the UK.

"Right." Hendricks' voice interrupted his reverie. "Please tell me about the case you're investigating and how these deaths could be connected."

Espinoza began a long and convoluted fabrication about drug smuggling, prostitution and human trafficking between the UK and Spain. It was an anodyne story that could have occurred anywhere in the world and Hendricks looked suitably bored until he said, "I identified Lambert during my investigation in Spain and I'm convinced he fled to South Africa to save his skin when the net started to tighten." Here he strayed somewhat from the truth, but said to himself, *The end justifies the means.*

"So you think he was murdered because of his involvement in the Spanish business?"

"According to my information they have interests over here too. I believe he was killed by an 'associate' to prevent him from betraying the organisation."

Now the South African was becoming interested. "We're aware of the links between our country and Europe. I hear there's a lot of organised crime in the South of Spain. What do you know about the 'associate'?"

"I've heard a name and I've seen a photograph. It's a long shot, but I would recognise him if I saw him again."

"Is there a connection with the other body, in Polokwane?"

Here Espinoza was on thinner ice, since he couldn't easily create a connection between the two deaths without risking the truth. He was saved by a 'ping' from Hendricks' laptop.

"It's Dewar. Hmm, this looks bloody complicated. Apparently Lord Dudley asked for two phones to be traced by a company called

EzeTracker in England. One was supposed to be in Polokwane at the time of the death up there, then it was traced to Phalaborwa and then to Delmas. A second phone was traced to Delmas and now they've both moved to a different location. He thinks it's an apartment building in Diepkloof. That's a half hour south-west of here," he added.

It took all of Espinoza's mental fortitude to remain calm. *Diepkloof. That's Nwosu's precinct and where he lives. Bingo!* He said, "Can you send someone there to check?"

The other man looked exasperated. "Look, Espinoza. I'm in the middle of a double murder investigation. This phone tracking is obviously not relevant to my enquiry. Just tell me what you know about this gang killing."

Espinoza realised he'd sold the gang story too well and Hendricks was desperate to believe it. The man didn't think laterally.

"You're right of course." He replied. "It's unlikely that it's connected to your two murders. But there could possibly be a link to my enquiry because of the English connection. Since I've come all the way down here I have to exhaust every possibility. I can go on my own if you don't have the resources."

Hendricks still looked uninterested, but he was thinking fast. He had no leads at all in the murder enquiry and Espinoza hadn't told him anything of value. *But he obviously knows something and he's looking for a deal. If I humour him in this Dudley affair, he'll be obliged to help me and it might make a difference.*

"You can't go on your own, you have no jurisdiction." He looked at his watch. "I'll take you myself. It'll be a waste of time but you can check it out then we can get back to my murder investigation. OK?"

The Spaniard smiled to himself. "Good, thanks. I'll be entirely at your disposal when we return."

Hendricks took a pistol and holster from his drawer and fastened it on. "I'm not allowed to arm you, but it's probably a wild goose chase. Let's go."

Espinoza followed him out the door, hoping he wouldn't live to regret that statement.

London, England

Dudley, Esther and Slater were sitting in a room near the reception of the hotel. She served them coffee and croissants from a tray on a sideboard.

"I have received an email message on my mobile phone from Ms Stewart," Dudley announced with a beaming smile. He put on his spectacles and read from the tiny screen. "She informs us that she is attempting to raise funds 'from various sources' to make us a reasonable offer. We can expect a confirmation by Monday, which I think you'll agree is extremely promising. I can only assume that she is speaking with her sister, since that is the closest and most available source of substantial wealth and they're probably in the same house together. What do you think of that?"

"If my partner comes over this afternoon we'd better have a better story than that to tell. This business isn't justifying an investment of half a million dollars at the minute." The man looked confident and professional in his business suit but his nervous tone confounded the image.

"I believe we are about to receive some very good news. Following further arrangements I have put in place I am expecting a call in just a short while. I suggest being patient until we receive further news. In the meanwhile we can discuss the details of the payment procedure once again." Dudley gave a smug smile and sipped his coffee.

Esther and Slater looked at him in astonishment. Last night they had lost the boy and now it seemed he had been found again. They both sat back in their chairs, breathing a deep sigh of relief.

Vereeniging, Gauteng, South Africa

According to the brochure, the Vaal Riviera Hotel is exactly one hour's drive from Johannesburg. But the south bound highway of the N3 was under repair and it took Coetzee almost two hours to get there. It was after midday before they were installed in their rooms. The hotel was a four star establishment, comfortable and old fashioned. He had booked a double room for Karen and Abbi and two singles for Leo and himself.

The hotel had a floating bar/lounge and dining room on a motorised barge that sailed from one side of the river to the other. It was a beautiful day so they went for a coffee outside on the deserted deck.

Leo was still waiting to call his mother. He wanted to hear what Coetzee had to say. Especially what part he played in Blethin's demise. To get his own version right before he called her, and that might depend on what he heard from the South African. He sat waiting nervously for him to begin.

"I reckon I owe you all an explanation." Coetzee looked uncomfortable. "Where should I start?"

"How about the beginning?" said Karen and Abby in unison.

"Right." He took a cheroot from the pack and laid it on the table without lighting it. Then he told them the story of the Voice and Nwosu and Lambert and Blethin, and Leo. He didn't tell them about poor Jacob Masuku and his wife. He realised that some things were best forgotten.

Diepkloof, Gauteng, South Africa

Hendricks' unmarked Peugeot pulled up in front of the apartment building in Diepkloof at twelve thirty pm. As they got out of the car a black Mercedes with darkened windows and Zimbabwean plates drove away from the kerb, narrowly missing Espinoza.

"Fucking tourists! Their country is bankrupt and falling apart and they're driving around my country in fancy Mercedes spending money they've stolen from their own people and from foreign aid. It's disgusting." Espinoza nodded his agreement as Hendricks spat into the gutter in anger.

There were three entrances to the building and the information from DI Dewar hadn't identified which one it was. Espinoza didn't want to reveal that he knew the address, it would look suspicious. Fortunately it was the only apartment building on the street. They chose the first entrance and went into a shabby hall with post boxes on the wall. "What was the name you heard?"

"Nwosu. Jonathon Nwosu." Espinoza held his breath in case the policeman recognised the name.

"Nobody here called Nwosu." The name meant nothing to Hendricks. "We'll try next door."

Nwosu's apartment was on the top floor of the third entrance. They climbed the four flights, ignoring the various noises and smells they passed on the way. There was no one in the stairwell and they arrived at the apartment without seeing a soul.

Hendricks pressed the bell. There was no response and he pressed it again and knocked with his knuckles. Still no response. Espinoza turned the metal handle and the door swung open.

"Wait." Hendricks took his pistol from the holster and released the safety catch. They walked into a small hall with three closed doors around them. The first opened onto an untidy bedroom with a travel bag lying on the unmade bed.

"Look." Espinoza pointed at a policemen's jacket hanging over a chair back. There was a cap and an empty holster on the seat.

"Fucking Hell!" Hendricks looked in amazement. "He's a cop. A sergeant, no less!" He started to reassess the possible connection between Espinoza's visit and Dewar's message. A shower room with an adjacent lavatory opened off the bedroom. Toilet items were strewn on the shelf in front of the mirror.

The room on the right was a small kitchen. Two coffee mugs stood on a bench. The mugs were almost full. Espinoza felt one, it was still warm. Hendricks cocked the pistol and opened the third door.

It was a comfortably furnished room with a dining corner by the window. Lying on his back by the dining table, his upper body in a pool of blood was Sergeant Nwosu. His pistol was lying on the floor beside him. He was in his shirt sleeves, his freshly plastered right arm stretched out and a bullet hole in his temple.

London, England

Dudley was itemising the fictitious additional costs of the operation when his mobile rang. It was his contact in Harare. The others watched expectantly as a broad smile came to his face. "That's good news. Where is the boy now?" He listened again. "I see. And the policeman and the other man? What about your two missing agents? Very well, please let me know when the boy is safely in Beitbridge. Thank you for your intervention."

"Well?" Slater asked eagerly.

"Please wait for one moment while I make another call." Dudley went out of the room and called EzeTracker. "Simon, my dear boy. Could you possibly ask for a very quick update on our friends in SA?"

A moment later Pickford came back on the line. "Both phones are on the Western Bypass. It's a ring road that takes you west of Johannesburg to get to the N1 northbound. Is that accurate enough, Master?"

"It is more than enough Simon, thank you. I do apologise for having troubled you again. Have a wonderful day."

He came back into the room and closed the door, his smile even broader than before. "I now have independent confirmation that Leo Stewart is on his way to Beitbridge with appropriate security. We are once again in charge of the operation."

Esther and Slater exchanged relieved glances. "Thank God. When was this? And what about Coetzee and Nwosu?"

"It was earlier this morning and apparently there was some collateral damage. Coetzee was not at the scene, but Nwosu was. Unfortunately he didn't survive the event, which of course fortuitously removes another witness without any intervention on our part. I confess that I don't understand what has been happening recently but the essential point is that we once again have Leo Stewart in our custody."

"But where is Coetzee?"

"It's really quite irrelevant now. The boy is out of his control and will very soon be in an inaccessible and inhospitable place. In the event he is still alive, there is nothing Mr Coetzee can do.

He has no idea who or where we are and is now completely removed from this transaction. Our path to Ms Stewart is now clear."

"So you'll be sending the payment instructions today?"

"This evening, yes. If you don't object I prefer to receive confirmation of their arrival in Beitbridge, there have been rather too many false starts as it is. I'll return to my apartment with Esther and we'll prepare the message immediately. It will be sent as soon as I have the necessary confirmation from my contact. I apologise for the confusion of the last few days and if possible I'll discover more information for you, but I hope you'll agree that we are once again in control."

For the first time, Slater looked relieved and at ease. "Well done, Arthur. I'll call my partner. Coming over here will be a waste of time now." He went out of the room to make the call.

"Are you sure of this news, Arthur? We can't afford another fiasco, it would cost us a lot, both financially and possibly in other ways."

"Quite sure, my dear. My explanation was deliberately over-simplified and modest in the extreme. What actually occurred was that we traced both phones to an apartment in Diepkloof, which I knew, of course, to be Nwosu's home. I arranged for another agent to call at the apartment and retrieve the boy. Apparently the sergeant tried to prevent them taking him away and had to be subdued. I have just had final confirmation that both phones are on their way to Beitbridge, which probably means that Coetzee had previously been neutralised and Nwosu had recuperated his own phone. That was the guarantee I required to prove that Leo has been retaken. It seems that for once we have managed to kill two birds with one stone."

"And the two missing agents? I heard you asking."

"They have still not been located. Nwosu threatened the agent and was shot before he could interrogate him about them, but that, fortunately is not our problem"

Esther came over and kissed him on the cheek. "Well done, Arthur. You are the most resourceful man I have ever met."

Dudley flushed a bright red. The combination of the kiss and her heady perfume were almost more than he could cope with. The moment meant more to him than he cared to admit. His embarrassment was deflected by the door opening again.

"My partner will wait for further news before taking the flight. If we get confirmation tonight there'll be no need to come." Slater had ignored the sight of Esther moving quickly away from Lord Dudley's chair, he couldn't imagine that there might be the slightest cause for jealousy. "I'm assuming," he continued, "that once in Beitbridge there's no possibility of losing the boy?"

"I can assure you that once Leo Stewart is across the border in Zimbabwe, no power in the world can remove him if we do not want that to occur."

"Then you don't need me here either. I told you I wanted to leave today." He looked at his watch and stood up. "If I go now I'll just make my flight." He called to the concierge to bring his suitcase. "I'll be in touch this evening for further news. Well done and good luck."

He shook hands with them both, resisting the impulse to kiss Esther, and walked out to take a taxi to Paddington to catch the Heathrow Express.

Vereeniging, Gauteng, South Africa

Including fielding a barrage of questions from Karen, Leo and even Abby, it took Coetzee an hour and a half to tell his story. He was not a loquacious man and didn't enjoy speaking for so long but he knew they all deserved the full story, no short cuts or prevarications. He finished by saying, "Thanks to Leo's brainwave, I knew if I gave the phones to Jamie, the heat would be off us. If the Voice is still looking for us he'll be following Nwosu. I'm not proud of what I've done, but Nwosu is a butcher and he deserves whatever happens to him." He picked up the cheroot from the table, put it between his lips then put it back again, unlit.

"Why on earth did you get mixed up in this dreadful business?" Karen had sat in shocked silence as she listened to her ex-husband's confession. Although he had kept the story simple she knew the trouble he could get into and was already in. "You've spent your life protecting your country, saving lives, becoming a national hero and a shining example to people of all ages. Then you suddenly go off and kidnap an innocent young boy whom you don't even know and get involved in death and destruction on a massive scale. What's wrong with you, Marius?"

"Karen, the truth is, it's really your fault." Before she could respond, he went on, "For the last two years I've been totally lost. After you left me I walked out of the army, the only place where I've ever felt safe and useful. I set up a business which turned out to be a money pit and cost me my pension pot because I was too incompetent to manage it properly. I screwed up that business and now I've screwed up my life. I used to be clean living and fit and now I'm smoking, drinking and eating crap food because I can't be bothered to cook or go to a proper restaurant.

"Then, to cap it all, I joined up with a psychopathic killer and a bunch of crooks because I'm broke and thought I could make some money to get started again and look at the result. There's innocent people dead, my family were put in harm's way and a young kid who could be my son almost ended up in Zimbabwe. How smart was that?"

Coetzee took the cheroot and snapped it in two. Threw the pieces over the side of the barge. "The bottom line is I'm a total fucking disaster on my own. I need someone beside me to keep me in order. I need a boss, Karen. I had one in the army and I had you at home and now I have no one."

Leo was looking at Karen. Tears started to run down her face as he finished speaking. He turned to Coetzee and saw the same thing. Coetzee was crying now. *Tears of love,* he realised. *They're still in love.*

He took Abby's hand. "Let's go for a walk. See what we can find along the river." They walked down the stairs from the restaurant deck leaving Coetzee and Karen sitting at the table, saying nothing, just looking at each other.

FIFTY-EIGHT

Diepkloof, Gauteng, South Africa

"She says that's the policeman who went upstairs with Mr Lambert, Sergeant Bongani. She's sure of it." The desk clerk at the Hotel Packard was looking at a photo of Nwosu's dead face. Hendricks had emailed it to an officer in central Johannesburg who had gone straight to the hotel to interrogate the woman. He and Espinoza were still at the apartment as the pathologist confirmed the death from a bullet wound when they received the call. Two officers were also there searching the apartment and another was questioning the other occupants of the building, without success. No guns had been found, neither the murder weapon nor Nwosu's police issue pistol.

Hendricks gave instructions for the clerk to officially identify the body when it was taken to the morgue and closed the phone. "That's one crime solved since you got here, Pedro. We might never have put two and two together, certainly not so quickly. The PR people will make a big deal out of this. It makes great headlines when we actually get something right." He made no mention of Espinoza's supposed European connection. It would only complicate matters. *Keep it simple and close the case,* he said to himself.

The pathologist announced that the death had occurred less than an hour ago and the other injuries to the body were older and not directly connected with the murder. Both men tried to imagine what recent events had occurred to inflict such harm to the dead policeman. An accident treatment form from the Newtown Private Clinic was found in the pocket of Nwosu's jacket and the nurse who answered their call confirmed that he had been there earlier that morning. The clinic had no further information to impart. His appointment had been made by telephone and he arrived and left with a young man after his wrist was plastered, having told them nothing about that or his other injuries. Hendricks had sent an officer to check, but there seemed to be nothing to learn there.

There were several photos in the apartment of a young black man, hardly more than a boy, some showing him with Nwosu in very explicit poses. Some had messages written on the back and were signed by 'Jamie'. Nwosu was clearly a homosexual and Jamie had been his partner.

Emma's instincts were correct, reflected Espinoza. Now, Nwosu was dead and Jamie was missing. The policeman's laptop was taken away to be forensically examined. Hendricks hoped they'd find more information about the boyfriend from its contents.

One of the officers came over to them. "It's funny, but we haven't found a mobile phone. I don't think I've ever searched an apartment without finding one. A cop always has a mobile."

"Jamie probably grabbed it when he left. We'll get after him right away. But we've got Lambert's killer and that's a good score for the day." Hendricks sent the man back to his work.

He said to Espinoza, "It looks as if Jamie topped him for some reason when they got here and then pissed off. He can't be far. We've got a good chance to find him if we put out an alert with one of these photos."

Espinoza was less sure than the South African. He remembered the Zimbabwean car that had almost mowed him down outside the building. *They were certainly in a hurry to get away.* He was also not sure if the young man with Nwosu at the clinic was Jamie. *It couldn't be*

Leo, he reasoned. *If Jenny's theory was correct, he was with Coetzee. So if it was Nwosu's boyfriend, why did he kill him and where was he now?*

He said, "Is there any way to find the owners of that Zimbabwean car that drove off when we arrived? It was an old black Mercedes 220, number 294-TCE 87."

Hendricks looked at him shrewdly. "You're very observant, Pedro. If you're right, that's a diplomatic registration plate and we have no jurisdiction." He checked his watch. "Their consulate is closed for the weekend, but even if they were open it would be a waste of time. They'll be well on their way to Zimbabwe by now and if it was Jamie in the car he'll get there without any problems. And a few hundred Rand will get them through the border even if we make a fuss. I'm sorry to admit it but there's not a thing we can do."

Espinoza took advantage of the policeman's assumption, silently praying that Leo was not in the Mercedes. "Whether or not Jamie was in the car, you're probably right. We now know Nwosu killed Lambert. There was a young man with him at the clinic and now he's gone and Nwosu's dead. It seems reasonable to assume that it was Jamie who was with him, but we can check his photograph with the nurse at the clinic. I don't think there's anything more we can do here."

Hendricks nodded in agreement and gave a few final instructions to the police officers. They went down to his car. Espinoza said, "When do you expect the DNA report from Polokwane?"

"It might be there when we get back. Why?"

"I was wondering if they chose the Newtown Clinic by accident or whether there might be a connection." Espinoza had now found a way to link the two murders. The DNA would identify Blethin and it would look as if he had also been murdered by the same people. Hendricks would be happy to close the dossier on a bent cop and a corrupt doctor if they could be tied together and blamed on Jamie who was probably on his way to Zimbabwe. He might be able to convince him of that. If Leo was safe with Coetzee he wanted to get out of the murder investigation as soon as possible and concentrate on getting him back and tracing the organisers of the abduction.

"Chance would be a fine thing. I'll call and chase it up while we're driving back."

Espinoza sat back in the car. *So far so good.* His suggestion had been accepted without question. His mind turned to the other sore point which was now in the forefront of his thinking. Why were the phones being followed by someone in the UK? That had to be where the abduction had been masterminded. He knew he was still a long way from fulfilling Jenny's appeal; 'To get Leo safely back and then to bring the culprits to justice'.

London, England

"I estimate that they should arrive in Beitbridge by seven this evening. As soon as I get confirmation I'll send off the message. It's Friday so that may spoil their weekend a little, but needs must." Dudley and Esther had prepared the email with the payment instructions.

"I have to do some shopping and sort out one or two personal matters." Esther couldn't face another long day alone with him. "Do you mind if I go now and we can speak later?"

He tried to hide his disappointment. "Of course not, there's no need for you to stay. I'll call you when I've accomplished the task. Perhaps we can have dinner together and discuss tomorrow's negotiations for the money."

"Thank you Arthur, but I'm afraid I can't join you for dinner. I have another engagement."

He said, "Very well my dear, I'll send you a text message so that you can sleep peacefully knowing that everything is in order."

"Good, but you may want to ask for a photograph from Beitbridge. I'm not suggesting that anything's wrong, but it's probably a wise precaution."

"Indeed. I'll call them later to request that. Where are you off to this evening?"

"I don't know. An old friend from Paris called me and invited me to dinner. He's on his own in town, so I agreed. You don't mind, do you?"

"Of course not, I have no claim on your time." Dudley turned away. *Foolish old man,* he said to himself, *she's not one of my prized possessions.*

"Then I'll leave you and look forward to seeing you in the morning."

He helped her into her coat, delighting as always in the closeness of her beautiful body and fragrant perfume. "Have a lovely afternoon and enjoy your engagement this evening."

She turned and waved as she walked away. Dudley forced a smile again then went back into his empty apartment and closed the door.

Johannesburg, South Africa

"I've sent the DNA analysis to the Newtown Clinic. They've got records of all their employees going back ten years. If we get a match we'll have solved the Polokwane murder as well. And if there's a link to Nwosu that's good enough for me. Lambert comes from the UK or Spain and gets murdered by Nwosu. Nwosu then goes after another gang member in Polokwane, comes back after a fight and gets topped by his boyfriend. Some kind of gang warfare ending with the deaths of three gangsters. One of them probably from Zimbabwe. Case closed."

They had received photographic confirmation from the nurse at the clinic that it was Jamie who had accompanied the policeman, so Hendricks was feeling very pleased with himself. "It had to be Jamie who killed Nwosu since we have no reports of anyone else being in the building. And it looks like he escaped in the Mercedes and he's probably safely back in Zimbabwe. My report will blame Nwosu for Lambert's death and Jamie for killing his boyfriend. If I get good news from the clinic I'm wrapping it up."

Hendricks had also called the duty officer at Diepkloof precinct to ask about Nwosu and his current activities. He was told the sergeant wasn't working on anything except some cases of football hooliganism and had taken a few days off. They were expecting him back on Monday. He decided not to share any information with the man, not until he was ready to make an announcement.

"Thanks for coming over, Pedro. It might seem a wasted trip for you, but it was a lucky break for me."

"What are you going to tell Dewar?" Espinoza asked.

"I'm not getting side tracked with phone tapping from the UK. Just because somebody was tapping a phone it doesn't link them to a murder. We didn't find any phones so there's no reason to do anything. I'll tell him we've investigated his report and found nothing. He can take it from there."

The Spaniard was relieved. If Blethin was linked to the clinic, as he surely would be, the murders would be wrapped up and he could get on with his main task without interference from Hendricks. It seemed certain that it was not Leo who had gone off in the Mercedes so he could concentrate on finding Coetzee.

Before leaving he asked for Dewar's number. It would be useful if he needed information in the UK, especially about Lord Arthur Dudley." He wrote it in his notebook then said, "I might as well stay on for a few days and make the most of the trip. It's a long time since I visited Joburg."

Hendricks was already writing his report so he asked if someone could run him over to the Packard Hotel. It was the only place he could think of on the spur of the moment. *Besides, there might still be something to find out there.*

Marbella, Spain

Jenny was at the front door trying to understand Juan's explanation as to why the water fountain had suddenly stopped functioning when a taxi arrived at the gate. She pressed the remote switch and the car drove up to the house.

"Patrice. How lovely to see you again. It's been far too long." She embraced him.

"Jenny. You look wonderful. How are you?" He paid off the driver and took his bag into the hall. "I hope you haven't delayed anything on my account."

"Encarni is just about ready to serve the first course, so you've got time for a quick aperitif if you like."

He followed her out to the terrace. Emma was showing Leticia and Emilio her website. They both jumped up and ran across to him and he picked up the little boy. "*Salut p'tit bonhomme.* Hello little man. Did you miss me?"

"We all missed you chéri, but you're home at last." Leticia kissed him several times. "You must be exhausted with all that travelling. That's a very smart suit you're wearing. This is Jenny's sister, Emma, she's a famous writer. She's been showing us her books on her website. Come and sit down, I'll get you a glass of wine, nice and cold. It'll just take me a moment."

Jenny watched her run quickly off to find Encarni in the kitchen. *What a performance,* she thought. *She's as nervous as a kitten. I wonder why?*

"I'm pleased to meet you Emma. Jenny never told me her sister was so attractive. Brains and beauty, I see."

"French charm. He says it to every woman he meets." Jenny joked. Patrice glanced swiftly at her. He didn't seem to appreciate the joke.

"Santé. It's wonderful to be back home again. Sorry, Jenny, I mean your home, but still wonderful." Patrice settled back on a settee with Emilio on his knee and Leticia beside him.

"I hear you've been running about a lot these days. Business must be good. Making fortunes for your clients, I suppose."

He glanced at Leticia. "We're still trying to make up the fortunes we lost for our customers two years ago. This is a very volatile year so it's a hard slog, but we'll get there in the end."

"I didn't know you looked after clients in the UK? Aren't Spain and South America your stomping grounds?"

He took a sip of wine. "I go there a lot, actually. I can't stop my clients from moving around and London is very often a hub for their travel. It's easier for me to meet a Brazilian when he's in the UK than to fly down to Sao Paulo."

Leticia put her hand on his knee. "Jenny, I'm sure Patrice is much too tired to talk about his work. Let's forget about business and relax."

Why is she protecting him? Jenny wondered. "I beg your pardon, Patrice. I'm just fascinated by your jet-set life style. Did you know that I called you to come for lunch yesterday, because I thought you were here, but you'd already rushed off to London. I don't know how you do it."

Before he could respond, Leticia interrupted. "We're neglecting poor Emma. Have you heard from Leo? When is he coming over to see us?"

Jenny was still looking at Patrice. He moved nervously on his seat and turned to Emma. "I forgot all about Leo. Sorry, I wasn't thinking. Where is he?"

"He's in Estepona, staying with Nigel Dean's family. He's a school friend. I'm expecting him back for the weekend." Emma managed the moment calmly, trying to work out what Jenny was up to. *Why is she deliberately setting out to irritate him?*

"They've just returned from South Africa, you know, from the football." Leticia was still keeping the subject away from her fiancé.

"Of course, I remember, the trip of a lifetime. Lucky boy, he must have loved it. I wish I'd been there to see Iniesta's goal, it almost made me want to be Spanish, beating the Dutch like that. When did you get back?"

"I'll just make sure Encarni hasn't set the kitchen on fire," Jenny said and went into the house. *What on earth is going on? It was like a sparring match out there. Leticia is worried about something. Something to do with Patrice, but she can't pluck up the courage to tell me about it.*

Another thought jogged her memory; their conversation the previous day. The words came back to her. Leticia hadn't said, '*I heard you talking about it*', she'd said '*We heard*'. Patrice also knew about their trip. Espinoza had been right. The list of suspects had been tripled, not doubled.

Jenny was confused again and she didn't like it.

It was one hundred and fourteen hours since Leo had been taken.

FIFTY-NINE

Johannesburg, South Africa

Espinoza's mobile rang just as he finished unpacking his case in the Packard Hotel. A very satisfied Chief Superintendent Hendricks announced that the murdered man in Polokwane had been identified as Dr Ernest Blethin, a consultant on the Newtown Clinic medical team. "And the bullet that killed Nwosu was fired from a Makarov PM semi-automatic pistol. That's standard issue to the Zimbabwean hard men and that's good enough for me. You've closed this case for me in half a day, Pedro. I owe you. How can I repay you?"

Espinoza had been waiting for this opening. "You can help me with the European part of my case, Johannes. I need to identify the connection with the people over there. Can you possibly check Blethin's DNA with another data base in Europe?"

Hendricks confirmed he'd be happy to do so and took down the details. He could now get his case written up and wait for the plaudits from his superiors and the Johannesburg press contingent. He thanked Espinoza again and rang off with a rare feeling of fulfilment.

Espinoza took out the jigsaw puzzle he'd drawn in the airport and ticked off three points on his list. He wasn't there yet but he knew he was starting to move in the right direction. He checked his watch. It was three thirty, two thirty in Marbella. He called Jenny.

She saw his name and walked away from the others on the terrace. "Hello Pedro, we're all here, about to have lunch. What's happening?"

He quickly related the morning's news and waited for her reaction. Jenny was too clever for him to waste time with long explanations.

"So Nwosu murdered Lambert and Blethin and now he's the latest victim. I would like to say I'm sorry, but it wouldn't be true. If it was his boyfriend who did it then it's a kind of poetic justice I suppose. And if he's now in Zimbabwe then the whole team in South Africa is accounted for. Hendricks must have been impressed. It sounds as if your detective skills are just as sharp as ever and the whole plot is unravelling, thank heavens. But where are Coetzee and Leo in all of this? We're no nearer to finding the real culprits behind it all."

"Wait, Jenny. There's another development that I don't yet understand. Someone called Lord Arthur Dudley has been tracking phones from London, that's how we found Nwosu. I'm looking into that now. It may lead us to the brains behind the abduction. I don't know where Coetzee is yet, but if he has Leo safe, as we believe, then we must be very close to the final chapter."

Jenny was thunderstruck. "What? You mean there might be an English aristocrat involved in the scheme? That's what Emma said. So your theory could be right, that this whole business was organised from England. How did you find out?"

He briefly explained about EzeTracker and Detective Inspector Dewar. "The tracking has been going on for several days, apparently."

"I simply don't understand how all these people found out about me and Emma. It means that Emma's secret might be in jeopardy. I can't tell her about this, she'll go to pieces. I need to think about it."

"Please call me if you get any ideas, I've checked in at the Packard Hotel for now. I'm sorry it's still so unclear."

"I have to go. The others will be wondering what's going on. I'll call you later, Pedro."

Slipping his mobile into his pocket Espinoza went downstairs to get something to eat. *They might even have a decent glass of wine,* he hoped.

Geneva, Switzerland

Sam Bensouda opened his briefcase and placed the bundle of papers on the desk in front of him. In French, he said, "I think you'll find that to be exactly one hundred and fifty thousand dollars".

"I'll just check if you don't mind, Monsieur le Prince." Eric Schneider counted out the hundred and fifty bearer bonds, face value one thousand dollars. He held one up to the light and examined it carefully, nodding appreciatively.

"They're the same as the last batch I brought to you. I haven't just printed them this morning."

Schneider smiled, "Excellent work if you did so, Monsieur." He picked up the phone and called someone in. "When do you need the amount credited?"

"I need to make a payment of a hundred thousand with today's value. Can you manage that?"

"I'm sure we can meet your requirements, as always. Come in!" A young man of Asian extraction came into the conference room. "Nadeem, kindly take these straight down to Mister Advecht in the bond trading department on the second floor. Ask him to confirm them to me immediately."

The man left and Schneider pulled out a spotless white handkerchief and blew his nose enthusiastically. He turned back to Bensouda. "Let me serve you coffee while we wait for confirmation of the credit transaction, then you can give me your transfer instructions."

"What is the discount commission?"

"The same as on the last occasion, Monsieur." He took a bank statement from the file in front of him. "There it is. I hope it's satisfactory to you."

Another thousand dollars down the toilet, Bensouda thought. "Fine, as long as the transfer is done today."

The phone rang and Schneider said, "Excellent. Please process the transaction immediately with credit to account number Rabat 671-32. That's right, thank you."

"Now, Monsieur le Prince, do you have the account details for me for the transfer?"

Bensouda lit up his mobile phone and found the email he'd received earlier from Jolidon. He copied the account details onto the note pad on the desk.

"Thank you." Schneider called his assistant in again and handed him the paper. "This is for value today, without fail." The man took it and walked quickly out of the room.

"Is there anything more I can do for you today, Monsieur?"

"One last thing. Please let me have twenty-five thousand dollars in cash."

"Certainly. I'll call the cashier immediately."

Fifteen minutes later Bensouda walked from the bank to his limousine and stepped into the back seat. "Divonne Casino," he said to his driver.

Marbella, Spain

They managed to get through lunch without further upset, thanks to a lot of hard work from Leticia and Emilio. Fuente the cat also made an appearance which helped to lighten the tension. Jenny knew it was her fault, but she was struggling to cope with all the thoughts that were invading her mind.

Espinoza's last remark reverberated in her head. 'Someone called Lord Dudley has been tracking phones from London.' *That can only mean the abduction was planned there. And now those people, whoever they are, have certainly murdered Nwosu. So what's happened to Coetzee and Leo? Where are they and are they still together?*

Her mind continued onto a different track, as the others struggled to make small talk. There were now too many coincidences involving Leticia. *I have to face the facts,* she realised. *Leticia could be the link. Probably unknowingly, because she would never do anything to hurt anyone, especially my sister, but it's the only connection we have between Emma's trip and my money. Why did I see her face in my dream? It could only be the money. She doesn't want to talk to me about it because of Patrice. What is she afraid of? And Patrice keeps flying to England. Is that what the aeroplane is about in my dream? Is that the connection? Is it Patrice we should be worried about?*

"What do you think, Jenny?"

She started. Emma was speaking to her, trying to bring her into the conversation. "Sorry. I was lost in thought for a moment. What did you say?"

"I asked you if you preferred the life in Spain to Ipswich, although I think I know the answer."

Jenny managed to get through the rest of the meal but she filed away two vital points from her reverie; *I have to get Leticia to show me those papers and I must talk to Pedro again.*

Vereeniging, Gauteng, South Africa

"I've been thinking, Abby." Leo and the girl were watching a school of flying fish leaping out of the river, their silver scales flashing in the sunlight. They had walked for miles along the riverbank to give Coetzee and Karen time on their own. From Coetzee's story he'd learned that his mother was with his Aunt Jenny, in Marbella, so he knew she was safe. The South African had also absolved him from any responsibility for the events in Polokwane, blaming everything on a fight between Blethin and Nwosu. A fight between two criminals which ended in an injury and a death.

He felt as if a huge weight had been lifted from his shoulders. Coetzee had attached no blame on him. It was just something that happened as a result of their criminal activities. He had said, 'They went into this abduction with their eyes open and they were prepared to hand Leo over in Zimbabwe to whoever was there to take him, not caring what might happen to him. Just for money. They deserved everything they got.'

Now, Leo had carefully considered the whole episode and had come to a decision. An unusual decision, but he instinctively knew it was the right one.

He went on, "Besides Coetzee, only Nwosu is left alive from the kidnappers and I don't think he's about to make a fuss. He ended up in hospital by messing with Marius and he's terrified of what might happen next time after seeing him destroy those two gunmen. He's better off to keep his mouth shut about this whole business."

"And Jamie?"

"Even less chance of him talking. He's a complete wimp and totally devoted to Nwosu, for some strange reason."

She was quiet for a moment. "What about the two gunmen?"

"Did either of them call anyone from the house?"

Reluctantly she thought back to the tense period of waiting she and Karen had endured. "No. We all just sat there until you turned up."

"So the answer's the same. Even better, if you think about it. Nobody except Nwosu saw anything and he would just implicate himself if he talked about the fight. Whoever was following us via the mobile phones has no idea what happened to those two. They just disappeared and they'll never be found. Coetzee's too professional to have messed it up. The phones are in Jamie's car, so they can't follow us anymore."

"So what's your point?"

"My point is that I'm the only one who could get Marius into trouble. I mean if I made a report to the police or something. Otherwise we could just forget about the whole thing. There's been no ransom paid and I'm sure your mom won't let that happen and I haven't been harmed. In fact he saved my life a couple of times and looked after me pretty well, so I figure we're more or less quits."

"And you'd just let it go like that?"

"What would be the point of getting the police involved? It would just mess up his life and probably yours and Karen's as well. You saw how they feel about each other. You could be a family again and you'd have a dad. I know what it's like not to have one. I think Marius would make a good dad, he's a great guy when he's not killing people and he knows an awful lot of really interesting stuff."

"So what's your idea?"

"If I can manage to get a ticket I could just go home now. Then we all behave as if nothing has happened and get on with our lives again. I'm not keen on staying here and being interrogated by the police like a criminal. I just want to get home and put the whole thing behind me for good."

"That's very smart, Leo. That's a very mature, adult attitude."

"Says you! Thanks anyway. Can you lend me your mobile? I haven't got one at the minute. "

"Here. Who're you calling, Marius?"

"No fear. I'm calling my mum to tell her she can come for me. I'm going back to Newcastle."

London, England

Simon Pickford called at two o'clock. "I just thought you'd like to know that both phones are on the NI going north towards Polokwane again."

Dudley smiled to himself. "That's kind of you Simon. As a matter of fact I was already aware of the move. We now have contact with the people involved and the affair is being sorted out. There is no need to continue the surveillance I'm happy to say, so please thank your technicians for me and tell them they can switch off whatever machine you're using with such impressive efficiency. Your help has been most invaluable and I shall be forever grateful."

"You're welcome, Master. Please call me whenever I can be of assistance." Pickford gave instructions to suspend the tracking operations. He thought for a moment then he called DI Dewar.

Marbella, Spain

Lunch was finally over and Encarni had served coffee when Emma's mobile rang. A shiver ran up her spine when she saw it was a 027 prefix, a South African code.

She excused herself and walked to the other end of the terrace. "Hello, this is Emma."

"Hello Mum, it's me."

It was one hundred and fifteen hours since Leo had been taken.

SIXTY

Johannesburg, South Africa

Espinoza was having a well-deserved early evening nap when his mobile rang. It was CS Hendricks. He was so excited that the Spaniard couldn't understand anything he said.

"Please slow down Johannes, my English isn't so good. Tell me again so I can understand exactly."

"I said we've just received the DNA report back from France, from the St Christopher Clinic in Nice."

"And?"

"It's unbelievable. It matches with a sample from a doctor who used to work there until earlier this year. A Doctor Antoine Constance."

"Estaba en lo cierto! I was certain of it!" Espinoza mentally doffed his hat to himself, his hunch had paid off. "Blethin and Constance were one and the same person, there was no other reasonable explanation. Thank you Johannes, this is of the utmost help in my European investigation. I can go back and put this business to bed. I am deeply indebted to you."

Hendricks didn't ask for any further explanation. He had what he wanted, closure on three murders. Espinoza's problems were, fortunately, nothing to do with him. The two men exchanged a few more words then rang off.

Espinoza took his jigsaw puzzle and drew another square on it, ticking off an item on the list. He was making further notes when his phone rang again. "I was just about to call you, Jenny. For once I believe it was a coincidence. What news do you have?"

"Leo's free, Pedro. He's free!"

She breathlessly explained the chaos that had ensued at the end of their lunch when Emma had received the call. Somehow she had managed to get her upstairs and then blamed her hysteria to the others on too much sun and wine. Leticia was relieved to remove Patrice from Jenny's questioning and they decided to take Emilio to Marbella. They drove off in rather a hurry, Patrice looking suspiciously back over his shoulder as they went out the gates.

After his initial reactions of surprise and relief, Espinoza listened calmly, waiting for Jenny to get it all off her chest. He knew how much this revelation meant to her. The money had never been her main preoccupation, it had always been the safety of her nephew and the mental anguish of his mother.

When she finally stopped for breath, he asked, "Do you know where he and Coetzee are now?"

"Actually, Coetzee's wife and daughter are with them, but as we suspected they're not in Phalaborwa."

"As you suspected, not we. Your dreams could replace old fashioned detective work if they were less random. Is he close enough for me to take a car and bring him to my hotel?"

"He's apparently at a hotel a couple of hours south of Joburg, but Coetzee is going to drive him to meet you this evening, at about eight o'clock if that's OK?"

Espinoza considered for a moment, it now seemed that Leo would be returned safely, but he remembered Jenny's second instruction; 'bring the culprits to justice'. "Do you want me to arrange for the police to be here when Coetzee arrives? I could ask CS Hendricks to send someone over. Although the explanations would certainly complicate matters, especially for Leo."

"I was about to tell you. Leo himself has decided on that. He told Emma that he's convinced Coetzee became involved only because he was lost and broke after his divorce from his wife. He never had any intention of hurting him and when he saw that might happen he took him away from harm. He says he's been well treated and Coetzee just wants to get him back to us without any further delay. He also says, and I must admit I believe he's right, that it would only complicate everyone's life if the police got involved now. What do you think?"

"He's right. Making this public would prevent him from leaving here for some time while investigations were in course. And we have no idea where they might lead. The best thing we can do is to get him safely back to Emma as quickly as possible."

"I agree. I'll confirm to Coetzee that he should bring Leo to the Packard at eight. Now, why were you going to call me?"

The Spaniard quickly relayed the results of the DNA tests. "I suspected they might be the same person. They were both French and there were too many coincidences in their backgrounds and careers not to be the case. Aesthetic Procedures and Reconstructive Surgery are the same, what we laymen would call plastic surgery."

"And they both worked at that French hospital. I never put the two together. So this explains the transfer of knowledge between Constance and the South Africans. Blethin knew about Leo's birth because he was there. This business is so complicated that I suppose nothing should surprise me any longer."

The line went quiet for a moment. "Hello, Jenny, are you still there?"

"Yes. I was just thinking about Emma. She had a high regard for Constance. How is she going to react to this?"

"I think we'd better not inform her yet. When she has Leo back these unpleasant facts will be of much less importance."

"You're right, better wait until you get back. I suppose this news ties up our business in Johannesburg?"

"I believe so but the trail doesn't end here. Don't forget we're still missing the other links; how did they find out about your wealth and how did they know about the football trip. Constance couldn't have known that without help."

"Do you think that's where Esther Rousseau comes into the picture?" Jenny was praying that her previous experience with the French woman had not been the cause of Leo's abduction.

"It's possible, but I don't think she sent Constance down here to help with the abduction. There's still a connection somewhere that we haven't found and that means there are other culprits involved, but not here in South Africa. It has to be nearer to home. We still have a lot of work to do when I get back."

"We can start with that tracking business in London. There must be a way we can find out about this Lord Dudley person and EzeTracker." Jenny was also thinking about Leticia and Patrice but she decided not to mention it. She needed to find out more.

"I believe Nice is also an important focus but we can discuss it when I'm back in Spain."

"Then you'll want to come back right away with Leo?"

"Exactly. I've got Leo's passport with me, so can you please arrange flights for us as soon as possible and email the details to me?"

"I'll get onto it now. Congratulations Pedro and all our thanks for your help. We can't wait to see you and Leo here in Spain." Jenny closed the call and went to give the news to Emma. Leo should be home tomorrow!

Espinoza reflected on the consequences of the news. Leo was free, which could mean that Jamie had been mistakenly taken to Zimbabwe in his stead. The possibility had been preying on his mind but now it seemed most likely. His sympathy went out to the young man. *Another victim in this dreadful adventure,* he thought, but there was nothing he nor anyone else could do about it.

Vereeniging, Gauteng, South Africa

"I suppose you've talked with your mother?" Coetzee and Karen were still on the deck when Leo and Abby got back. "I hope she forgives me. I'm giving up a million dollar reward just to curry favour with you three."

"That's enough of that! Remember our deal." Karen interrupted. "Right, Abby and Leo. Mr Coetzee has made me a proposal. He is begging to come back to a peaceful, loving and civilised existence with us and I've set the conditions. On his side, the requirements are; no booze, no cheroots, no kidnapping and no murdering people."

"And on our side?" Abby caught on quickly.

"We promise to be loving, understanding and provide three square meals a day. What do you think, Guys? Should we take him back?"

Abby ran across and threw her arms around Coetzee. "Please come back. We've missed you every single day since we left."

"I've got one more condition, if you don't mind," Leo said. "Can we get something to eat before you take me back? I'm starving."

London, England

Lord Arthur Selwyn Savage Dudley was in a maudlin mood. Even the call from his bank in the Bahamas, confirming that one hundred thousand US dollars had been received on his account that afternoon hadn't cheered him up. *Prince Sam Bensouda obviously has too much money,* he reflected. *I should have asked for more.*

He was sitting in front of the TV with a glass of *Gevrey Chambertin.* In the light from the screen it shone with a deep ruby hue. This was his third glass, on an empty stomach. A performance of Verdi's *La Traviata,* with Anna Netrebko, was playing but his attention kept wandering off. He was thinking about Esther. He was jealous. Dudley had never had a relationship with a mature person, male or female and had never previously been tempted to embark on one. But being in close proximity to Esther for the last week had stimulated his desires more than he could ever have imagined. Her flattering remark to him that morning, her kiss and the fragrant beauty of her form had gone completely to his head. He was in love. At the age of fifty-nine, Lord Arthur Selwyn Savage Dudley was in love with a woman half his age about whom he knew virtually nothing, except that she was as corrupt as he.

He took another sip of his wine. It was just after six o'clock, another hour before he could expect news from Harare. He'd asked for a photo of Leo to be sent as soon as they arrived in Beitbridge. He'd spent the afternoon imagining the worst possible events, not concerning Leo Stewart, but Esther and her friend from Paris. In his experience Frenchmen were arrogant, ignorant bullies with no civility or even common manners. He shuddered at the thought of him having dinner with such a beautiful creature. Other thoughts, much more intimate, crowded his mind but he refused to countenance them. Esther wouldn't be attracted by a person of that ilk, she was too refined, too lady-like, too … perfect.

Marbella, Spain

"When's the earliest flight they can get?" Emma was impatiently watching her sister looking for flights from Johannesburg.

Jenny was trawling through a series of cost comparison websites, looking for single stopovers and the shortest transit time. "They can't fly direct, and so far I've only found one-stop flights tomorrow evening. There don't seem to be any in the morning, so they wouldn't get back until Sunday."

She saw Emma's disappointed expression. "Wait. What about tonight? It's only just after six over there. If there's a flight late enough, they could make it. See, there's a departure with Swiss at ten fifteen this evening to Zurich. It gets in at nine in the morning, and then they've got a connection for Malaga at ten twenty, getting in at ten past one. What do you think?"

"I think we should call Pedro right away and get him moving."

Johannesburg, South Africa

Espinoza looked at his watch. "It's six twenty now. We should be able to make it if Leo arrives within an hour or so. It all depends on the traffic between Vereeniging and here. We only have carry-on luggage so we have should time for the transfer in Zurich."

"I'll call Coetzee right away. I was looking at the map and it would be quicker for him to take Leo straight to the airport. The R59 goes directly there from Vereeniging and avoids central Joburg. You could go and wait for him and be sure of being in time." Emma's voice sounded strong and decisive. Her sister had wisely let her take over the proceedings, it would do her good to feel in charge of her family again.

"Jenny's reserved the seats and you just have to check in. Pedro, thank you for everything. You've been amazing and I can't wait to see you and Leo in Malaga tomorrow."

Vereeniging, Gauteng, South Africa

They were eating hamburgers at the deck restaurant when Abby's phone rang. "Hi. Is that Abby? This is Leo's Mum, Emma. I'm looking forward to meeting you. Can I speak to Mr Coetzee please?"

Coetzee reluctantly took the phone, a pained look on his face. "Hello, Emma. Look, I'm sorry about what happened, I….."

"Mr Coetzee, please save your breath. You did a very bad thing and now you seem to be putting it right. I just want to get Leo back and forget about this whole business and that's what Leo wants too, so listen very carefully." She quickly explained their plan.

He responded just as rapidly. "It's six forty-five and we can leave in ten minutes. I can be at the airport by eight thirty latest. Is that good enough?"

Emma described Espinoza, an easy task because of his shortness and red hair. "He's an ex-Chief Inspector of Police and a very clever detective, so be nice to him and don't cause any more trouble."

"I don't intend to and what's more important Karen isn't going to let me. Thank you, Emma, I hope you'll come back to South Africa one day and we can meet under better circumstances."

"One thing at a time, Mr Coetzee. Get my son to the airport, pronto. Then I'll believe you've turned over a new leaf."

Johannesburg, South Africa

Since he wasn't going to stay the night, Espinoza went down to reception to negotiate a reduced rate for his room When he mentioned he was a friend of Ms Stewart and had managed to locate her son, they cancelled the room charge, refunded his credit card and offered him dinner. *Every little helps,* he reflected as he went back up to repack his bag. He could have something to eat and still get to the airport in good time and make his calls while he waited for them to arrive. He was looking forward to his business class seat and getting to know Leo over a glass of champagne. Leaving his bag at reception he took a table in the almost empty restaurant and ordered dinner, with a glass of Merlot.

Marbella, Spain

Leticia and Emilio returned at seven thirty without Patrice, explaining that he was tired and had gone home to get an early night. After she had put her son to bed she came down and sat with Emma and Jenny on the terrace. She looked tired and unhappy.

"Is there anything you want to tell me?" Jenny knew she could talk to her like that, she sometimes had to behave like a mother to the younger woman.

Leticia looked at Emma. "No, it's nothing, I'm just a bit tired."

Emma said, "I've got some writing to do. I'd better get on with it." She went into the house and upstairs to her room.

"Now talk to me, Leticia. I feel there's something wrong. You know you can trust me and perhaps I can help. Why don't you get it off your chest?" She went over to sit beside her.

"Oh, Jenny. I'm so unhappy. I don't know what's going on with Patrice and it's causing such problems. I sometimes think he doesn't want to have the wedding in October. I don't know anything anymore." Tears ran down her cheeks.

"Let's take one thing at a time and we'll talk about them. Do you want to start with the papers you mentioned to me? The financial papers?"

"All right. He told me not to ask you about them, but it's such a lot of money and I don't know how it happened. It's my account at the *Banco de Iberia.* Wait. I'll get the file."

She went along to her apartment, leaving Jenny wondering what was going on. Patrice was a manager at the bank and looked after Leticia's account. Jenny had asked for a different manager to handle her own affairs, not wanting to mix business and personal matters. She sighed, *something else to worry about.*

"Let's sit at the kitchen table, so we can look at the papers properly," she said when Leticia returned with a thick green file, *Banco de Iberia. Statements 2008* - written on the front.

"You know after Charlie died, we divided the money in Spain between us?"

Jenny remembered very well. Charlie had foreseen the upcoming crash in early 2008 and had sold off his investments. The balance on his account was eight million Euros. Patrice had set up accounts for each of them and they had transferred the funds equally to the new accounts. "It was almost exactly four million Euros each. I remember you said you didn't know there was so much money in the world."

Leticia smiled wryly. "It turned out I was right. Patrice told me it was a waste to have so much money sitting in cash. It would lose value because of deflation."

"You mean inflation, but I understand his point of view, after all he's a banker. So you invested it?"

"Not straight away. And that was lucky, because when the big crash happened I didn't lose anything, I still had all that cash. But afterwards, at the beginning of last year, he told me that the markets were very low and it was a good time to buy shares."

"Again I can't disagree with him. It was a very good time to invest, depending on the investments you bought."

"That's what I don't understand. Look." She opened the file and showed her the last statement, dated June 30th 2010.

Jenny gasped. The total on the bottom of the statement was two million nine hundred and sixty thousand Euros. Over a million

Euros had gone from the account in less than eighteen months. "That's twenty-five per cent of your money gone. Are you sure you haven't been spending it on silly extravagances?"

"No, Jenny. I know you think I spend a lot, but it's really only on clothes and trips and on Emilio, after all, it's really his money. But I budget myself every month and I know that over the last two years I haven't spent that amount. It would be impossible to spend it unless I bought a yacht or something. We have three cars here, the house has no mortgage and I pay my mother and Juan five thousand Euros a month between them. I couldn't have spent such a huge amount."

"Have you looked carefully at these statements?"

"Yes. But there's so many transactions and currencies and debit and credit notes that I get completely lost. Patrice has a *Poder* on the account and he's managed it since I started investing last January."

"A power of attorney, you mean. So he just buys and sells shares when he feels like it, without discussing it with you?"

"No. He always tells me what he's doing, but when he says I should buy shares in a company I've never heard of doing stem cell research or oil and gas exploration or something else I don't understand, how can I give an opinion? I just agree with what he says."

"And have you asked him about this loss? He must have talked to you about it, explained why it has happened. You can't lose twenty-five per cent of someone's money, especially your fiancée's, without explaining what happened."

"Every time I ask him he says it's only a temporary problem and that my account is in very good shape. He says it will be back to the normal value by September and I just have to be patient."

"But at the moment you've lost a million Euros, after your own expenses. He's not much of an investor, is he?"

"But he is. According to everyone at the bank he's a marvellous investor. Last year he won the award for *Best Investment Forecaster of 2009*. And everyone knows that all the markets went up, so why has my account gone down like this?" She burst into tears.

"You're right, even I made some investments last year. It was almost impossible to lose money between January and December and it's more or less the same this year. So what you don't want to tell me is that you suspect something? That there might be another reason for this missing money?"

"I don't know. All I know is that there's something wrong. He's become so nervous lately and he's been travelling such a lot I hardly ever see him, and when I do… Well, that's something else."

"Do you want to share it with me? If you don't I'll understand."

"No, it's OK. It's just, when we first got together he was very, you know, he couldn't get enough of me."

"You mean he's lost his sex drive? He doesn't make love to you as much as before?"

"Hardly at all. When he gets back from travelling he's too tired. When he's here, he has an early morning meeting or is about to travel again. It's over two weeks since we had sex, It's not normal, we're not even married yet!"

Jenny supressed a smile. *Now she no longer sounds tearful,* she thought. *She's indignant; her fiancé doesn't want to make love to her. She's more upset about that than about the money.* She said, "Can I keep the file tonight and look through it? I might spot something. It's probably not what you think, but if you want me to I'll go through everything with a fine toothcomb."

Leticia handed over the file with a palpable sense of relief. Prior to Charlie's death she had been a housekeeper on a frugal salary. She had never had money and was still not used to handling large sums. "I trust you so much, Jenny. I'm sorry to be so ignorant on these things."

"Let's look on the bright side. Our money in Switzerland hasn't been affected. Since we settled the business with Klein Fellay it's with Philippe Jaquelot at the Banque de Commerce and he's doing very nicely, nothing earth shattering, but safe and steady." Jenny thanked the lucky stars that Leticia had agreed to appoint Philippe as her manager. *But,* she wondered,*what exactly is there to worry about?*

SIXTY-ONE

OR Tambo Airport, Johannesburg, South Africa

Espinoza looked nervously at his watch for the umpteenth time. It was after nine o'clock and he was waiting near the check-in counter for Coetzee to arrive with Leo. Since he had Leo's passport the woman had let him check them both in to save time. The boy had only a carry-on bag, so they could go straight through security. He was annoyed that he'd forgotten to ask Emma for a contact number for Coetzee, he had no information and no way of knowing what was happening. The travelling and lack of sleep were catching up on him and he was having difficulty keeping his eyes open. He tried to concentrate on his notepad and was adding a new piece to his jigsaw puzzle when he heard, "Dr Espinoza, I presume."

The speaker was a burly, square-built man in a safari shirt and cotton trousers. He needed a shave and he carried a wheelie bag as if it weighed nothing.

"Mr Coetzee?" He stood up, registering the several inches difference in their height and standing as erect as he could. "You're a little late. I thought you'd run off with Leo." He gave the South African a disapproving look, but said nothing further. He didn't want to get into a difficult discussion when they were already tight on time for their flight departure.

"No chance," said the boy beside him. He almost towered over the Spaniard, who tried to stand even taller.

Holding out his hand, he said, "How do you do, Sr Espinoza. I'm Leo Stewart and this is Karen and Abby. The whole family's here." Leo was understandably nervous, worried that Espinoza might not be as forgiving as his mother.

The Spaniard shook hands with them all. "Unfortunately, we have very little time to get to know each other, since our flight will be called shortly. My main concern is to get Leo on the plane home to his mother."

Coetzee said, "Can I see Leo's passport and the boarding cards? In the hurry we didn't arrange any identification password or whatever. I'd just like to be sure that he's finally in safe hands."

"Of course." Espinoza showed him the documents. "I appreciate the professional attention to protocol."

He picked up his travel bag and Karen said, "We'd love Leo to come back and visit us some time. When things have settled down." She wanted everything to finish on a positive note.

"You can bet I'll be back. Marius owes me a proper safari in the Kruger, I didn't see a single dangerous animal so I can't wait to do it properly."

"It's a deal, Leo. Karen is going to sort out my company so that I can actually make some money for a change. Come back next year and we'll do you proud."

"It's time we were going, Leo." Espinoza shook hands with them all again and went towards the fast track security gate, leaving the others to bid their farewells. He was still irritated that Coetzee had arrived with no time to spare. *No time to ask him any awkward questions,* he thought. *Very well calculated from his point of view.*

"Please come back to see us again, Leo and keep in touch by email or on Facebook. I was really pleased to get to know you." Abby put her arms around him and kissed him on the cheek then turned away, a tear in her eye.

Karen kissed him then Coetzee shook his hand firmly. "Travel safely, Leo. We'll miss you and all the excitement and mayhem you seem to create around you."

He laughed, "What a team we make. I start it and you finish it off. See you soon, Marius."

Going through security into the Business Class departure lounge Leo was wide eyed. It was the first time he'd experienced the comfort of anything beyond economy class. They settled down in a corner near a TV monitor and he fetched a coffee and a soft drink. "This is really cool," he said, sitting back in the armchair.

"How do you feel, Leo? Do you have any ill effects from the last few days' events?"

"I actually feel great, thanks. No ill effects whatsoever. It's been a few days since the drugs wore off and Cooetzee's made sure I've eaten properly and had plenty of sleep. I'm really fine now."

Espinoza couldn't argue with this reply. Leo looked fit and well, showing no signs at all of illness, stress or worry. He sipped his coffee and looked at the TV screen, thinking of the questions he needed to ask.

The evening news was on, the headline story and ticker tapes full of the successful unravelling of the triple murders in Johannesburg, Polokwane and Diepkloof. Espinoza's attention was captured when he heard Hendricks' name. The two minute press conference with the Chief Superintendent was almost certain to win him a promotion or a salary raise, or perhaps both.

He supressed a smile when the policeman stated; *"Working with information received from a reliable source, my officers went to an apartment in Diepkloof where they found the owner dead. He had been shot. His name will be released when our investigation is completed. We have identified the deceased as the murderer of Mr Barry Lambert, the British hotel manager who was found dead earlier this week at the Packard Hotel in Mayfair.*

"Intensive detective work has also resulted in the identification of the body found on Thursday in Polokwane. The victim is Dr Antoine Constance, a French doctor, who was travelling under the name of Ernest Blethin. Dr Constance was

also killed by the deceased murderer. We believe that the killer was then murdered by a male friend of his who has subsequently fled across the border out of South Africa.

"Information from the same source suggests that all of these persons were involved with a drug syndicate based in Europe. Thanks to the impressive work of our officers here in Johannesburg, we have been able to assist the authorities there in identifying these criminals and potentially dismantling the syndicate."

Leo was listening, a shocked expression on his face. "Is that Nwosu he's talking about?"

"That's right, Leo. Although he fully deserved it from everything I've learned, I don't approve of murder under any pretext. On the other hand it has closed the case here, which is better for everyone concerned, so I suppose justice has been served in an oblique fashion."

"Poetic justice, you mean. And that man Blethin who kidnapped me with Lambert, he's really a French doctor called Constance. Shit! Why would they set up an international gang to kidnap me?"

"Didn't Coetzee explain it all to you." Espinoza was feeling his way, trying to find out how deeply the South African was involved.

"I don't think he knew what it was all about either. Does he know how it's all finished up?"

"Probably not. This is the first official announcement I've heard, so I suppose he'll learn about it from the TV like everyone else. I doubt he'll be very upset in the circumstances."

Leo was trying to hide his reaction to the bulletin. *This is fabulous news! If Nwosu's a goner there's nobody left who knows what really happened in Polokwane except me and Coetzee.* He thought about the rest of the story. *Who was the male friend who fled across the border? It couldn't have been Jamie, he's not capable of murder.*

He decided to say nothing about Nwosu's boyfriend, it would open up the trail to the Zimbabwean thugs' attack and murder. If Espinoza didn't know, that episode was a closed book. Aloud, he said, "So the whole lot of them are dead and the case is closed. Why is that policeman talking about a drug syndicate?"

"It was the only way I could tie the three of them together and get the case closed over here. The South African police have got enough problems of their own, so Hendricks was happy to leave it to the UK police to handle the matter from now on."

For the first time, Leo looked worried. "Why are the UK police involved if it's only a fictional plot?"

"Don't worry, they're not and they won't be. I was talking about Hendrick closing off the case. As far as you're concerned the whole business is behind you."

"Oh, I see. That's cool, thank you. My mum told me that you only arrived here this morning. How did you get all this done so fast?"

"It was pure good fortune. I happened to arrive at the right time and I had some knowledge of the circumstances which led me, fortunately, to the correct conclusion. I was just lucky."

"So who are you, exactly? How come my mom's in Spain? She told me hardly anything on the phone. Only that she's at Aunt Jenny's house."

"I'm just a simple detective and a friend of your aunt's. She asked me to help, but I'll leave it to your mother to explain everything to you when we get back." Espinoza paused, his suspicious mind still undecided. He was an ex-policeman and he needed to know for his own peace of mind what had happened in Polokwane. He framed his next question as carefully as he could. "Most of the story I pieced together from the various parts I found out from the SA police and my other sources, but the bit I don't really understand is how Constance, or Blethin, as you knew him, came to be killed in Polokwane. You were there, I believe. Do you know anything about his death?"

Leo was ready for the question. He had to make sure there was only one culprit, a dead one, Nwosu. Even if he didn't like doing it, he had to stick to the story.

He said, "Coetzee decided to stop in Polokwane so I could get something to eat. I'd been drugged for days and I was starving. We got burgers and we were sitting in the car in this field and the three of them started arguing. Did you know they hardly knew each other and they argued all the time? "

Without waiting for a response, he went on, "They were banging on about whether to go on or stay the night there. The doctor got out the car and Nwosu followed him, it was pitch black, you couldn't see a thing. Then he came back and said Blethin had attacked him and he'd had to bash him in self-defence. We got out with the torch and Blethin was lying on the ground with his head smashed in."

"So Coetzee had nothing to do with his death?"

"I swear Coetzee didn't even know about it until too late. He was really angry with Nwosu." Leo chose his words carefully.

"I see. That was a key point I was unsure of. So what happened next? They undressed the body and left him in the field and then you continued on?"

"Yes, but we didn't continue on. That's when Coetzee saved me. They were going to take me to Zimbabwe. Apparently it's a really dangerous place and he didn't want anything to do with taking me there. He got Nwosu's gun and left him behind then drove me to the Kruger to get time to think. He's a pretty tough guy, but only with people who deserve it. He treated me really well and now he's going to get back with his family again."

So that's the connection with Zimbabwe! The conspirators must have some kind of relationship there. I was right about the car. That's where Nwosu's murderer came from and that's presumably where they took Jamie. If it's true, Coetzee certainly saved Leo's life. Espinoza knew if Leo had been taken there he'd never have been heard of again. He decided to say nothing about Jamie and his probable mistaken abduction. Neither Leo nor Emma should ever be told of it.

But he was still undecided about Leo's story. *I wonder why he's so determined to clear Coetzee's name? Is he hiding something, has Coetzee threatened him with some kind of reprisal?* The Spaniard was still suspicious, it was in his DNA.

"Where did you get the phone? The one you texted your mother with from Polokwane and Phalaborwa?" He hoped to take the boy by surprise with this question out of the blue, but Leo was up to it.

"It was Blethin's. I found it on the ground when they were moving his body. Coetzee told me to put it in the glove compartment.

I managed to send the message but then I couldn't get hold of it again until we were at the lodge and the battery had died. I didn't know the messages had gone, I never got any reply."

Espinoza ignored this remark. "Why do you think Coetzee took you to Phalaborwa?"

"I think he was trying to work out what to do. He didn't want to be involved with Zimbabwe or Nwosu and he just needed time to think. He told me he'd sent the reward message with my photo but after he spoke to Karen he changed his mind. Then he drove me to the hotel and I called Mom with Abby's phone. Nobody stopped me from calling."

"You'd make a very good character witness, Leo. And since the other members of this gang are dead, there is no one who can argue with your story. I suppose that Mr Coetzee was with you this morning when Sergeant Nwosu was murdered in Diepkloof?"

"We were all together at the hotel. He couldn't have had anything to do with it."

"It's what I assumed. Well, Leo, if Mr Coetzee is not a murderer I have no intention of disturbing his life ever again. His wife and daughter seem to be devoted to him and I wish them every happiness and success."

"Oh, I almost forgot." Leo fished in his case and handed some documents to the Spaniard. "Marius gave these to me. They're from Blethin's stuff, I mean Constance. His passport and a couple of other papers."

Espinoza took the documents and opened up the French passport. He assumed that it had been Constance who had administered the drug then pushed out the wheelchair, but he didn't recognise the photo, the man in the CCTV clip couldn't be seen properly. The passport seemed to be quite normal, but he would have it examined by an expert when he returned to Malaga. The other documents were personal items, a couple of letters and a bill from a McDonalds restaurant in Polokwane.

He was composing another question in his mind when they heard the flight announcement. They walked to the departure gate, each preoccupied with his own thoughts. Leo was breathing a sigh of relief. He'd got through the worst part of the conversation, it could only get better. Espinoza hadn't finished his interrogation but he still had a ten hour flight to find out more.

SIXTY-TWO

Marbella, Spain

The house was in darkness but Jenny was still wide awake. She was in her nightdress at the desk in her bedroom studying the file of bank papers given to her by Leticia. She knew she wouldn't sleep if she didn't look for the problem now. To save time, she looked only at the monthly statements, starting in January 2009 when the account was still entirely in cash and the first investments began. The balance was almost three point eight million Euros, so Leticia had spent about one hundred and fifty thousand in nine months. She had told her the truth; she wasn't frittering away her money.

After the investments began, the value of the account slowly increased month by month, until by December 31st it had climbed to over four million. During the first quarter of 2010 both the number of transactions and the increase in value continued to grow, then suddenly in April, the value fell by a half a million. It fell again in May and in June, ending with the amount of two million nine hundred and sixty thousand she'd first been shown. She looked quickly through the statements for large sales, but there were very few. Now Jenny was becoming worried. *It could only have been cash withdrawals or payments, but Leticia wasn't spending that kind of money.*

She decided to compare the statements month by month from April of last year and in ten minutes she found what she was looking for. Amongst the first investments made by Patrice, in January 2009, were two amounts of five hundred thousand Euros each, in the names of *Asian Atlantic Multi-Diversity Fund and Asian Atlantic Life Sciences Fund,* a total investment of a million Euros. By September the values had already grown by five per cent and by year end were ten percent higher. But by April, they were reduced by a third, then again in May and in June they had both disappeared from the statement. *A million Euros, plus the profit, gone just like that. Why?*

Looking through the individual advice notices for June she found a simple debit note. It said, '*Reserve against potential loss: Asian Atlantic Investment Funds: €1,100,000'.* The value of the investment had been written down to zero!

Jenny opened her laptop and looked up the company website. Nothing came up except a notice saying, *Closed for business until liquidation of relevant holdings.* She typed in *Asian Atlantic Investment Funds.* There were hundreds of recent articles. The last newspaper extract had been published ten days previously with the headline, *Asian Atlantic Investment Funds Managers Arrested for Fraud and Embezzlement.*

She read the article with a sense of déjà vu. Asian Atlantic Investment Funds was a holding company which owned five subsidiary funds. Although the funds specialised in investing in mid-sized Asian, US and European companies, she saw that the holding was registered in the British Virgin Islands, the directors were mostly Brazilian and the head office was in Dubai. The company had been created immediately after the Lehman debacle, in December 2008 amid a considerable fanfare. The top strategy manager was Alwyn Forsdyke, a Wall Street legend who had, allegedly, foreseen the last three economic crises and made a fortune in the process. His book, *Why Will They Never Learn?* published at the same time as the launch of the Asian Atlantic Investment Funds, became the US best-selling financial exposé of 2008.

In December and the first quarter of 2009, over a billion dollars poured into the five sub-funds and this inflow continued until mid-

April, when Alwyn Forsdyke was killed in a motor accident. Rumours abounded and the newspapers were full of contradictory reports surrounding his death. An investigation into the 'accident' was set up in late April, apparently after a dossier was passed to the FBI by his one-time secretary. The dossier was reputed by the financial press to contain a lot of background on the dubious dealings of Asian Atlantic Investment Funds, its founders and directors.

Immediately after this announcement a run of substantial customer withdrawals commenced, causing a halt in the growth of net asset values and a shortage of liquidity. By May, clients were waiting up to thirty days for repayment of their funds and by June the funds were closed to new investors and all repayments were postponed indefinitely. On July 1st AAIF was shut down by the Securities and Exchange Commission and several criminal warrants were issued.

The latest newspaper report implied that Forsdyke had been eliminated because he discovered that the directors of the fund were operating a massive *Ponzi* scheme, paying dividends from new incoming cash. The underlying investments were proving difficult to locate or were worthless 'special purpose vehicles', set up just to receive money and pay it to the directors and their cronies.

She sat back from her laptop. *Another Madoff,* she thought. It was in December 2008, the same month that this fund had been set up, that Bernard Madoff had cost investors, including members of his family and lifelong friends, almost twenty billion dollars in the biggest Ponzi scheme in history. *At least he didn't murder anyone in the process,* she reflected. *Or at least not as far as they know.*

She turned her mind back to the problem in hand. *So Leticia has lost twenty-five per cent of her money in Spain because of Patrice. He didn't steal it, which is a good thing, but why didn't he liquidate the investments when he saw the writing on the wall?* Then another thought occurred to her. *He told her that it was just a temporary problem. It would be back to normal by September. What was he expecting would happen before then to put it right?*

Jenny closed her laptop and put the file aside. Worrying thoughts crowded into her mind as she lay trying to fall asleep.

Thoughts about Patrice flying around and being in London so often, especially this week. Lord Dudley, whoever he was, tracking people in South Africa from London. Esther Rousseau and Leticia's face in her dream. Doctor Constance, Emma's friend who had suddenly become Leo's kidnapper. And Leo himself, victim of an abduction plot whose perpetrators demanded ten million dollars and still hadn't been found. She finally fell into an uneasy sleep, full of invasive and frightening dreams, the kind she had experienced after Ron's death, the kind she thought she had got over long ago.

London, England

A 'ping' from Dudley's laptop woke him. He'd fallen asleep and had a crick in his neck and a dry mouth. He looked at his watch, it was almost eight thirty. Laboriously he got to his feet and went to the toilet, drank a glass of water then came back and looked at the screen. There was a new message, from Harare. It had no subject or text, just an attachment. He opened it up. It was a photograph.

Sydney, Australia

"Thanks Rolf. Is that everything?"

"That's all I could find, Mac. Come back to me if there's anything I've missed."

Detective Sergeant 'Mac' McCallister reread the notes he'd made from his call. He was starting to understand Espinoza's obsession with the Forrester case. None of this information had been available to his department previously because the accident had been handled by the Perth police force and then filed away when the death was officially registered eighteen months previously. He had asked for a copy of the whole file to be FedEx'd to him

He looked at his watch, it was two in the afternoon, midnight on the previous day in South Africa, Espinoza might still be up. He didn't want to send an email. Digging up a closed case, especially in another jurisdiction, wasn't encouraged unless there was reasonable evidence that a serious mistake had been made. All he had was a query from Spain and a possible line of enquiry into a confirmed case of accidental death. He pressed Espinoza's number on his mobile.

There was no reply and he got the answering service, in Spanish. He left a short message, just enough to pique Espinoza's curiosity. *This'll put the cat among the koalas,* he thought to himself. *Let's see what it's all about.*

London, England

Dudley's phone rang several times between nine o'clock and midnight. Both Esther and Slater were calling for news, but there was no reply and he never called back. After receiving the message from Harare he had finished off the bottle of *Gevrey Chambertin.* He was drunk and fast asleep.

Johannesburg, South Africa

"So what did you think of Leo, Abby?" Coetzee and his newly reacquired wife and daughter were driving back to Delmas.

"He's nice. I really like the way he talks, his accent is lovely. Shame he's gone back to the UK." She smiled shyly.

"So at least you have a new pen pal, or I should say, Facebook pal. Keep in touch and I'm sure he'll come back to see us again. He's mad keen on visiting the Kruger properly so we can organise a safari and invite him."

"Only if you start making some money from the business." Karen had the upper hand for the moment and she intended to take full advantage of it.

The drive home was relaxed and comfortable. Coetzee already felt he belonged again, that he had someone to report to and two people to feel responsible for. He was also looking forward to finishing Emma's book when they got back.

Over South Africa, en route for Zurich, Switzerland

"I'll have a glass of champagne, please." Espinoza was settled comfortably in his seat, a blanket over his knees and his feet up on the folding stool. He turned to ask Leo what he would like but the boy was already out like a light, snuggled down into his seat and snoring gently. He had been looking forward to chatting with him, getting to know Emma's son and finding out more about Coetzee and Lambert, the abduction and especially about Constance's death, but it would have to wait.

He must be more exhausted than me, he mused. *After everything he's been through, if anyone deserves an undisturbed rest, it's this boy.*

The cabin attendant placed the glass on his table with a packet of nuts. "Thank you," he said. "Could you show me how to operate the television? It's not a system I'm used to and I'd like to watch a movie." If he couldn't talk to Leo, he was determined to get the most out of the flight before he went to sleep.

London, England

Slater called Esther at midnight, after trying Dudley's number one last time. "What the hell is going on?" He almost screamed. "I've been calling Arthur for two hours and he's not answering. I've come outside to call you so my partner doesn't hear me, but I can't keep this quiet for long. It's all going to blow up if we don't get any news." His voice trembled and he stumbled over his words as if he'd been drinking.

"I've been calling too and I'm none the wiser. I agree it doesn't look good, but we shouldn't jump to conclusions. Maybe he hasn't heard from Harare, or he's gone out somewhere, or he just doesn't feel like talking to us. He's a peculiar man, so leave him alone tonight. I'll go to his apartment first thing in the morning and find out what's happening and then call you. Just relax and remember we'll soon be together and we can forget this whole business."

"OK. I'll try to keep a lid on it until tomorrow, but call me as soon as you can. I can't take much more of this uncertainty.

Goodnight darling."

Esther switched off her mobile and sat on the bed in her shabby hotel room, reflecting on the situation. *He's cracking up,* she thought. *He doesn't have the balls to manage a crisis. He's not half the man Ray d'Almeida was.*

She still hadn't got over her Angolan lover and didn't think she ever would. He had been a strong, clever and resourceful man, nothing could stand in his way; he was indomitable. And he was the most accomplished lover she had ever encountered, unlike this second rate substitute. The six months they had been apart when she was working with Schneider at the bank in Geneva, preparing the groundwork for their master plan, had been almost intolerable. He had been able to come down from Haute Nendaz on just a few occasions, but she had remained true to him until their plan was ready to execute. One night with Ray was worth a lifetime of waiting and the waiting was almost over.

But somehow, on the night that should have been the start of a new life together, he was suddenly gone and it was over. She had never found out exactly what had happened but she knew it was the work of that bitch, Jenny Bishop, the daughter-in-law of Charlie Bishop. The man who had condemned Ray's family to a life of poverty and hardship and caused his mother and father's premature deaths while he and his 'Angolan Clan' of thieves were living high on the hog in big houses with swimming pools, spending Ray's money. Money that had then gone to Bishop's Angolan girl friend and his bastard son and to the Bishop woman. The fortune that had been stolen from Ray and that she was determined to recover. It had been her lover's inheritance and it was rightfully hers to reclaim.

The abduction plan was a work of genius. Apart from a few minor hiccups it had been well executed and she had been confident of recuperating at least a part of Ray's fortune. *Until,* she reflected, *this evening.*

Now it was time to face the facts. For some reason it looked likely that Dudley's confident announcement of this morning was unfounded. Otherwise why would he not answer the phone? He was embarrassed and he was hiding from them, so Leo Stewart must not have arrived in Harare, there was no other explanation that made sense. The scheme was compromised and there would be fallout, there always was. Recriminations, blame, arguments and ultimately the risk of disclosure and punishment and that wasn't part of her plan. The other conspirators were just cogs in the machine and meant nothing to her. If there was no future in the ransom plan then it was time to move on and regroup. There were still ways in which she could come out of this mess ahead of the game. She had learned from the Angolan Clan disaster that she needed a backstop and she had taken some wise precautions, but first she had to extricate herself from the potential repercussions of tonight's news, or rather, lack of it.

She went to the British Airways website on her iPad. There were seven flights the next day from Heathrow to Belfast. The two o'clock flight was ninety-nine pounds and there were a few seats available. She knew if she booked it the next morning it would be even cheaper. The Heathrow express cost twenty-one pounds, so that was a maximum of one hundred and twenty pounds and she had an Oyster card for the tube to Victoria. Slater had paid the hotel bill including tonight, so she owed nothing for her room. In her purse she had four hundred and seventy pounds and the train from Belfast to Dublin would be about forty-five Euros. She could manage for a few days in the inexpensive B&B she would go to.

She quickly made up her mind, as she had been forced to do many times in the last couple of years. *I'll go to see Arthur first thing in the morning. If he hasn't got confirmation that the boy is in Harare then it's over. I'll take the train to Heathrow for an afternoon flight.*

Esther cleaned her teeth and went to bed. She fell asleep almost immediately. Unfortunately, she was becoming used to things going wrong.

DAY SEVEN

SATURDAY, JULY 17, 2010

SIXTY-THREE

At sea, between Antalya, Turkey and Marseille, France

The cargo ship *Erzurat* was making eleven knots between Antalya and Marseille. Flying a Greek flag, she was a medium size ninety metre Norwegian vessel, built in 1970 and rebuilt in 1979, with a 2,000 HP MAK engine and 2,900 dead weight tonnage capacity. The ship had left Latakia in Syria two weeks previously, carrying a cargo of shoes, boots, handbags, travel goods and other leather, plastic and rubber articles insured for five hundred thousand dollars. A stopover had been made in Turkey, which produces over half of all TV sets and twenty per cent of white goods manufactured in Europe. In Antalya, on the southern Turkish coast, sixty containers containing ten thousand flat screen television sets, various types of audio equipment, refrigerators and other white goods were loaded, with an insurance value of three million dollars.

During these loading operations, under the strict control of Captain Bahadir Yilmaz, one of the containers was opened on the dockside and fifty of the television sets were removed and taken into a warehouse. They were extracted from their cartons and polystyrene packaging and the back panels removed and emptied of their components, leaving only the screen and the panel intact.

The components weighed four kilos and were easily detached with a screwdriver and a pair of sharp pincers. Inside the four centimetre deep compartment thus created in each TV, four waxed paper packages wrapped in cellophane, measuring thirty by twenty centimetres and weighing one kilo each, were placed and packed around with wood shavings and coffee grounds. The back panels were then replaced, the TVs restored to their original packaging, marked with a new bar code and reloaded into the container amongst the other sets. The twenty foot metal box was then loaded onto the ship alongside its fifty-nine identical partners and the Erzurat was ready to sail for Marseille.

The two hundred kilos of material inside the packages had a value of over sixty million dollars on the street, or thirty million dollars in bulk, a fraction of the three and a half thousand tons of the same material, valued at over fifty billion dollars, which was shipped from Afghanistan through Pakistan annually. It was heroin, the most potent and most valuable of the mind altering substances available to the two hundred and thirty million people in the world who use hard drugs. Captain Yilmaz had been paid fifty thousand dollars for his attention to this cargo, equivalent to almost two years of his salary.

The heroin now hidden inside the television sets had come on a long trip. It had started life in an opium poppy field near Jalalabad in Nangahar province, Afghanistan, near the border with Pakistan and more importantly, close to one of the busiest ports of entry for people and goods moving between Afghanistan and Pakistan, at Torkham - the historic Khyber Pass. After being refined from two thousand kilos of opium locally, on June twentieth, the two hundred kilos of pure heroin had been brought across the border in a horse drawn cart carrying a family of farmers and leading a small herd of cattle. The cart was full of chicken feet, already beginning to decompose and smelling so badly that the customs official accepted a very small bribe to avoid investigating the bloody, stinking mess. Even if this had not been the case, the money that changed hands ensured discretion. Jobs at border crossings are highly valued and equally competitive, as money earned from corruption usually exceeds actual salary. These posts are commonly awarded along familial, tribal or friendship lines. As a result of corruption and inefficiency on both sides of the frontier, Torkham border is favoured by drug smugglers as ineffective and not threatening to their movements.

Once comfortably over the border, the two hundred packages were transferred to cavities built into the side panels and floor of a battered and broken down lorry filled with second hand bicycles and spare parts. It took three days, including stops for two flat tyres and a broken fan belt, to cover the fourteen hundred kilometres that brought them to the coastal area of Balochistan, on the Arabian Sea. In the port of Karachi the merchandise was transferred to the *Lady Guinevere,* a cabin cruiser kitted out as a fishing boat and flying Gibraltar colors, where it was hidden underneath the cabin floorboards in the hull space.

The thirty-one foot 1972 Trojan Express cruiser, powered by its Mercury Mercruiser twin inboard/outboard engines, set off at twenty knots westward towards the Gulf of Oman at seven in the morning on the twenty-sixth of June. The boat passed Ras Al-Kaimah and Dubai in the United Arab Emirates in the evening of the twenty-eighth, sailing through into the Persian Gulf. Off the coast of Qatar a customs boat came alongside, but after a short discussion and an exchange of several packages of cigarettes, the *Lady Guinevere* was sent on its way and entered the Port of Shuaiba, in Kuwait, on the twenty-ninth.

The next transfer was into a compartment built in the floor of an ex-US army canvas roofed Chevrolet C/K truck, with Kuwaiti military plates. The lorry was then packed with a heavy load of scrap copper, recuperated from bombed-out electricity stations, and the lorry's speed was accordingly compromised. The driver had the necessary papers to drive out of Kuwait, through Iraq and into Syria. He set off on the morning of June thirtieth and after leaving the tiny state, headed north-west, averaging forty miles an hour on Route 1 towards Falluja in Iraq. From there he continued in a westerly direction on Route 12, a secondary road, reaching the Al Qaim-Abu Kamal crossing on the Euphrates River belt after another twelve hours drive. He drove into Syria without any problems on the morning of July second and the following evening the merchandise arrived under cover of darkness in the port of Latakia, on the north western coast of Syria. The packages were removed from the lorry and stored that night in the warehouse of *MediShip*, a small Turkish shipping company.

The next morning, the fourth of July, the Erzurat came into harbor from Marseilles and offloaded a shipment of French pharmaceutical products and optical, technical and medical equipment. The new cargo of Syrian exports of leather, plastic and rubber articles was loaded, together with the merchandise from Afghanistan. The cargo ship sailed to Antalya that afternoon and arrived on the night of the 6th July to load the sixty containers waiting on the dock. The packages were taken off the ship into the warehouse once the fifty TV sets had been opened up to receive them. Loading of the containers was completed during the following two days. The Erzurat sailed for Marseille on the evening of the second day with a full cargo and had now been at sea for nine days. The whole delivery mechanism up to this point had taken twenty-seven days and it would take another day and a half to arrive in Marseille.

The price paid to the drug lab in Afghanistan for the two hundred kilos of pure heroin was four hundred thousand dollars. That price is not much higher than unrefined opium, but heroin is easier to smuggle and the sales price more profitable. The drug smugglers and their transport, plus the additional costs of bribing district officials, insurgents and warlords to permit the merchandise to pass their jurisdictions amounted to six hundred thousand dollars, including the organiser's commission and Captain Yilmaz's fifty thousand dollars, making a total cost of one million dollars. This was the investment made by the funder, without any additional bribes.

The price of heroin is typically valued at eight to ten times that of cocaine on European streets, making it a high-profit/low volume substance for smugglers and dealers. The average street price is one hundred dollars per gram with thirty-five per cent purity. One kilo is worth three hundred thousand dollars at the user level, or about one hundred and fifty thousand dollars in bulk to dealers. Two hundred kilos is worth sixty million dollars on the street and has a bulk value of over thirty million dollars, making a profit of at least that same amount to the funders. Erzurat was carrying one of its most valuable cargos ever, uninsured, and it was just a day and a half away from its destination.

Delmas, Mpumalanga, South Africa

"Breakfast!" Karen shouted the order, or invitation, from the kitchen. Coetzee was still upstairs in the bathroom and Abby had just returned from walking the two dogs. The house was busy and happy; she felt as contented as she believed was possible. Last night Marius had made love to her; gentle, tender but passionate sex, made all the more enjoyable for both of them after their two years of abstinence. She had felt a change in him, perhaps the two year separation and the difficulties with his business had taken the edge off his rather arrogant macho persona. The hard, disciplined, military side of his nature seemed to have been replaced with a softer, more feeling disposition. She was falling in love with him all over again.

For once she agreed to put the TV on while they had their meal. It was usually not allowed but he wanted to see if there were any reports about the recent events, he was still nervous that Nwosu would try to cause him problems. Coetzee had learned the hard way that paranoid psychopathic sadists never gave up causing problems for those unlucky enough to be around them. But his fears were wrongly directed.

They watched a repeat of Hendricks' press conference in silence, all of them leaving their food to get cold on the plates. Coetzee was trying to work out what part Espinoza had played in the investigation.

He was astonished by the revelation of Blethin's real identity but doubted that the Johannesburg police could have discovered it, he hadn't even known it himself. All he'd known was that he was French. The Spaniard was obviously a lot smarter than he looked. Short and red-haired, Coetzee had not been impressed by him at first sight.

What was also obvious was that it was Nwosu who had been murdered and it couldn't have been by Jamie, the kid wouldn't hurt a fly. It seemed though, that Hendricks was closing the case with runaway Jamie as the culprit. *He can only be in one place, Zimbabwe. That means the Voice sent in another team to grab Leo and get rid of any unnecessary witnesses. Jamie was there and they took him by mistake. The poor kid. He doesn't deserve to be abducted to Zimbabwe, if that's what happened.*

"What's that all about? And please eat your eggs." Karen and Abby started on their meal.

He decided to give them a sanitised version of events. "It means that this business was more complicated than I thought. Dr Blethin turns out to be a Frenchman called Constance and Nwosu has been killed by Jamie who has run away to Zimbabwe. The main point though, is that they haven't mentioned Leo or his kidnapping and the investigation seems to be closed."

"So it's over?"

"It seems like it. I think we can get back to normal life and forget the whole thing," Coetzee said confidently and turned his attention to his breakfast. He wasn't as confident as he sounded. If the Voice had sent down some more gorillas to get Leo and they had failed, then they were likely to come back. They would also be trying to find out what happened to the first pair of goons. And they knew where he and his family lived. He decided to prepare for the worst.

Kloten Airport, Zurich, Switzerland

Espinoza switched on his mobile as the Swiss Airbus A340-300 taxied to its bay, fifteen minutes ahead of schedule. Both he and Leo had slept well during the flight and were feeling fresh and alert.

There was a message from his friend Mac, in Australia. He had more news and wanted him to call back. He checked his watch, it was just before nine, seven in the evening in Sydney, not too late. There was no queue at security and they were in the departure lounge in less than fifteen minutes. He called the number.

"Good evening, Mac. I hope I'm not too late in calling."

"Pedro, where the hell have you been? I've got more information than the seven o'clock news bulletin." DS MacCallister had been running out of patience. He couldn't wait to share his findings with the Spaniard.

"I just arrived back in Europe. I got your message a few minutes ago."

"Right then. Get a giant size note pad."

It took the Australian twenty minutes to repeat the news from his colleague in Perth, interspersed by Espinoza's questions. The Spaniard made detailed notes and became more and more animated as his friend finished the report.

"Thanks Mac. You've given me a few new lines of enquiry. I'll get back to you when I have some kind of confirmation, it shouldn't be long. If you've got a photograph could you scan it and send it to my email address? You have, excellent." He thanked the policeman and rang off.

"You look a bit excited, Pedro. What's going on?"

"It's nothing to do with South Africa, Leo. Just another line of enquiry I'm following up." Espinoza was now wary of what he told the boy. Over breakfast he had attempted to interrogate him further about the circumstances of the abduction, Constance's death and the reason for the trips to Phalaborwa and the hotel in Vereeniging. Instead, he had somehow fallen into the trap of giving an autobiographical account of his police career in Spain. He had learned absolutely nothing about the abduction and he was certain that was Leo's objective. *It won't happen on the next flight,* he told himself. *Two can play at that game.*

He took out his jigsaw puzzle sheet, ticked off several more items on his list and drew two more boxes. Then he made two phone calls, one to France and one to Switzerland. He spoke French each time, in case Leo was listening.

The flight was called and they boarded the plane and took their business class seats. As the aircraft was taxiing away, he sent a text to Emma. *On Malaga flight with Leo. Everything OK and on time. See you soon.*

London, England

The time was coming up to eight thirty as Esther walked from Piccadilly underground station to Lord Dudley's apartment. It was already a warm day under an overcast sky and she was sweating slightly in her blazer and jeans, pulling a wheelie case along behind her and carrying a large shopping bag. She didn't want to pay for a check-in bag if she had to take the flight to Belfast.

She pressed the bell beside the unnamed letterbox at the side of the plain black windowless door. After a few seconds she rang again. A few seconds later she rang once more, keeping the bell pressed down whilst simultaneously knocking with her knuckles. "Arthur, it's Esther. Please open up, I need to speak to you." There was no letter box to shout through and the only window on the street façade was grilled so she couldn't bang on it or look inside. After knocking and calling several times more there was still no response from the occupant of the flat

Finally, she called his number, but like the previous evening there was no reply. If Arthur Dudley was at home he clearly didn't want to see her. Esther turned and walked away from the building, her head held high. As she had decided last night, she would take the tube to Paddington and then the express train to Heathrow. Book her Belfast flight on the train journey while she considered what to do with the dossier in her bag and the recordings on her iPad. Her mobile rang and she looked at the caller's name then replaced it in her pocket without answering.

From behind the curtain of the kitchen window, Lord Dudley watched Esther walk away from the flat towards the tube station. He looked at her lithe sensual figure and swinging hips with genuine anguish. Realising he would probably never see her again, his eyes welled up with tears. It had taken all the strength of mind he could muster to refrain from opening the door. After her display of affection for him yesterday in the hotel he had nurtured high hopes. She had called him, *'the most resourceful man I have ever met'* and kissed him and he had almost swooned with emotion. But that was before he had learned that the boy who had been taken to Zimbabwe was not Leo Stewart. He didn't know who it was, but it was irrelevant. Leo was gone, God knew where, and his reputation, at least with Esther, was gone as well. There was no point in wasting his time, she obviously had a penchant for Frenchmen anyway. He had other fish to fry. He went into his office and consulted his phone list.

Marbella, Spain

Emma went out to the terrace and showed Espinoza's text message to her sister. "They're on their way!"

"That's a great start to the day. We should crack open a bottle of champagne," Jenny laughed.

"We will soon. And I'll be toasting you and Pedro. I can't begin to think what might have happened if you hadn't taken charge of the whole horrible business. Thank you for everything you've done. I'll never be able to repay you."

"Just try to contain yourself for the moment. Leticia's coming down with Emilio. I can hear her talking to Encarni. Now," she continued in a whisper, "we need to get the story right. You simply tell her you're going along to Nigel's house in Estepona to pick up your son. In the taxi you explain it all to him and Pedro so they can play the game when they get back. Now that Leo's safe we've got lots of time to talk about it with them later, when Leticia's not around."

Geneva, Switzerland

"I assume that everything is still on track for tomorrow?" Prince Sam Bensouda was in his suite at the Kempinski Hotel speaking to Claude Jolidon. As the deadline drew nearer he was becoming more and more anxious about his million dollar investment.

"I've just received confirmation from the agent in Marseille. The ship is due in tomorrow evening, on schedule. Everything is proceeding as planned."

"And the hand-over arrangements are carefully programmed?" Under no circumstances did he want to be present at such a potentially incriminating event. In his position it would be a risk too far.

"The merchandise will be available to be picked up in Marseille on Monday morning at eleven. The buyer's agent is going to meet our agent at the dock and will make the transfer to the escrow account against reception of the merchandise. I will then send it on to your account, minus the remaining expenses and commission."

"And the exact amount of the transfer to my account will be?"

"Exactly twenty-nine million dollars, Monsieur."

Bensouda didn't mention the additional commission they'd extorted from him. It was just an unfortunate extra cost he had to accept. The profit still represented more than twenty times his investment. *The best deal I've made in a long time,* he thought. *In fact, the only deal. This will settle quite a few problems.*

"Very well. That seems to be in order. I'll call you at eleven on Monday just to be sure there are no delays."

"Thank you, Monsieur le Prince. Have a pleasant day. "

Bensouda chose another number from his Favourites list. "Good morning, darling. How are you?"

"Sam. How lovely to hear your voice. I've been missing you." Jenny moved to the end of the terrace away from the others. "Where are you?"

"I'm in Geneva, just finishing off a transaction I've been working on."

"When will you be back? I can't wait to see you." Jenny had decided to take her sister's advice. A little out of practice and trying not to sound too eager, she blurted out, "I was thinking we could maybe go off for a weekend somewhere. Emma will be leaving in a couple of days, so I'll be as free as a bird. I've heard great things about the *Finca Courtesin*. It's just a half hour along the road. What do you think?"

"That's a great idea. I should be back on Monday evening, so I'll have time to see Emma and meet her son before they leave. Go ahead and book it."

"Good, that's very good." Jenny felt both relieved and guilty, as if she'd lured an unsuspecting fly into her spider's web. *Never mind, no half measures,* she decided. "I'll call and book right now."

Emma looked enquiringly at her as she walked back towards the others. Jenny winked, as if to say, *Job done, as instructed.* A frisson ran down her spine, a feeling she hadn't felt for a long time.

SIXTY-FOUR

Over France en route for Malaga, Spain

"I don't remember anything about the first couple of days. They kept me drugged, in a room on my own. It was like a hospital ward, but without any equipment, just a bed and a table."

Espinoza didn't mention that he knew about the room and had learned a lot from the photograph of it. He had finally got him talking again and he didn't want him to stop. With a little prodding he learned about the visits from Coetzee, the lies he'd told about his mother and how hard he'd tried to find out about his father. Leo described the moment when Blethin injected him before they left for Zimbabwe, how it had brought back the memory of the abduction, the first injection in the toilets with Lambert holding him. How he'd woken up when they arrived in Polokwane and Coetzee had bought hamburgers for everyone.

All of these memories Espinoza could believe. They were vividly described and related without hesitation, a pure memory play. Then he noted a more hesitant note in Leo's voice as he talked about the argument in the car and the death of Constance, as they now knew him to be. He sounded almost as if he was reciting a well-rehearsed script.

The Spaniard ignored this hiatus in the story and asked about their trip to Phalaborwa. Now the narrative became alive again, his descriptions vivid and detailed in their clarity, as if he'd enjoyed the visit to the Kruger and Coetzee had suddenly become his close friend. He talked at length about the beauty of the surroundings, the animals, birds and the river life. It was as if he didn't want to leave that memory and move onto the next one.

"And then you drove down to the hotel in ... where was it again?"

"Vereeniging, the Vaal Riviera Hotel. It's got a bar and restaurant on a barge that floats across the river. It's really cool."

Once again the story didn't ring true to the Spaniard. It didn't seem reasonable that they would drive all the way to the south of Johannesburg from the Kruger "It must be at least eight hours drive. Why do you think Coetzee decided to go all the way down there?"

Leo offered up a very unconvincing tale about Coetzee wanting to take him home to meet his wife and daughter but they happened to be staying at the hotel, so they drove down there to join them.

"Where do they actually live?" He asked.

Here, the boy's story became even more vague and disjointed. He explained that Marius and Karen were divorced, he lived in Johannesburg but she and their daughter lived in Delmas, in a big farmhouse with dogs. The daughter, Abby was adopted, (as Espinoza had of course surmised), and now they were going to live together again and get his security business back on its feet.

A dozen questions jumped into Espinoza's mind. *How did he know they had a farmhouse and dogs in Delmas? Why were Karen and Abby in Vereeniging? How did he know about Coetzee's business? How did he know they were going to live together again? What had caused that reconciliation?*

He asked, "Was that the reason for his involvement in your abduction? Problems with his business?"

"That's right. He said it was only for the money. He didn't even know who had organised it all. When we got to Vereeniging he told us that Nwosu was the original contact in South Africa and he hired Marius but it was only because he had the security contract for the stadium so they could grab me. There was this man called the 'Voice' who gave all the instructions but they had no idea who he was or what the reason for the abduction was. Everything was done by phone and email and they just had to follow his orders if they wanted to get paid."

Espinoza's ears pricked up at this snippet. "He told you they called the organiser the 'Voice'? Why did they call him that?"

"He said he talked like William Shakespeare. Very good English but old fashioned words and phrases. He sounded like a school teacher or a lecturer, but he never told them what the plan was. Just that they had to abduct me and look after me. That's why Marius kept asking me questions about my family, so he could work out the reason for the plan. But I don't have a clue what they wanted so I couldn't tell him anything."

Filing this away in his memory, the detective asked, "Why do you think they took you away from Johannesburg?"

"I have no idea. They injected me again and the next thing I knew we were in the car on the way to Zimbabwe. But at the first chance Marius took me away from the others and looked after me."

"And he told you that he tried to get money from your mother to return you?"

"He said he'd asked for a reward and I told him we were skint. My Mum spent all her money on the trip down here, so I know she's broke right now."

"And did he tell you why he thought he could get a reward?"

"He said my father must have money, but I don't know where he got that from. I've never even seen my father and I told him I didn't think he'd be keen to throw money around for a kid he doesn't even know."

"But then he let you go without asking for a ransom. Why do you think that was?"

"It's obvious. It was because of Karen and Abby, when he phoned her before we drove down. Once he started thinking about getting his family back, he just dropped the whole idea of the ransom and took me down to meet them. I could have walked out in Phalaborwa if I'd wanted to, but I knew Mom would be worried if I was on my own so I waited until we got nearer to Joburg and then called her straight away. In the end he's brought me to safety and he's asked for no money, so I think we're quits. Don't you?"

Although they were still a lot of unanswered questions in Espinoza's mind, he was reaching some conclusions. *It seems Coetzee didn't know about Leo's birth or Jenny's wealth. He wasn't a key person in the conspiracy, he just happened to have the security of the stadium under his control and had financial problems. When he saw the danger Leo was in, he pulled the plug on the operation and thanks to him, the boy is safe.* "I think I agree with you," he said. "No more questions for now, I promise."

"Can I ask one? Do you have any idea who came up with the abduction plan and why they picked on me?"

"I have some preliminary thoughts, but there's still a lot of detective work to be done, so there's no point in speculating for the moment. The main thing is that you're safely back. That was my promise to your mother. If I can follow the trail up to the real culprits all the better, but it won't affect you or her anymore and that's always been my main objective."

"I never said thank you, sorry. Thank you for all you've done for me and my mom. She must be so relieved that this is over, I know I am." Leo settled back in his seat, his mind at ease, although he suspected that Espinoza was not a man to leave any stone unturned. But as long as he stuck to his story he should be OK. He couldn't afford to tell the truth about Constance's death, nor about the gorillas from Zimbabwe. *Anyway,* he thought, *that's all behind me in South Africa and I'm going to leave it there.*

Espinoza was now thinking about the mysterious 'Voice'. Was he the key to the conspiracy? He went back over Leo's words, 'He sounded like a school teacher or a lecturer.' *Or,* he thought to himself, *perhaps Lord Arthur Dudley who was tracing their phones all over South Africa?* He took out his jigsaw puzzle and added a new box. The picture was starting to become clearer.

Marbella, Spain

"I've just checked and the flight's on time. It's landing in forty minutes." Jenny and Emma were still out on the terrace. Leticia and Emilio were up at the lake at the top of the garden.

"I'd better get moving. Does Juan know we're going to the airport?"

"He knows, but don't worry. I managed to find enough Spanish to tell him to say nothing to the others. He'll go straight home when he's brought you back. He usually doesn't work on a Saturday and by Monday everyone will have forgotten about it."

"Listen, Jenny. I have to tell Leo about his birth, about Rwanda and about Mutesi. I was summoning up the courage to do it one day, but after what's happened I have to do it now. It's going to be a big shock to him but if I explain it properly I'm sure he'll understand. The main thing is that he's always been loved and cherished and he knows that. But I can't tell him about Galaganza. He can't be told that his biological father was one of the organisers of the greatest human catastrophe since the second world war. It's too much for anyone to cope with. So it has to be kept secret and never disclosed to anyone. After Tony and Dr Constance's deaths, no one except you and Pedro and I know this and you must promise never to divulge it. Never."

After promising that the subject would never be discussed again by her with anyone and that Pedro would abide by the same promise, Jenny saw her sister off then went up to find Leticia at the lake. Emilio was throwing handfuls of fish food and the carp were threshing about, thrusting up their open jaws to grab the food from the surface. There must have been fifty of the enormous creatures, of every hue imaginable, creating what looked like an underwater rainbow as their scales flashed in the sunlight. It was an impressive sight, reminding her of what may lie just beneath an apparently calm surface.

They walked back down the steps to the house, listening to the little boy's chatter about *les poissons,* the fish. He had evidently decided to speak French that day, so his mother obligingly helped him with his vocabulary. Jenny was increasingly impressed by Leticia's ability to pick up languages. As well as Portuguese, her mother tongue, she was fluent in Spanish and English and now she was mastering French. *That's thanks to Patrice. Lovers and languages, it's a good formula for fluency.*

"Emma's gone off to get Leo, so she'll be a little while," she said to Leticia. "Come and sit with me and I'll explain about your accounts. I checked them over last night and I think I know what's happened."

"Is it something bad?" Leticia looked fearful. She couldn't face a rift with her fiancé.

"It's not as bad as we may have imagined, but let's look at the statements and you can see for yourself."

Jenny opened up the file and pointed out the transactions involving the *Asian Atlantic Investment Funds.* Then she went online to the newspaper articles and explained to Leticia what a Ponzi scheme was and where her million Euros had gone.

"Meu Deus! My God. I can't believe people can do such things. These people just took the money and disappeared. So there was nothing Patrice could have done."

"That's right. In fact, apart from that crooked scheme, Patrice hasn't done a bad job. Ignoring the lost million, after your living costs he's actually produced a profit of almost ten per cent so it's not such a terrible result."

"But I'll never get back the money from this Ponzi scheme?"

"No. I'm sure it's gone forever, unless there are other assets that the SEC discovers. But I wouldn't hold out any hope for that, they sound like a really callous bunch of criminals. The money will be hidden away in offshore accounts all over the world." She had a fleeting vision of d'Almeida in the kitchen just behind them, two years ago, boasting about transferring twelve million dollars on a Sunday night. She shivered and said, "Did you notice that there were a lot of pension funds that had invested? Stealing people's pensions, it makes you want to throttle the lot of them."

"Patrice said it was just temporary, that he would make the money back by September."

"If he said so, he must have something up his sleeve, I suppose." Jenny tried to sound confident, hoping against hope that her suspicions were unfounded. Despite having Leo back, they still hadn't uncovered the identity of the conspirators and she was afraid of what might be found. She was especially afraid of what Leticia might learn.

London, England

Lord Arthur Dudley was working on his laptop. Although he liked to give the appearance of total incompetence in all things computer and Internet related, he was quite skilled at most tasks. After a number of false starts, partly because his written French wasn't equal to his conversational ability, he found the correct website and printed out the details he was looking for.

Then with the help of the online translation programme, he prepared a short email and practised reading it out loud until he was confident of the result. Ready, he called a number in *Montreuil, Seine-Saint Denis,* a Commune in the eastern suburbs of Paris. He used the French mobile phone with the Bouygues SIM. The number rang out and he switched on the voice distortion system, just enough to disguise the distinctive tone of his voice but not enough to sound like a robot. After several rings, a recorded message advised him that the office was closed on Saturday and gave him another number for emergency calls. He went through the same procedure again and this time a bored-sounding woman answered the number. He assumed that like most civil servants, especially in France, she objected to working on the weekend, but she deigned to listen to his well-rehearsed reading of the message.

As he had expected, she then asked for his name, address and other particulars, all of which he answered with convincing, but incorrect details. Finally, she told him she'd forward the information to the appropriate office but he had to confirm the details in writing. Dudley noted down the email address, thanked the woman and rang off. He went back to his laptop and completed the message with the email address and the name of the person she'd given him. After rereading it one last time he sent it to *IPsend* in the Philippines from where it was automatically forwarded to Montreuil. Dudley waited to ensure that the message had been sent then went back online. He was in a cleaning up mood and there was more to do.

Heathrow Airport, England

The Internet banking system asked for the amount of the transaction. Esther took a deep breath and entered two, five, zero, zero, zero, full-stop, zero, zero, then pressed *Submit.* A moment later the confirmation came onto the screen. She gave a gasp of relief then looked around the departure lounge self-consciously. No one had witnessed the transfer of twenty-five thousand dollars from Arthur Dudley's *Joburg* account with the Private Bank of Panama to her own account at the Credit Bank of Guadeloupe. That was the daily limit of the authorisation given to her by him to operate the account in the event of an urgent payment if he was indisposed. She knew he would cancel the authorisation when he thought about it, but he hadn't yet done so. There was more than two hundred thousand dollars in the account, but she couldn't get more today. She could try again tomorrow, but it would probably be too late.

The Guadeloupe account was in the name of Esther Bonnard, her maiden name, which she had used since fleeing Switzerland after d'Almeida's death. She had renewed both her passports, in that name and her married name, Rousseau. By using the passports alternately she was able to move between countries without leaving a complete trail. Although she had no information on the police enquiry after the Klein Fellay robbery she assumed she had become a suspect, so she was taking no chances of being found by Interpol, nor of the little money she had managed to accumulate being taken away from her. No one, including Dudley and Slater knew her married name.

The balance on her account was now close to fifty thousand dollars, nothing like what she'd hoped for with the ransom plan, but better than nothing. And she wasn't yet finished. She was sure she could extract more cash if she handled the next step well. Her mobile had rung five times on the train and as she waited for her Belfast flight. Now that she'd kept him waiting and had made the first successful transfer, it was time to call Slater back. She had rehearsed her story and was ready. She called his number.

"Sorry, chéri, I was rushing for the train and then going through security so I didn't manage to phone you back earlier."

"You mean you're on your way back?"

"No, not yet. I'm leaving in an hour for Geneva." For the moment she had to keep the door open, although she was going to slam it shut fairly soon.

"Why Geneva? Have you spoken to Dudley? I've been trying to get him all morning but he isn't answering. I don't know what in hell's going on."

"I went to his apartment this morning, as I promised. That's why I'm on my way to Switzerland. To get the transaction back on track"

"So the deal is still alive? Are you sure? Have they got the boy in Zimbabwe?"

"Apparently so," she lied convincingly and heard a deep sigh of relief at the other end. "But it seems Arthur's connections are not what he led us to believe. The Harare people are actually managed out of Geneva and with all the recent activity they've realised that they've been underselling their assistance. I'm going over to sweet talk the boss into clearing the way for the transaction to continue. It's going to cost us some money, but Arthur has dropped the ball and I'm going to pick it up again."

"I don't fucking believe it! You know how difficult it is for me to get money from my partner. It's like blood from a stone. How much is it this time?"

Esther quickly weighed up the odds of getting a small amount easily or missing out by asking for too much. "I think I can resolve it with twenty-five thousand dollars in cash and some feminine persuasion, but I'd need it in my account immediately so that I can settle the matter on the spot."

"What do you mean, 'feminine persuasion'? You mean sex, don't you?"

"Chéri, we're talking about you and me and the rest of our lives together, nothing is more important than that. And if I have to be a little generous with my attentions to arrange that, I'll do it willingly, as long as I know it will work. But for that I need to have the cash available."

"Who is this man?"

"He's called Sébastien. Sébastien du Pasquier. He's apparently half Swiss, half French and he's an ex-banker. Arthur told me he's now the Zimbabwean money manager in Geneva." Esther skilfully embroidered her story with more details. She knew that the more elaborate the lie the more easily it was believed.

"When are you meeting him?"

"Tomorrow night for dinner, so I should to be able to get it agreed by Monday morning. That's when I'll need to make the payment."

"And you'll come straight back here to be with me?"

"You know I will, I can't wait. As soon as I can get a flight, I promise."

There was a long moment of silence, then, "Are you sure this will fix the problem and we can finish the transaction?"

"I can't promise until I meet the man concerned, but I'd be astonished if I failed to get him to do what I want. Don't you agree?"

He knew her powers of persuasion better than anyone. But was she using them on him? And what about this man she was proposing to seduce? Another thought came to him. "What if I could find the twenty-five thousand myself? We might be able to rearrange the participations. If we save the situation we have every right to demand a larger slice. What do you think?"

"It's a brilliant idea. I should have thought of that. If you can convince your partner, I can certainly persuade Arthur. They're both desperate to produce some real money from all the work that's gone into the plan. We could do very well out of this setback if we handle it properly." Esther couldn't believe how naïve this man was, but she wasn't about to argue.

"Right, I'll do it. Send me the account details and the funds will be there by Monday first thing."

Esther walked to the departure gate for her flight to Belfast, congratulating herself on the conversation. *I haven't lost my touch,* she told herself. *That's fifty thousand dollars recovered from a dead deal. And I still haven't finished.*

SIXTY-FIVE

Malaga Airport, Spain

Espinoza stood aside as Emma hugged and kissed her son for a long moment. Leo looked around the crowded arrivals hall in an embarrassed fashion and pulled away from his mother as soon as he reasonably could. "I'm fine, Mom. Don't worry, I'm really fine."

Reluctantly she released him and turned to embrace the Spaniard. "You must be exhausted, Pedro. You've been travelling non-stop for days and you've kept your promise to me. I'll never forget it. I don't know how to thank you."

"I was rather lucky, Emma, but I'm happy that everything has ended this way. Now you'd better get Leo home. It's lunch time and he's probably hungry. He seems to be hungry all the time." He tried to lighten the emotionally charged atmosphere.

"Actually, the food on both flights was really good. Nothing like the plastic stuff in economy. How did you manage to wangle business seats?" Leo grabbed his bag and started off towards the exit doors.

"I'll explain it all to you in the car. It's a very long story."

They walked along to the parking area where Juan was waiting for them in the Jaguar. "Are you coming back with us, Pedro?"

"I'll take a taxi home and relax with my family if you don't mind. I've actually only been away for two days, but it seems a lot longer. And," he continued thoughtfully, "I don't want to cause any unnecessary speculation in Leticia's mind. I'll call later this afternoon." He shook them both by the hand. "By the way, have you got a photograph of Tony Forrester?"

Emma looked a little embarrassed. "Actually, I've got one here. I keep it just for old time's sake." She opened her purse and handed him a small plastic case with a well preserved colour photo inside. It was of a good looking, fair haired man with an appealing smile, in his late twenties. She made sure that Leo didn't see it.

"May I take a copy and bring the original back to you?"

A sense of foreboding entered her mind, but she said nothing in front of her son. "Of course."

They climbed into the Jaguar and Espinoza watched them drive away then walked over to the taxi rank. *I wonder,* he said to himself.

"I think some parts of Leo's story are invented, but in the end I don't think it matters." Espinoza had called Jenny from the taxi to give her a more detailed account of everything that had occurred in Johannesburg. "It seems that Coetzee was not involved at a high level. He took this job to solve his financial problems and when he realised what it entailed he backed out. But he didn't leave Leo to his fate, he removed him from danger and probably saved his life. If you know anything about Mugabe's country you'll have an idea of what would have happened to him if he'd been taken there. "I would say he has probably learned his lesson and if Leo wants to leave it at that, we should let it go."

"It sounds as if Coetzee's wife might have been the key to his change of heart." Jenny said. "Although, judging from his previous background he can't have been very comfortable in this scheme. He's a life saver, not a life taker. To have Leo back is all that really matters and if he doesn't want to testify against Coetzee we can't force him to. But what about the people at the top, the real conspirators? We still know nothing about them."

"That's not entirely true, I know quite a lot about them. But I'll have more information over the weekend and I'll keep you informed as soon as I get a clear picture. In the meantime, enjoy a quiet time with your family." He had decided to say nothing about Leo's revelation of the 'Voice'. No need to disturb their enjoyment of Leo's homecoming. It could wait until Monday.

"A quiet time thanks to you, Pedro. Thank you for everything. Take care."

London, England

Hmm. She's quick off the mark! Arthur Dudley was looking at the *Joburg* bank account in Panama on his laptop. He immediately saw the transfer of twenty-five thousand dollars that morning to Esther Bonnard's account at the Credit Bank of Guadeloupe. He supressed a laugh, *Cheeky creature.* He could have reversed the transaction, since the value date was not until Monday, but he decided to let it go. *She deserves some recompense for her efforts and for that kiss. Besides, I'm still two hundred thousand to the good.*

He transferred the balance to the Swiss Credit Bank of Lugano, with Monday's value date, leaving a balance of one hundred dollars to cover any late costs and to avoid further contact by the bank. The Lugano account was in the name of *Arturo D'Uddlio,* which he found quite amusing. He'd been a client there since long before the compliance restrictions on banks had made it almost impossible to open new accounts and it was a useful transit point. Finally, he transferred two hundred thousand dollars from Lugano to his account in the Bahamas with Tuesday's value date to permit the arrival of the funds from Panama. It wasn't a perfectly secure trail, but it had always served him well in the past.

Already that morning, Dudley had deleted the Internet browsing history and every single document and message in the Leo Stewart dossier from his laptop and iPad and then permanently deleted them from the Trash files. A few years previously he had acquired a software programme written by one of his star former pupils at Cambridge, which scrambled files of every type when they were permanently deleted. Even if the files could be restored by a professional IT technician or hacker they would be incomprehensible. In his line of business he could not afford to leave traces of any kind. He replaced the Bouygues SIM from the French phone with a new one then spent an hour feeding every document concerning the abduction transaction into his shredder. He was certain that there was nothing incriminating on the T-Mobile SIM, but he replaced that one too. Although it was July, there was a fire in the grate in his office and he threw the SIM cards and paper strips onto the flames.

He was disappointed with the outcome but he had survived many such disappointments in his career. The plan had been a good one and had failed only due to a combination of unfortunate circumstances. He had earned a reasonable fee for his services and in his estimation that was the end of the matter. He was convinced there was nothing to fear from any of the other participants. No one in South Africa knew anything about him, and Esther Bonnard and Slater had as much, if not more to lose than him. In any event, he was not directly involved in any of the criminal events that had occurred. If everyone kept their mouth shut it would be a case of mutual protection and not mutual blame.

Dudley looked at his watch. It was twelve forty-five. He had a table booked at the Petrichor in the Cavendish for one o'clock. It was a beautiful day, so he set off on the fifteen minute walk, already savouring his champagne aperitif.

Marbella, Spain

"So who's this guy, Tony Forrester? Is he my father?" Leo and his mother were in the taxi on the way to Marbella. She had coached him in what to say to Leticia and he reluctantly agreed to keep to himself what was to him an incredible adventure story. He and Emma had always been totally open with each other and now it was his turn to ask awkward questions.

"I was expecting that. No, he's not your father, but he had a lot to do with you becoming my son. I've got thirty minutes to tell you about him and why you were abducted. But first I have to tell you about an incredible girl. Your real mother, Mutesi." Emma gathered her thoughts and began the story for the second time that week. The story of the Rwandan genocide and Leo's biological parents.

Malaga, Spain

"Buen provecho amor mio. Bon appétit, dearest." Espinoza clinked his glass of rioja against Soledad's glass and took a slice of the delicious Iberian ham. "Did you miss me?"

"I didn't have time to miss you. You were hardly gone at all. How did you get back so quickly?"

"It was partly thanks to you. You made me think about the problem in a different way and suddenly it became much clearer. You saved me a lot of time."

"So the case is closed? Does that mean you get paid a big bonus?"

"It's almost closed. Unfortunately, I have a feeling that it will never be fully wrapped up, it's all rather complicated." He had received an email with the photo he'd requested from DS MacCallister in Sydney, but it didn't tell him anything for the moment.

"You didn't answer my question. What about the bonus? If I was of so much help I should get at least a part of it."

Espinoza laughed and leaned over to kiss her. "I'm sure my client will be very generous. Enough to buy you flowers in the market."

Marbella, Spain

"Come and walk with us, Leo." Jenny led the way through the house to the garden. Fortunately, Leticia and Emilio had gone to meet Patrice at the beach so that the boy's arrival at the house aroused no complicated explanations. Jenny was overjoyed to see her nephew again and they had enjoyed a pleasant lunch on the terrace, just the three of them. Encarni didn't speak English so they were able to talk freely about the recent events. She was happy and relieved to see that Leo seemed to be unfazed by his mother's story, he was used to having no father and in his mind he now found that he'd had two mothers, both of whom had obviously loved and cherished him. Many of the kids at school had unhappy home lives with absent or abusive fathers or mothers or both, and he was content to have a close and loving relationship with Emma, however it had come about. But he was hiding his feelings well.

Emma had never talked to him previously about Rwanda, restricting her short involvement in the aftermath of the genocide into a brief summary with very few details. In the taxi she didn't disclose the identity of his presumed father, just that Mutesi had been a rape victim and she had helped her give birth before she passed away.

At that point, he said quietly and thoughtfully, "My God. She was younger than I am when she gave birth. And then she died. That's terrible."

After Emma managed to explain how she had smuggled him out of Rwanda and into England, he didn't speak for a while. "Isn't that illegal?" He finally asked.

"I suppose it is. But if you love someone enough, doesn't it become perfectly legal?"

"Is that why you did it? I was just a little African baby."

"Not to me. I helped to bring you into the world. Who else could care for you when Mutesi died?"

Leo didn't speak, just took her hand and looked at her in a way she'd never seen before.

When she finished the story, he asked many questions about her experience at the clinic and the work she had done to save mothers and their children. What kind of a man was Tony? Why had he left her and the child he had rescued to go off with another woman? How had those events affected her life back in the UK? Leo understood the principles of cause and effect.

As far as he could see, she had handled it brilliantly, bringing him up and looking after them both whilst finding the time to earn a living as a successful author.

When they arrived at York House he helped her out of the taxi and gave her a tight hug. "Thanks for saving me from an African orphanage. I much prefer being Leo Stewart and having you as my mother."

Now, they climbed the stone staircase alongside the stream that Charlie had designed four years before at the wheel of a tractor and came to the small lake on the plateau above the house. Looking to the South, Leo had never seen such a wonderful vista. Visibility was so good that the Atlas Mountains in Morocco stood out clearly, one hundred and fifty kilometres across the Mediterranean. On arriving at the house he had realised that Aunt Jennie must be a very wealthy lady; the place was simply fabulous, but she was the nicest and most modest person he'd ever met. Over lunch they hadn't talked about his abduction, she'd shown a lot of interest in his life, his schooling and hobbies. He knew she'd been a school teacher and had lost her husband and wondered why she hadn't remarried and had children. He didn't like to ask such personal questions, he'd find out in due course.

His mother had also told him that she was prepared to pay the ransom money. *She must be incredibly fond of my mom,* he thought. *She paid for her to escape and she was ready to pay the ransom to free me.*

"Do you know anything more about the people who abducted me? I mean the real organisers? Pedro told me that he had some ideas but he wasn't sure yet, it needed more detective work. He seems to be really smart, he tied the murders up in South Africa in just a few hours. The police chief was on TV taking the credit, but I know it was Pedro who did all the work."

"Let's put that aside for now. We'll leave it to him and just enjoy our few days together. You're on holiday now."

London, England

Dudley had put his US mobile onto silent to avoid disturbing the other clients at the Petrichor. He had spotted two cabinet ministers at the bar and a group including a couple of TV celebrities and he didn't want to attract attention to himself. The phone vibrated gently on the table four times whilst he was eating, always showing the same 0033 number. It was his contact in Marseille, no doubt calling about the merchandise on the Erzurat. The ship was due to dock there the following day and he had given no delivery instructions, nor did he intend to. He had employed that channel of delivery several times over the last several years, but never before involving drugs. He had always known the time would come when he would have to close it before it became compromised and him with it. That time had now come.

The email he had sent yesterday to the Directorate-General of Customs and Indirect Taxes in Montreuil, Seine-Saint-Denis, (DGDDI), would have caused quite a stir. A haul of two hundred kilos of pure heroin was substantial enough to demand immediate attention. Either the authorities had already intercepted the Erzurat at sea or they were waiting at the container port in Marseille. Whatever the case, the cargo would be confiscated and the available perpetrators, namely the ship's captain and his contact in Marseille, would be incarcerated in a French prison. *Just as it should be,* he told himself. *Drug smuggling is a vile business and they deserve to be severely punished.*

The trail would end there, since there had been no traceable contact with either himself or Claude Jolidon, the originator of the funding of the transaction. Both of them had used the Philippines ISP and deviated prepaid phones with foreign SIMs, which would lead nowhere. Jolidon could still be useful to him in his position at Ramseyer, Haldemann, so he had no intention of casting him aside for the moment. He wondered vaguely whether Bensouda might attempt to extract his revenge on the man, but thought it unlikely, since they could each blackmail the other and he didn't imagine that Bensouda was the murdering type. *In any case, it's not my problem. There's always some collateral damage in these transactions. It's part of the risk/reward ratio.*

On his way back to his apartment he walked across St James Park to the lake in the centre. He removed the SIM from the phone and threw it into the water. Even though the chances of it being traced were next to none he didn't want to risk it. He had another AT&T SIM in his office. The park was quiet and he decided to sit by the lake and enjoy a few minutes of sunshine. It was a shame not to enjoy such a lovely day.

Malaga, Spain

Espinoza awoke abruptly from his siesta. The clock on the bedside table showed seven o'clock. He got off the bed and took the mobile from his wife. "Since I'm now awake I might as well answer it. G*racias,* Soledad," he said with a smile.

Recognising the 4122 Geneva prefix, he answered, "*Bonsoir* Andréas. Thanks for calling back on a Saturday. I assume you have some news for me?"

He listened for a few minutes then said, "Esther Rousseau, née Bonnard. I see. Why wasn't this discovered at the time? I assumed she was a single woman."

The explanation didn't seem to impress him and after a few further exchanges he said, "Never mind. I'll do what I can with this new information. *Merci et à bientôt.*"

He went downstairs where Soledad had made him coffee. "Is something wrong?"

"I need to make two quick calls, the last for this evening."

The first was to Marcel Colombey, his contact in Paris. Colombey was a Senior Inspector in the Central Directorate of Judicial Police; a high-ranking officer. "Esther Rousseau, née Bonnard. That's right. And I want you to check on another possibility." He gave the details to the Frenchman. "It's a long shot, but we might just get lucky."

Then he called Jenny, to ensure that all was well in York House. "I've got one or two ideas about the perpetrators," he added. I'll call you when I have more news."

He put away the mobile. "Now, Soledad. Go and get yourself ready. We're going to Antonio's for dinner to spend some of my bonus."

Dublin, Republic of Ireland

Esther Bonnard-Rousseau was eating ham and eggs in the bar of the Liffey Landing pub in Rainsford Street in Dublin. That afternoon she had taken the train from Belfast, managing to avoid showing any identification, then come straight to the pub on the bus so no one knew where she was. She'd stayed there several times; it was close to the Guinness storeroom where tourists came to taste the black bitter ale straight from the keg. Her shabby but comfortable room had everything she needed and the owners respected her privacy.

She had come across the pub two years before, after being stranded in Luton when she realised Ray d'Almeida wasn't coming for her and had made the same trip by a cheaper route, the train to Liverpool then the ferry to Belfast and another train to Dublin. With only four hundred and fifty pounds to her name she had gone into the pub looking for a cheap room and had ended up helping out as a barmaid. The proprietors, Seamus and Susan McCaffey, were large, friendly and discreet. They paid her in cash, with no questions asked. After working there for six months she had saved enough money to survive for a while and had cultivated a great ambition to make a lot more.

Now back in Dublin again she felt safe and ready to renew her attack on the world for compensation for the losses she'd incurred, namely Ray d'Almeida and twelve million dollars. She rehearsed in her mind the messages she would send in a day or two. Meanwhile she needed a good night's sleep. She asked Susan to pour her a pint of Guinness. That should do the trick.

DAY EIGHT

SUNDAY, JULY 18, 2010

SIXTY-SIX

Malaga, Spain

Marcel Colombey at the French National Police called back as Espinoza was having his second coffee that morning. Soledad had gone to church with Laura, their daughter, but he wanted to catch up on his jigsaw puzzle. Several new ideas had come to him in the night and he needed to explore them in the quiet of the empty house. He would meet them in the tapas bar for lunch later on.

"*Bonjour, Marcel.* I'm impressed to see you working on a Sunday. *Quelles nouvelles?*" He listened for some minutes, making notes on his pad as always. "Nicole Charpentier. Well done," he said eventually. "How did you find that out? A *Casino Employees Recruitment Register?* And then you searched through the employment records at the casinos in the Nice area, I suppose."

He listened again. "Even with all the data bases at your disposal, it's still excellent detective work. We're getting close to solving this case and it's you who should get the credit and you'll deserve it. Can I ask you one last favour?" He explained his request, adding, "I'll send the photos to you now and if you could possibly get someone to research them today, it would be of great help."

Espinoza sent off the photos he'd received from Emma and

MacCallister then filled out two more of the boxes of his crossword and ticked off several items on his list. He grunted with satisfaction. There were very few boxes left to fill and the unticked items were diminishing rapidly. He went to make himself another coffee.

London, England

"*Bonjour M Jolidon,* how are you today?" Lord Dudley had been expecting the call from Geneva since the previous day when he had failed to respond to his contact in Marseille. He listened patiently as the Swiss man told him what he already knew.

"I'm sorry that you find yourself in this situation but unfortunately I am unable to give the appropriate instructions to the agent."

There was a pause, then Jolidon said, "In that case give them to me and I'll send them to our agent. This is urgent so that nothing goes wrong tomorrow morning. The agreed identification codes will be exchanged, the transaction will be executed and we will receive our commission."

"M Jolidon, I have been confidentially advised that information about the cargo has been notified to the French customs authorities. The ship will be apprehended, the merchandise impounded and there is nothing we can do about it. We need to stay as far away as possible from the matter to preserve our integrity."

"*Putin de merde!* How did this happen? Where did you get this information?"

"I'm afraid I can't reveal my source, but I am absolutely certain of the truth of the information."

"That means our agent will be arrested. Do you know what the penalties are for bringing in this material?" Even on a secure line he didn't dare use the word heroin.

"I am painfully aware of them and I agree that the poor man will not be well treated. That is the bad news and it is most regrettable. However, the good news is that we still have two hundred and fifty thousand dollars under our control, which means that you have just earned one hundred thousand dollars. What do you think of that?"

Dudley heard a sharp intake of breath. From Esther Rousseau, he had learned the exact amount of Jolidon's debt to the Casino de Divonne. It was seventy-five thousand Euros, about ninety thousand dollars. The Swiss man would now be able to throw away another ten thousand on the tables.

"That is most generous, Monsieur. But what shall I tell Favre?"

"You have had no written contact with him, as I recommended. Is that right?"

"Everything was done by telephone and he knows me as M Valentino, but I don't see what…"

"Then, M Jolidon, I suggest that you simply replace the SIM in your US phone and he will be unable to contact or find you. This will save you a disagreeable conversation which would, in any case, be of no value to either party. What will be, will be."

"And the Prince Bensouda?"

"The Prince took a gamble, M Jolidon. A risky gamble that unfortunately hasn't succeeded. We have fulfilled the terms of our contract and deserve to be paid. Regrettably there will be no remaining funds to return to the Prince. As you know better than I, that is the unfortunate downside of gambling."

The two men talked for a few minutes more and agreed to say nothing to Bensouda. He would find out about the aborted shipment soon enough. It was better for them to remain out of the picture, wait for his call and then commiserate with the loser.

Dudley reflected on the conversation. He had said nothing that could incriminate him in the forthcoming apprehension of the cargo and the identifiable perpetrators. Most important of all, he had not disclosed that there was no purchaser for the drugs shipment and never had been. He disapproved of drug abuse and would not contribute to the distribution of heroin on the streets of European cities. The whole transaction had been concocted by him with the assistance of various contacts in Afghanistan, Syria and Turkey. Contacts whose fees had been paid from Bensouda's funds, along with the other costs of the operation.

According to his own contrary personal moral compass, Lord Arthur Selwyn Savage Dudley had acted correctly. He approved neither of drugs nor of gambling and he felt vindicated for the actions he had taken. Apart from the agent, who had been an unfortunate victim of collateral damage, every person involved in this month long transaction had been properly remunerated. But the gambler had lost. This so-called Prince Bensouda, who had been willing to destroy an unknown number of lives by delivering a supply of deadly drugs worth sixty million dollars on the street, in a risky gamble that he could obviously afford to lose.

The end had also justified the means. The escrow account with the balance of the money was under his control and the additional commission was in his bank in the Bahamas. The generous payment to Jolidon would buy his loyalty for the foreseeable future and encourage him to recommend more of his clients at Ramseyer, Haldemann.

He finished shredding the documents from the Bensouda file then burned the remains in the grate and raked the ashes. The transaction had never existed and if it had, he had not been involved. The weather was fair and he decided to go for a walk and have a coffee at the Italian café near the park. He had done enough work for a Sunday morning.

Dublin, Republic of Ireland

Esther Bonnard-Rousseau was working on her laptop in her bedroom in the Liffey Landing pub. It was foggy and pouring with rain outside and she felt warm and secure in her room. She reread and modified the emails she'd prepared, double checking the addresses of the two recipients. She wouldn't send them until after she'd seen the transfer from Slater in her account on Monday, but she couldn't sit around doing nothing. She wanted to be ready for the next steps in her recuperation plan.

Marbella, Spain

Pedro Espinoza called Jenny in the afternoon to say he was following a promising trail, but still had nothing definite to report. He would call her if he had more information on Monday. She didn't mention her suspicions about Patrice, time would tell if there was anything in it. For Leticia's sake she hoped it was only her suspicious mind and there was a simple explanation for his peculiar behaviour and the promise of expected funds.

London, England

"Identitity of Joburg and Polokwane murderer revealed."

The news headline screamed out from the *Africa Online News* item. Dudley had consulted the site several times since the disappearance of Leo Stewart and was already aware of CS Johannes Hendrick's claim to have solved the murders of Lambert and Blethin. The doctor's real identity had been a surprise to him but he didn't consider it of any importance. When he saw that a murder had been committed in Diepkloof, he had immediately assumed it was Nwosu and now it seemed he was correct.

He had no idea who had been abducted in the place of Leo Stewart, but it was no longer relevant, he was in Zimbabwe and likely to stay there. The deaths of Lambert, Blethin and Nwosu marked the end of any possible links between him and South Africa. Coetzee, he assumed, was either in hiding with the boy, trying to negotiate a ransom, or the boy had escaped and was perhaps reunited with his mother. In either case the South African was in no position to cause any problems for him, since he knew nothing and was himself a potential target for the police, either as a principal or an accessory. Esther Bonnard had paid herself off and disappeared and it was too dangerous for her to reappear and the same applied to Slater. The circle was completed; Lord Arthur Dudley was, as usual, in the clear.

Marseille, France

The Turkish cargo ship Erzurat tied up in the Port of Marseille's Northern Terminal at seven o'clock in the evening. The port authority was closed on weekends and no work was carried out. Unloading was scheduled to start at seven am the following day.

Shortly after the docking, two unmarked Peugeot 308 police cars from the *DCPJ,* the French Serious Crimes Division, arrived alongside the ship together with a Citroen Jumper bearing the insignia of the *DGDDI,* the French Customs and Excise Directorate. Eight passengers emerged from the vehicles, three DGDDI officers, three policemen in uniform and two more in plain clothes. One of them, wearing a leather jacket and cap, asked a seaman at the gangway to call for Captain Yilmaz.

The captain was a short, burly man with a scruffy beard. He had donned a grubby officer's jacket and cap before coming down to the dockside which made him look even more unscrupulous. Before anyone could speak, he announced that he spoke no French then burst into a long monologue in Turkish about the cargo of TV sets, fridges, etc. The visitors listened for a few moments until the leather jacketed man interrupted him in his own language, introducing the group as a joint task force from the DGDDI and the French National Police. He was Alexandre Treboux, Divisional Superintendent of the DGDDI, responsible for the Marseille area and he described the visit as a routine inspection of goods coming from the Middle East in view of the ongoing strife in the whole region.

After some discussion they went up to the captain's quarters-cum office and he produced the bills of lading from Syria and Turkey. One of the DGDDI men installed himself at his desk and started going through the paperwork. Superintendent Treboux asked Yilmaz to assemble the crew in the canteen. Eighteen crewmen arrived in the room and he instructed the captain to order everyone to surrender their mobile phones. No one would be allowed to go ashore until unloading was completed the following day and that three customs officers would be stationed on the ship that night and three policemen would guard the gangway and the dock.

By now Captain Yilmaz was looking extremely nervous and unhappy. He confirmed everything to his crew, giving the example by placing his phone on the table, then left the canteen and went into the lavatory. After locking and bolting the door, he took another mobile phone from his inside pocket and called a local number. Speaking French now, he said, in hushed tones. "*C'est foutu! Les douaniers sont là.* It's fucked, the customs people are here."

He listened for a moment then said, "I don't give a shit about that. I'm getting off this ship tonight and on my way back to Antalya. They'll never find me in Turkey."

The other person spoke again and Yilmaz said, "OK. I'll meet you there in the early morning. I'll call when I'm out of the port."

He put the phone back in his pocket and went to join his crew, trying to look unconcerned.

Geneva, Switzerland

Prince Sam Bensouda had stayed away from Divonne Casino yet again, having convinced himself his gambling and drinking days were over. Now he had regained a substantial part of his family fortune, or so he believed, he was determined to change his ways and start a new life. He wanted that new life to include Jenny Bishop. It was time for him to settle down and she seemed like the ideal partner to keep him grounded. In addition to being a very lovely looking woman, she was sensible, charming and apparently independently well-off. His family would applaud a union with her and the black sheep would be welcomed home with open arms.

He poured himself a Chivas Regal and consulted the Room Service Menu.

DAY NINE

MONDAY, JULY 19, 2010

SIXTY-SEVEN

Marseille, France

Captain Bahadir Yilmaz slid hand over hand down the rope he'd cast over the port side of the Erzurat and slipped into the oily, murky water of the Port of Marseille. It was two o'clock in the morning but the water was still warm. He was wearing only his jockey shorts and carrying a set of clothes in a waterproof rucksack on his back. In a slow breast stroke, without causing a single splash he swam across to the side of the harbour furthest away from the ship. On the dock he dressed in a dark outfit and pulled a balaclava over his head. He walked towards the charging station of the railway that served the facility, alongside the high metal fence with CCTV cameras and other electronic security devices that surrounded the fourteen hectare property. It was a cloudy night and the area was deserted.

Keeping under the line of cameras he found the point he was looking for, the break in the fence where the rail track went through. There were control posts on both sides of the track, but they were unoccupied at that time of night. He slipped around the fence and crawled under the sliding gate then walked away from the dock, as free as a bird.

* * *

From inside the southern control post, Superintendent Treboux looked out the darkened window as Yilmaz, speaking on his mobile, walked across the periphery road towards the A55 heading west. He went down to the waiting unmarked police Peugeot and they drove just near enough to watch for the car that the captain must have called. There was no hurry. It would be interesting to see who came to pick him up and where they went.

Malaga, Spain

Espinoza was watching the morning news on TV when Marcel Colombey called back from Paris. Whilst they were talking he sent through a scanned photo. Espinoza compared it with the two photos he'd sent over then exclaimed, "How did you obtain this?"

"I arranged for an agent to go round to her apartment building yesterday afternoon. He talked to one of the neighbours then waited until she came out with her boyfriend. His name is Harry Slater, he's English and apparently they've been living together since she came back from Australia, eighteen months ago."

"That means I got hold of the wrong end of the stick completely. Now I'm totally confused. Let me think about it and I'll get back to you as soon as possible."

He prepared a quick email to DS McCallister and sent it off with the photograph attached. It was four in the afternoon in Sydney and he asked the policeman if he could turn it around quickly. It was time to close this case. He found the number given to him by Chief Superintendent Hendricks and called DI Dewar in London.

Marbella, Spain

"Good morning Patrice. You're just in time for coffee." The Frenchman had arrived without warning and Leticia was in the garden with Emilio. Jenny took him out to the terrace. "You know

Emma of course and now you can finally meet Leo. He came back from his friend's house on Saturday. I'll go and call Leticia."

Patrice sat opposite Leo, seeming to scrutinise him carefully. "How was the match, Leo? It must have been quite exciting, waiting for over two hours for a single goal right at the very end."

"The whole trip was exciting actually. Mum and I had a great time, but I'm really happy to be back in Europe, to be perfectly honest. Especially here in Aunt Jenny's house. It's fabulous."

"It's a nice coincidence having a friend living just along the road. What was his name again?"

"Nigel Dean. He's our head boy. Brainy but rubbish at football. It's not their house anyway, they're just renting it for a month. It's on the beach but not half as nice as this one."

Emma had tightened up imperceptibly at Patrice's first question, but she was impressed with her son's performance. "Tell Patrice about the day out at Lion Park," she said, to move him onto safer ground. He didn't need to invent that story.

As he started his account of their trip, Jenny came back with Leticia and Emilio. "Chéri, what a lovely surprise." They embraced and he lifted Emilio up in his arms.

"I'll have to wait for the rest of your story, Leo. My next appointment is at ten so I've only got a few minutes," he said. "There's something important I need to tell Leticia and it can't wait. We'll go by the pool where we can talk quietly. You don't mind, Jenny?"

She shook her head and looked quizzically at her sister as he took them into the garden, speaking to Leticia in French in an animated fashion. "What was all that about?"

"It started off as a bit of an interrogation, but Leo was more than a match for him. I'm not sure what's going on with that man."

"I sometimes wonder that myself."

London, England

Detective Inspector Dewar was cleaning up his desk. He picked up the dossier on Lord Arthur Selwyn Savage Dudley. The email from

CS Hendricks had thanked him and advised him that the murder cases were closed and he didn't consider the phone tapping to be relevant to his investigation. Dewar's last information from Simon Pickford was that Dudley had apparently made contact with the targets and didn't need any further tracking. He had a lot on his plate and was about to send the file back to records when he received a call from Pedro Espinoza.

The Spaniard introduced himself as an ex-Chief Superintendent of Homicide who had been assisting Hendricks in the South African murder hunt but had been intrigued by the phone tracking story. He asked if Dewar had any information on Lord Dudley.

"I'm afraid I can't comment on that, Mr Espinoza. I don't know you and in any event as an ex-policeman you know that such information is restricted on a 'need to know' basis. I'm sorry but I can't help you."

"I applaud your caution Detective Inspector, but perhaps you can do two things for me. Firstly, if you would like to check my credentials with CS Hendricks that may allay your worries, and secondly, I doubt that the name of your contact at EzeTracker would qualify as 'need to know' information and I would be very interested in learning a little more about the technology involved."

Smart approach, thought Dewar. *There's no reason not to assist his technical education.* He replied, "I'll contact Hendricks and I'll also call EzeTracker. If my contact wants to speak to you I'll give him your number in Spain." He read Espinoza's number from his phone. "That's the best I can do. OK?"

Dewar rang off, wondering if this might somehow lead to a new angle on Dudley. It would be nice to finally get something more than circumstantial on him, the man was obviously a nasty piece of work. He would help Espinoza as much as he could within the rules. He put the file back on his desk and called Simon Pickford.

Port-de-Bouc, South-West France

Superintendent Treboux and Lieutenant Grandville were in *Port-de-Bouc,* a seaside commune of twenty thousand inhabitants on the south-west coast of France. The Peugeot was parked at the side of the *Quai de la Liberté,* on the east side of the slipway from the marina. From the car they looked straight across the water to *La Leque,* the central tourist area on the other side. More importantly they looked directly at the *Ancre de La Leque,* a small three story hotel with a brasserie on the ground floor. It was ten in the morning and Captain Yilmaz and the man who had picked him up had been in the hotel since arriving there at three o'clock. The two customs officers had taken turns to catnap in the car, and Grandville had walked across to the brasserie to bring back coffee and croissants at eight o'clock. The town was still quiet at that hour and they had an uninterrupted view of the hotel entrance.

"*Regardez*! Look!" Treboux sat up and rubbed his eyes. Yilmaz and the driver were coming out of the hotel. A swarthy man carrying a leather bag walked up to them from the direction of the *Port Renaissance,* the small yacht basin adjacent to *La Leque.* They shook hands then scanned the street around them and set off back towards the port. The officers locked the Peugeot and crossed the bridge across the waterway, keeping the others in sight.

The men walked alongside the rows of private yachts and climbed aboard a white Jeanneau fishing boat with blue and red stripes along the side. They quickly cast off the lines and the craft headed out of the port.

As he and Grandville ran down the quayside, Treboux pulled out his mobile phone. "They're just pulling out. It's a red and blue striped Jeanneau."

"I see it," replied the voice on the other end. "Hang on a minute."

The officers lost sight of the boat as it exited the marina. The man's voice came back. "It's heading west to go south from the looks of it. Probably heading for Spain but it'll be hours before they cross into Spanish waters."

"Then on to Turkey, I suppose. We're almost at the lower quay, you can pick us up there."

They reached the end of the quay just as the unmarked M15 High Speed customs inshore patrol boat pulled alongside the jetty and they jumped aboard. The vessel pulled away immediately and headed back out to sea, going west after the Jeanneau.

Treboux called one of his team at the Port of Marseille. "Anything?"

"Not yet. One of the crew has identified the last container to be loaded and we've taken it off and opened it, it's full of TV sets. They look OK but the dog handler's on his way. I'll call as soon as we have something."

Geneva, Switzerland

"Quoi? Ce n'est pas possible. It's impossible. "

"I'm afraid it's true. I wouldn't joke about something like that, M le Prince." Jolidon was trembling. He had just announced to the Moroccan that the cargo had been seized by the French customs.

"Fucking Hell, it can't be true!" Bensouda was in his suite at the Kempinski. He sat on the settee, a cold sweat suddenly covering his forehead. "What about my investment?"

"It was entirely consumed by the purchase of the merchandise and the costs of transporting it to Marseille."

"You mean there's nothing left? What about the last hundred thousand I sent? That can't be gone as well."

"I tried to recuperate it for you this morning, M le Prince," Jolidon lied, "but it had already been transferred on to the other party."

Bensouda gasped for air. "One moment." He went to the bar in the suite and poured out a measure of Chivas Regal and drank a large swallow. "I have to come and see you. You can't just call and tell me I've lost over a million dollars like that. There must be something we can do. I'll be at your office in a half hour."

"Unfortunately I am not in Geneva today, Monsieur. I came to Zurich last night to ensure that the transaction was executed correctly by our bank here and I just received this dreadful news by telephone a moment ago." This was also untrue. He was actually in Lausanne, not to execute a transaction, but to keep away from Bensouda.

"What exactly did they tell you? Are you sure you didn't get it wrong?"

Jolidon gave a brief fictional account of the telephone call. "You can rest assured that your involvement in this matter has not been and never will be disclosed to anyone." This subtle threat went unnoticed by the troubled Moroccan. "But I'm worried about my own position, Monsieur. If my involvement in the transaction has been discovered, I could be facing very serious charges. I may stay away from Geneva for some time. Until I know what transpires."

After a few minutes more of begging and pleading for some respite Bensouda was finally lost for words. He rang off and went to get another whisky. He was shaking with rage and with fear. There would be no more jetting around the world, no more living like a lord in Marbella, no more chauffeur-driven limousines, no more throwing his family's money away in casinos, no more suites in fancy hotels. *The game's over. That was my last throw of the dice and I lost. Time to pay the piper.*

He found his uncle's name in his phone and with trembling fingers he pressed the number.

Marbella, Spain

Leticia waved Patrice off from the front entrance then came running back to the terrace with Emilio. "Jenny," she called excitedly. "I have important news. Get your iPad please?"

"I've got it here. What is it?"

"We'll go for a stroll and leave you to it." Emma and Leo went off into the garden.

"Right. What do I have to look up?"

Leticia handed her a sheet of note paper with *Banco de Iberia* embossed on the top. "Here. Patrice says it explains everything. I think I understood, but you can explain it properly to me."

Jenny typed in, *Regina Oil & Gas Inc, Saskatchewan.* There were several items on the page, all with variations of the same headline, *Regina Oil & Gas Strike. Saskatchewan's Biggest Find, Ever.* She opened the Bloomberg item, as Patrice had indicated and read the article to Leticia.

"Regina Oil & Gas, one of Canada's newest and smallest oil exploration start-ups, announced yesterday that their third exploratory drilling, near Sask, in the Bakken formation in the southeast part of the province, has delivered the goods in style. Using a combination of horizontal drilling and hydro fracturing technology Regina discovered a large contiguous pool of sweet, light crude oil. The company estimates that the pool could deliver over a billion barrels of oil over the next several years, making it the largest single discovery in Saskatchewan's history. Trading in Regina stock was suspended on the Toronto Stock Exchange yesterday after the share price more than tripled in frenzied trading.

"Fetch me your bank file will you?"

Leticia came back with the file and Jenny leafed through the statements. She drew in her breath. "Now we know what Patrice meant when he said he'd make the money back by September. Look."

She showed her the June 30th statement. Included in the list of shareholdings was five hundred thousand Ordinary Shares of Regina Oil & Gas, at a value of four hundred thousand Canadian Dollars. This small oil and gas company had now discovered a massive pool of oil worth a fortune and their share price had risen from eighty cents to two dollars fifty cents.

Jenny looked up the exchange rate against the Euro. "They were valued at about three hundred and twenty thousand Euros and now they're worth almost a million. You've made about six hundred and fifty thousand already and it sounds like it'll still be going up when they open the markets today."

Leticia clapped her hands. "We'll make back the money we lost on that Ponzi scheme. That's why he was rushing about so much. It was this Canadian customer who had a lot of meetings in London but it was very confidential. He was involved in their PIO, I think he said."

Jenny was so relieved at the news that she laughed out loud. "You mean IPO, it's when they went public on the Canadian Stock Market, I suppose. That means he's been involved with them for a long time. He must have a good nose. I should ask him for some tips."

So that's what all his travelling and stress was about. She felt embarrassed that she'd harboured any suspicions about him. *Thank heavens we can all get back to a normal relationship now.* "I'm putting a bottle of champagne on ice for lunchtime. We're going to celebrate."

Sydney, Australia

DS McCallister compared the photos sent by Espinoza with those in the dossier he'd received from his colleague in Perth. There was a background file with pictures of everyone involved in the case; Tony and Nicole Forrester, the staff at N-Jet and the two executives lost in the crash.

He sat back in astonishment. "Shit! I don't believe it. This is going to add some spice to Pedro's paella." He checked the two images once more then scanned the photo from his file and sent it with a quick note to the Spaniard. He wasn't allowed to send the dossier to Espinoza, who was no longer a police officer, but he now expected to receive a request from the French National Police. He asked his assistant to prepare a scanned copy to be emailed as soon as it was requested. Then he left the station and drove to an Outback Steakhouse along the street. It was eight o'clock in the evening and he was famished. He switched his mobile to vibrate and laid it on the table in case Espinoza called.

Marbella, Spain

"Cheers! Here's to Leo coming home, Leticia getting marvellous news and the renewal of my social life."

No one understood Jenny's toast completely but they were all happy to raise their glasses. Even Leo had a glass of champagne in his hand and joined in the celebration. There was an air of cheerfulness in the house that hadn't been there for a while. They relaxed on the terrace and chatted happily, Leticia getting to know another part of her new family and everyone enjoying the moment.

Jenny's phone rang and she excused herself and walked away from the others. "Sam, how are you. Are you back in Marbella?" She listened for a moment then said, "Morocco? I don't understand. I booked at the Finca Courtesin for next weekend. How long will you be away?"

After a few minutes Jenny walked back to the others, fighting the tears from her eyes.

"What is it?" Emma jumped to her feet. "What's wrong, Jenny?"

She took a deep breath. "It was Sam. He's going back to Morocco. He doesn't know for how long, perhaps for a long time, he said."

Malaga, Spain

Pedro Espinoza had been on the phone with Paris, working out an arrest procedure with Marcel Colombey when the email arrived from MacCallister. He didn't yet know who they were going to arrest, nor under what names, but he was sure the moment was not far off and he wanted to be ready. He looked at the screen in disbelief and grabbed his mobile again.

"Sorry to disturb you Mac, but I'm sure you were expecting my call."

"Too right, Pedro, only I expected it sooner. I just ordered a T-Bone so I've got five minutes."

The two men talked for a short while then the Spaniard thanked him and rang off. He called Inspector Colombey back. Now he knew who to arrest, although he could hardly believe it.

At Sea, en route for Barcelona

It was a clear day and the patrol boat, doing ten knots, had been trailing the Jeanneau for over four hours at a distance of just over one kilometre. The sea was quite choppy and the fishing boat was hugging the coastline. This suited the customs pilot since there was a lot of tourist traffic and he could keep the boat in sight without being noticed.

Although Superintendent Treboux's position with the French Customs Directorate gave him the authority to detain Yilmaz and the other man at any time, he didn't want them taken into custody until the drugs had been found and impounded. It was easier to obtain an arrest warrant backed up by irrefutable proof and much easier to get the men to talk when they knew they were facing many years of imprisonment. These men were just the low hanging fruit. He wanted to find the people at the top of the tree, those who were flooding Europe's streets with deadly narcotics and fuelling the never-ending escalation of crime in his country.

They had just passed *Saintes-Maries-de-la-mer*, about forty nautical miles from Marseille, when his mobile rang. "*Oui, Jean-Philippe*?"

"Two hundred kilos of pure heroin stuffed into the backs of fifty TV sets. A first for me, I've never seen that before. Really professional as a matter of fact."

"Have you asked for the arrest warrant?"

"I've just emailed it to you now. You're set to go. Good luck."

Treboux called to the pilot, "Let's join them. It's Happy Hour!"

The pilot opened up the throttle and the twin Man engines propelled the craft forward, closing in rapidly on the unsuspecting Jeanneau.

He printed off the warrant in the cabin then pulled out his 9mm Sig Sauer SP 2022 pistol and went back on deck, ready to make the arrests. This was the part of his job he enjoyed.

Dublin, Republic of Ireland

"*Parfait*! Perfect!" Esther Bonnard saw that her account with the Gaelic Bank of Belfast had been credited with Slater's twenty-five thousand dollars. She had been running messages for Susan McCaffey all day to earn her keep and hadn't had time to check until then. She immediately transferred the amount to her account in Guadeloupe, where it would be safer. Although the address she had given to the Irish bank was fictitious, she didn't trust European banks any more. Esther had worked at Klein Fellay, a Geneva bank, for over a year and she knew how easily private information could end up in the wrong hands. She also knew how valuable such information could be.

Her mobile had rung incessantly during the afternoon until she finally switched it off. She knew who was calling and wasn't interested in talking to him. It was a prepaid phone, so there was no chance of her being located from any records filed with the network provider. She had already decided to get a new phone the next day.

She checked her lipstick and went downstairs. Susan had asked her to help in the bar that night. Esther didn't mind what she did, so long as she was paid accordingly.

Malaga, Spain

"Thanks for your explanation Mr Pickford, it clears up a number of points. I'll tell DI Dewar how helpful you have been and I'm sure there will be no repercussions as far as you are concerned. After all you simply provided a service that you are established to deliver."

Espinoza rang off and considered what the EzeTracker boss had told him. Dudley's background and previous requests for tracking pointed to a very sophisticated criminal. One who used other people to carry out his dirty work. Dewar's response on the telephone had also told him a lot. He knew Dudley, otherwise he would not have quoted, 'need to know basis'. There was obviously a dossier on the man and Dudley had simply confirmed the fact with his reply. *Maybe deliberately*, thought the Spaniard. He returned to his jigsaw puzzle and notes and summarised what he knew of Dudley from Pickford, Dewar and Coetzee's comments as reported to Leo. The picture was taking shape but there were still a number of missing features.

Nice, Côte d'Azur, France

Harry Slater had called Esther a dozen times during the afternoon without success. He had transferred twenty-five thousand dollars to her account that morning, almost all the money he could find, but had received no word from her. She was supposed to have arranged the Leo Stewart business with the Zimbabwean money manager that morning. If she hadn't, he hated to think of the consequences.

He looked up the Geneva online phone book for the name she'd given him, Sebastien du Pasquier. There were five persons of that name, two with no professional details, a dentist, a teacher and a garage mechanic. No bankers or financial experts. His mind went numb. *What a gullible amateur I am. Why didn't I look it up before?* He rehearsed a story to tell his partner. This wasn't a time to panic. There had to be an explanation for the delay. He called her again then put the phone on vibrate in case she called while he was having dinner.

Marbella, Spain

Jenny was lying on her bed feeling sorry for herself, wondering what she'd done to deserve being dumped by Sam before they'd even become an 'item', when her mobile rang. It was Espinoza and he sounded excited.

"We've had a breakthrough. It's too complicated to tell you on the phone, so I'll come around tomorrow morning to explain it to you. Is that alright?"

"Of course, Pedro. Come whenever it suits you."

"You don't sound your usual self, Jenny."

"I'm just a little tired, thanks. I'm sure I'll feel much better tomorrow."

"It's probably the anti-climax of recovering Leo after a stressful week. Goodnight, Jenny. Sleep well."

DAY TEN

TUESDAY, JULY 20, 2010

SIXTY-EIGHT

Nice, Côte d'Azur, France

"Who the hell can that be at this time of day?" It was eight thirty in the morning and the doorbell of the apartment in the swanky area of *Mont Boron* had just rung twice. Nicole Forrester and Harry Slater were having breakfast on their terrace and enjoying the bright, clear vista over the Vigier Park across to the sea. It was pleasantly warm and the smell of mimosa filled the air. Slater was as nervous as a cat, still wondering what was going on with Esther and Dudley. He had called them incessantly the previous day with no success. Deep inside he knew he'd been played for a fool, but he couldn't admit it to his partner. She had the money and if he didn't continue to keep up the pretence he would be out on his ear, flat broke in a country where he couldn't even speak the language. He knew he was running out of time but he had no other option.

"I'll go." He went to the door and was confronted by two gendarmes in uniform and two men in casual wear. A cold shiver ran down his spine. "Bonjour, Messieurs." He realised his French would let him down and was about to call Nicole when one of the plain clothed men showed him his ID card.

"I'm Inspector General Colombey of the DCJI and this is Police Commissioner Lefèbre. We have some questions for you. May we come in?"

Nicole came to the door and pushed Slater aside. "What's this about?" She blustered. "Why are you disturbing us at this hour in the morning? It's a scandal, an abuse of power. You have no right ..."

"Madame, I have every right to question you in connection with a crime we are investigating. You can either invite us in or you can come to the *Commissariat* and we can question you there. The choice is yours."

The dossier had arrived in Paris from Sydney the previous evening and Colombey immediately requested his superior officer to assign the case to him, as an international and not a local investigation. He had taken a late flight to Nice and organised the arrest team with the help of the Regional Commissioner. After spending the night at a local hotel he was up at five am and at eight he and the team were on their way to Mont Boron.

The couple led them into the apartment, "Just keep your mouth shut and let me do the talking," Nicole whispered to him. "These *flics* know nothing." The two detectives followed them in, leaving the policemen outside the door.

"So, what's so important that you threaten to arrest us and take us to the station?"

Colombey ignored the jibe and addressed Slater. "I understand you're a British citizen, Sir."

He moved uncomfortably on the chair. "That's correct."

"And you, Madame. You're French, I believe?"

"Yes I am. What of it?"

"May I see your passports?"

Slater looked at Nicole but she avoided his eyes and said nothing. She went out of the room and returned with both passports, handed them to the policeman.

"Harold William Slater. Is that your full name?"

"Yes, it is."

"Do you know anyone by the name of Robin Little?"

At this, Slater shivered as if he had a chill. "I don't think so. Who is he?"

Again Colombey ignored the question. "And you are Nicole Mireille Charpentier?"

"Yes."

"Was your married name Forrester?"

"I've had enough of this interrogation. I'm going to call my lawyer now."

"Please do so, Madame Forrester. In the meantime we are confiscating your passports, computers, laptops, iPads and phones and you are coming to the *Commissariat* to assist us in our enquiries. Your lawyer can meet us there."

Marseille, South of France

"Nothing. They've told us nothing and I'm starting to think they don't know anything."

"*C'est du Bullshit*! I don't believe it. Yilmaz might know nothing but the agent must know who he was working for. You're telling me Favre doesn't know who his bosses are?"

Superintendent Treboux and Lieutenant Grandville were in the offices of the French Customs Directorate in Marseille reviewing the interrogations of the two captives. The captain of the Jeanneau was a local seaman who had been hired by telephone by the hotel and they had released him after a few perfunctory questions.

"He says he only had phone conversations and his contact told him nothing except his name, M Valentino."

"What about the phone records?"

"We've traced the number he was calling but it's led nowhere. It was a prepaid US number and it's gone dead. We can't get any further on that track. The only other related calls are to Yilmaz."

"Emails?" Treboux was becoming irritated.

"Nothing. None sent and none received from anyone in connection with the merchandise except Yilmaz. It's the same with the captain's phone and emails. It's a dead end. This is a very sophisticated operation. Looks like it was set up in two halves; the receiving end here and the sending end over there."

"And never the twain shall meet. Fuck!"

"There's one possible loose end, but I don't know where it fits."

"I'm listening."

"Favre says he had some conversations with another man, someone he's done business with before, not drugs, but he wouldn't tell me much about it."

"And?"

"We've checked the calls and it's another dead prepaid US number. There's no trail there either." Treboux looked impatient, so he continued, "He never learned the man's name but he was certain it was an Englishman."

"Why was he so sure?"

"Favre lived in London for a while and he said the man spoke with a posh accent. You know, when they speak French as if it's just an English dialect."

"And that's all we've got?"

"One last thing. The second man told Favre to queer the pitch. He had to tell the other contact that the deal was off, so they could squeeze more commission for him. After that they just cut him off and he didn't know who the purchaser was, nor how to contact him. Then we turned up and they pissed off to try to get to Spain."

Treboux's mind was spinning. The informer's original call to the DDGGI in Montreuil had been recorded and although the voice was slightly distorted it had been identified as an English speaker. The email had also been written by a non-French person. Now there was an Englishman who had told the agent 'to queer the pitch'. *It had to be the same person. He set the transaction up then pulled it down and presumably raked in his commission without delivering the merchandise.* Treboux was impressed and infuriated by the realisation. Once again he was no nearer to identifying the top dogs and would have to make do with the messenger boys.

Despite repeated interrogations of the two captives and many costly man hours trying to identify the mysterious English informant and track the merchandise back to its origins, Treboux was still left with only the low-hanging fruit. Favre and Yilmaz would have to pay for the crimes of the organisers, as was so often the case. Lord Arthur Dudley had been right. He and Jolidon had left no evidence of their involvement in the heroin transaction and been well paid into the bargain.

Dublin, Republic of Ireland

Esther Rousseau, née Bonnard, was in her room at the pub, revising the emails she'd prepared. With some luck they might bring her more than the measly fifty thousand dollars she'd earned from the aborted abduction. She now knew, from the online South African news reports, that the late Sergeant Nwosu had been blamed for the murders and therefore Dudley and his partners, including her, were in the clear. However Leo Stewart had disappeared and she wondered if Jenny Bishop, whom she hated like a venomous snake, had been involved in the débacle.

Esther knew Ray would have been proud of her plan to get some of his money back; it was clever and audacious, like him. After his disappearance two years ago she didn't go back to Switzerland from Ireland; it was too dangerous. She returned to France under her maiden name, staying as far as she could from the capital, in Nice, on the south coast. But she never forgot the diamonds; she was still determined to get her share, Ray's share. Her first step was to find a way to cultivate a friendship with Claude Jolidon, at Ramseyer, Haldemann in Geneva. He was the guardian of the diamonds and, as she had learned from d'Almeida, he was also an inveterate gambler at Divonne Casino. She signed up with an agency specialising in casino employees and her looks and sharp brain quickly earned her a job at the Casino d'Azur in Cannes. From there she networked her way through to Jolidon. A quick visit to Geneva had cemented their relationship. She was adept at appealing to people of all sexual inclinations and always felt safer with gay men than heterosexuals who had only one thing in mind from the moment they saw her.

The decision to take the casino job turned out to be a monumental piece of good fortune. In July 2009, Nicole Charpentier, a French woman newly arrived from Australia came to work at the casino. Nicole was a status seeker and she deliberately let slip to Esther that she had come into a lot of insurance money when her husband, Tony Forrester, had died in an accident in Australia. Money was a great motivator with Esther and she began to socialise with Nicole and her partner, Harry Slater. Casual 'girl talk' in the casino and loose chatter after a few glasses of wine revealed that she had stolen Tony from another woman, Emma Stewart, in Rwanda. The name immediately rang a bell with Esther and she remembered from her investigation of Jenny Bishop that Emma was her sister. The penny dropped when Nicole told her 'confidentially' that with Tony's help, Emma had illegally adopted a Rwandan child and smuggled him into the UK.

The last coincidence was the one that clinched the story for her. One of the regular players at the casino was an old friend of Nicole's. Dr Antoine Constance had worked with her in Rwanda. He was now a reconstructive surgeon at the nearby *Clinique Saint Christophe.* Like most men she met, he fell for her and often stayed late in the evening to buy her a drink and try to seduce her. With each drink Constance became more and more indiscreet and she learned a lot about him, including the profitable side line that paid for his losses at the gaming tables. She used her sexual favours to glean as much information as he could supply and also obtained from him a very valuable service which could prove useful to her in the future.

His drunken, rambling narratives included a vital anecdote which confirmed Nicole's story. He had been at the clinic in Rwanda and assisted at the birth of a boy called Leopold who disappeared at the time that Emma returned to the UK. Esther knew she was onto something. Something potentially very valuable.

Emma's son would now be fourteen years old, still a juvenile. From online research of UK law concerning juveniles she learned that he could be taken away from Emma if she had acted illegally. A plan began to form in her mind. She pulled together the various strands of the story into a scenario to make Jenny and her sister pay for Ray's disappearance. She carried out constant surveillance on them, via Emma's web page, her and Leo's Facebook and Twitter accounts and through Claude Jolidon and other contacts she'd made in Switzerland. Then she began to plant the seeds for what she dreamed would blossom into a full-blown revenge on Jenny Bishop and her family.

In November, Constance left the *St Christophe* and moved abroad. Esther knew the reason. He was about to be arrested for his involvement in a fraudulent passport scheme and had fled to South Africa to escape punishment. She also knew he had changed his identity and was now known as Ernest Blethin.

From her surveillance she then discovered that Emma was taking Leo to South Africa, where Constance, or Blethin, was in hiding. They were going to the World Cup in July, 2010. She had six months to prepare a plan to be executed in Johannesburg.

Her first step was to start an affair with Harry Slater and that had been the easiest part. Ray had taught her tricks that would drive any man mad with desire and she had been an eager and adept pupil. After Slater had fallen head over heels for her, it was a simple task to get him involved in the scheme then to get Nicole's agreement and more importantly, the funding. She was the one with the money.

Lord Arthur Dudley was recommended to her by Claude Jolidon as a 'facilitator' and he was a hard nut to crack. Together they sketched out an abduction scenario to force Emma Stewart to pay a ransom which could only be financed by her sister. Before his disappearance, Ray had cornered Jenny Bishop in her house and recovered twelve million dollars from the Angolan Clan, but they hadn't been permitted to enjoy it. Based upon her inside knowledge gained as Eric Schneider's assistant, Esther knew the woman's wealth must still be substantial. However Dudley had been unconvinced; until February, when Jolidon confirmed to her that the diamonds were still at Ramseyer, Haldemann and Jenny Bishop had both keys. Then the stakes became immensely high and he was immediately hooked.

Dudley had lived up to his reputation in planning and implementing the strategy and she had been impressed by his professionalism, his decisiveness and his extensive knowledge and contacts. He was a truly amoral person, ready to sacrifice anything or anyone in the pursuit of his objective. Ray would have greatly admired him. *If he had been younger and better looking,* she mused, *I might have been attracted to him as much as he was to me.* Unfortunately that wasn't the case.

Under Dudley's management they had assembled the abduction team and put the plan into operation. With Nwosu, Coetzee and Blethin in Johannesburg and Lambert, a friendly Englishman at Emma's hotel, they had an abundance of talent, experience and local connections. Apart from a few minor hiccups the abduction had been highly successful and the plan was progressing well. Until someone, *probably Jenny Bishop,* she guessed, had somehow screwed it up and with it her chance of recovering Ray's legacy.

But that was all in the past and Esther always looked to the future. Now it was time to send her emails. She reread them one last time, checked the attachments then pressed Send. *That should create some surprises,* she thought to herself.

SIXTY-NINE

Marbella, Spain

"That's how the whole plan started. The common themes were Nice and gambling casinos. On this occasion a poisonous combination." Espinoza was at York House with Jenny and Emma. Leo had also been invited into the discussion since he was the principal character in the plan. The Spaniard didn't yet have final confirmation of the last details but he had just explained his theory about Esther's involvement and how and why Nwosu, Coetzee and Lambert were involved.

He confirmed that Nwosu had been found dead in his apartment but didn't mention that Jamie had probably been abducted in the place of Leo. Nothing could be done about it and it would only cause upset and feelings of guilt. He also said nothing of his suspicions about Dudley for the moment. If he was right, that might complete his jigsaw puzzle, but he still had no real proof.

"In Johannesburg the whole matter is now filed away in Hendrick's successful solving of the triple murder case, so if we ignore Coetzee's apparently unwilling participation, the only other culprit we are certain of is still at large; Esther Rousseau."

"Incredible!" Jenny said. "After two years she's still blaming me for d'Almeida's death and still trying to get her hands on my money." She turned to Emma and Leo. "I'm so sorry. I feel terribly responsible for what's happened."

Espinoza replied. "You're underestimating your contribution to Emma's escape and to the ultimate outcome. Your dream was prescient, as usual. Esther has turned out to be as ingenious as her late lover. We're fortunate they weren't working in tandem again. The outcome might have been different."

"Where is she now? Have they managed to catch up with her?"

"For the moment we don't know where she is, but it's possible that we'll have further news of her later."

"You worked all that out? They should call you Sherlock Espinoza."

The Spaniard laughed. "That's generous praise, Leo, but the truth is that my detective powers have not been quite up to the task."

"How come?"

"There is still one link that I haven't been able to connect. We still don't know how Esther or Dudley knew about your trip to South Africa and it's causing me an immense amount of annoyance."

Leo looked thoughtful. "I think I might know that. It could be really simple." He went to fetch his laptop from the kitchen. "Look." He scrolled back up the timeline on his Facebook page to December 2009 and showed them the status update:

LEO'S MIND-BOGGLING CHRISTMAS GIFT.
MY BRILLIANT MOTHER IS TAKING ME TO THE WORLD CUP IN JULY!
WHO SAYS EXAMS ARE RUBBISH?

"And by that time Esther was obviously following your account." The Spaniard shook his head in disbelief. "So simple and so obvious and I never even thought of it."

"Welcome to the digital world, Pedro. Everyone knows everything and understands nothing." Emma said. "Except that Esther understood exactly what an opportunity it was to kidnap Leo while we were in a hostile and unknown environment on the other side of the world. You're right. She's an ingenious woman."

Espinoza's mobile rang and he got up to leave the room. "Excuse me, I'm waiting for one last piece of information and this may be it."

A few minutes later he returned, a resigned expression on his face. "I think my reputation as a detective may have been redeemed, although I'm very unhappy at the price. Now I can continue with the rest of the story."

He sat next to Emma and took her hand. "There is no easy way to tell you this, but Nicole Forrester and her boyfriend, Harry Slater, have just been arrested in Nice for the murder of Tony Forrester and three other people in Australia in the airplane crash in 2008."

Espinoza paused to let everyone cope with their shock and distress. The first to speak was Jenny, "That's dreadful news about Tony, but I think we're all trying to work out how Nicole fits into the abduction scheme."

"And this man Slater," added Emma. "We have no idea who he is."

The Spaniard put his notes in order. "I'll explain as simply as I can," he said.

"The story starts in Perth, where Tony and Nicole were running N-Jet, their private airline business. In late 2007, a young Englishman joined the company. His name was Robin Little. He was a pilot and engineer, good looking, ambitious and apparently what you would call a lady's man. He started an affair with Nicole Forrester, his boss's wife, and she became infatuated with him. Early in 2008, they hatched a plot to get rid of Forrester so they could start a life together. It was a diabolical plot.

"The company had a weekly flight arrangement with a large oil firm which had regional offices in Perth, Hobart and Sydney. In the first week of July they were flying two executives from Perth to Hobart, then on to Sydney. Forrester and Little were scheduled to fly the plane in tandem. On longer flights they always had two pilots on board in case of sickness, fatigue or other possible problems. A young woman cabin attendant would also be on board. The weather forecast was predicting severe storms, which are common in winter time at that latitude.

"The morning of the flight was stormy, as the forecast had warned. It was not a good day for flying but Forrester knew his passengers were used to conditions of this kind and it wouldn't put them off. A couple of hours before the flight Little rang to say he had food poisoning and had been ordered by his doctor not to fly. In addition he couldn't risk bringing a viral infection onto the plane. Forrester didn't want to fly alone and asked Nicole to find a replacement for him. She pretended to make several calls and told him there was no one available at such short notice, but another pilot could join him in Hobart to complete the flight. This wasn't true of course, but Forrester believed her. The flight time to Hobart was only four and a half hours so he decided to fly the first leg alone then take the other pilot on from Hobart to Sydney. Nicole and Little had counted on that decision, which turned out to be a fatal one for Forrester.

"As I mentioned, Little was an engineer and the previous night he had interfered with the aircraft fuel supply, so that it would fail about half way into the flight when they were at the most vulnerable point, far out over the deepest part of the ocean, hundreds of kilometres from land. And that was what happened. After two and a half hours, Nicole received an emergency call from Forrester to say he was having problems with his fuel supply, just as Little had calculated. She informed the coastguard and the aviation authorities and opened up the call to their wavelengths. It was difficult to hear clearly because the transmission was broken up by the effects of the storm. All they could make out was that the fuel supply was failing. Then within a few minutes the call was cut off. They heard nothing further from Forrester; his plane had come down in the Indian Ocean."

The Spaniard paused again, waiting for this terrible news to sink in. No one spoke, they sat in silence, mesmerised by the story, waiting for him to continue.

"Nicole had ensured that the paper work for the previous day's prep and service of the aircraft were in order and had filed the flight plan showing that her husband and Little were flying together that day. The various emergency services were deployed to look for the plane but as we know, it was never found and nor were any survivors. The 'accident' had been perfectly planned and executed and Tony Forrester and three other innocent people had disappeared.

"So Nicole organised these deaths just to go off with this man, Robin Little?" Jenny interrupted. "I don't understand. Why go to all that trouble to get rid of Tony? All she had to do was to divorce him and marry Little."

"That leads us to the motive, Jenny. You know my theory about motives and crime and that's why I asked for the file from Perth. As is so often the case, it was simply money. Tony Forrester was well aware of the risks of flying small jet planes, so when he set up N-Jet, he took out a life insurance policy in favour of his wife for one point five million dollars, with a double indemnity clause for accidental death. Six months after Tony died in the air crash, Nicole collected three million dollars."

Emma shuddered and took a deep breath. "I can't believe it. How could anyone be so callous? To execute the premeditated murder of four innocent people in cold blood, just for money."

"Unfortunately it's true. Both Jenny and I have previously come across similar crimes. You can't imagine what people will do in such circumstances."

"So that's insurance fraud to be added to their list of crimes as well."

"It's becoming a very long list."

"And now Little is living with Nicole under the name of Harry Slater? How does that work" Leo was intrigued by the cast of characters.

Espinoza took out his jigsaw puzzle and list of questions and laid them on the table. He ticked off the second last item. "We have almost come to the last remaining square on my puzzle. That was a question I wondered about a lot – where and how does Constance fit into the plan and why was he fired from several jobs if he was so competent?

"The first answer is that Constance and Nicole knew each other before they went to Rwanda. They had both worked for *SOS Médicale* in Paris and he arranged for her to come down to replace Emma and that's when she met Tony Forrester."

Emma put her hand to her mouth. "I thought he'd been having an affair with her in Paris. I've misjudged him all these years."

"Whatever the case, he jilted you and married her, so I don't think you misjudged him too badly. Anyway, Constance had kept in touch with Nicole while she was in Australia and she knew he had changed jobs several times and was now working at the St Christopher Clinic. And she knew why. He was an excellent plastic surgeon, but also an inveterate gambler. He gambled more than he earned and found a way to supplement his income to finance his losses.

"That brings us to the second and key reason. When Constance left Rwanda he went to work in Toulouse and played in one of the casinos there. He met a local fraudster who was involved in people trafficking; immigrants, young girls, etc. The man was a forger, creating false documents to permit the movement of people across borders. They went into partnership together, Constance would change people's looks and his partner would provide them with a new identity. They carried on this business for several years, but he was very indiscreet under the influence of alcohol and he was found out and fired from several hospitals. He was never prosecuted because they didn't want any scandal and they had no concrete proof. But that was how Nicole learned about his part time occupation."

"And that's how Robin Little was transformed into Harry Slater."

"Exactly. After Forrester's death, Little stayed in hiding in Perth while Nicole came over to France and acquired a fake passport for him through Constance. He then installed himself in Nice, as Slater, waiting for Nicole to cash in the insurance and join him.

It took six months, but in the end the plan worked perfectly. Until they made a terrible mistake."

"They got involved with Esther Rousseau."

"Yes, Jenny. Nicole became bored and got a job in the casino. She became friends with Esther and they swapped stories. When Esther and Dudley came up with the idea of the abduction, knowing Nicole had come into a fortune, she seduced Slater and he became her lover. She was already preparing the ground to finance the plan if Dudley would agree to go ahead. When he did, she and Slater convinced Nicole to provide the funding. Constance was already in Johannesburg with a new passport so everything was in place to carry out the abduction."

"How did you get the story in such detail?"

"Slater broke down and started talking. Marcel told me they couldn't shut him up. Nicole is a very tough nut but she finally cracked when she knew he'd told them everything."

"So the police know about the abduction plan. What about me and Leo? Will there be any repercussions for us?

"Not in France. It may seem cruel and heartless, but Marcel Colombey isn't concerned with Leo's abduction. He doesn't know why it was planned and since Leo is safely back home, it's of no importance to him. He has helped to solve a multiple murder case in Australia and isn't interested in anything else, especially a boy and his mother in the UK."

Emma breathed a sigh of relief. "And what happens to Slater and Nicole now?"

"They'll be held in France until Mac gets the paperwork ready to take them back to Sydney for trial. It's in his jurisdiction now, so he'll get a lot of brownie points. He's a very happy Aussie. Marcel gets a lot of credit too. The French helping the Australians; that's quite a coup."

"I'd better get back to Malaga now and leave you and your family to absorb all this news. I'm afraid it has upset Emma a lot. She feels guilty for bringing all this upon her family and is very upset about what happened to Forrester." Espinoza and Jenny had left Emma and Leo together and were talking in the hall.

"There's something I realised during your explanation," she said. "Our research into Mutesi's experience with Galaganza was actually irrelevant. They seem to have known very little about it, only that Mutesi had a child, probably by a genocidist and Emma took him illegally to England."

"You're partly right. Because of Dr Constance and Nicole Forrester's involvement we assumed that it was an important event, and in reality it was just a red herring. Against my own experience and convictions I have to admit that the timing of Galaganza's death and the organisation of the abduction was purely a coincidence. He may not even have been Leo's father; we just don't know. But your overall analysis was correct and it helped us in many other ways to work out what was going on in South Africa. In the end though, the whole abduction scheme and the deaths of many people were caused by nothing more than a fortuitous conversation in a casino and a combination of greed, sex and revenge. What a sad indictment of our civilisation."

"All the more reason to never mention anything about Galaganza to Leo. He and Emma need to put this behind them and get their lives back on track. You've solved this case brilliantly, Pedro. Emma and I can never thank you enough. Leo is safely back and doesn't seem to have come to any harm; in fact I think he enjoyed the experience in a perverse way. We now know why it happened and some of the people responsible.

"But there's one thing we haven't discussed. You remember our agreement, 'get Leo safely back and then bring the culprits to justice'. We know the participants who have been arrested or killed were not the brains behind this plan. Esther Rousseau was definitely one of them, but she must have had help to carry it out. What are the chances of finding and punishing her and the other culprits?"

Espinoza took her hand and in a conspiratorial whisper, he said, "Wait until this evening and we'll see what happens. *Hasta luego,* Jenny."

SEVENTY

Nice, Côte d'Azur, France

Robin Little, alias Harry Slater's laptop was in the data retrieval room at the National Police Commissariat in Nice. An IT technician was interrogating the machine for any information relating to the murder of Tony Forrester and the subsequent cover-up and counterfeiting of passports and other documents.

An incoming email flashed across the screen and he opened it up. It was from someone called *Esther* and came from an ISP in Thailand. There were several attachments, including a recorded conversation. The material didn't seem relevant to his search criteria but the technician transferred everything onto a memory stick and sent it up to the fifth floor, addressed to Inspector General Marcel Colombey.

London, England

Lord Arthur Dudley was watching the midday news when a message arrived on his laptop, it was from Esther. He grunted with surprise when he saw she had used an ISP in Thailand.

He read the short message and opened up the various attachments with an increasing sense of anger. *That unfaithful hussy. She led me to believe she had feelings for me and now she's resorting to blackmail!* Once again his perverted sense of justice distorted his reaction. Blackmail against a common foe, such as Emma Stewart, or Jenny Bishop, was acceptable, they were the opposition and fair game to be targeted. But he and Esther were partners; they had worked together in a united cause and he had developed feelings for her which he thought were reciprocated. It was simply unacceptable for her to act so spitefully.

He considered the situation. If she disclosed this information to the authorities he might be compromised, although he had never failed to escape from such situations before. His London lawyers, De Franco & Berlinger, were the most expensive and sought after criminal defence firm in the UK. She couldn't risk confronting him in person, since she would be equally compromised. In addition, he was wealthy and she wasn't. He would wait and see what transpired. *Probably nothing,* he decided. *It's a last futile attempt to get money from me.* He deleted the message and its attachments twice from the machine. Thanks to the scrambling software there would be no incriminating messages to be discovered, if ever it came to that.

There was another nagging worry in the back of Dudley's mind. He'd received a call the previous evening from his contact in Harare. The two agents sent down by them seemed to have disappeared from the face of the earth. There was no trace, neither of them nor their car. One of them was an old and experienced agent, personally known to the President and he was likely to ask questions. The man did not want to incur his wrath, he needed to find them, or risk suffering serious consequences.

"Did they have family in Harare?" Dudley had asked.

"Those guys never have close friends or family, that's why they get chosen. Plato's a widower, lost his family during the war. He's a bitter man. The kid, Greg, is an orphan. His folks were purged years ago. I don't know the details, it was before my time, but he's what you'd call a career gangster, no allegiances."

Dudley suggested that the usual reason that people disappeared was because they wanted to. There had been no confirmation that they had arrived in Delmas and that was probably because they had never gone there in the first place. Otherwise Nwosu would not have been allowed to continue on to Diepkloof, he would have been eliminated by them in Delmas. If they had nothing to stay for, everything pointed to them deciding to take the opportunity to escape from Zimbabwe.

He didn't insinuate any reason for such a decision but the man in Harare seemed to consider the suggestion possible, or even probable. He would continue to investigate but if they didn't turn up he would try to bury the news, like many other matters he'd buried in the past.

After the call Dudley had speculated further on the events in Delmas. There was still a missing link and that was Coetzee. He had assumed that Nwosu had got rid of the security man in Delmas, which was why he wasn't with him when the Zimbabwe agent arrived at his apartment, but it might not be the case. *I wonder. Could he have somehow turned the tables on the two hit men in Delmas and escaped? But why would he let Nwosu go free if he had the upper hand?* He knew he would never get to the bottom of the matter, but it was still lurking in his mind.

His thoughts turned back to Esther. He was still furious at her insolent disrespect but there was nothing he could do to teach her a lesson. He had no idea where she was and any action on his part could backfire on him. He watched the news programme for a long while, not registering anything, fuming inside at her disloyalty and the possible loose ends that he had assumed were tied tightly. Loose ends that could just possibly lead back to him. Finally he made a call, using his US phone with the new AT&T SIM, making a mental note to get rid of it later. Then he made an online transfer of twenty-five thousand dollars from his Lugano account. He began to feel a little better.

Malaga, Spain

Espinoza received a call from Marcel Colombey at two pm Spanish time. While they were speaking, an email forwarded from the

Commissariat in Nice arrived on his laptop. He read it with satisfaction. "Très bien. I'll get back to you when I've looked at the attachments. *Merci,* Marcel."

London, England

DI Callum Dewar received Colombey's forwarded email at two thirty pm UK time and called Espinoza as soon as he had read and listened to the content. "It seems Simon Pickford was right to suspect Dudley's motives. Thank you, Sr Espinoza, this could be the break we've been looking for to nail this so-called Lord."

"I recommend immediate action, Detective Inspector. Dudley has probably received a similar message and he will be destroying everything that could compromise him. I think you have no time to lose."

"I'm taking charge of this myself. I've asked for a warrant and we'll be knocking on his door in less than half an hour. Wait for my news later this afternoon and thanks again."

Dublin, Republic of Ireland

Esther Bonnard had received no response to her emails to Dudley and Slater. This didn't surprise her. Given the content of the messages it would take them some time to react. She knew, though, that if they resisted her blackmail attempt, there was nothing further she could do. The abduction plan was almost irrelevant compared with the murders in South Africa and the emails and recordings she had safeguarded were highly incriminating in that regard. But she couldn't go public with the information without setting off another manhunt targeted at her, and this time she might not be so lucky. If her threats brought no reward she would have to regroup and devise a new strategy to recover her lost inheritance from Jenny Bishop.

London, England

DI Dewar arrived at Lord Dudley's apartment just before three pm accompanied by DS Holden. A police Vauxhall Astra, warning lights still flashing and a uniformed driver at the wheel, stood half on the pavement in front of the building, adding to the usual disruption in the London street.

Dewar didn't beat about the bush. He made his introductions, then immediately announced, "Lord Arthur Selwyn Savage Dudley, I am arresting you in connection with the recent deaths of Barry Lambert, Ernest Blethin and Jonathon Nwosu in South Africa."

Dudley was dumbfounded. How on earth had this detective, in London of all places, connected him with Leo Stewart's abduction in South Africa? He summoned up his most unctuous tone. "I haven't the faintest idea what you're talking about, Detective Inspector. I've never heard of the persons you mention, but I suppose you have some obscure reason for this unpleasant disturbance. If you don't mind I'll call my lawyer, Sir Archibald Berlinger, who I'm sure will assist us in rectifying this misunderstanding."

"You can ask him to join us at Scotland Yard, Lord Dudley and please provide us with your computers and mobile phone."

When he tried to bluster his way out of the demand, Dewar showed him the warrant he'd received fifteen minutes earlier. "Since you seem to be unwilling to cooperate with us we'll look for the items ourselves."

They collected the laptop from the table in the living room together with a mobile phone. A quick look around the other rooms revealed nothing, but one door in the apartment was locked. After prevaricating as long as he was able Dudley opened the door with a terrible sense of foreboding. His inner sanctum was about to be violated and he couldn't bear the thought of it. The other mobile phones and his iPad were in there. The police technicians were bound to be able to break into his private world. *Why didn't I simply destroy and replace everything?*

He sat silently in the living room, his confidence ebbing away, leaving a frightened middle aged fraudster who knew the game was up.

* * *

An hour later, Lord Dudley was in an interview room at Scotland Yard, with his lawyer, Sir Archibald Berlinger. Sticking to the lawyer's advice, he was denying all knowledge of everything that was said to him. His confidence was slowly returning. Thanks to his obsessive paranoia the scrambled delete software meant they could obtain no information from his computers. His choice of ISPs and SIMs might appear peculiar, but they proved nothing at all. *They have no actual proof of anything,* he realised. *It's all circumstantial evidence based on hearsay. But who have they been listening to?* He racked his brains to work out who their source could be. *Slater's in France, Esther has disappeared and Coetzee is somewhere in South Africa. There's no one else.*

Finally, Sergeant Holden said, "Do you know a man called Harry Slater?"

Dudley supressed any reaction. "I don't believe so. Should I?"

"You might know him as Robin Little?"

"Never heard of him, I'm afraid."

"You may be unaware that Mr Little changed his name to Slater. We have been speaking to him and he says he knows you."

"I think I would remember if I had spoken to him, Detective Sergeant, and I can assure you that it's not the case."

"Then perhaps you can explain this, Lord Dudley." He hit Enter on the laptop on the table and Harry Slater's voice rang out:

> *How do you know he's telling the truth? It could all be a purely fictitious story. Nwosu may even be there and he doesn't want to talk to us. Maybe they've worked out a different agenda. This whole plan is falling apart. Isn't there anybody there you can trust? Fucking Hell! How could you let things get so out of hand?*

Then Dudley heard his own voice reply:

> *Please remain calm, Mr Slater. I believe our South African colleague is telling the truth. We have some independent verification*

of the local situation. There are reports of two murdered white men in South Africa in the news today. The first is Lambert, the hotel manager, in Johannesburg and the second is an unknown man in Polokwane. That must be Blethin, the doctor. This corresponds exactly with what he has told us. I will instigate a means of locating the others and report back to you this afternoon.

Fifteen minutes later, Sir Archibald left them, pleading another urgent meeting. Dudley knew it would cost him a good deal of money to see the lawyer again, the situation wasn't good. It was the same recording that Esther had sent him that morning. Holden had obtained it from Slater, but he still didn't know why. All he knew was that Esther had played him for a fool. He had misjudged her in many ways and it looked like it might cost him dearly.

He decided he had nothing to lose by satisfying his curiosity. "May I enquire what Mr Slater has done to merit your questioning him, Detective Sergeant?"

"All I can tell you is that Robin Little, whom you know as Harry Slater, has been detained by the French Police in a totally unconnected murder investigation. From your point of view, Lord Dudley, I'm afraid it is simply an unfortunate coincidence."

That's the problem with being an intermediary, Lord Arthur Selwyn Savage Dudley reflected resignedly. You're never really sure what's going on elsewhere.

Marbella, Spain

"So your theory was correct. It was this British Lord, Arthur Dudley, who teamed up with Esther Rousseau to plan Leo's kidnapping?" Jenny, Emma and Leo were on the speaker phone listening to Pedro Espinoza as he related the latest events in Nice and London.

"Yes, Emma. Esther originated the plan and Lord Dudley was hired to execute it. I didn't mention him this morning because we had no definite proof of his involvement. But thanks to her vengeful nature, she has provided us with proof and we are now certain of their partnership. A very gifted pair of criminals."

Emma asked. "What's happening to them?"

"Dudley will face charges of conspiracy and complicity in the murders, perversion of justice and whatever else they can find from his computer records, although DI Dewar told me that everything had been deleted and they haven't yet managed to reconstitute any files. They may have to rely on the recordings and messages sent by Esther, but they are very damaging."

"And Esther Rousseau?" Jenny felt physically sick at the thought of the woman escaping justice.

"No one knows where she is. She seems to have become an expert in disappearing since the d'Almeida business. There is an Interpol alert out for her, but I think she's too experienced to be caught. Time will tell."

"But now the English police will find out about Leo's abduction and Emma's illegal adoption. Can they get into any trouble?"

"That's what I wanted to discuss with you. I know that both of you want to see Dudley and Esther punished for their crime against Leo. But this leaves us with a difficult choice.

"At the moment, in the UK, DI Dewar has no knowledge of Leo's birth and adoption, nor the abduction plan. He is aware only that Dudley is somehow connected with the murders in South Africa and he'll be talking to CS Hendricks. Their sole objective will be to tie Dudley into the murders. In Paris, Marcel Colombey is interested in helping DS McCallister convict Nicole and Little for Tony Forrester's death and he's not interested in the abduction.

"Then Dudley himself is facing a potential murder charge and is not about to worsen his situation by opening up a can of worms involving child abduction. Esther Rousseau is in hiding, probably alone, because the whole organisation has been destroyed. She's won't risk giving herself away or exposing Emma unless she can plot a new way to extract Jenny's money and that would require resources she doesn't have.

"So, if there is nothing in Dudley's files, which seems to be the case, I don't see how the truth could ever be exposed."

"You mean, unless we bring it up?"

"Exactly, Leo. That is the choice you have to take. We have identified the chief criminals but we cannot prosecute them without exposing your secret."

Jenny said, "And Dudley may be tried for something else entirely if he can be linked to the murders. But Esther Rousseau is going to get away scot free for the second time."

No one spoke. They were all thinking the same thing. *Esther Rousseau has not gone forever. She'll be back again. One day.*

"You were right, Aunt Jenny. Pedro is a terrific detective. Did you see that jigsaw puzzle he prepared? It had every person and every event from start to finish and he just worked his way through it all until he came to the right solution." They were sitting on the terrace going back over their recent conversation.

"I knew you'd asked him to find the culprits, Jenny, and he did. Thank you for seeing it through all the way."

Jenny said, "Leo's right, you have Pedro to thank for that. But it's true what you say. A great crime was committed and several people, innocent or not, were killed or hurt and I don't think we can just walk away and say, 'Well, it ended OK for us, so we'll just forget it'."

She gave a deep sigh. "It's funny though. I thought it would make a great difference to us knowing who had done this thing and that they would be punished; a kind of closure. But I don't feel any different at all. I'm just happy that Leo's back and we're nearer to each other than we were before. That's the best closure we could have."

A little while later, Leticia came out with Emilio. Emma was typing furiously on her laptop and Jenny was reading. "The oil shares are almost at four dollars," she said to her in a conspiratorial whisper.

Jenny gave her a high five. "So you've made back the Ponzi money. Well done Patrice."

Emma looked up quizzically and Leticia asked, "What's the title of your new book?"

Jenny interrupted. "It's called *Red Sky over Orkney*."

"No it's not. I've scrapped that one. It was rubbish. I've started a brand new story with a different set of characters altogether. It's called *My son, the Hostage*."

Leticia didn't notice the glance that passed between the two sisters. She said, "You must have a marvellous imagination, Emma."

EPILOGUE

Delmas, Mpumalanga, South Africa
July 2010

Skelton limped quietly towards the door at the end of the hall, it was ajar *and light was escaping from the room. He was wearing rubber soled boots and carried his silver headed walking cane but was careful not to lean on it to avoid making a noise. As he approached the room he heard a voice, it was Murdoch, speaking in his whining, nasal twang. He stopped outside the door and listened to the man's words.*

"This is all your fault, Ms West. You and that bloody Scotsman, poking your noses into other people's business. I would have disappeared without a trace, long gone with a fortune in the bank and nobody any the wiser. After all, accidents do happen and that was the most perfectly contrived accident. Why would you have to imagine that Delaney's death was anything but accidental? Why did you have to hound me down and deprive me of what was rightfully mine?"

A woman's voice was speaking now. Low, soft tones. He knew it was Tory, but he couldn't make out the words. Ignoring the sharp pain from his right ankle, he knelt down and looked through the gap almost at floor level, knowing the man was less likely to notice something low down than at eye height. Murdoch was standing near a huge fireplace with his back to him. The log fire was blazing and the sight of it made him aware of how cold the hallway was. A wide, low oak table stood in front of the man and his hand rested on a high backed armchair to his side. In his other hand he held a pistol, not in a menacing way, almost casually.

Skelton poked his head around a little more and saw Tory. She was sitting in a similar armchair on the other side of the fireplace facing Murdoch. She was looking intently at the man and didn't seem to have noticed his intrusion. He wasn't sure but it looked as if her hands were tied. Now he could make out what she was saying.

". . . don't think you understand the seriousness of your actions, Commissioner Murdoch. Hundreds of thousands of pounds of public money have been embezzled, two innocent people have died and two more are in hospital in a serious condition. This is not just about Sergeant Delaney and even if it was, murder is murder. If Angus and I hadn't poked our noses in, as you put it, justice would have been badly served and a murderer and embezzler would have walked free. How can you pretend it's our fault? This crime spree started two years ago and we just happened to put two and two together in the last few days. The best thing you can do is to give yourself up and confess to your crimes. You have no other alternative."

"You're wrong, Ms West. I have one last alternative, because you have made a fatal mistake. You and Skelton have kept this information to yourselves. Foolish arrogance! No one knows you're here except your dear partner and I fully expect him to arrive at any moment. As you can see, his visit doesn't concern me in the slightest. He is old and lame and much too weak of character to present any kind of a challenge to me. As a matter of fact I let him discover where we are with exactly that in mind. When he arrives my new plan will be ready to execute, a verb that is well suited to the plan.

"While we are waiting for Mr Skelton I will share a little confidential information with you. This manor is very well insured, far in excess of the amount of the mortgage. It's been in my family since it was bestowed upon one of my illustrious ancestors in the sixteenth century along with the title of Earl of Branceworth. In fact it's the only part of my family inheritance I've managed to save, because I love the place. It's the one anchor that I've always been able to hang onto when everything else went wrong.

"But I cannot take it with me when I leave, and leave I must, as soon as possible. So I'm obliged to kill two birds with one stone. Nothing will be left of it, including the unfortunate occupants, who will never be identified in the ashes. Fire is a terrible obliterator of identity and as I said before, accidents do happen. One more or less is irrelevant."

Murdoch picked up something from the floor and held it up in front of Tory. Skelton could see it in the firelight. It was a jerry can. He unscrewed the top and sniffed the contents. "You'd be amazed at how much damage this small amount of fluid can cause. My officers have investigated many cases over the years and on very few occasions have we been able to prove that a fire was caused intentionally. So you might say that I have some expertise in that area and can be reasonably sure that my insurance claim will be rewarded."

'He's as mad as a hatter, finally gone completely round the bend'. Skelton waited to hear no more of the Commissioner's speech. He pushed the door open and deliberately dropped his cane to the floor then scrambled clumsily to pick it up as he looked around. He was in the largest room he'd ever seen in a private home. It was almost devoid of furnishings and the massive fireplace stood imposingly against the south-most wall. A long way away on the opposite wall, at a height of two and a half metres, a minstrel's gallery juxtaposed the almost five metre high ceiling. He realised it was the old baronial hall, where lavish feasts and musical entertainment predated television in the life of the wealthy classes in medieval times. But now it looked dark and foreboding, the only light provided by the leaping flames in the fireplace.

Murdoch looked across at him without any sign of apprehension, as, leaning heavily on the cane, he limped painfully across the enormous room towards them.

"Welcome, Mr Skelton. Exactly on time as all self-respecting gentlemen should be. As you can observe, Ms West is already my guest and now the invitation is complete. I'm afraid I can offer you nothing more than a warm evening by the fire, away from the freezing cold outside. Please come closer and I'll make sure that the room is quite warm enough."

He waved the pistol vaguely towards Tory. "Sit over beside Ms West. With any luck your remains will be strewn together to make identification even more difficult, not that it matters any more. Once you are gone, this unfortunate accident will be only that, nothing more or less."

Skelton could now see that Tory's hands were tied, but not her feet. He limped closer and made as if to skirt the table to sit beside her. As he turned, he lashed out to his right and was rewarded with the painful sound of a 'crack' as the steel-cored cane caught Murdoch full on the left kneecap.

"Ouch!" Involuntarily the policeman reached for his knee and the can slipped in his grasp, spilling petrol onto his clothes and onto the floor. He grabbed the can with his other hand and the pistol went spinning onto the hearth.

"I'm awfully sorry, Commissioner," he said. "I'm old and lame and unable to control my movements properly."

"You interfering old idiot!" Murdoch put down the petrol can and went to pick up the pistol. A spasm of pain from his knee made him slip in the pool of petrol and he fell towards the fire, reaching out to the fender to hold himself.

Skelton helped Tory to her feet. "Come on, my dear. Commissioner Murdoch is right. We've kept this business to ourselves for too long. It's time to file our report." They started walking back towards the door.

"Stay where you are. There'll be no report filed." Murdoch pulled himself to his knees and leaned forward to recuperate the gun again. As he reached out towards the hearth the heat of the fire caused his petrol soaked sleeve to burst into flame. He stood up and desperately took off his jacket and threw it down. With a 'whoosh' the fire ran across the floor and licked towards the jerry can. Murdoch was now standing in a pool of fire, the flames leaping up around his feet and legs.

"Help me. For Christ's sake help me!" He screamed, as the petrol on his trousers caught fire.

"My God. We have to save him." Tory tried to wrest herself from the Scotsman's hand.

He pulled her away. "It's too late. There's nothing we can do except get downstairs and out of here before the petrol can goes up."

They had just exited the main door when a massive explosion seemed to shake the huge building. A blast of hot air came rushing down the staircase like a tsunami, almost blowing them off their feet. Angus untied the rope from around her wrists and gently massaged the chafing away then took off his overcoat and placed it around her shoulders and they walked across to his car.

As they walked, he called the emergency services. "Murdoch Manor Hall is on fire. The whole place is going up in flames. Yes, that's right, Murdoch Manor Hall, in Branceworth. There is a fatality." They reached his car and got in out of the cold. He switched on the engine and put the heating up to maximum.

They sat in the car, watching, transfixed by the scene, as room by room the fire consumed the whole of the second floor of the manor house from end to end. Tory was weeping and he held her hand gently. Then the flames leapt simultaneously upwards and downwards until all three floors were a burning furnace. The sky was illuminated by the fire as the magnificent building burned ever brighter until it was almost as light as daytime.

Skelton put his arm around Tory's shoulder. In his soft Edinburgh brogue, he said, "Now that's what I would call an extravagant death."

They could hear the sound of the sirens now, increasingly loud as the blue and white flashing lights of the emergency vehicles came towards them up the long driveway. In the lightened sky they saw it was starting to snow.

THE END

Coetzee was sorry to reach the end of the story, he'd gotten to like the principle characters and decided to download the previous volumes. He turned to the last page of the Kindle book. A very pretty Emma Stewart was smiling at him from the screen. He looked fondly at the photograph, remembering their verbal tussles and regretting that he hadn't got to know her better. Another thought occurred to him, *If Emma is as tough as that, what's her sister like? Maybe one day I'll find out.*

He switched off the device and put it away. It was almost midnight and Karen and Abby were asleep upstairs. He had stayed up to enjoy the remaining few chapters of Emma's story in the quiet with his one whisky of the day.

The dogs were waiting at the door and he put his jerkin on and took them out for their last evening walk. A million stars sparkled like diamonds across the clear sky and the full moon was so bright it looked as if you could grab it with your hand. The night air was cold and he shivered and pulled the leather jacket tighter around himself.

Coetzee walked along Groot Street to the path that led across the open farming land then let the dogs off their leads to run off any remaining energy. As he followed them over the field he felt a sudden desire to smoke a cheroot, the first time since he had got back together with his family. He didn't have any, so the temptation wasn't hard to resist. After a ten minute stroll he whistled for the dogs and they came running back to him. He put them on their leads again and headed along the road towards the house.

"COETZEE!" The shout came from behind him and he swung round, reaching for the pistol in his pocket. Three shots rang out and he felt the bullets smash into him, throwing him against the hedge at the side of the road. The gunman ran along to the end of the street and climbed into a car hidden behind the trees, leaving Coetzee unconscious and bleeding under the hedge, the dogs whimpering and scratching around his body. The engine revved up and the vehicle sped off, it was a black Mercedes 220 with the number plate 294-TCE 87.

THE END

Christopher Lowery is a 'Geordie', born in the northeast of England, who graduated in finance and economics after reluctantly giving up career choices in professional golf and rock & roll. He is a real estate and telecoms entrepreneur and inventor and has created several successful companies around the world. The genesis of **The Rwandan Hostage** was his daughter's work as a delegate for the International Committee of the Red Cross in Rwanda, after the genocide of 1994. Chris also writes technical patents, poetry and children's books and has recently produced an album of his songs. He and his wife Marjorie live between London and Marbella. Their daughter, Kerry-Jane, now a writer and photographer, lives in Geneva and London.

URBANE